RIPPED VEIL

A MAFIA ROMANCE

NICOLE FOX

Copyright © 2021 by Nicole Fox

All rights reserved.

No part of this book may be reproduced in any form or by any electronic or mechanical means, including information storage and retrieval systems, without written permission from the author, except for the use of brief quotations in a book review.

* Created with Vellum

MAILING LIST

Sign up to my mailing list!
New subscribers receive a FREE steamy bad boy romance novel.

Click the link below to join.
https://sendfox.com/nicolefox

ALSO BY NICOLE FOX

Romanoff Bratva

Immaculate Deception

Immaculate Corruption

Kovalyov Bratva

Gilded Cage

Gilded Tears

Jaded Soul

Jaded Devil

Ripped Veil

Ripped Lace

Mazzeo Mafia Duet

Liar's Lullaby (Book 1)

Sinner's Lullaby (Book 2)

Bratva Crime Syndicate

Can be read in any order!

Lies He Told Me

Scars He Gave Me

Sins He Taught Me

Belluci Mafia Trilogy

Corrupted Angel (Book 1)

Corrupted Queen (Book 2)

Corrupted Empire (Book 3)

De Maggio Mafia Duet

Devil in a Suit (Book 1)

Devil at the Altar (Book 2)

Kornilov Bratva Duet

Married to the Don (Book 1)

Til Death Do Us Part (Book 2)

Heirs to the Bratva Empire

Can be read in any order!

Kostya

Maksim

Andrei

Princes of Ravenlake Academy (Bully Romance)

Can be read as standalones!

Cruel Prep

Cruel Academy

Cruel Elite

Tsezar Bratva

Nightfall (Book 1)

Daybreak (Book 2)

Russian Crime Brotherhood

Can be read in any order!

Owned by the Mob Boss

Unprotected with the Mob Boss

Knocked Up by the Mob Boss

Sold to the Mob Boss

Stolen by the Mob Boss

Trapped with the Mob Boss

Volkov Bratva

Broken Vows (Book 1)

Broken Hope (Book 2)

Broken Sins *(standalone)*

Other Standalones

Vin: A Mafia Romance

Box Sets

Bratva Mob Bosses (Russian Crime Brotherhood Books 1-6)

Tsezar Bratva (Tsezar Bratva Duet Books 1-2)

Heirs to the Bratva Empire

The Mafia Dons Collection

The Don's Corruption

RIPPED VEIL
BOOK ONE OF THE RIPPED DUET

I got pregnant the first night we met.

It was my wedding night...

But he wasn't my fiancé.

What happened was this:

My family made me marry a monster.

I ran from my wedding...

Into the arms of another man.

I thought he was my savior.

But I was wrong.

He was just the beginning of the real nightmare.

After it happened, I tried to run from him, too.

And for one year, I thought I'd gotten away.

But then reality came crashing in.

He's back on my doorstep now.

And he's already furious.

Just wait until he finds out about our baby.

RIPPED VEIL is a secret baby, arranged marriage romantic suspense novel. It is Book One of the Ripped Duet. Phoenix and Elyssa's story concludes in Book Two, RIPPED LACE.

1

ELYSSA

SOMEWHERE IN THE DESERT OF NEVADA

To serve is to find peace.

To obey is to find happiness.

To listen is to find truth.

The words repeat in my head like a dirge. How many times have I said them? Too many to count. Every dawn, noon, and dusk for the last nineteen years. Every day of my life.

Fumbling shapes flit through my subconsciousness. My head hurts. So do my legs.

I can smell the strong accents of incense and fire. Patchouli oil. Desert sand.

And something else beneath all that, something sharp and wet and metallic.

My eyelids remain stubbornly closed as if I'm not in control of my own body. It's easier to remain blind sometimes. It keeps you from seeing the monsters.

Heat suffuses the dry air around me and seeps into my body. That's what finally forces me to open my eyes—the heat. Why on earth is it so hot?

My vision blurs as I push myself into an upright position. More questions bubble to the surface. Why am I on the ground? Why do I feel the indents of the floorboards on the side of my cheek?

I blink a few more times, temporarily distracted by the layers of tulle draped in front of my face. I'm so used to simple cottons and softened white linen—the uniform I've worn all my life, the same one my parents wear, and my friends, and everyone I've ever known—that the tuille over my head feels invasive, strange, unwelcome.

I swat at the fabric, but it follows my every movement. My head spins and the room tilts for a moment, forcing me to take stock of where I am.

This... isn't my room.

Fear pierces through my body as the thought settles. My room has roughened adobe walls that I'd painted an ugly yellow when I was too young to know better. It has a thin mattress lying bare on the floor and a loose board in the corner where I stash all the books I don't want Mama and Papa seeing.

This is not my room.

In here—wherever "here" is—the walls are polished wood. The floor doesn't creak. The bed frame is iron and ornate, far fancier than anything I've ever seen, and the sheets are twisted and half-ripped off the bed like someone has thrashed them to the floor in the throes of a nightmare.

Everything is tilted and leery and wrong. But *what* is wrong? I can't remember anything about how I got here. Like today is the first day of my life.

I wait for the unsettling disorientation to fade, but my memory is still patchy. Gauzy flashes wisp across my mind, but they don't linger long enough for me to decipher them.

I decide to focus instead on what I see right in front of me. But it's so hard to see, to make sense of things. The world keeps spinning, colors bleeding together.

It reminds me of the time when Father Josiah made all the women and girls gather in the main hall of the Sanctuary to drink the purity water. He said it would cleanse us. But all it did was make a lot of us sick.

Mama couldn't eat for two days. Carrie Wilson vomited her guts out after just one sip. Old Mother Hobbs had taken right to her bed.

Father Josiah insisted that the purity water had worked exactly how it was meant to. "You're cleansed!" he'd boomed in that gravelly voice of his. "All your sins swept away like desert sand after a rainstorm."

To make sure, he had met with all the women individually after the fact. I'd been exempt because I was only six. Mother Hobbs was exempt, too.

Not that it mattered much. She died three days later.

We held a prayer circle after the burial to thank Father Josiah for purifying Mrs. Hobbs's soul before she was taken by the powers that be. He stood in the middle and soaked up our prayers and told us to say them louder. "I've been sent to guide you to salvation," he said again and again. "Let me guide you. Let me guide you."

My finger slips in something sticky and warm. I look down at my hand and as I do, my confusion intensifies.

I didn't even realize I was holding something until now. Something heavy and solid. I hold it up in front of my whirring eyes. The first thing I notice is the graceful curve of dark wings carved into the metal. They rise up a swooping swan's neck to the point of a beak.

It's a paperweight, cast iron and expensive by the looks of it.

And the whole thing is drenched in blood.

Panic starts to pulse through my frozen body, but it hasn't yet crested. I have to avoid hysteria. *Hysteria is just another outlet for sin,* Father Josiah always says.

I struggle to my feet. I fall a couple of times, still so dizzy that it feels like I'm on a ship at sea, but I keep trying until I'm upright.

The room spins again. I refuse to fall back to the ground, though I do think about how easy it would be to succumb to the disorientation and simply fade away.

Because the alternative is remembering how I got here.

And I'm not sure I want to do that.

I finger the folds of my tuille dress. Another realization hits me like a slap in the face. It's not just any dress: it's a wedding dress.

The confirmation is on my head.

Filmy material tickles the side of my neck and when I go to bat it away, I realize that it's attached to my head.

A veil. I'm wearing a veil.

Oh God… If this is my wedding night, then something has definitely gone very, very wrong.

The panic surfaces again, but I push it down. Hysteria is the enemy. I cannot react. I should not react.

I drop the paperweight. It clunks to the floor. My fingers come away from it, sticky with dried blood clinging to me like a second skin. Without thinking, I brush my hand against the folds of my dress. Of course, it leaves a dark crimson smear.

Don't panic, Elyssa. Don't panic. Do not panic.

Shivering, I take a step forward and stop short when I notice something sticking out from around the edge of the bed.

A naked foot.

My shivering worsens. I hear the howl of a coyote from somewhere in the distance and my gaze flits instantly to the bedroom window. I can see only darkness beyond the glass, but I've grown up on this land. I don't have to see the rolling acres of desert to know what's out there.

My eyes slide from the window to the mirror propped against the adjacent wall. Beneath it—and beside it and lining every available surface in the room—are hundreds and hundreds of candles, all lit and flickering. The flames look almost blue in the moonlight.

That's why it's so hot in here. That's why I'm sweating.

My reflection swims in the mirror. Confirmation of what I suspected when I first came to—it is a wedding dress I'm wearing, and it is a veil on my head. The smear of blood on the skirts does not belong to me.

Scariest of all is my face. It's not even the expression, which is both terrified and confused. It's the makeup caked onto my skin.

Rouge on my cheeks, a dark red lipstick on my lips, a pale foundation applied with a heavy hand. I look so white I'm nearly lifeless. A corpse made of clay.

I've never worn makeup once in my life. I wouldn't even know where to start with it.

Which means... I've done none of this.

Automatically, my gaze falls back to the foot peeking out from behind the bed. I can't ignore it anymore. I take a shaky step forward, my stomach roiling uncomfortably as the man takes shape before me.

He's tall. He's wearing dark pants and no shirt. He's fallen facedown, but his head is turned to the side.

"No," I whisper to the empty room. "No!"

The candles seem to flicker manically, spurred by the burgeoning panic that's turning my chest into a block of ice.

I lurch forward, my hand reaching out to touch him, but I stop at the last moment. Instead, I fall to my knees next to him. I want to touch him, but fear has taken my hands captive.

"Father Josiah," I whisper.

I can't tell if he's breathing or not. But I can see the nasty crater on one side of his face. It looks like paint. It looks like syrup. It looks like…

I forget about the sin of hysteria in that moment. I gasp as the shocking realization scorches through me like a lightning bolt. I collapse and scurry backward on my hands and knees, as far away from Father Josiah's body as I can get.

"Oh God, please, no…" I beg to no one in particular.

I stare desperately at the flickering candles as tears start to run down my cheeks. Each drop carves a track in the thick makeup.

"Stop," I plead helplessly to my reflection in the silver mirror. "Stop staring at me."

The simple facts click together ruthlessly. I woke up with a bloodied metal swan in my hand. There's a dead man in the bed with a hole in the side of his head. One plus one equals two.

I killed him.

I killed him.

I killed him.

The candles flicker brighter, as if they know what's going on inside my mind. I rip the veil off my head and hurl it at a cluster of candles in the corner. It catches fire immediately and starts to crackle.

The shivering comes back. As do the memories—some of them, at least.

Tonight was supposed to be my wedding night. We'd spent weeks in preparation. The event of the decade: Father Josiah had finally decided to take a wife. And he had blessed my family with the highest of honors.

He had chosen me.

But even though the past few weeks start coming back to me, the last twenty-four hours are a complete blur. A black hole that hides the secret to what happened in this bedroom.

I shake my head, unable to look at Father Josiah's body. I'd agreed to marry him. Of course I had. He was the leader of our commune, the Sanctuary. He was strong and brave and kind and honest. He was the savior of so many families, including my own.

I'd been chosen.

And then I'd... killed him?

I look down at the paperweight where I dropped it, waiting for the last piece of the puzzle. But nothing comes. All I have are black shapes, wavy images, and fleeting emotions that I don't recognize.

But the facts are the facts. I killed Father Josiah. I killed my husband.

I don't quite understand what comes over me in the moment that follows. All I know is that my eyes drift to the burning wedding veil in the corner. I stand and rush over to it, though it feels like I'm not even in control of my actions. An out-of-body experience, I think they call it.

I snatch up the biggest candle. Hot, molten wax sears my skin, but I barely feel it.

It's not a conscious decision. But I am distantly aware of the hysteria twisting into something else. Something that feels like... survival.

I push the open flame against the filmy material of the curtain tied up on to side of the window. It catches fire immediately and the roar grows quickly. The fire spreads fast.

Then I throw the candle at the bed. I don't look to see where it lands. I just turn and run.

Down the stairs.

Out the door.

My high heels sink into sand as I cross from the patchy yards of the commune out into the wild desert. Gasping, I kick them off and keep running.

I don't look back. My eyes are on the glow of lights in the far distance. I know those lights. I've watched them my whole life.

Las Vegas.

I've never been myself, despite it being right at our doorstep. The Sanctuary is all I've ever known. To want more was to accept sin into your life. To venture beyond was to turn your back on the commune.

But I've murdered the heart of our community. The shepherd to our flock. I've handed my soul over to the devil. There's nowhere else for me to go now.

So I go toward the lights.

I keep running, even when the heels of my feet start tearing and bleeding. I pant through the pain in my side and the pain in my heart. My eyes never leave the lights ahead.

And little by little, they get brighter. More blinding. The Sanctuary disappears into the vast blackness behind me.

But it doesn't seem to matter how much distance I put between myself and my family, myself and my community, myself and the only home I've ever known.

No matter how far or how fast I run…

I can still smell the lingering hints of patchouli following me through the shadowy desert.

2

PHOENIX
LAS VEGAS, NEVADA

Wild Night Blossom. A haven for the depraved. A hellhole of debauchery.

On the surface, it's all class. But that's a cold-blooded lie.

I know better.

So does the man I've come here to meet.

It's a meeting that's been three years in the making. *My* making. And tonight, all this shit finally comes to an end.

I circle the room I've just been shown into. The walls are black, but you can barely tell, thanks to the dozens of framed, mismatched mirrors hung at every height. Some are small and square with thin iron frames. Others are massive splays of rectangular glass with thick, gilded edges.

Five uniform chandeliers hang from the high ceiling. Made of crystal and flickering with candlelight, they're barely bright enough to beat back the shadows crowding in every corner.

There are no windows, of course. Not one. Privacy is of utmost importance to a man like Viktor Ozol.

The master of this whole circus of sin. The motherfucker who has plagued my peace of mind for three years.

Ever since Aurora...

Ever since Yuri...

I'm pacing hard, but the sounds of my footsteps are swallowed whole by the burgundy carpet. The music pulsing beyond these walls is felt more than it's heard. The whole point of this room is to shut out the unsavory nature of what this club was built for: sex in all its forms.

I'd come to the club alone, as per the agreement between Ozol and myself. And as expected, it was a fucking orgy of flesh from the second I stepped foot in the door. In every booth, beneath every table, on every possible surface, there were people fucking. Groans and moans filled the air.

They say the sex is an expression of freedom. *Strip yourself of inhibition,* reads the ornate sign over the door. They think it's a cute little double entendre.

Sex is power. Sex is confidence.

What a fucking farce.

I'd surveyed the faces of the men and women in each booth I'd passed. Some hid their pain behind robotic moans. Others made a show of enjoyment, despite their vacant expressions.

They were all young.

They were all beautiful.

They were all breathing fucking corpses.

My hand twitches automatically towards the waistband of my pants, but I remember I don't have my gun anymore. My weapons were confiscated at the door.

I made a lot of concessions to gain this meeting. I'm still convinced it's worth it.

Or rather it will be… once I have the fucker within my grasp.

Ozol agreed to meet me in this room at precisely ten-thirty. The silver clock on the wall tells me that it's ten forty-three now. The bastard is late.

I doubt it's an accident. Nothing Viktor Ozol does is ever an accident. I'm sure he thinks this deliberate power move will assert his dominance over me.

He's wrong if he believes I'll be intimidated. He's wrong if he thinks I earned all the things I have—the money, the power—from sheer fucking nepotism.

The blood that runs in my veins is pure mob royalty. I am Phoenix Kovalyov, son of Artem and Esme Kovalyov, the reigning king and queen of the Los Angeles-based Kovalyov Bratva. Nephew to Cillian and Kian O'Sullivan, dons of Ireland's O'Sullivan mafia clan.

But the blood I've spilled to earn my place at the table was done with my own two hands. I carved this empire in Las Vegas myself. Made my own way. Built my own legacy. And I made sure that my reputation would stand on its own two feet, far removed from the dynasties that my mentors built.

Ten years ago, I left my Uncle Kian's tutelage in New York City and came here to erect something from scratch. I did exactly that. I am a don in my own right. Nothing can touch me. No man can hurt me.

Or at least, that's what I used to believe.

Until three years ago.

When I was foolish enough to let an enemy take advantage of the one vulnerability that I'd allowed myself in the last decade.

I glance at the time. Ten forty-nine. This asshole is really fucking with the wrong man. But I force myself to be patient. I've waited three years for this meeting. I can stand to wait a few more minutes.

My muscles ping with adrenaline, preparing for a fight that I've imagined in my head a thousand times over.

Uncle Cillian always says that revenge is the wrong reason to fight. But I disagree. It's the strongest motivator I have left. It's the reason I've made it my life's mission to expose and destroy Astra Tyrannis, the organization that Viktor runs.

Three fucking years… and I can finally feel the end coming.

For one of us.

I hear a sound from just outside the door. I wait, ears piqued, but the door remains closed.

Frustrated and growing increasingly impatient, I stalk over to the gigantic bar that covers the entire end wall of the room. The shelves are set against polished glass, weighed down with endless bottles of liquor.

All rare. All expensive. All bought with blood money.

I don't kid myself that I'm some kind of crusader. I'm no saint. And I'm definitely no hero.

I've killed without reason. I've stolen without compulsion. I've lied without guilt. But even among thieves and murderers, there's a fucking code.

You don't fuck with women or children. And Viktor Ozol has done both.

There's no evidence to pin to him. No proof to nail him with. Just a fuck ton of rumors and the stink of corruption that pervades through every single establishment he owns, through every nasty place his fingers have ever soiled.

He's been avoiding me, though. I'd scored this meeting only because I'd lied about the reason for it. *A temporary truce* is what I told him. An attempt to broker a mutually beneficial deal between the two biggest players in Las Vegas. It was too tempting an offer for Ozol to pass up, so I'd secured my meeting.

But I'm starting to smell a rat. Because there's no excuse for this kind of delay.

Ten more minutes and his absence will go from rude to insulting. And the only answer to insults in the underworld… is violence.

I'm about to reach for the shiny new bottle of Isabella's Islay —when the door bursts open. I whip around, abandoning the whiskey to face Viktor Ozol.

Except it's not Ozol at all.

The person standing in the doorway is a frail blonde who looks like she's been plucked off the poster of some Gothic horror movie. She's wearing a ripped wedding dress, torn in several places, dusty and bloodstained at the hem.

She stares at me without seeing as she stumbles blearily into the room. I walk towards her cautiously, wondering what kind of game Ozol is playing with me.

My hand strays towards the tiny knife I managed to conceal from security, but I resist pulling it out. No sense in showing my cards before I have to.

The girl—I suppose she's a woman, but she looks so young and innocent that "girl" seems more appropriate—looks up at me. She has huge amber eyes fanned with thick black eyelashes and ringed with smudged mascara. Her blonde hair has lost its sheen to sweat, and her breaths burst from her in small, pain-filled gasps.

She looks like every other girl I've seen here tonight: beautiful. Young. Broken.

The only difference is that, on her... it shows.

"Who the fuck are you?" I snarl.

She blanches, her eyebrows furrowing as though she's trying to shake off the voices in her head.

I look around the room, but it doesn't appear that we're being watched. Of course, that means fuck-all. There are a million places to hide a camera in here if someone with bad intentions wanted to observe.

I turn back to her, unmoved by the tear tracks leaving streaks down her hollow cheeks. She still hasn't answered my question.

"I asked you a question," I repeat. "Who the fuck are you?"

"Please," she whispers, as though terrified to speak out loud, "don't curse."

I raise my eyebrows. Did she just tell me to watch my language? I almost laugh. I'm thirty-two years old, and it's been more than two decades since someone has told me to watch what I say.

Her eyes dart from side to side and her hands twitch at her sides. I look down and notice that her fingernails are bloody. She seems to be shivering, too.

"I... I... The lights were so bright," she stammers. Her words slur. "I was just trying... trying to get away from everything... A door was open... I went... I came in here... and there were... I saw... I saw..."

The trembling is more pronounced now. Her eyes are unfocused. I've seen this before, more times than I care to relive.

She's drugged.

"Listen to me," I order, raising my hands palms up. I don't touch her, but I take a step closer. "Calm down. Breathe."

She complies instantly, melting with innocence and looking into my eyes like she's desperately waiting for my next instruction.

This girl doesn't fit the mold of a spy or an assassin. She can't possibly be working for Ozol. But maybe the fact that she's an unlikely recruit is exactly the reason he's sent her in here.

"How do you feel now?" I ask.

"I..." She shakes her head, and a fresh tear squeezes from the corner of one eye. "I'm scared," she admits, her voice breaking.

"Did someone bring you in here?"

"No. I was on the streets... There were so many lights, so many people... I just wanted some quiet. I needed to think." Her eyes dart around the room. Whatever she notices clearly doesn't make her feel any better, because she clams up instantly. "I shouldn't be here."

"No," I agree, "you shouldn't."

Any minute now, a very bad man is going to walk through that door. The only thing that would keep her safe is the very bad man who's already in here.

Me.

"But I can't go back out there," she pleads desperately. "There were men and women. They were everywhere. They were..."

"Fucking," I offer coldly.

She flinches at the curse. There's no way this woman works for Ozol. There's no way this woman has spent any time in the underworld at all.

But then again, she's standing in front of me in a bedraggled wedding dress and bare, dusty feet. And there's literal blood on her hands.

So she can't be as innocent as she looks.

"I was trying to get out," she says in a small voice. "But I just… The rooms got worse. There were men and they looked at me… They tried to touch…"

Her breathing is getting panicked again.

"It's okay," I interrupt. "I'm not going to hurt you."

"I know," she replies instantly. Her answer seems to surprise her. It sure as hell surprises the fuck out of me.

I frown. "You know?"

Her brow wrinkles as she tries to gather her thoughts. Her eyes keep going in and out of focus. Whatever she was slipped, it's strong. She's still fighting the after-effects, even if she doesn't yet know it.

Before she can respond to my question, the door opens slowly. Acting on instinct, I grab her hand and push her behind me.

This time, the person at the door is exactly who I expect to see.

"Viktor," I greet coolly, trying to salvage the situation despite the desperate girl trembling behind me.

He's dressed to kill in a navy suit and a white collared shirt. His cufflinks catch the candlelight—a pair of black swans, set in metal. His alarmingly light blue eyes linger on me for a mere second before they fall on the unkempt bride trying to disappear under my shadow.

"What the fuck is this, Kovalyov?" Ozol asks, his tone rippling with annoyance. "We agreed to meet alone."

"She's not part of this," I snap back.

He looks at me suspiciously. So I'm right in assuming she's just a cosmic fluke that's stumbled into the wrong place at the wrong fucking time.

"You told me you wanted to meet to discuss a truce."

"Among other things."

His eyes narrow dangerously. Movement flickers from just beyond the door. Enough to let me know that Ozol is not alone like he claimed to be.

"What kept you, Ozol?" I drawl. I know I need to play this smarter, but my hatred for the man runs deeper than he could ever imagine. It takes so much effort to keep the black rage from pouring out of me. "You were scared to meet me alone?"

"Says the man who brought the bride of Frankenstein to the party," he retorts. "Why the hell is she dressed like that?"

The way he looks at her has me seething. Is that the way he looks at all his victims before he tears their lives apart?

I step right in front of her, blocking her from view. "Like I said, she's not part of this. She stumbled in here moments before you did. Wrong room."

"And yet you seem keen on protecting her."

"From you?" I say. "Someone has to."

He glowers at me. "You didn't come here for a truce, did you, young Phoenix?"

"Oh, I did," I tell him, my fingers twitching with anticipation. "And I plan on seeing it through."

I push the girl to the side, forcing her behind one of the wing-backed armchairs. Then I whip out my knife.

Ozol moves at the same time. But when he raises his hand, it's a gun he's holding.

He sees the blade glimmering in my hand and laughs. "You brought a knife to a gunfight? Stupid Russian."

I'm not scared for myself as I stare down the barrel of his gun. Death stopped scaring me a long time ago. My only point of concern is the terrified girl cowering behind the black armchair.

Viktor stalks closer. "Stupid, stupid, stupid. Stupid to ask for this meeting. Stupid to think you could walk onto my turf and leave in one piece."

I spit on the floor at his feet. "I'm still standing, *mudak*."

A slow smile pulls up the corners of his mouth. "Not for long."

3

ELYSSA

I'm caught between two angels of death.

The man closest to me is all darkness. Dark hair, dark eyes, dark, handsome features. He's wearing dark pants and a black t-shirt underneath a black leather jacket that fits him perfectly, accentuating the raw power of his arms.

The man standing against the open door is his opposite. He's got light hair and pale blue irises. His skin is ashen, almost sallow. And he's dressed as though he's going to a wedding.

Somehow—of all the rooms in all the buildings in all the world—I've managed to stumble into the worst possible one I could have chosen.

And I'm forced to look to a devil for protection.

There's no denying that the dark-haired man is a devil. It's radiating from every inch of him—raw, brutal power. The way he spoke to me, the way he grabbed me, the pure fury in his eyes when I first opened the door.

And yet, of the two, he's the less threatening one. Because even though his words—"I asked who the fuck you are"—hit me like a whiplash, there was something almost like concern dancing on the edge of them.

"You going to shoot me, Ozol?" my dark-haired protector asks. "Before we've even discussed terms?"

"Discussed terms?" the man called Ozol asks. "Something tells me that you don't want to discuss terms at all."

He looks at the gun in Ozol's hand without the slightest trace of fear. It may as well be a toy for all the effect it has on him. "Why wouldn't I?"

"I know you've been keeping tabs on me for a while now," Ozol says. "Did you really think I wouldn't be doing the same with you?"

"Find anything interesting?"

Ozol smiles. I shiver automatically. It's a disgusting, sinister smile. He makes my skin crawl, without reason or explanation.

"I've discovered a vendetta you've decided to lay at my feet. Unjustly so."

"You're going to stand there and deny it?"

"That is exactly what I'm doing," he snarls.

My protector looks furious. But even in his state of fury, he contains his reaction. He doesn't give into hysteria like I would have. He's the kind of man that Father Josiah would have been impressed by.

Father Josiah. Just thinking about him sends me into a tailspin of guilt.

I glance down to my bloodied fingers, and I have the sudden urge to rip them from my hand.

My vision blurs, but I'm not crying. Truth be told, I don't think I have any more tears left to cry. On top of that, the fogginess keeps draping over me in waves at the most unexpected times. Sometimes, I feel as though I've got my bearings, and just then, my body seems to quit on me.

It's *his* voice that pulls me back from the horrific truth of my sins—of what I'm running from.

"You may have everyone else fooled, Ozol. But I know who you are. I know how you make your money."

"My dealings don't concern you."

"They have in the past."

"I had nothing to do with their deaths. You ought to run a tighter organization, Kovalyov."

Deaths? I seize up, caught between wanting to know more and wanting to never hear another word either of these men speak.

"I'll ask you again…" Ozol begins, his tone twisting into darkness.

For some reason, it reminds me of Father Josiah when he was angry. That didn't happen often. But when it did, it was like a rolling storm that sent bolts of lightning down in every direction. Purposeful and merciless.

"…Who is the girl?"

His light blue eyes land on me.

I duck back behind the sleek leather armchair, but I don't quite manage to make myself small enough to disappear completely.

"I already told you," my protector growls. "She has nothing to do with this."

"I find that hard to believe. You came here to kill me," Ozol says. "Is the girl meant to be a distraction?"

"The girl is what I said she is," he replies. "Just an innocent bystander in the wrong place at the wrong time. But you're right about the first part—I'm exactly where I intended to be."

I scream when the first gunshot pierces through the relative silence.

All I can register is fear.

Not for myself—but for the dark-haired man who decided to protect me when he could've fed me right to the beast.

I scramble forward, ignoring the voice in my head that's telling me to stay put. I expect to see him on the floor, blood pouring from his body.

But I realize he hasn't been hit at all.

He's feinted to the side, his body moving with a grace that belies his massive stature.

"Mikal! Vlad!" Ozol screams as he fires off another round of bullets.

I look up in time to see my protector fling the knife in his hand. It twists through the air, with an aim so true that I marvel at the technique.

The knife bites into Ozol's gun-wielding arm. His weapon clatters to the floor a few feet from me. My first instinct is to recoil from it. I've never held a gun in my life. I don't intend to start now.

But fear is not an option. And despite the pounding in my head, I'm not naïve enough to believe that doing nothing is an answer.

I can't bring myself to pick it up, so I kick the gun towards my protector. It spins across the floor, dragging in the carpet but still managing to get to within his reach.

His hand lances out so fast that by the time I've blinked, he's grabbed the gun and bounced up on his feet.

I grip the broad back of the armchair and use it to pull myself upright. My legs are still weak and wobbly. The two guards that Ozol yelled for come hurtling in at the door. But Ozol has disappeared, leaving behind only a few droplets of his blood.

My protector shoots three times. The first bullet misses, but the second two both strike the first guard in the chest. He plummets to the ground immediately, leaving the path clear to the second guard.

The man's features go slack with fear. He acts to survive, not to attack.

Unfortunately for me, I'm part of his plan.

He lunges to the side and grabs me, forcing me in front of him. My back is pressed against his chest, and now I'm facing my protector. Somehow, despite all the chaos erupting around me, that's what keeps me calm.

Until the haze kicks in again. My vision blurs behind another bout of dizziness and his features swim before me for a moment.

"Let her go," I hear him growl. "Or I will kill you slowly."

"Let me go and I won't hurt her," the man behind me bargains.

My protector's eyes narrow with dangerous promise. "You're fucking with the wrong man, *mudak*."

"Spare me and I'll let her go," he practically yells in my ear. "I swear it!"

"Very well," my protector nods. "Let her go now."

The bodyguard shoves me forward into the man's arms. My cheek collides the hard muscle of his chest as he clutches me close. I have long enough to register his smell—a dark, swirling cologne mixed with the faintest hint of whiskey—before another sound erupts just inches from my ear.

The sound of a gunshot.

I scream. Then, trembling, I look up at him.

My protector's face is impassive, his eyes hooded. It's his darkness that makes him so beautiful. In my delirium, I think about telling him exactly that.

But a question comes out instead.

"You killed him?"

He nods. "Yes."

I start to turn, but he wrenches me back towards him. One hand on my jaw, forcing me to look at his eyes and not at the bleeding corpses behind me.

"But... he let me go," I whisper in a tiny voice. "You promised you'd spare him."

"Some promises are not worth keeping," he rumbles. "Come."

I don't look down when I step over the two bodies lying on the stained carpet. I just walk blindly, allowing myself to be pulled by my protector.

I know I should be scared of him. But I'm not.

Then again, I'm not myself at the moment. I'm someone else.

A woman who set a fire to cover up a murder.

A woman who ran without a backward glance.

A woman without a home or a family or a name.

So when he opens a door and pushes me through, I go willingly.

It takes me a moment to recognize where we are. It looks like a bathroom, but it drips of opulent luxury. The taps and faucets are gold. The tile is marble. The high ceiling bears clusters of glittering stars, hundreds of them. It reminds me of the candles in the bedroom I left behind and I almost vomit at the thought.

CLICK. I glance behind me to see that my protector is locking the door.

When he turns to me, I freeze, suddenly aware of the fact that we're strangers. Just because he hasn't hurt me so far doesn't mean he won't do it now.

"Should I be scared of you?" I ask, my voice trembling.

His eyes flash. "No."

He doesn't offer me any evidence, but I don't need it. For some godforsaken reason, I believe him.

"Who are you?" he asks.

"I… I wish I knew," I say, a tear slipping loose from the corner of my eye.

It's a stupid answer, but an honest one. Who am I anymore? I'm no longer Elyssa Redmond. I'm a killer in the night. A ghost in the desert.

"You don't know?"

"Not anymore."

I stare down at my hands, wondering when my fall from grace really began. There's so much I can't remember. And at the same time, there's so much I wish I could forget.

He moves closer to me. This time, I don't back away. I don't want to. There's something comforting about his presence. Something that soothes the jagged edges of my anxiety.

"You've been through something," he guesses.

It's not really a question, but I nod anyway. I can't find my voice.

"Come here," he says, taking my hand and leading me to the bathroom counter.

His hands grip my waist. In one smooth motion, he's lifted me onto the counter as though I weigh nothing at all. While I sit there, wondering what he's doing, he grabs a hand towel from a ring next to the sink and runs it through water. Then he lifts to my face and dabs carefully, almost… tenderly.

When the towel comes away, I realize it's smeared with dirt and dried blood. I hadn't even realized I'd been hurt.

Then again, maybe it isn't my blood at all.

The realization makes me feel light-headed all over again. My vision blurs and fresh tears fall.

"Listen to me," he rasps softly. "There's no point thinking about it. Whatever it is."

"But—"

"Can you change it?"

"N… no."

"Then don't torture yourself."

He works on my face again patiently, his eyes lingering on my lips for a moment before he dips the towel in water once more.

"Thank you," I whisper.

He just nods.

"Who are you?" I ask.

He meets my gaze. I feel my insides shiver. The intensity in those dark eyes has me leaning in, just the tiniest fraction of an inch.

"You chose the wrong place to seek refuge," he warns me. "This place is not safe."

"Why are you here then?"

"Because I can handle myself," he says. "You can't."

I drop my head, unable to argue.

"You have to leave," he adds.

I bite my lip to keep from saying the words that are dangerously close to spilling out. *I don't want to leave you.*

But I'm not his problem. I'm my own problem now.

The drugged haze has mostly cleared away by now, though the fear still remains. He reaches up and brushes away one of my tears. Our eyes meet again, and I recognize something in him. Probably because it's the same thing twisting inside of me right now.

Restlessness.

Conflict.

Two sides of himself warring with each other.

"Thank you," I murmur.

"You've thanked me already."

"Not enough."

And then, before I can stop myself, I reach out and cup his cheek with the palm of my hand. He jerks away momentarily from the sudden gesture, but I force it and he allows me to touch him.

I can't read much about him. But in this moment, I know that neither one of us knows what's happening right now. There is a connection here, but it's too muddied in the chaos of what's just passed for either one of us to unpack.

Maybe that's why, when he leans in, I lean towards him, too.

Because that is the only way we can think of to diffuse some of the tension growing between us.

His lips fall on mine like a cloud. Soft. Supple. Tender. I've never been kissed like this before. So, when his hand wraps around my neck, I crane it up for him, giving him better access to my mouth.

I sigh and the sigh unlocks my lips. His tongue enters with quiet confidence. When his hands snake under my dress, I part my legs for him until he steps up between them. I'm trembling again—but this time, it has nothing to do with fear.

His lips leave mine and fall to my neck. I hear myself moan. The sound is so foreign that it forces my eyes open. I've never moaned like that in my life.

And I don't even know this man's name.

When he pushes aside my panties, I tense up a little. He pulls his lips from the side of my neck and looks me right in the eye.

"Say the word and I'll stop."

I stare at him. "Please, God… don't."

He keeps his eyes on me when he pushes himself inside me for the first time. It's not as gentle as his kiss, but it doesn't need to be. I want him to take the memories away—by any means necessary.

I feel his length sink into me, aware for the first time of an aching pain between my thighs. The pain lasts for several thrusts, but his eyes distract me.

And when the pain clears, only pleasure is left behind.

My hands move to his shoulders. I'm suddenly shy. Shy to touch him, shy to hold him, shy to give myself over to him in a way that I desperately want to.

I don't know what's come over me. Having sex with a stranger in the bathroom of a horrible club goes against everything I've been taught.

But then again, I'm not the same girl anymore. I'd made sure of that when I set that fire and started running.

It feels like I've peeled off the layers of who I used to be. And in her place is another girl.

Someone reckless and wild.

Someone desperate and alone.

And maybe…

Just a little bit brave.

4

PHOENIX

She clings to me as though I'm her last lifeline. Her breathing comes in staggered gasps that makes her entire body tremble. Everything about her screams of frailty and vulnerability.

Maybe that's why simply looking at her is a complete mindfuck.

Because despite all that innocence, she's sitting here in a ripped wedding dress—with bloody fingernails that prove she can fight back.

Her eyes find mine as I thrust into her, reveling in the tight clench of her pussy. The thought that I might be taking her virginity flickers across my mind. But I cast it off. There's no way a virgin would part her legs for a stranger so willingly.

In any case, I'm past the point of caring.

I'm definitely past the point of stopping—unless she says the word.

That doesn't seem likely. Her moans are soft, pleated with tentative desire. Like she doesn't want to make a noise. Doesn't want to lose her inhibitions completely. She's tense, even while I fuck her.

And that only makes me more determined to make her unravel.

I push her back against the bathroom counter and bear down on her, pushing myself deeper. Her eyes pop open with shock as I consume as much of her as I possibly can.

She doesn't stop me. Doesn't seem to want to. She just looks amazed that I can make her feel anything at all.

And that's when I get it—it's not that she's never had sex.

She's never had *good* sex.

She doesn't yet understand what her body is capable of when she gives everything to me.

I desperately want to rid her of the old-fashioned wedding dress she's wearing. I want to rip the aged fabric off her and gaze at her naked breasts as they bounce with every plunge of my hips.

I settle for running my hand over her chest. She whimpers as I brush against her nipples. Her lips part. Her eyes are limpid with lust.

But I can sense the desperation in her. It's probably that very desperation that's causing her to go with this in the first place.

This is total fucking madness, after all. She just saw something that not many people live to tell about: two of the most powerful dons in Las Vegas—hell, two of the most powerful dons in the world—squaring off with gunfire. And now we're in the bathroom of this nightmare club, and we're *fucking?* I'm sure her mind is completely screwed.

Her body is about to be completely screwed, too.

A moan rips from her lips as I increase the speed and intensity of my thrusts. Apparently, I need this release more than I realized. It's been a minute since I last let off some steam. I haven't fucked like this since...

"Oh, God," she whimpers softly. "Oh God... what's... what...?"

She doesn't even finish the sentence, because a second later, I feel her orgasm break. Her walls pulse around my cock, trying to choke me out for what feels like minutes before she finally calms and dissolves into a puddle of near-silent moans.

Just when her orgasm recedes, I let myself go, spurting inside her with a heavy load that's a result of months of abstinence. Her nails dig into my back, keeping me as close as she can get me. I welcome the sharp burst of pain.

I don't stay inside her long after that. When I pull out without warning, she nearly falls forward off the counter. She gasps, but I manage to catch her in time.

Her hands latch onto my shoulders, preventing me from moving away like I'd planned. And all I can think is…

What the fuck have I done?

How have I allowed that shit show to devolve into a quick, filthy fuck in the bathroom of one of the seediest clubs in Las Vegas?

It was her innocence that did it.

No—not *only* the innocence. It was the combination of the innocence and the violence.

Blood on a wedding dress.

A body like sin with eyes like hope itself.

I try and move away again, but her nails dig into my arms. "Please," she begs, "wait." She's looking down as though terrified of the request she's just made.

"Who are you running from?" I ask.

Her answer is immediate. "Everyone," she whispers. "Everyone."

I zip myself up and then stroke a finger underneath her chin, forcing her to meet my eyes. "How bad is it?"

She hesitates for a long time. "Bad."

"And you can't go back?" I ask, wondering where "back" even is.

She shakes her head, doesn't say a word.

"Do you have anywhere else to go?"

She shakes her head again.

Fuck. I can't play the hero to this little lost lamb. And yet, I want to. Which is inconvenient at best—and self-destructive at worst.

"Fine," I growl. She looks slightly cowed by my intensity. "First things first… we need to get out of here."

"We?" she repeats, dumbfounded.

I nod. "I can't leave you walking the halls of a sex club on your own."

Her expression screws up with distaste. "I didn't mean to come in here. I didn't know…"

"Well, you picked wisely. One of the most expensive of its kind in the country."

She shudders. "It was an accident."

"They didn't teach you sarcasm where you're from?"

"They taught me not to ask too many questions."

I raise my eyebrows. That explains a lot. "In case we get separated out there, you go to Weston's Diner. Corner of Las Vegas Boulevard."

"Why would we get separated?" she asks, her voice turning panicky instantly.

I put my hand on her shoulder instinctively. "Because there's a lot of people out there who want me fucking dead." She flinches the moment I swear, but I keep going as though I don't notice the tic. "Most of them have connections, and if they don't, they *are* the connection."

She looks at me with a baffled expression on her face. Clearly, what I'm saying is making zero sense to her.

When's the last time I spoke to someone like her? Someone wholly untouched by my world and its schemes, its sins, its prices?

Aurora... She was the last. She was the only person I can remember who had eyes like that, pure and clear. The only person who—

A gentle flicker against my cheek pulls me back to the present. I realize that she's cupping my face again.

The first time, she was asking for comfort.

This time, she's giving it.

"You went somewhere dark," she tells me bluntly. "I wanted to bring you back."

Bring me back? Does anyone have that power?

But the way she's touching me... Tenderness, mixed with comfort... I haven't felt that in a long fucking time.

I didn't think I ever wanted it again.

I jerk away from her touch. She recoils, her hand suspended in air for a moment before she lets it drop.

"Ozol will have put a hit out on me before he ran like the coward he is," I say. "Stay behind me at all times. But if I tell you to run, you run."

She looks terrified by the very notion of leaving my side. I glare at her, hardening my expression so she knows I mean business.

"Do you understand me? If I tell you to run," I snarl slowly, "you...?"

"Run," she whispers. But there's nothing remotely confident about her tone.

I take a step closer. She needs to understand what's at stake here. "Listen to me," I say urgently. "The men out there? They want me dead. And now, they think you're with me. If they get their hands on you, they will do worse than kill you."

She looks baffled for a moment. "What's worse than death?" she asks innocently.

I shake my head. Where the fuck has this girl come from? Who the hell is she?

"Lots of things," I retort grimly. "And I hope you never have to find out what."

I grab her by the hips and lift her off the counter. She feels so fucking weightless in my arms. Feather-light and trembling.

"Now, come. We have to move."

I head to the door and unlock it gently. When I open it and poke my head out, there's no one standing in the broad, dimly lit hallway.

I wish she was wearing anything other than the bridal gown she has on. It's pretty fucking conspicuous. But we're short on time and options alike.

I follow the wall down the corridor while she shadows my footsteps, knocking into me twice in the space of a minute. She apologizes every time. I have to remind her to be quiet.

When we reach the end of the wall, I glance around the corner. There's a large common area with plush red sofas arranged around the circular space. Behind each sofa is a door that leads to private playrooms. There are a few men on the sofas, each one with a woman or two draped all over him.

It's a dead end. *Goddammit.*

I cross the opening and keep walking. When I don't feel her behind me, I turn. She's still tailing me, but she's fallen behind by a foot or so.

"Come on," I say impatiently. "Stay close."

She moves fast, but her expression is troubled.

"What's wrong?"

She shakes her head.

"Tell me."

"I just never knew…"

"Knew what?"

"…that places like this existed."

She looks stunned. But whether she's stunned by the fact that sex clubs exist or stunned by her own ignorance, I don't know. And now's not the time to find out.

The thundering of footsteps has me pulling out my gun. And just in time, too. Two men burst into the corridor from the circular room we've just passed. I grab the girl and push her behind me as I shoot.

My bullets fly blindly, but it's enough to force the men back and put them on the defensive. I keep firing as I press back against the corridor. One of the attackers collapses to the floor, but two others appear to replace him.

"Fuck!" I growl.

It's the first time she doesn't flinch at the swear word.

"Remember what I told you?" I ask as more men come pouring out of the woodwork brandishing firearms.

She freezes. Looks up at me with those endless amber eyes. Her blond hair catches the light. The blood on her wedding dress looks dark and vicious. It doesn't belong on a girl like her.

"Run," I growl at her. "Now!"

To my dismay, she hesitates. Gunfire is pouring down around our position. We're running out of time.

So I grab her arm hard, no doubt bruising her in the process. Her eyes go wide with pain. Then I push her back away from me hard.

"If you want to live, you fucking run."

Her eyes glaze with fear. But this time, she listens.

She turns and starts running. The folds of her dress trail behind her in wispy waves. I don't have the time to watch her disappear—the guards are coming my way.

I duck into a room in the opposite direction. A deliberate attempt to throw them off her tail.

I don't know why it's so important that she gets to safety. The girl's a stranger to me. She doesn't factor into any of my plans.

And yet, I'm actually worried.

Will she make it out of here in one piece?

Will she be captured when she tries to get out?

Will she find the diner?

The guards thunder into the room behind me. I'm ready for them this time. I duck for cover while letting out another round of bullets. I manage to shoot three different men, but my ammo is running out. I need to make a quick escape.

Right on cue, I hear a storm of gunshots going off down below. I move to the edge and glance down to see a handful of my men bash through the main entryway.

I've never been one to smile in triumph. But this time, I'm definitely smiling on the inside.

I aim at the glass and send my last bullet hurtling into it. The bullet cracks the surface, sending glossy little fissures in every direction. I toss my gun to the side and run towards the window.

I hit it, legs first, causing the entire glass window to shatter as I fall to the dancefloor below. I land on my feet with nothing more than a few cuts on my arms. Thankfully, the drop is only about six feet. Any further and my landing wouldn't have been quite so flawless.

The screams that punctuated my landing have all but disappeared as I straighten up. It's late enough that the dancefloor is relatively empty. It's the private rooms that are packed to the brim.

Not that I'm very fussed about casualties in this particular venue. Apart from some of the women, the people that frequent this joint are fucking scum like Ozol.

None as bad as him quite yet—but some men just need a little more time to rot all the way down to their souls.

My men rush to cover me as they shoot back more of Ozol's goons. Within minutes, the fight is over. Each side is just interested in getting out intact at this point.

The moment we're back out on the streets, my men gather around me with their guns still drawn.

"Didn't go well, boss?" Ilya asks.

"You can fucking say that again."

My black Wrangler is brought around. I head for the driver's seat immediately.

"The rest of you get into the other vehicles and head back," I order.

"Boss?" Konstantin calls back, looking confused. "You're not coming with us?"

"No," I reply. "I have a stop to make first."

5

ELYSSA

Is it possible for your heart to jump out your throat? That's how it feels as I run blindly through the club, hoping to stumble on a way out.

I don't look back. But I don't need to do that to know I'm being pursued.

Thundering footsteps echo in my ears. They're closing in—fast.

I just ran God-only-knows-how-many miles barefoot through the desert to even get here. The soles of my feet are raw and bleeding. There's no way I can outrun these masked monsters for much longer.

"Fucking grab her!" yells a man with a voice like a chainsaw. A sickly spice cloaks the air as I dart past a room filled with more naked, gyrating patrons.

I turn my head back in the direction I'm running just in time to avoid colliding into a server girl holding a tray of beverages. She's wearing a tiny black triangle of cloth over her breasts and private parts. It doesn't cover much. I suppose that's probably the point.

"Hey!" she hisses. "Watch it, zombie bride."

Zombie bride? It registers only a second later that I'm still wearing a ripped, bloodstained wedding dress. I stick out like a sore thumb.

But, considering the alternatives for clothing on display around me, I actually prefer to be wearing this.

I mutter an apology as I dart through the room. Some of the men barely notice me. Others look up in amusement.

"Why don't you slow down and hang out for a while, babe?" I hear one man call out to me. "I wouldn't mind ass-fucking a little she-devil newlywed."

I don't have time to cringe at the terrifying comment. Instead, I fly out of the room through a door on the opposite side.

The space I enter is massive. Lights hang from the ceiling, each one a different color that pulses unnaturally, setting off a chaos of swirling patterns on the floor below. My eyes go crazy at the disorienting sight and the pain in my head worsens.

Dancers cluster in the center of the room, grinding together just below the lights. The smell of alcohol burns my nostrils as I try to maneuver past them, but they bump and flop and crash into me as if I'm not here at all.

I turn on the spot, trying to find a door out of here. But I don't see anything. And the world just keeps spinning faster and faster, those bright lights flickering and pulsing, the people whirling and writhing…

"Hey there, bridezilla, wanna dance?" I cringe away from the reedy man who snares my arm.

His fingers encircle my wrist painfully, so I act on instinct. My free hand lashes out in the shape of a claw and I swipe at his face.

He shrieks in pain and releases me immediately. When he looks back up, hate in his eyes, I realize I've left three long, bloody scratches down his cheek. Before he can recover enough to take his revenge, I fly in the opposite direction.

Door, door, where's a door?!

Just when I think I've escaped my pursuers, I notice them at the far end of a massive room. It takes them only seconds to spot me. I pivot once again, trying to avoid both the man I'd clawed and the guards on my trail.

And that's when I see the door, haloed in white light, like a beacon calling to me.

Ignoring the pain burning in my feet and the throb between my thighs, I hoist up my tattered skirt and start running again.

But when I burst out onto the street in front of the club, I feel a moment of relief.

I've made it out of the club. Now, I just need to get to the diner.

My flustered mind grapples to find the name that my dark-eyed protector told me. *Wiley's... Waco's... What was it?*

I close my eyes and picture those full lips moving. That jaw, covered in a rough, three-day beard that burned my face when he kissed me...

"Weston's Diner." *That's what he said.* "Corner of Las Vegas Boulevard."

I turn on the spot and search for street signs. When I find none, I grab hold of the first woman who passes me. She jerks away from me, but I keep a tight grip of her anyway.

"I'm sorry," I stammer, "but please, where's Las Vegas Boulevard?"

She looks like she's about to tell me to go to hell. But something in my expression softens her. She jerks her chin forward. "Go straight two blocks and turn right."

"Thank you," I mumble. I let her go and she hurries away.

I head in that direction, praying that I'll find the diner easily. But more importantly, I pray that my protector will be there waiting for me.

I follow the woman's instructions and end up on Las Vegas Boulevard. This place is like something out of a dream—or a drug-induced nightmare. Everything is glowing neon, people moving, cars honking, signs flashing and flaunting and flickering in the desert darkness.

After everything I've been through, this might be what does me in. The straw that breaks the camel's back. It's just too much to process.

I cast my eyes down to my feet. That's the only safe place to look. The only thing that won't drive me insane.

One foot in front of the other. One bare, bloodied, dust-covered, aching foot in front of the other. That's all I have to do. Step and step and step.

I can do this. I can make it.

I limp down the street until I sense someone approaching me. "Excuse me," I say, trying to keep my eyes shaded downwards to avoid the harsh glare of the flashing signs, "do you know where I can find Weston's Diner?"

The man blows right past, ignoring me completely.

I try again with the next pedestrian. "Excuse me…"

Same result. The stranger breezes by as if I'm not even there.

The third person just shakes their head. "No idea, little lady."

I sigh, swallow past the bitter fear in my throat, and go back to looking at my feet. *Left foot, right foot, left foot…*

It's right then that a hand snakes out suddenly and grabs me by the wrist. I'm pulled into a darkened alleyway that smells like stale bread and urine. I'm about to scream, but a whiff of gardenia makes me stop.

That's not the scent of a man who wants to hurt me.

I turn to the face of a woman about my age. She's got slanted blue eyes and dark hair piled high on her head. She's also wearing an oversized trench coat, but it's open wide enough that I can see what she's wearing underneath.

Which isn't much.

Straps of black see-through fabric push up her breasts and highlight her nipples. It looks extremely uncomfortable… and extremely familiar.

I gasp. "You work at that club…!" I say, backing away from her.

She reels me back into her, but her touch is gentle. "Hey, hey, shh, it's okay. I'm here to help."

"You do work there?"

"Well, shit, girl, don't hold that against me."

I frown, unsure how to react to this woman. I've never come across anyone like her in my entire life. She radiates confidence, sass, and a cunning intelligence.

"I'm trying to help you," she explains. "I saw you earlier running around the club with those brutes behind you. I thought you could maybe use a little help."

That much is certainly true. I need more help than she could possibly provide.

"Hold on," she says, walking around me to the edge of the alleyway. She looks right and left, and her shoulders relax a little. "Okay, cool. All clear."

"All clear?" I repeat stupidly.

She turns to me with curious eyes. "I know those guys who were after you. Hulk One and Hulk Two have many admirable traits, but a third brain cell isn't one of them."

I barely follow what she's saying. And it doesn't help that she's talking really fast.

"I think the first thing we need to do is get you out of that dress," she says, assessing me from head to toe. "It's a little on the conspicuous side, even for Sin City."

I glance down instinctively, still trembling with fear and exhaustion.

"Hey, girl, hey," she croons, "everything's gonna be okay. Let's take a step back. You don't have to do anything you don't want to. I'm just trying to help. I've been where you… well, you need some help, I think. So let me phrase it as a question: Will you let me help you?"

I appreciate the question. Maybe that's why I nod immediately. In any case, I don't really have the luxury of turning down help.

She smiles, revealing a dimple in her right cheek. "Then follow me, little lamb."

Instead of leading me back into the street, she goes to the opposite end of the alleyway. I assumed it was a dead end, but then I realize there's a nondescript door nestled in the corner.

"It leads to the restaurant out front," she explains, sensing my confusion. "The one you just passed."

She opens the door. I follow her into a bright space that looks like a storeroom of some kind. I can smell frying meat in the air. My stomach churns with hunger.

"My name is Charity, by the way," she says, turning to me and gesturing for me to sit down.

"Charity," I repeat. "I'm…"

I pause. She's the first person in the outside world I'm offering my name up to. It feels momentous somehow.

"Hey, I'm not asking for your blood type or Social Security number," Charity says with a knowing smile. "Just something to call you that's better than, 'Hey, you there.'"

As she talks, she steps past some shelves stacked with boxes and moves to a thin cupboard wedged in the corner. She opens it up and starts pulling out normal clothes. One set for her. One for me.

Then she removes the coat, revealing the full extent of her outfit.

She's wearing a bra that leaves little to the imagination. Her body is lean and tight, but very curvy. The panties she's wearing are black lace. When she turns, I realize it's a thong.

As I watch, still too traumatized to move on my own accord, Charity pulls a pair of jeans up over the thong but discards the black bra for a more modest one before shrugging a t-shirt on top of that.

When she turns to me, I realize I'm gawking. She smiles. "So, you gonna tell me your name or are you gonna make me guess?"

I shake myself out of my reverie. "Um, my name is Elyssa. With an E."

Her smile gets wider. "Well, Elyssa-with-an-E, here you go," she says, offering me the second stack of clothes. "Something to help you blend in."

I examine the clothes she's offered me. A pair of black leggings and a white t-shirt similar to the green one she's wearing.

"I'd offer you a pair of jeans, but you're much smaller than I am. The leggings are a one-size-fits-all kind of deal."

Again, I barely follow her words as I struggle to unzip myself from the dress.

She notices my struggle and swoops over. "Oh. Right. Let me help you."

She drags the zipper down the back and the dress falls off my shoulders easily. I shiver instantly once I've been parted from the material. Beneath it, I'm wearing white cotton panties and a matching bra. The same kind of thing I've worn my entire life. Unlike Charity's undergarments, mine cover up everything they're supposed to.

"Wow," she remarks with a chuckle. "I've only ever seen underwear like that in my grandma's drawer."

I blush, bringing my hands up and around my body. Charity's expression softens as she takes in my reaction.

"You want me to leave while you change?"

I nod gratefully. She gives me a reassuring smile and then heads for the door.

"By the way, the pink door to the side is the bathroom. Feel free to use it however you like. I'll make sure no one bothers you in here."

When she opens the door, sounds and smells filter in, including the scent of cooking oil and sizzling bacon grease. My stomach roils again, but I ignore it.

The moment Charity leaves, I shuffle to the bathroom. It's small but well-stocked, with full soap and a fresh hand towel hanging from a nail in the wall.

I take a deep breath and look into the mirror. My face isn't as nightmarish as I'd expected. With a jolt, I remember why: because my protector cleaned and washed me back in the club's bathroom.

I touch my fingers to my lips, remembering the all-consuming way he had kissed me. I still can't quite believe that happened. What's even more shocking is that I don't regret it. I still ache from where he entered me, from how he grabbed me and molded me to him. But it's a good kind of ache.

The kind of ache that wipes away all the pain that came before it.

I use the bathroom sink to wash most of the grime and dirt off my body and dab the hand towel around to dry off. By the time I'm done, the off-white towel is patchy with dirt. Embarrassed, I hide it under one of the shelves and head back into the storeroom to get dressed.

Charity's tights are snug and the t-shirt is comfortingly loose. I feel so much better in normal clothes than I did in that godawful dress. There aren't any chairs in the room, so I sit down on one of the larger storage boxes. It's firm enough that I can put my weight on it without worrying that it'll cave in.

Then I take a look at my feet. I'm bleeding in several places from long, jagged cuts. Scrapes from rocks in the desert and the rough city sidewalk will only get worse in the coming days. Overall, despite the damage to my body, the adrenaline and exhaustion is keeping the pain at bay. But I need medical supplies or walking is going to get difficult very soon.

Just then, the door opens and Charity returns. She's carrying a bottle of water and a plate. The savory smell hits me immediately and my mouth waters.

"You looked like you needed a little TLC," she says, setting the tray down on a box next to me. The plate is laden with a gargantuan cheeseburger balancing on a mountain of crisp French fries.

"Thank you," I say gratefully, reaching for some fries.

Charity nods and leans against the wall I'm facing. "Jesus, girl, you did a number on yourself. We'll have to take care of those feet. What did you do? Run through hot embers for miles on end?"

"Something like that."

She raises her eyebrows in shock. "Well, fuck."

I've heard that word more in the space of an hour than I have my entire life. It's weird how quickly you can get used to it. Sort of.

"Am I right in assuming you're on your own?"

I hesitate. "Yes."

"Okay, well, if you're interested, I know this great place that'll help you get on your feet. It's a women's shelter, the best one in Las Vegas."

"A women's shelter?"

"Yes, ma'am. There are even jobs available. They'll pay you. It won't be much, but you can save up over time if you're careful."

"Do you work there, too?"

She smiles. "I used to. Before I realized that I could make a fuck ton more money at the clubs."

I try not to cringe at the thought of what she's required to do to make money in places like the one we just left. It's not for me to judge.

"Do you know where Weston's Diner is?" I ask abruptly.

Charity raises an eyebrow. "Uh, yeah. It's across the street, a couple doors down from here. Why?"

I bite my lip, but I decide to trust Charity. After all, she decided to help even though she has no reason to. "I'm… meeting someone there."

She frowns. "I thought you said you were alone."

"I am. Or, I mean, I was…"

"Who are you meeting?"

"Um… I don't know his name," I admit.

Charity's expression goes from curious to worried. "You don't know his name? Where did you meet him?"

"It was… at the club," I tell her, a sinking feeling overriding my desire to meet him. "I met him tonight."

"And he told you to meet him at Weston's?"

"Yes."

"Elyssa, honey, I don't know how to break this to you... But Weston's has connections to the mob. The Russian Bratva, to be more specific. They're dangerous guys. I'm not sure that's the best place for you right now."

I tense, but I can't say I'm all that surprised. He may have been my protector tonight. But I'd sensed he was dangerous from the beginning. And I didn't need to see what he could do with a gun to confirm that, either.

"He helped me tonight, though," I stammer, feeling foolish.

"That doesn't mean he doesn't have ulterior motives," Charity says gently. "The men that frequent Wild Night Blossom... they're not good men, Elyssa."

"I don't think he wanted to be there." I don't know why I'm defending him, even in the absence of a real reason to do so. Just something in his eyes, I suppose.

"I'm sure that's what he told you to get you to meet him at Weston's."

I look down as the sinking feeling in my chest grows. There's so much I don't understand about what's happened to me tonight. The world I thought I knew seems utterly broken.

Charity moves forward and sits down next to me. "Elyssa, you're clearly a nice girl, but you're also clearly not from around here. So let me be the first to say this: you can't just trust people blindly. Especially men. This can be a dangerous city for a young, inexperienced girl who's on her own. Don't let anyone take advantage of you."

I want to tell her that my protector was different. But I know how it would make me sound. Like some naïve little hick who believes in fairy tales.

Which, to be fair, is probably exactly what I am.

"It's clear you have a past," Charity says, her flickering towards the bloodied, discarded wedding dress in the corner. "But that past doesn't have to determine your future. Forget it. Bury it. Leave it in the past. No one has to know where you came from. The only thing that matters is where you plan on going. What I'm saying is, keep your secrets to yourself so that no one can use them against you. Understand?"

As I look into her strong, confident eyes, I realize that I do understand. I'd sort of made the decision already when I set the fire and ran. But that was all done in a haze of confusion, fear, and whatever drugs were pumping through my system.

This is me making the decision consciously, in full control of my wits.

Forget everything that happened before this moment and start fresh.

I think about my dark-eyed protector for a moment, regret curdling in my belly.

Then I breathe out and let him go.

I choose myself.

6

PHOENIX

I don't park in front of the diner. It's common knowledge that Weston's is tied to the Bratva. Nothing definitive, of course. But rumors carry weight. Especially if you repeat them often enough.

I grab the extra jacket I keep in the back of the Wrangler and walk down Las Vegas Boulevard towards the unassuming little diner.

I'm not exactly sure what I'm feeling as I walk to meet her. Wariness? Uncertainty? Annoyance?

Why the fuck have I gone and made her my problem? It's not as though I don't have enough shit on my plate. The sting of tonight's failure pierces through the fog of my thoughts. Maybe that's the real reason I'm heading towards the diner right now: it's the only distraction I have.

Because after three fucking years, I'd finally managed to hook a meeting with the man I've spent all this time trying to kill. The mastermind behind Astra Tyrannis.

Only to let him slip through my fingers.

And for what?

Some runaway bride who flinched every time I swore.

I might have assumed she was working for Ozol. But watching his expression when he'd first laid eyes on her had disabused me of that theory. Her presence in the club had been a fluke. A big "fuck you" from the universe.

My phone rings, but I ignore it. I already know who it is. I don't need to look at the screen and I sure as fuck don't feel like talking to them.

I switch my phone on silent and keep going until I get to Weston's. Considering the time, there's only a couple of young guys sitting slumped in one of the booths, nursing large mugs of coffee. Probably trying to stave off the hangover they're likely going to face tomorrow.

Mischa is wiping down the counter as I take a seat on one of the fading brown barstools. "Evening, boss," he grunts.

Mischa has been running this place ever since it was established more than half a century ago. He's as much an institution as the diner itself.

"Mischa," I greet with a nod. "Has a girl been in here recently?"

Mischa smiles. "Nice to hear you talking about a girl."

"It's not what you think," I say brusquely.

"With most women, it never is."

I don't bother asking him what that means. Talking to Mischa is like talking to the Sphinx. Every question is answered with another. Riddles on riddles. It's fucking exhausting.

"So you haven't seen a girl in a wedding dress come by here?"

He frowns, looking up at me with an expression that's clearly concerned. "A wedding dress?" he repeats. "No, sir. I would have remembered that."

Fuck. I glance around, but one sweep has the diner covered. Besides—Mischa remembers everything.

I turn my attention to the streets, still lively despite the hour. There's no sign of an astonishing, shell-shocked blonde in an ugly wedding dress. I turn back towards Mischa, but I'm looking right past him at the bottles lining the back wall.

"Need a drink, boss?" he asks.

I think about it. For a long fucking time.

"No," I decide at last. "Another time."

I spin around on the barstool and keep my eyes fixed on the street. Maybe she got held up somewhere. Maybe she's on her way here right now.

I don't know why I care. I don't know why I'm invested.

Maybe because I need the distraction. But something tells me it's more than that. Something that's excruciatingly hard to put a name to.

Fuck it. I glance over my shoulder at Mischa. "Actually, I'll take a whiskey. The strongest one you've got."

"I'll bring out the good stuff for you, boss," Mischa replies.

He disappears into the back. When he returns, he's carrying a crystal glass half-filled with a burnt umber liquid that looks smooth as fucking silk. He sets in down in front of me and slides it closer.

"Enjoy."

I pick up the glass and take a whiff. The oaky notes hit my nostrils first. Then I get the subtle tones of vanilla. I take a sip, swirling it around on my tongue first before I swallow.

"Well?" Mischa asks, as though he's personally responsible for the whiskey I'm drinking.

"Fucking fantastic," I say approvingly.

He nods, his impressive silver-white whiskers twitching up. "That whiskey is meant to be drank on a bad day," he tells me. "You look like a man who could use it."

"Truer words have never been spoken," I grimace, glancing out the window again.

"Does this girl in the gown have a name?" Mischa asks innocently. "In case she comes in when you're not around?"

I hadn't even asked for her name. Not even when I'd been buried inside her. Then again, she hadn't asked for mine, either.

My fingers curl around my whiskey glass as I curse myself out internally. Fucking her was a massive mistake. I should have known better. I should have been stronger. Instead, I'd acted like a horny college student on his first spring break.

"No name," I reply. "And I don't think it matters at this point." I take another sip of the whiskey. "I don't think I'll see her again."

"You never know," Mischa says, a glint in his wizened eyes. "This is a strange city."

I finish the rest of my drink and push the glass away.

"Another one, boss?"

"No," I say firmly. I have to draw the line somewhere. One was bad enough.

I feel my phone vibrating against my pocket, and I grit my teeth. Second call in the last ten minutes. They're persistent.

"Get some sleep," I tell Mischa as I get off the barstool. "You can't work forever."

He chuckles, a sound like boulders smashing together. "Watch me."

I snort and head out of the diner.

My phone's still vibrating, so I pick it up and glance at the screen. They're getting really fucking predictable in their old age. Pushing down my frustration, I take the call.

"It's late, Mama," I say wearily.

Esme Kovalyov just clicks her tongue and sighs. *"Mijo...* What happened?"

She still talks to me like I'm five fucking years old. I'd told her so once and she'd just shrugged in response. *"You'll always be five years old to me,"* she said.

"Shit went down," I tell her. "Things didn't go according to plan."

"I never liked the plan in the first place."

"That's why I didn't tell you about it until it was already in play."

"Your father tried calling you earlier."

"I know."

She sighs audibly. "He worries about you," she says. "I know it doesn't always show, but—"

"Can we not do this now?" I interrupt.

"The two of you," she says. "You're too alike; that's the whole problem."

I snort. "Papa would never have botched the job like I did tonight."

She laughs out loud. "Your father didn't get to be the don he is today without making a few mistakes along the way."

"Yeah?" I ask. "You wanna give me the list? Just in case I need ammo for a future argument."

I can tell she's smiling even though I can't see her. "Get some rest, son," she says. "You sound exhausted. I'll call you tomorrow."

"I really wish you wouldn't."

"I wouldn't need to call so much if you'd visit more often."

"Las Vegas is my city now."

"What does that mean?" she asks curtly. "You can't visit any others?"

I smile. "One city can't contain the both of us, Mama."

"That's probably true. Both your egos in the same zip code might not leave enough oxygen for everyone else."

"Gee, you really know how to make a man feel special."

She laughs gently. It still carries the same melody it used to when I was a boy. She's older now, but just as beautiful. Time hasn't taken that from her. "Goodnight, son."

"Goodnight. Tell the old man I'll handle things."

"Tell him yourself."

"He likes you better."

Before she can argue, I hang up, knowing full well I'll catch hell for it the next time we speak. Still—worth it.

I walk down the road, telling myself that I've stopped searching for the girl even though I know damn well that's a lie. Anytime I catch sight of a blonde with a slender physique, I find myself taking another look.

I remember the way she'd looked at me back in the club. Pure terror—that's what I'd seen in her eyes.

This was a girl who's never been alone much in her life. She needed a security blanket and she'd found me.

Maybe it's a good thing that she's disappeared into the ether. I don't have the fucking time to protect anyone.

Bad things happen when I try.

And still, my eyes dart from one corner of the street to the other. Even if I do happen to run into her, I don't have a plan. It infuriates me that I'm still preoccupied with this. Especially given the mess I've made of what was supposed to be a simple kill mission.

Victor fucking Ozol. I'd stood barely two feet away from him and I'd missed. Solely because I'd been worried about the terrified child bride cowering behind the wing-backed armchair.

"Hey, handsome."

I whip my neck to the side in the direction of the soft, feminine voice. The first thing I see is blonde hair curled over a half-naked breast. But a moment later, the excitement curdles in my chest.

The woman's similarities to the girl from the club are hollow at best. A pale imitation, nothing more.

"You look like you could use some company," she says with a seductive smile and a curled finger. She's wearing a red leather skirt that barely covers her pussy, knee-high boots, and a V-neck vest that puts her sheer bra on full display.

"Have you seen a girl in a wedding dress go by here by any chance?" I ask on a whim.

She raises her eyebrows with interest. "No, honey. You searching for your missus or something?"

My hopes plummet. I start walking away into the night.

But she follows me. "Where you off to, good-looking?"

"Stop following me."

Her eyes spark the moment my tone turns harsh. Some women are just suckers for pain. "What if I don't want to?"

I stop and turn to face her. "I'm not fucking interested."

She looks me up and down, making no secret of the fact that she likes what she sees. "I won't charge you."

"Your pimp's not gonna like that."

"Fuck him. He's not in charge of my body."

I snort. "I think you need to look up the definition of a 'pimp.'"

Her eyes flash again, and she grabs my hand. "I can make you feel better, honey. I promise."

This has turned into a challenge for her. She doesn't know how impossible that challenge really is.

"No," I snarl, "you can't."

Her bottom lip trembles for a moment, but she recovers quickly and with such finesse that I'm forced to admire her for it.

"Fine, then," she grumbles defensively. "Your loss." She turns and struts away like she doesn't have a care in the world. She almost nails the exit, too. Unfortunately, she fucks it up by turning and looking back over her shoulder.

I sigh bitterly. She can't be more than eighteen or nineteen. And she was so ready to give herself to me for nothing.

Maybe that's what's wrong with the world. Too many women out there, willing to give it all up for a man who can keep them safe. Who can make them feel loved.

I think about the beautiful blonde with the haunting brown eyes. I wonder what her name is. I wonder if she's okay now.

But a part of me is glad she's somewhere else. Somewhere away from me.

Because what do I have to offer her?

Only one thing: pain. Lots of it.

7

PHOENIX
ONE YEAR LATER

I'm driving fast when the call comes in on the video phone in my car. I don't know why Konstantin had it installed in the first place. Thing's a fucking nuisance.

So is the person calling.

"Jesus," I growl when I see the name lighting up the screen.

I don't have the time for this conversation, especially when I can probably predict word for word what they're about to say. But I've avoided calls for a week straight. The longer I do that, the more frequent they become.

So I hit the answer button. My parents' faces fill up the small screen propped up just over the dashboard.

Artem and Esme Kovalyov. To anyone who knows anything about our world, they're two of the most fearsome faces in existence. King and queen of the Kovalyov Bratva. Infamously wealthy. Infamously powerful.

To me, though, they're just an infamous pain in my ass.

"Are you driving?" my mother asks before I can get a word in edgewise. She's as beautiful as she's ever been and aging gracefully all the time. Long, dark hair, though there are a few more grays in there than I remember. Those shimmering eyes that see everything in an instant.

"You two realize that I'm not an eighteen-year-old kid living under your roof anymore, right?" I demand.

"Then why are you acting like one?"

I suppress a sigh. "Nice to see you too, Papa."

It's been over a year since I've met them in the flesh. Too long. My fault.

But I've been focused on my mission. And every time I pop up for air, I realize another few months have passed.

My father's features have darkened with age. His features have taken a more severe bent. I suppose it's the inevitable culmination of decades of being a don.

I wonder if the same will happen to me. But deep down, I know it's already happening. The last vestiges of softness disappeared from my face five years ago, when Yuri and Aurora disappeared.

I've always looked a lot like my father on the surface. But the older I get, the more my eyes start to look like his, too. Sharp. Brutal. Dark as midnight.

"Is it true?" Papa asks.

Fuck. "Any number of things could be true," I reply evasively.

"The hit on the warehouse two nights ago," he asks, leaving me no way out.

"That was necessary."

"Phoenix," my mother sighs, "where was the evidence?"

"Those men were seen with Ozol last week."

"You don't know why."

"And I don't care," I reply. "Anyone connected with that fucker is bad news."

"We're getting some disturbing reports," Papa warns.

I tense. It's true that I've been chasing bloodlust of late. But that's the only language men like Viktor Ozol seem to understand. The only way to get through to them.

He's become even more evasive in the last year. When he surfaces, it's for short bursts of time and he's always surrounded by security fit for a fucking emperor.

And yet, despite all that precaution, Astra Tyrannis has become even more active.

Last month alone, seventeen more women were sold on the black market. Most of them were under eighteen. My sources are well-placed but I still find myself a day late and a dollar short every goddamn time. I get news, but it's always a little too late to do anything about it.

That's one of Astra Tyranni's strengths. The organization moves fast, and it covers up its tracks with expert skill.

They leave behind no trace. Women are stolen, sold, violated, and in many cases, left for dead. Their bodies and their stories surface. The men behind the horrors never do.

"I wouldn't pay attention to that shit," I say dismissively.

"Phoenix," Papa says firmly. "My son, you've carried out seven different hits in the last two weeks alone. You're starting to concern even our allies."

"I'm doing what needs to be done."

"You don't have evidence that Ozol has anything to do with these crimes."

"I have my gut."

"Your gut is not proof!" he thunders.

I notice Mama's arm linger on his arm for a moment, calming him, before she speaks. "*Mijo,* we're just concerned about you," she says. "And we're not the only ones."

I narrow my eyes as I take a sharp left towards the tip-off location. According to my GPS, the route to my destination should normally take forty minutes. At the speed I'm driving, it'll only be probably half that time.

"There's nothing to be concerned about," I reply brusquely. "I have the situation under control."

"You lost nine men last month."

"No one ever said this business was clean or easy. They knew what they were signing up for. You're telling me you never lost men?"

"Those fights were necessary," he growls. "A good don knows when to engage an enemy and when to hold off."

And there it is. The *Good Don* talk. An Artem Kovalyov Classic, patent pending. That didn't take long at all.

"Some enemies only take advantage of that," I counter. "If I back off, the whole thing gets much fucking worse."

"*Mijo,*" Mama says in the gentle tone she uses when she's afraid to upset me, "I know what you went through when… when they disappeared."

"For fuck's sake, don't—"

But of course, she doesn't listen to me.

"Obviously, you want revenge," she continues. "Obviously, you want to see the people responsible burn. But you're turning this into a personal vendetta."

"That's exactly what it is."

"But you are not acting alone," Papa interrupts. "You are a don; you have men that follow you. You need to be smart."

You need to be smart. I feel like I've heard that my whole fucking life.

"Just because I'm not doing it your way doesn't mean I'm doing it the wrong way," I tell him.

"You're acting rashly," my father says, his voice taking on the hardened authority he's spent decades cultivating. "You're acting from a place of emotion. You're making it personal."

"Astra Tyrannis abducted my wife and son!" I snap with anger. "They rounded them up like cattle and slaughtered them like pigs. Of course it's fucking personal."

Silence reigns for a moment. My hands are tight and sweaty on the steering wheel. The speedometer ticks up and the engine roars as I press the pedal harder into the floor.

"A good don knows how to separate emotion from a mission," Papa says finally, his tone chipping at the edges.

I notice Mama's hand stroking a little faster now. It's the gesture she uses to calm him down when she knows he's getting riled up.

I wonder for a moment what it must be like for her—living in between two Kovalyov male egos her entire life.

No wonder she's going grey.

"Guess I'm not a good don then," I fire back hotly.

"You're being childish."

"I know what I'm doing," I say.

I hate how much I'm forced to repeat myself any time I talk to my father. He makes me feel like I'm thirteen again.

"You've been saying that for five years now."

"Ozol is a slippery motherfucker. But he can't escape me for long."

"You're antagonizing a viper," he says calmly. "Sooner or later, he'll strike."

"That's what I'm counting on."

"You're trying to draw him out?" Mama cuts in before my father can say anything. "You're trying to goad him into an open war with you?"

I know how it sounds.

Reckless.

Short-sighted.

Stupid.

To which I say: fuck all that.

I'm strong enough to take a few hits to my reputation. I'm strong enough not to care.

"If I keep attacking him, he'll have no choice but to answer in kind."

"You're endangering your men."

"This isn't day camp. I'm not here to babysit them. This is the fucking job. It comes with the territory. If my men have a problem with how I'm running things, they can fucking say so to my face. I will not stop anyone from walking away. But if they stay, I expect them to follow my orders. Because in this city, I am the fucking don."

"*Dios*, Phoenix," my mother says, sounding close to tears now. "Do you even hear yourself?"

I can feel her worry through the screen. For the first time, a smidgen of discomfort manages to weasel its way past my defenses. I'm glad my parents don't know everything.

Even if ninety percent of my activities will travel back to them, ten percent manage to stay hidden out here in the desert.

Like the death of one of Ozol's loyalists.

I'd tortured the bastard for seven days straight. On the eighth day, when he still refused to give me anything, I made good on my promise.

I'd flayed him until he begged for mercy. Then I'd ripped him from chest to groin and watched his insides fall to the floor in front of me.

And I'd fucking enjoyed it—he deserved worse.

Even as I stood in the open desert and torched his remains until there was nothing left but ash, I wish I could have made him hurt more for all the sins he'd wrought.

His disappearance has definitely been noticed, but no one can connect him with me. Well, perhaps one man can. Fortunately, it's the one man I want to make the connection.

The hit was a personal message to Ozol. One I know he will understand loud and clear.

"Son, please… you're losing yourself to this mission," she says heavily. "You've become obsessed."

She says it like it's a dirty word. Hell, maybe it is. I've lost the ability to tell any longer.

"I'm not obsessed. I'm focused."

"No?" she asks. "You live, sleep, and breathe it. Tell me, when was the last time you did anything fun?"

Jesus. *Fun*. What does that word even mean?

Of course, I'm proving her point. Which only serves to piss me off further. So I just opt for the easiest response—escape.

"I have to go."

"Phoenix, don't you dare—"

My father's warning dies as I disconnect the call. The timing is perfect. I would have had to hang up anyway. I turn the corner and spot the location I'd been sent earlier.

I park far down the street, but I make sure I have a clear view of the entrance to the nondescript house with the rusted gate.

According to my source, the man who lives here is a decorated, fifteen-year veteran detective on the Las Vegas police force. He's spent most of that time cultivating contacts in all the wrong places.

The motherfucker's hands are dripping with innocent blood. He helps facilitate trafficking operations within city limits. Making it easier and more convenient for bastards like Ozol to kidnap, transport, and sell women in broad daylight.

It took a handful of long, arduous interrogations before his name came up at all. I'm not letting this lead slip through my fingers.

So I slide down against my seat and wait. A text pings onto my screen. I glance down, expecting to see a message from my mother.

But it's not her.

It's Matvei Tereshkova.

The fucker has been a thorn in my side for the past several years, ever since he arrived in Las Vegas from Europe and told me he was a hired killer in need of a job. It's sheer dumb luck that he also happens to be my closest friend.

Please don't tell me you're actually tailing the cop on your fucking own?!

I smile and ignore his text for the time being. But the smile slips off my face when I notice a tall figure moving towards the gate. Detective Jonathan Murray steps outside wearing dark trousers and a black t-shirt. He looks to be in his mid-forties. Well-built and slightly burly. He definitely doesn't look like a cop.

But then again, he seems to be working off the clock here.

As I watch, he gets in his shiny black Lexus, a far nicer model than a working detective should be able to afford. He doesn't scan the area before he gets in his car. Totally relaxed. Unconcerned.

Idiot.

That makes it easier for me to follow him at a safe distance.

I get another text notification, but I don't even glance down to see who it is. I keep my eyes trained on the Lexus in front of me.

We drive for ten minutes before we arrive at a ramshackle building on the outskirts of the city.

I read the sign out loud. *"Las Vegas Women's Shelter… What the fuck?"*

Definitely not what I'm expecting. But it doesn't change anything. No matter where he goes, Jonathan Murray cannot be saved.

Tonight, one way or the other, he's going to tell me everything he knows about Viktor Ozol and Astra Tyrannis.

And then he's going to die.

I park several yards away and watch as he leaves his car and heads to the entrance of the shelter. My blood starts boiling as I watch his confident, purposeful gait. There's only one reason a crooked cop connected to Astra Tyrannis would come to a women's shelter…

Fresh meat for the market.

8

ELYSSA

LAS VEGAS WOMEN'S SHELTER

I close the door softly, careful not to make any noise. Once I'm in the inventory room, I relax a little and pull out my trusty pad.

I've got columns upon columns of inventory that I need to take account of. I only finished half the list yesterday. The sleepless nights have been hitting me hard lately, but I refuse to be defeated by them. Work is work and it needs to get done. Not just so I earn my paycheck—but so all the women who come here desperate and hungry the way I did a year ago can be taken care of.

I move over to the far corner of the room where our new supplies have been stored. One item at a time, I go down the list, noting quantities and marking what needs to be replenished.

Spam. Check.

Boxed cereals. Check.

Breakfast bars. Check.

Some of the items are past their use-by date. I eye them suspiciously, but we can't afford to be picky. The shelter's been struggling lately.

Too many women and not enough resources. But I'm glad that I've been able to do my part.

Learning the ropes those first few months was hard for me. Not just in the sense of this job in particular, but in the sense of the world as a whole.

For a while there, I'd felt like I was drowning. Heck, I may very well have drowned if it hadn't been for Charity. She was the lifeline that kept me afloat while I found my footing in Las Vegas, battling constant sickness and my new reality.

"I know it's hard," she used to tell me. "Suck it up and keep going. It'll make you stronger."

There were days when I hated her for the tough love. But eventually, just like she'd promised, the smoke cleared. I emerged from the fog feeling more confident and more capable than I'd ever felt at home in the commune.

I had more on my plate than any woman should have to handle at one time. Especially a woman on her own. But I'd made decisions and I live every day now with the consequences, head held high.

There's no going back, even if I wanted to.

I frown. My clipboard says that there should be ten pallets of canned vegetables. But when I count the large brown boxes in front of me, I only get eight.

"Damn," I breathe, one of the few curse words I'm comfortable using.

Charity likes to tease that she'll make a potty mouth of me yet. But that's one thing I don't mind keeping from my old life.

I move to the old cord phone lodged into the back of the room next to the water cooler and dial in our supplier's number. It takes at least ten rings before Miles answers.

"Yeah?" he grunts into the phone.

"Miles? It's Elyssa."

"Yeah?"

I sigh. "You made a delivery to the shelter yesterday. We ordered ten pallets of canned meats. We only have eight."

"Why didn't you tell the driver this yesterday?" he whines.

I suppress another sigh. "I didn't accept the delivery," I explain. "One of my colleagues did and he clearly didn't check."

"You know you're supposed to confirm receipt on delivery."

"One could argue that you're supposed to deliver the goods ordered and paid for," I say as politely as possible. "But yes, my colleague should have checked, too."

"Well… we're not making deliveries out that way until next Thursday."

"We'll run out of supplies by then. I've got women I need to feed."

"Tell them to share."

"They already do!"

"Yeah, yeah, yeah. When do you want the extra pallet?" he sighs.

"Two pallets," I remind him. "And they're not extras; they were part of our original order."

"I get it," he says impatiently. "When?"

"We can make it with what we've got until tomorrow."

"I'm gonna charge you extra for the delivery," he huffs.

I grit my teeth, but I've never been much of a fighter. *Don't rock the boat.* That's my motto. It's a credo that pisses Charity off to no end.

"That's ridiculous!"

"I dunno what to tell you, hon. Time is money."

I grit my teeth and close my eyes for a moment. "Fine," I reply. "That's fine."

He hangs up without so much as a goodbye. I'm left standing there, irritated and wanting to fling the phone across the room.

The shelter has a small stash of cash for little expenses like this. But it's dwindled fast as of late. I decide to pull the money for the extortion fee from my own cash.

Charity would tell me to stop being a bleeding heart, but when it comes to the shelter, I don't mind doing extra. This place gave me a home, a job, and a support system when I had nothing. I'm not going to forget that anytime soon.

I go back to inventory, ticking off items on my list, feeling slightly better about our situation. It looks like our supplies will hold for at least a week. If we don't have too many new walk-ins, that is.

Although, with the way things have been going lately, that's far from guaranteed.

I'm almost done with inventory when I hear a battering from the front entrance. I stiffen instantly, very aware that it's late at night and I'm currently manning the fort all alone. Everyone else is dead asleep.

I wait and hope whoever it is leaves. God only knows what kind of monsters are wandering the streets of outer Las Vegas this far past midnight. But the battering only gets more intense.

Reluctantly, I sidle up to get a vantage point of the door. The moment I get to the front, though, I see Charity's face pressed up against one of the side windows.

I smile, but the smile slips off my face when she doesn't return it. As I move closer to the stained glass, I realize that she doesn't look good at all.

I rush forward to unlock the door for her. When I throw it open, Charity all but jumps into my arms.

But not before I notice the blood and bruises all over her face.

"Oh my God, Charity!" I gasp. "What happened?"

Tears stream down her face as she clings to me. Her entire body is trembling, and she can barely get her sobs out, let alone an explanation. I just hug her, rubbing her shoulders until her crying subsides somewhat.

"Hey, hey, hey," I soothe. "It's okay. You're here now. You're safe."

It feels strange to be the comforter. Typically, that's been Charity's role in our relationship. I'm oddly grateful for the change.

But I hate that she's suffering. And my blood boils at the thought of the man who did this to her.

"I'm sorry. I shouldn't have come like this, but… but… I didn't know where else to g-g-go."

"You came to exactly the right place," I tell her firmly. I pull away just enough so that I can look at her face. My stomach twists as I take in her split lip, black eye, and the purple bruise erupting on the right side of her face.

"Oh, Charity," I whisper.

"I thought I was going to die, Elyssa," she whimpers.

The thought of losing Charity fills me with deep-seated dread. I can't even imagine a world where she doesn't exist.

"But you didn't die," I point out. "You're right here. With me. Now, come on. Let's get you cleaned up."

She's wearing a tight black faux leather dress. It's got a built-in bustier corset that pushes up her ample breasts and clings to her curvy figure like a second skin. I notice a few bloodstained rips at the hem.

I've always worried that this very thing would happen to Charity one day. Being a prostitute in Las Vegas isn't easy, but no amount of pleading can get her to change lines of work.

She always said that sticking to the high rollers actually keeps her safe. That men with influence, money, and power don't bother hurting the working girls.

I always argue the exact opposite. Powerful men don't care about who they hurt because they'll never have to answer for it. They do what they want out in the open and walk away laughing.

I just never wanted to be proven right.

I lead Charity to one of the empty rooms in the back of the shelter and sit her down on the hard, single bed. She's still crying but silently now. Her right eye has swollen completely shut. It must hurt terribly.

"Let's get you out of that dress," I suggest gently.

We don't talk as I help her get undressed and clean her up. She just sits there like a rag doll, moving when I tell her to, but otherwise staring off at the opposite wall as though she's in some sort of trance.

The damage isn't limited to her face. I find a nasty indigo flower blooming across her lower abdomen and more bruises snaking up and down her legs.

Anger momentarily blinds me, but I push the red spots away and try to focus on Charity and what she needs right now. Once she's wearing a pair of grey sweats and an oversized t-shirt, I sit down next to her on the bed.

"You want to lie down?"

She shakes her head without looking at me.

"You want something to eat or drink?"

She shakes her head.

"You want to tell me what happened?"

Just when I think she's about to shake her head, she turns to me, with tears still slipping from her one good eye. "How bad is it?" she asks.

"Your wounds will heal," I tell her, taking her hand. "Trust me. The bruise will clear, your eye will open, the scars will go away."

"I... I won't be able to work 'til they do."

I squeeze her hand. "Charity," I say with a small amount of desperation, "forget that. Look at yourself. How did this happen?"

She looks down as though she's embarrassed. "I was working a high stakes poker game at the Bellagio," she explains. "I was just meant to serve the drinks, flirt with the high rollers who were there to play."

I nod and wait for her to continue.

She swallows a sob and goes on. "The short version? The wrong man lost. He was doing really fucking well, but then he got cocky. He lost about two million at the table in two minutes flat."

Two million. Jesus.

"He enlisted my services for... after," Charity says, her voice cracking a little. "It's not unusual for one of the players to want to fuck me after the game. I thought he just wanted to blow off some steam. And he did... But not the way I expected."

"He hit you," I say with outrage.

She nods.

"Charity..."

"It's never happened before, Elyssa," she says. "I've always known how to handle men. But this one... He was so angry... And when he looked at me, it felt like he wanted to kill me. I thought he *was* going to kill me."

"How did you get away?"

I know I'm probably holding her hand a little tighter than is comfortable, but I don't care. And she doesn't seem to care, either. She needs it.

Her trembling ramps up a bit. "I managed to grab hold of something. I don't even know what. But it was hard and heavy. I hit him with it and I just… I—I ran."

"Good for you."

"I heard him roaring as I ran, but I didn't look back."

I wrap my arms around her and pull her close. I hold her tight until her trembling subsides. "You were so brave, Charity," I tell her softly. "So, so brave."

She burrows her face in the crook of my neck. "For the first time, I'm scared of my job."

I want to tell her that I've always been scared of her job. I've spent the last year worrying about her every time she's gone out to work. But why rub salt in the wound? What she needs right now is a friend, not a kick when she's down.

I can't deny that it's unsettling, though. To see someone like Charity so out of sorts, so broken down…

She's the confident one. The experienced one. The smart one. Nothing scares her. She's always been so damn unflappable. She's been my strength every time I've faltered over the last year.

To see her like this—it's sobering.

Not to mention terrifying.

"Charity, what he did to you, it's assault. It's a crime. We should report it."

Her one good eye goes wide. And I read the hopelessness there. "Report it?" she repeats. "To who?"

I hesitate. "To... to the police?"

"The police?" she echoes again. "That's a joke. The cops in this city don't give a shit about people like me. I'm just a whore to them. A cheap, disgusting, filthy whore."

"Stop! That's not what you are."

"It doesn't matter, Elyssa," Charity sighs. "What I am doesn't matter. All that matters is what they think I am."

"Well, then..."

I struggle for a moment to find the right word. The word that conveys the enormity of this situation. The word that'll mean the most to Charity.

"Fuck them!"

Charity turns to me, and, despite her busted face, I can see the shock there. "You swore," she says in laughing amazement.

"I... I did."

"How did it feel?"

I sigh. "Weird."

A bubble of laughter escapes her lips. She groans almost immediately. "Ow, that's fucking painful. But it was worth it."

I smile. "Glad I can help."

"Thank you," Charity says seriously, placing her head on my shoulder for a moment. "Sometimes, I don't know what I'd do without you."

"Back atcha," I say.

We're sitting in the silence when I hear another knock on the door. This one is calm. Unhurried. But for some reason, I'm wary.

One knock in the middle of the night is strange.

Two knocks is trouble.

Charity looks at me with trepidation and I realize that, today, I have to be the strong one. I have to be the fearless one.

"Wait here," I tell her, giving her hand one last squeeze. "I'll go see who it is."

"Elyssa…?"

"Yes?" I ask, turning to her.

"Do you think it's… him?" she asks, fear drenching her tone. "Do you think he followed me here?"

I'd been thinking the same thing. But I force a look of disbelief onto my face and shake my head confidently. "No, no way. It's probably just some random woman who needs a place to stay for the night," I say. "Or Miles decided to be a Good Samaritan and make a late-night delivery. Don't you worry. Whoever it is, I'll deal with it. Okay? Just sit tight. I'll be right back."

She pauses for a second. "Okay."

I give her a reassuring wink and head out of the room. I make sure to close the door behind me before I head to the main entrance.

The whole time, my heart is pounding frantically against my rib cage.

"Come on, Elyssa," I tell myself. "Baby steps."

I take a deep breath as I approach the door. This time, the person on the other side is shielded from view completely.

"You don't need to be brave," I tell myself. "Just a little braver than before."

9

PHOENIX

FIFTEEN MINUTES EARLIER—IN HIS CAR OUTSIDE THE WOMEN'S SHELTER

"What the hell are you up to, motherfucker?" I growl under my breath, watching Murray step up to the front door.

The shelter is in need of repair. Roof shingles are missing like bald spots, windowsills sag, weeds burst through the concrete walkways. It's a broken home for broken women.

Murray peers in through the side door, but he doesn't knock like I expect. He doesn't pull out a weapon, either. Instead, he cases the joint with care, his eyes darting from side to side in search of something.

I lean down lower in my seat in case he glances this way. But he seems too preoccupied to notice anything outside of his immediate vicinity.

I glance at his car. He's got no one with him, and no one else has shown up. No backup that I can see.

He may have made stealing women his side hustle. He may even have it down to a science, but doing it alone seems risky. He has no idea how many women are in there.

Unless, of course, there's another explanation for this whole visit.

The thought gives me pause. I'd assumed that he was coming here in order to pick up more fodder for Astra Tyrannis auctions.

But what if there's another reason? What if he's working *with* someone in the shelter?

I stiffen as I realize the theory actually has merit. Allying with someone who works in a place like this would guarantee continuous access to young women. Women with no home and no family. Women who are young and vulnerable and more likely to be desperate because of it.

It's the perfect fucking plan. A funnel straight from the streets of Las Vegas into the gaping maw of Astra Tyrannis.

Adrenaline is pumping through my veins as I wait for the fucker to make his next move. I'm just about to get out of the car and go after him when he pivots on his heel and goes back to the car. He lumbers into the driver's seat.

Frowning, I wait for the vehicle to take off, but it doesn't. He's just sitting there. Waiting. For what, I don't know.

My phone vibrates again. I look down at it with a preemptive sigh. When I see Matvei's name on the screen, I decide to answer.

"Jesus Christ, Phoenix," he says the moment I answer. "You're following the lead on your own, aren't you?"

"Nah, just out for ice cream."

"You asshole."

I smirk. "I can handle this."

"You say that about everything," Matvei says harshly. "Some might accuse you of having an ego problem."

That earns a snort. "You been talking to my parents or something?"

"Why, are they saying the same thing I'm saying?"

"If you're going to accuse me of being obsessed with Astra Tyrannis, then yes."

"Great minds think alike," Matvei says. "Where are you right now?"

"Went for a drive."

"You went to his house."

"A minor detour. Nothing crazy."

"And?"

"And then he left the house and started to drive, so I kept the detour going right along with him."

"Jesus."

I roll my eyes. "Hadn't pegged you for the religious type. But you do call on the big guy a lot."

"Having you to deal with, I just might turn to religion."

"Ouch. Am I really that bad?"

"We're supposed to be working together, Phoenix. Since when do you work alone?"

"Since people started accusing me of being obsessive."

"Where is he headed?"

"We're parked outside a women's shelter on the outskirts of the city," I reply.

"A women's shelter?" Matvei repeats. "Fuck. Do you think the son of a bitch is… recruiting?"

"*Recruiting?*" I hiss, balking at the word. "Is that what you call stealing and trafficking women?"

"Sorry," Matvei says quickly. "That's not how I meant it."

I remind myself that Matvei is not like some of the other men in my circle. I know him; I know his intentions. I know he didn't mean it that way.

"I know," I say brusquely. "Anyway, he's just parked outside the place now."

"Waiting for someone?"

"Maybe. Not sure who that'd be."

"I take it you're going to wait there until something happens."

"You're a smart man, Mr. Tereshkova."

"If I were, I'd have given up on you a long time ago."

I smile at that. "There's time yet."

"You should have at least told me."

"You would have insisted on coming with me."

"And what's wrong with having a little backup?" Matvei demands.

"If shit goes down, I want all the glory," I fire back.

Matvei is quiet for a moment. Which is never a good thing. He's a thinking man. And thinking men never stop planning.

"I also have another theory," I say, just to distract him. "What if this fucker is working with someone in the women's shelter? Think about it: whoever works in this place has all the intel. They know the women, know their stories. They can pick out the most vulnerable girls and offer them up to Astra Tyrannis on a silver platter."

"It's a possibility…"

"But what?" I ask.

"I've done extensive background checks into Murray's past. Nothing suggests he's involved on that kind of level."

"The Ozol loyalist we caught gave us Murray's name before he died."

"I don't doubt the legitimacy of the source," Matvei says dismissively. "I mean that Murray may not be as big a player as we think he is. The informant was being tortured. He needed to give us something. Why not a name that's legitimate but not all that important?"

That's what I mean about thinking men. They ruin everything with their fucking logic.

"Doesn't matter," I say fiercely. "We got a name. Which is more than we had before. Once I have Murray backed into a corner, he'll start talking, too."

"And what if he has nothing to give?"

"Then he dies painfully," I snap. "Like all the rest before him."

I can sense Matvei wants to say something, but he's holding back. I'm glad of that. I don't have the patience to stave off his doubt, too.

"Well, what's happening now?" Matvei asks.

"Nothing yet," I say. "He's still sitting in his fucking car."

"You think he knows you're tailing him?"

"Nah. He can't even see me from here."

"I can come to where you are," Matvei suggests.

"I'll be fine. You just sit there and be pretty."

"What if whatever's about to go down requires some manpower?" Matvei asks.

I roll my eyes. "I'll handle it."

"Fucking hell, Phoenix. Quit this now. You know where the fucker lives. That's all we need. We'll get him another day. When you have your men behind you."

"The men don't need to be involved until they have to be. That goes for you, too."

"You know that your parents are right about this, don't you?"

"I don't care," I reply. "Astra Tyrannis is a fucking stain on the world and I'm going to wipe it out."

"And I am completely behind that plan," he tells me. "But not the way you're doing it."

"If you're about to call me reckless again, I'm hanging up."

"Brother," Matvei says, his tone growing cautious, "Astra Tyrannis is a century old. Their systems have been in place forever. All their members have been active since the inception, and we don't even know their names."

"We know one," I growl. "Viktor Ozol."

"And he might as well be a ghost in the wind, for all the good our hunting has done in getting us close to him again. You're running a personal war on instinct alone. It's a bad idea, Phoenix."

"My instincts have never let me down so far."

"There's a first time for everything."

"Thanks for the pep talk. That's just what I want from my second."

I can tell Matvei's smiling. "That's exactly why I'm your second. I'm not going to feed you lies or stroke your ego. You do that plenty yourself."

I squeeze the phone hard. "I can't just sit by and watch this shit happen in my city, Matvei. Aurora wouldn't want that. Yuri wouldn't want that."

Their names still taste like fucking asphalt coming out of my mouth. But sometimes I force myself to say them anyway.

It's the fire I need to keep going.

"That's not—"

"Everyone assumes that I'm so consumed with revenge that I can't see straight enough to make certain decisions. But it's possible to want revenge and think clearly, too."

"You haven't properly mourned them."

"I've mourned them plenty," I snap. "I've got the scars and the tattoos to prove it. Now, I just need to avenge them. I won't stop until I do."

"You're missing out on life in the meantime."

"This *is* my life, Matvei. I don't want anything else."

"Okay," he sighs. I can hear the taint of defeat in his tone. "Okay. There's no stopping you."

"A smart man would have realized that sooner."

He chuckles darkly. "I don't know why I take this abuse."

"Because you know I'm right."

"You can't be right every time."

I'm about to make some quippy remark when I notice movement in the far distance. Murray perks up in the front seat.

The person running towards the shelter is moving fast. When they burst out of the shadows, I see it's a woman. A woman wearing a tight black dress. The kind of dress that marks her as either a hostess or a hooker.

My money's on the latter.

"Phoenix?" asks Matvei on the phone. "What's going on? Did something happen?"

She turns to check over her shoulder as if she's worried she's being chased. As she does, the light illuminates the blood and bruises on her battered face. I can barely make out her features because of all the swelling.

She shudders, turns back, and starts banging both fists against the shelter door.

"Are you still there? Phoenix?"

She's calling out but I'm too far away to hear what she's saying. Even when I roll down my window, I can only hear the muffled sounds of gasping cries.

Then the door opens, and she disappears into the shelter. I can't make out who's opened the door, but one thing's for certain: something's about to happen.

"Fucking hell, Phoenix!"

"Quiet down, will you?" I snap. "He's getting out of the car."

"Why?"

"A woman just appeared. A hooker, by the looks of it. She looked like someone beat her to a bloody pulp."

"Murray?"

"Fuck knows, but I'm going to find out."

"On your own?"

"Yes, Matvei. On my fucking own."

Impatiently, I hang up and watch as Murray lights a cigarette and leans against the hood of his car. He takes his time smoking it. When he's done, he heads towards the shelter door.

"What's the move now, *mudak*?" I whisper.

He raps on the door and waits patiently. It takes a while, but then it finally swings open. I see only the silhouette of a woman standing in the doorway.

Then I notice Murray reach around to his back.

He pulls out a gun.

And that's when I get out of the car and start running.

10

ELYSSA

I approach the door with nervous trepidation. "W—who is it?" I ask, hating that my voice trembles.

"Evening, ma'am," a deep voice calls. "I'm Detective Murray. I'd just like to talk."

Why is there a detective at the door? My first blindly fearful thought is that I've been found out. The Sanctuary hired a detective to track me down, drag me back, hold me accountable for the crime I'd committed over a year ago now.

That can't be happening, right? There's a logical little voice in my head going on and on about how far-fetched that is.

But it's drowned out by the screams of panic. Emotions ping through my extremities, reminding me of that terrified, lost girl who'd run across the desert with bloody feet and a raging fire behind her in the night.

The night I'd met *him*—my protector. One year later, and I've still never thought of him as anything else.

Whenever we talk about it, Charity is dismissive. She still thinks he was a bad man with bad intentions. But in the rare, quiet moments when I allow myself to think back on what happened, that is how I think of him.

As a guardian angel.

I saw the war raging in his eyes—and yet he helped me anyway. He saved me when I was too weak and feeble to save myself.

"Ma'am?"

I jerk out of my trance. I tend to do that a lot. Slip into the past, lose myself to people I used to know. I've shut out so much of my past life that it surfaces in random moments when I least expect it.

The detective pounding repeatedly on the door is not helping me keep my demons at bay.

It's not unusual to have cops come to the shelter. Sometimes, the women who find their way here are brought by police. Or else they're fleeing demons of their own—abusive spouses, criminal pasts—and the cops come calling for other reason.

I've grown used to dealing with men in blue asking pointed questions. I don't like it, but I do it.

But for some creeping reason, this feels different in a way I like even less.

"Ma'am, I just want to talk. Can you open the door, please?"

He's polite—for now. But I know from experience that he probably won't stay that way for long. Especially if he thinks I'm trying to hide something.

So I swallow my fear and open the door.

The man standing there is tall and lean. In his forties, I'd guess, but he looks good for his age. His eyes dart past me into the shelter.

Immediately, I stiffen. My bad vibe radar is pinging off the charts. "What can I help you with, Detective?" I ask.

He smiles. My stomach twists instantly. I don't like his smile at all. All shiny, almost pretty.

But sharp. The kind of sharp that cuts deep.

"I'd like to speak to Ms. Charity Longoria."

I frown. "Charity?"

He nods.

"What about?"

"I'd prefer to discuss that matter with her, Miss…" He trails off, waiting for me to offer up my name.

"Charity's not in at the moment," I say instead.

He raises his eyebrows, though the smile never leaves his face. I want to cringe, but I don't want to antagonize him any more than necessary.

"Funny. I saw her running up to this very building not fifteen minutes ago."

Shit. I stare at him, but I've never had much of a poker face. Ironic, really, considering the many secrets I've kept all these years.

"Uh, what I meant to say was… she's indisposed."

"That's okay. I'll wait."

His persistence is another bad sign. Whatever—or whoever—drove Charity here, the fact that a detective showed up shortly afterwards and insists on speaking with her does not bode well.

I need to find a way to get him out of here.

"Detective… was it Murray?"

He nods.

"I'm sorry, but she's really tired at the moment. I don't think she's ready to see anyone just yet."

"What's your name, ma'am?" he asks directly.

"Elyssa."

"Elyssa," he repeats. "I've been given a tip off about your friend. A witness saw her flee in a panic from the Bellagio. I need her to come down to the station to make a statement."

I hear a sound from behind me. I adjust my position and see Charity standing there in my peripheral vision. She's probably been listening to our entire conversation this whole time.

I pull the door forward a little so that the detective won't be able to spot her. Charity takes the opportunity to inch closer.

Floating my hand behind the door so that the detective won't be able to see, I gesture for her to get to one of the back rooms. But of course, she doesn't listen.

"Uh, listen, Detective—"

"I'm Charity." Before I can stop her, she's rounded the door and is standing in full view of the officer, a few feet behind me.

His eyes rake over her. "Wow," he murmurs. "It's as bad as they said." The sympathy in his tone doesn't quite translate to his eyes, though.

"Who told you?" Charity asks. "What witness?"

He clears his throat. "An anonymous source saw you running from the hotel," the detective repeats, sticking with his story. "He called the station and reported it."

"And you just knew where to find me?" Charity asks dubiously.

"The witness tailed you here to the shelter."

Charity and I exchange a glance. I can see it in her expression: she's not buying this load of crap either.

The policeman is lying.

"Some random stranger saw me run out of the hotel, he followed me here, and then called the cops to report a crime?" she asks slowly.

"Yes."

"It sounds a little hard to believe."

"Stranger things have happened," he says with a shrug.

His tone is even. Almost calm. But I can see his patience start to unravel beneath the surface.

"Why don't you come to the station with me now?" he suggests. "I can help you make a statement."

Charity squares her shoulders. "Thank you, Detective. I appreciate that. But it's not necessary."

"Excuse me?"

"I don't want to press charges against anyone. So I don't need to make a statement."

His eyes bug out a little. "You're going to let whoever did *that* to you," he says, gesturing to her face, "get away with it?" Again, there's concern floating on the surface of his words, but something about this guy doesn't sit well with me. My gut is churning more and more with every passing second.

"Yes," Charity replies without missing a beat. "That's exactly what I'm saying."

"Why would you do that?"

"Because I know how things work in this city," she says. "It's my word against his. And no one cares about me. After all, I'm just a hooker."

Murray narrows his eyes. "Or maybe you're involved in things you don't want the police department to be aware of."

Charity rolls her eyes. "Sure, why not? This is why people hate cops."

"In my experience, the only people who hate cops are the ones who have something to hide."

Charity stiffens and huddles a little closer to me. "I've got nothing to hide. I just don't want to go down to the station only to be told it's my fault for putting myself in a dangerous situation in the first place."

"Detective," I say, interrupting the two of them, "thank you for coming, but my friend is okay now."

He takes a step forward, planting his foot in the doorway so that I can't shut it. "You're making a mistake."

I glance at Charity. "She's not coming with you."

"I'm afraid this is non-negotiable."

I see a flicker of fear in Charity's eyes. "Since when do cops force victims to make statements they don't want to make?" she asks.

"Since some victims may not be victims at all," he replies dangerously. The smile that has stayed plastered on his lips this whole time finally disappears. His eyes darken.

Now, he looks like a predator whose prey is about to slip free.

"It's late and we have things to get back to, Detective," I say. "If you'll excuse—"

I'm about to slam the door shut—on his foot if I have to—when he leans in and growls at me, "One last chance."

I shake my head, and a second later, I'm staring down the barrel of a gun.

Charity grabs my hand and tries to pull me behind her. She's always protecting me. But this time, I feel like it's my duty to protect her.

So I keep my body in front of hers as I stare at the grim-faced detective.

"You're not a cop."

"That's right; I'm not a fucking cop. I'm a motherfucking detective, and I demand respect. Especially from filthy little whores like you two." His voice is slick with fury and condescension. No more politeness to be found.

The insult hits me the wrong way, too. It's not just the word itself; it's the tone. The look of anger and resentment in his eyes when he flings it at us like a weapon.

"You need to leave, Detective."

He brandishes the gun in my face. "Not happening. Now, either you invite me in and be polite, or I put a fucking hole in your whore mouth. What's it gonna be?"

Charity's nails dig into my arm, but I'm glad for the sharp, stinging bite of pain. It keeps me focused. Reminds me of how much I stand to lose.

We have no choice here. Just have to pray that something saves us.

Trying my best to quell my shaking, I step back and let him enter, never taking my eyes off the gun.

But just before he's about to step through the door, something propels him forward. His foot catches the threshold as he stumbles and grunts. He's still clutching the gun, but he's out of sorts. Flustered. Stunned.

I glance at Charity, and I see the message blaring in her eyes.

Go for the gun.

11

PHOENIX

Murray never sees me coming.

I cross the darkness from my car to the front stairs of the shelter at a full sprint. He draws the gun and takes one step inward.

That's when I hit him. A hard blow in the center of the back that sends the wind rushing from his lungs. He stumbles into the shelter and his jaw clacks hard on the tile floor.

I take stock of the two women standing a few feet away, but I don't focus on either one. First, I need to make sure Murray isn't a threat. Then I can deal with them.

But before I can move towards the prone Murray, both women make a grab for the gun in the cop's hands. He's just flustered enough that the dark-haired woman is able to tear the weapon from his fingers.

He gets a grip at the last moment and sweeps at her ankle. She's badly injured, enough that she stumbles back despite his lack of strength, dropping the weapon in the process. It gives him enough room to bounce up to his feet—just in time for the blonde to charge forward and claws at his face.

Something about her is strangely familiar, but I'm too distracted by what's happening to puzzle it out.

This shit needs to end. Now.

The blonde retreats backwards and manages to scoop up Murray's gun from the floor. But he's on the offensive now as he closes the distance to her while unholstering the Taser from his belt.

He's milliseconds away from unleashing it on her…

When I crack the back of the head with a crisp elbow. Immediately, he slumps to the ground. His face hits the floor hard enough to break something. I hope he's still conscious enough for that shit to hurt.

It's only the beginning of the pain he'll face tonight, though.

I look up, satisfied with my handiwork—to see the blonde brandishing the gun in my face.

"Don't move," she orders.

Her voice wobbles.

Her gun doesn't.

I freeze in place. My eyes track slowly from the gun to her trembling hands, down those skinny arms and up to her face.

A face I thought I'd never see again.

She sucks in her breath at the same moment cold realization floods through my body. *Chto za khuynya? It can't be...*

Her eyes go wide. I know she recognizes me, too. But we don't even have names for one another. Just the memory of one hot, hazy night over a year ago.

"Oh my God…" she breathes.

Her huge, amber eyes are just as mesmerizing as I remember. Her chest rises and falls, but she doesn't drop her hands. The gun trembles in my direction. It's obvious that she's never even held a gun before, much less fired one. One wrong twitch would leave me with a hole in my chest.

"Why don't you put that down?" I suggest coolly.

"No."

Her brunette friend stares between us from the floor, suddenly aware of the recognition that's burning between the blonde and me. "Elyssa, what's going on?"

Elyssa. I feel as though a year-long mystery I've been chasing has finally been fucking solved. It suits her. Feminine. Pretty.

Elyssa glances at her friend with a tiny hint of annoyance. But then her eyes find mine again.

"Who are you?" she demands. She's trying to appear unfazed. But I hear the tremor in her voice.

"I should ask you the same thing," I retort, looking between her and Murray. "How do you know the cop?"

"I don't."

"That's tough to believe. Because it's really fucking curious to me how every time you show up, shit's going down with men involved in Astra Tyrannis."

She blinks in confusion. "I don't even know what Astro, Astra… Tyran… whatever it is you just said is."

She's convincingly confused. But seeing her again, like this… it's too fucking convenient. What are the chances that the same woman who crashed my meeting with Victor Ozol would show up again when I'm closing in on a corrupt Astra Tyrannis henchman?

On the other hand, even if she is connected with Ozol somehow, she's certainly not trained or experienced in any way. The way she's holding the gun tells me that much. As does the fear surging in her eyes.

Murray groans at my feet, his body lurching upwards slightly.

"He's going to come to soon," I inform both women. "I didn't hit him that hard."

"Who are you?" the brunette asks, finally getting to her feet.

I scan her face, but she's unfamiliar. In any case, her features are obscured by the beating she's taken. The wounds are fresh. Whoever did this to her did it recently.

She notices me watching her and jerks her chin up proudly. "What do you want here?" she asks when I don't answer her first question.

"I want this fucker," I say, gesturing to Murray. "You two just happened to be in my way."

My gaze moves to Elyssa. She flinches under my stare. But before she can say anything, her friend interrupts. "Okay, back to the first question: who are you?"

"You first."

"I'm nobody," she replies immediately.

I smirk. "So what's the story?" I ask. I look at the brunette. "You got a boyfriend who likes to box or something?"

"Maybe I do."

I narrow my eyes. "I'd tell the truth if I were you."

"Why?" she demands. "Because you're dangerous?"

I take a menacing step forward. "You tell me."

Her irises are a bright, beautiful blue that reminds me of my Uncle Kian's. But it's overshadowed by the ugly bruises marring her face. She seems to be extremely protective of Elyssa, stepping in front of the girl to shield her from me.

"Why don't you put that away before you hurt yourself?" I tell Elyssa again.

Her brown eyes spark. *That's new*, I think to myself. The last time we crossed paths, she had been so completely passive, so helpless, that she'd clung to me, a complete stranger.

I can still recognize some of the same passivity in her. But there's a little more steel now. If I had to guess, I'd say that's probably the friend's influence. Which isn't a bad thing for her, insofar as staying alive in Las Vegas requires a little steel sometimes.

Just an inconvenient thing for me right now.

"I know what I'm doing," she says. But there's no confidence in her tone. She's saying the words that she thinks she's supposed to say.

"Do you?"

Doubt flickers across her eyes and she sighs. "No," she says, letting her hands fall.

"Elyssa!" the friend snaps, snatching the gun before Elyssa can lower it all the way down. "What are you doing?"

"He's right," she says innocently. "I don't know how to use that thing. It feels wrong to even hold it."

"It's called self-defense."

"He hasn't threatened to hurt us," she says in a voice so low I almost don't catch the words.

"Yet!"

"I don't plan on hurting either one of you," I tell them both, but I keep one eye on Murray. "Can't speak for this motherfucker, though."

He's writhing around a little extra now, still bleating softly in pain.

"Like I said, I came here for him. He's the one I'm following," I continue. "My question is, what does he want here?"

"Me," the friend says at once. "He wanted me to come with him."

"For what reason?"

She frowns. "That I don't know. And that's the honest truth. We were trying to get rid of him when you showed up."

"I see." I look down at the cop again, then back up to the girls. "Do you have rope?"

"Rope?" she repeats, confused.

"For our friend here. He's waking up. I want to make sure he can't run when he does."

The friend hesitates for a moment. Then she looks at Elyssa. "Gary keeps a ton of shit in the back room, doesn't he?" she says. "You might find some rope there."

Elyssa looks uncertain about leaving her friend alone with me, but in the end, she goes without a word.

The moment she's gone, her friend turns her one good eye on me. "You're him."

"I might be."

"That guy she met that night," she continues bluntly. "The night she showed up in Las Vegas in a wedding dress."

"So she's mentioned me."

A strange expression flits across her face. I don't know why, but it makes me feel uneasy. "You could say that," she says at last.

I frown. "What aren't you telling me?"

She looks away before I can read her expression. "It's not my place to give you explanations. I'm not even sure you have the right to ask for them."

"The fuck is that supposed to mean?"

Before she can respond, Elyssa walks back into the room with a bunch of thin cord. One look tells me it's not going to hold Murray for long.

"Will this work?" Elyssa asks, offering me the rope at arm's length as though she's scared to come too close.

"It'll have to do."

I take the rope and bend down to tie Murray's arms with quick, sure hands. He comes to just as I get the last knot together.

"What the… get the fuck off me!" he mumbles, trying to sound intimidating. "I'm a fuckin' cop!" It's hard to sound tough when you're hogtied on the ground, though.

I flip him over so that he can look me in the eye. At first, he can't see past his own anger. Then his eyes go wide, as he takes in my face, recognizes me.

"You… I know you."

"Do you?" I ask calmly. "How flattering."

I can feel Elyssa and her friend watching me. Waiting for an answer as to who I am. Murray's going to give me away, but I don't care. I don't even know if my name is going to mean anything to either one of them anyway.

"Kovalyov," he whispers. "You're the son."

I try not to let my anger show. It's an immature reaction I'd picked up as a teenager, but even after a decade as the lone Kovalyov don in Las Vegas, it's stuck.

My father's name has always come first, then mine.

To an extent, I understand it. He is the top don of the Kovalyov Bratva. That is an honor he deserves. But living in his shadow robbed me of the ability to stand on my own, away from his legacy, his reputation.

"I'm the only one who matters to you," I reply icily. "Because I'm the one who decides what happens next."

"Phoenix Kovalyov," Murray murmurs.

I'm watching the two women out of the corner of my eyes. Elyssa doesn't react to my name at all. But her friend does. She reaches out and grabs Elyssa's arm. They exchange a look, but I can't tell what it holds.

"You've been interfering with Astra Tyrannis operations for the last several years," he snarls.

I smirk. "And now we get to chat about it. Just the two of us. Lucky night."

Murray bares his teeth at me. "You don't know what you're getting involved with. You don't fuck around with Astra Tyrannis."

I smile. "Why don't you let me worry about that? How about, for right now, you worry about yourself? And believe me, my friend—you should be worried."

"What do you want?"

"Isn't that obvious?" I ask impatiently. "I want answers."

"All you'll get is a painful death," he snarls. "I'm not alone, you know. I've got backup."

"Where are they now?"

"On the way," Murray replies. "I called them in before knocking on the door."

"Thanks for the heads-up."

I know he's trying to scare me off. But all he's done is warn me about the impending danger. If it is in fact true.

"Wait," Elyssa's friend says, stepping forward. "Do you mean that the cops are coming here? Now?"

"Yeah," Murray snarls, answering her even though his eyes are still fastened on me. "They're coming. Two squad cars with more on the way."

"And none of them know you're working with Astra Tyrannis?" I ask conversationally.

He snorts. "Is that your way of threatening me?" he asks. "I've been on the force for a long fucking time. Those men on their way here are my friends. Whereas you are a crime lord with a bad fucking reputation. I can pin all kinds of shit on you. I can make your life really fucking difficult."

"Are you threatening me now?" I ask with faux amusement. "Because from where I'm standing, it doesn't look like you have much in the way of bargaining power."

"All I want is the whore," he says, jerking his chin towards Elyssa's friend. "Let me take her and you won't have anything to worry about."

Elyssa moves in front of the brunette instantly, her body stiffening. I can tell she's terrified to intervene, but she does it anyway.

"No one is touching her," she says proudly.

Murray looks at her with complete disdain. "Careful, little bitch," he snaps. "You might be next."

He doesn't see my fist coming. I don't think any of them do.

I just hear two gasps and a very loud, very shocked yell as my knuckles collide into Murray's face. Cartilage crunches and the bleeding starts almost immediately.

"What the fuck… you motherfucker…" he moans.

Just then, I hear a siren off in the distance. It's faint, but a sobering reminder that we might in fact have company soon.

"I told you backup was—"

I punch him again. This time, the aim is to knock him out cold. Sure enough, he goes out like a light, his head cracking against the floor as his eyes roll back in his skull.

When he's limp and unresisting, I hoist the man onto my shoulder like a sack of potatoes.

"Wait! What are you doing?" the brunette asks urgently.

"Leaving."

"You're just going to leave us?" she asks.

I raise my eyebrows and resist the urge to look at Elyssa. The night we met was… unique.

But I've spent enough fucking time thinking about it in the year that's passed since then.

I let her distract me once before, and it cost me my best shot at Ozol. I won't let her do it again. So, despite the fact that I'm aching to look at her one last time before I leave, I bury the desire underneath resolve. I focus on the reason I'm here in the first place.

I came for Murray.

I have Murray.

Time to cut and run before the backup gets here.

"Leave you?" I repeat. "Neither one of you are my fucking responsibility. I saved your asses from a life of enslavement. That's my contribution here."

I turn to leave.

"Wait!"

Her voice stops me in my tracks, despite the siren sounds drawing closer.

"You have to take us with you," she says.

"Give me one good reason."

In response, she nods, then turns and runs deeper into the shelter.

"Where the fuck is she going?" I demand. "I haven't got all fucking day."

"Give her a minute," the brunette snaps at me, as though I'm being the unreasonable one here. "This is important."

That look is back in her eye. The look that suggests she knows something about me that I don't.

"Elyssa?" the brunette calls out as the sirens grow ever louder.

"We can leave through the back door," Elyssa calls from out of sight.

With the sirens blasting as if from right out front, I know I can't risk taking that exit out of here. So when the brunette starts walking, I follow her, lugging the unconscious cop along with me.

We reach an ugly crevice that leads to a backdoor, when Elyssa emerges from an adjacent door to the left.

Except, when she reappears, I see that she's not alone.

She's holding a groggy infant against her chest. A dark-haired boy with deep brown eyes shaped like almonds.

Elyssa looks at me with big guilty eyes. And for a moment, my brain feels like it's short-circuiting.

This can't be happening...

"Well?" the brunette asks without a shred of sensitivity. "Aren't you going to say hello to your son?"

12

PHOENIX

I stare at the apple-cheeked baby in Elyssa's arms.

His face is turned away from me now. He's tiny. No more than a couple of months old. Which of course adds up.

Kakogo chyorta, I curse silently in Russian. *What the fuck...*

"I didn't think I'd ever see you again," Elyssa says tremulously.

I still don't know what the fuck to say to this revelation. So I focus on the one thing I do know how to do: handle an imminent threat.

I pull out my phone and call Matvei. He answers on the first ring. "Phoenix? Are you okay? What happened?"

"Meet me out by Eastern Ave and the Beltway. Bring a big car. Come fast."

"On my way."

He doesn't blink, hesitate, or ask questions. That's why he's my closest ally in this world.

The line goes dead. I turn back to the two women who are both watching me carefully.

"Come on," I order. "Let's go."

A shadow of disappointment flits across Elyssa's face. It ignites the guilt that's starting to build slowly inside of me.

But I can't worry about that right now. Because the cops are on their way, and I don't want Murray stirring while we're on the run.

"Where are we going?" the brunette asks.

"Away."

"You said the Beltway. That's like a twenty-five minute walk from here. Longer with a baby."

"We can't use my car," I snap gruffly. "It's parked out front and the cops are definitely going to notice the unconscious body over my shoulder. Also, it wasn't a question. Start walking."

The brunette seems like she wants to balk again, but Elyssa places a reassuring palm on her forearm, and she falls silent. I eye them fiercely for one more moment before I turn and stride towards the back exit.

As we slip out the door and down into the thin thicket of trees that will give us enough coverage to get away from the shelter without being seen, I notice the flash of sirens in the distance.

"We need to hurry."

I take the lead, making sure to keep several feet of distance between the women and myself. I don't even look back as I charge ahead.

"Will you slow down?" the brunette calls after me. "We've got a baby here!"

I hear the gurgle of the boy in Elyssa's hands, and I stiffen instantly. It's a primal reaction. Carved into my soul like scar tissue.

The body remembers even when the mind wants so desperately to forget.

When Aurora and Yuri had first disappeared… The helplessness, the uncertainty…

I vowed to never feel so out of control ever again. The ironic part is that it isn't the kind of promise that any man has the control to make in the first place.

Not even a man like me.

I force myself to slow down just a little, though I still make sure to stay ahead of them. I don't want to talk to Elyssa or to even look at the boy right now.

Murray is getting heavier against my shoulder, but I don't want to drop the pace. If I slow down, then all my mistakes will catch up to me.

"Jesus, hold the hell up!" the brunette calls. "Elyssa, you okay?"

I glance around to see Elyssa panting softly, her cheeks flushed with color. She's cradling the baby to her chest, trying to soothe him, but he's starting to cry anyway.

"You okay?" the brunette asks her again gently.

Her tone takes a different edge when she talks to Elyssa. It's kind. Maternal. Her hand flickers over Elyssa's shoulder and then to the baby.

The dark hair throws me for a fucking loop.

It's just like mine.

Yuri favored his mother. He was born with Aurora's teal blue eyes and strawberry blonde curls. I said again and again that his hair would darken with age.

We never got the chance to find out.

My gut twists uncomfortably and I feel the gasping need for alcohol. Anything to numb the steel-edged pain of old memories.

"You're tired," the brunette says. "Let me carry him the rest of the way."

"I can manage," Elyssa replies.

She looks at me and I see the soft determination in her eyes. She doesn't want to look weak in front of me. She doesn't want to look like she's not capable.

"Don't be silly. You've been carrying him for ages. Let me take him."

Before Elyssa can protest, the brunette plucks the baby out of her arms and cradles him against her chest like he's her own.

"Hey, handsome," she coos to the baby as she starts to walk again. "We're going on a little adventure."

As she moves closer, my eyes can't help but go straight to the baby's face. His eyes are shaped like mine. Their color is more complex, though. Not too light. Not too dark.

Instinctively, I look at Elyssa, only to find she's looking right back at me. She blushes hard and averts her gaze, but not before I make a mental note of her eye color. Caramel brown with subtle flecks of green, like toasted hazel. Mine are a dark, inky brown that might as well be black.

The baby's eyes are a perfect blend of the two.

"If you're done gawking, we can keep going," the brunette chides.

I throw her an annoyed look and resume hustling through the night.

"There's no reason to look at me like that. Especially when the person you're really mad at is yourself."

I stop, pivot, and stare at her with irritated disbelief. "You met me five minutes ago. What makes you think you know me?"

She shrugs. "I know men."

I bark out a harsh laugh. "I bet you do."

She twists around a little to find Elyssa, who's walking a few feet behind us. I resist the urge to check on her, too.

The baby starts fidgeting in the brunette's grasp. "Hey now, little cherub," she coos fondly. "Your mama is right here. I've got you, okay?" She flicks her gaze up to me. "Don't you want to know his name?"

"No."

She glances at Elyssa again, as though she's worried her friend might have heard. Then she lowers her voice. "Don't be a fucking asshole."

The baby starts crying and she's forced to turn her attention back to him. "Hush now, handsome. We're almost there."

"I think your face is scaring him," I point out.

She glares at me with her one good eye just as the infant devolves into a full-on cry.

"Charity, you can give him back to me," Elyssa calls up.

"Charity?" I scoff. "That's a fucking joke."

"It's not a joke; it's my name," she snaps. "And it's a good one."

"You think so?" I drawl. "Doesn't really suit you."

Elyssa joins us and takes the baby back. The moment her hands are free, Charity flips me the bird.

Smirking, I adjust Murray slightly, ignoring the growing ache in my shoulder as I guide us back onto the main road and come to a halt behind a manicured hedge.

This street is relatively quiet, but I don't want to linger in the open any longer than necessary. You never know who's watching you in the Las Vegas night.

"What are we waiting for?" Charity asks when I stop walking.

"My ride."

I drop Murray roughly to the ground and crack my back, thankful to be rid of the fucker for at least a few moments.

"*Our* ride," she corrects quickly, as though to remind me that I've committed to taking them along.

I'm about to make some flippant comment, but I take one look at Elyssa and stop myself. She's holding the baby tightly and he's quieted down. One of his chubby little fists clings to the front of her dark blue t-shirt. It's a couple of sizes too big for her, but somehow it suits her perfectly. He's pulling the neckline down enough to expose the gentle curve of her cleavage.

"She's not a piece of meat, you know," Charity says quietly, noticing where my eyes have fallen.

I grit my teeth and turn to her. "I'd watch my words if I were you. You're very close to being left by the roadside."

She smiles. "I bet I can convince you otherwise."

"First of all, I'm not that kind of guy," I tell her straight. "And second, even if I were, you're in no fit state to bargain on your looks right now. You look like hell warmed over."

"What 'kind of guy' is that?" she inquires innocently.

I'm conscious of Elyssa watching us, but she's standing far enough away that I'm confident she can't hear the conversation. "The kind of guy who gets his head turned by a perky pair of tits."

"Oh yeah? Then how do you explain the night you met Elyssa?"

I have to bite back a wry laugh. This woman can certainly hold her own. But even with all her feistiness and misplaced anger towards me, it's easier to focus on her than on the blonde and the baby right behind me. Those two are an enigma I cannot let consume me.

Not now. Not yet.

"What happened to you?" I ask instead of answering her question.

"Long story."

"Give me the short version."

"Why do you care?"

"Because he does," I say, gesturing to Murray's back. He's face-down on the ground. I'm pretty sure he'll wake up to a mouth full of dirt. It's the least he deserves. "He came to the shelter in search of you. Why?"

Confusion and fear flickers across her face. "I wish I knew. The only reason I can think of is the man that did this to me must be important."

"Who is the man that did that to you?"

She hesitates. "Does it matter?"

"Yes."

"Why?"

"Because maybe I can stop him coming after you."

She studies me carefully. "Right. Phoenix Kovalyov," she murmurs. "I've heard of you."

I'm surprised to hear a faint hint of reverence when she says my name. Or is it fear? Doesn't matter either way, I suppose. I've never really cared about the difference.

"Yeah? I'm flattered."

"Don't be. I just couldn't have imagined that you of all people were Theo's father. Wonders never cease."

A jolt of adrenaline surges through my body when she says his name. I echo it unthinkingly: "Theo…"

"Your son."

I nod and clench my jaw, trying to act as though this information means nothing to me. That's when I hear the rumble of an engine. A fast-moving vehicle.

"Stay here," I order Charity.

I step out from behind the hedge and go stand at the edge of the road. The car is a black SUV. Nice and big, just like I requested. One look at the license plate tells me it's one of the Bratva's plethora of cars.

Matvei cruises to a stop right in front of me and reaches across to throw open the passenger side door.

"Thank fuck. Been waiting long?" he asks.

"My whole goddamn life," I grumble. "What took you so long?"

"I was at the safehouse," he says. "And I wouldn't have needed to come get you at all if you'd just taken me with you."

I roll my eyes. "Let's do this later. I got Murray."

"No way. Where is he?"

"Rotting away over there." I jerk my thumb back at our little alcove near the hedge.

"I'll get him," Matvei says, putting the car on park before he leaps out.

"I'll help."

He leaves the car in the middle of the road like he owns it. In a sense, we do. Then he follows me back to the shadows.

"Wait, is there someone else there?" Matvei asks as we approach Murray's near-lifeless body.

"Yeah," I sigh. "Long fucking story."

Charity chooses that moment to step forward into a beam of moonlight, her eyes widening slightly as she takes in Matvei.

"Are you the brainless henchman?" she drawls.

Before he can answer, Elyssa steps up next to her with the baby in her arms. It seems he's fallen asleep. A single lock of dark hair drapes over his eyes. As I watch, my fingers itch with the urge to smooth it away.

Matvei just turns to me slowly. "Jesus, brother. How long of a story is it?"

"I'll explain later."

"I'll give you the short version," Charity offers, giving me a conspiratorial wink and smile. "I'm Charity, the hooker that this fucker was trying to abduct."

She gives Murray a kick to illustrate her point.

"And this is Elyssa," she adds, jerking her thumb at the blonde, "the one-night stand that your friend here ghosted a year ago. But at least he was kind enough to leave her with a little souvenir of their night together. His name is Theo."

Matvei has a stellar poker face. He gives nothing away. Instead, he turns to me with a deadpan expression. "Seems like she hit the key points pretty efficiently there, pal."

"Don't fucking start with me," I snap.

"Is it all true?"

I'm looking at Elyssa, trying to gauge her reaction. She's blushing fiercely and looking down at her son. "Apparently," I mumble. "Now, help me pick up this son of a bitch and let's get out of here."

Matvei and I grab the slumped Murray by the wrists and ankles and haul him over to the trunk. The women slip into the back seat.

Once Murray's settled, Matvei shuts the trunk and turns to me. "Is this for real?" he asks. "Like, for real for real?"

I can see Charity's silhouette twisting around to watch us through the rear window.

"Now's not the time to discuss this. I need to get Murray to a secure location so that we can question him."

"Really? That's what you're focused on right now?"

"That's the *only* thing I'm focused on right now," I retort stubbornly.

Then I head to the passenger side door, effectively ending the conversation. Matvei follows behind, watching me.

"Where to?"

"The mansion," I answer at once.

The drive there is quiet, punctured only by the sporadic sleeping murmurs of the baby in Elyssa's arms. He wakes up just as Matvei steers us up the private driveway.

"Jesus, this place is huge!" Charity gasps, doing nothing to mask her amazement as she takes in the three-story estate.

Elyssa's expression is more difficult to read. She looks more overwhelmed than blown away. And kind of nervous.

When the car comes to a stop in front of the ivy-laced brick façade, Charity pops out at once. I walk around to Elyssa's side to open the door for her.

She struggles to get out without disrupting the baby, but I resist the urge to offer her a hand. Touching her seems like it might be a little too much at the moment. She seems to feel the same way.

We all snake through the front entrance. Charity steps inside and does a double take as she takes in the interior.

"This place is like something out of a fairy tale. *Beauty and the Beast* meets *Scarface*."

Matvei ogles Charity before turning to me. "I'll have Murray taken to the basement cell," he says softly. "Then I'll meet you in the office." He takes off before I can say otherwise.

The bastard thinks he's slick, leaving me alone here to confront this situation.

"I appreciate the support," I snap at his receding back.

He doesn't answer. When he's gone, I turn to Charity and Elyssa.

"Um… Phoenix?"

Honestly, my body shouldn't react at all. But the moment she says my name, I feel as though I've been touched by fucking fire. It's the weirdest feeling I've ever experienced.

"Yes?"

"Theo needs to be changed."

"Right," I say gruffly, refusing to look her in the eye. "Follow me."

I take them up to the second floor, to one of the numerous and rarely used guest rooms. "I'll send someone out for baby supplies," I tell Elyssa as I escort them in. "There should be a pen and pad somewhere in the desk drawer. Write down a list and I'll have someone collect it at once."

Then, before either one can say a word, I shut the door on them and walk away.

But it doesn't matter. Refusing to acknowledge this won't make it disappear.

I've learned that lesson the hard way.

13

ELYSSA

INSIDE THE KOVALYOV MANSION

I turn to the door at the definitive clicking sound that can mean only one thing: we're locked in.

Swallowing back my fear, I cradle Theo and turn to Charity. She's not even looking at the door or at me. Her eyes are fixed on the massive glass doors overlooking the private balcony.

"This is fucking amazing," she mutters. "Who the hell does this guy think he is?"

I'm so unnerved to be here at all that I don't even scold her for the language the way I used to. "Charity," I hiss instead, grabbing her arm and pulling her around to face me.

"What?" she asks. She's still looking around in awe. "Lys, just look at how high the ceilings are!"

"I think he locked us in!"

Her eyes snap to mine. She walks straight to the door and pulls on the handle. It doesn't budge. She pivots back around slowly. "Okay. So he locked us in here. Let's not freak—"

"Oh my God," I gasp, fidgeting on the spot. "Charity, we should never have come here."

"Of course we should have," she replies. "He's Theo's father. He won't hurt us."

I wince. We hadn't really had much time to discuss him or who he was to me. Who he *is* to me.

But Charity is sharp. She understands people in a way I don't think I ever will. She read the situation. Saw the truth on my face.

And she used it to save us.

"He's Theo's father," I echo. My voice wavers and breaks.

"Hey now," Charity murmurs, coming forward and putting her hands on my shoulders. "It isn't all bad. We're in the penthouse suite, baby. At least we didn't get the basement cell like that cop asshole."

A bubble of desperate laughter escapes my lips. "True, I guess."

"We couldn't stay there, Elyssa," she says with a sad, gentle smile. "That dirty fuck called backup. It wasn't gonna end well."

"I know, I know," I say, trying to look at the situation logically. "It wasn't safe. But… to come here? To accept his help?"

"I might not have thought it was a good idea," Charity reasons. "But you have the trump card."

I frown. "Huh?"

"Theo, dummy!" she says, pointing at the baby in my arms. "We have Theo."

I curl my hands around him protectively. "My son is not a trump card, Char."

She sighs and nods. "I'm sorry. Bad word choice. That's not what I meant. I just meant that he's not going to hurt you or Theo."

"If he even believes me…"

"Why wouldn't he?"

"I don't know. It was a one-time thing," I sigh. "Like a nightmare. And he basically accused me of being a spy working for some… horrible organization."

"Astra Tyrannis," Charity says at once. She doesn't stumble on the name at all.

My eyes go wide. "You've heard of these people?"

"I've heard the name mentioned before," she admits. "It pops up now and again in the circles I work in."

"And?" I press. "Who are they? What do they do? Why does he care about them?"

She hesitates slightly. That's how I know it's bad.

And yet, the hesitation irks me anyway. I've contributed to it, and God knows there's plenty about this world I still don't understand. But sometimes I hate that Charity treats me with kid gloves. Like I'm too fragile to handle certain truths.

I walk over to the bed, set Theo down against the covers, and gaze at him with new eyes.

My son. Phoenix's son. Is he a miracle, like I've always thought?

Or is he the anchor that's about to drag us to the bottom of a dark and stormy ocean?

I shudder and busy myself with checking him over. His diaper is full, which reminds me of the list of supplies I'm supposed to be writing.

"Can you look for a pen and paper?" I ask Charity. "I need some things for Theo."

Clearly relieved for the distraction, she searches the sprawling mahogany desk jammed along one side of the room. "Here we go," she says triumphantly. "What do we need?"

"Diapers and formula. A couple of onesies. Diaper cream. A swaddle cloth, a milk bottle…" I trail off as I try to think of what else I might need. "A soft towel so I can wash him."

Charity writes quickly and then looks up. "What about for you?"

I frown. "What about for me?"

"Don't you want anything for yourself?"

"No," I say immediately. The thought of owing Phoenix anything is nauseating. We shouldn't be here. The locked door is proof enough that whatever we've found ourselves caught up in is bad news indeed.

Maybe my dark-eyed protector should've stayed hidden in the shadows.

"Come on, Lys," Charity argues, gesturing around the room. "The guy's clearly loaded. We're talking Bratva money here. That's serious fucking cash."

"Language," I hiss.

"Theo's three months old," Charity points out. "He can't understand a word we're saying."

"You don't know that."

Charity gives me a long-suffering sigh and looks down at her list before adding a couple more things.

"What are you writing down?" I ask suspiciously.

"Stuff," she mutters, just as a knock sounds through the door.

It swings open before either of us can even get up. I'm expecting to see Phoenix, but it's not him. There's a stranger standing in his place. A tall, tattooed stranger we've never seen before.

He's got a prominent, hawk-like nose and dangerously alert eyes. Something about him radiates violence. I have to force myself to suppress the shiver running down my spine.

"I'm here to collect a list," he informs us without a trace of emotion.

Charity hands it over and gives him a flirty wink. An impressive feat, considering she has only one eye to wink from at the moment.

"Anything else you wanna collect?" she asks coyly. "I don't mind delivering."

He doesn't react. "Just the list."

He takes it, steps back outside, and closes the door on her smile. Again, the click of the lock echoes throughout the room.

"Damn," Charity says, turning to me. "He was hot."

"Are you serious?" I ask, staring at her in disbelief.

"What?"

"He's dangerous. He's probably, y'know… killed people," I say, lowering my voice.

She sighs. "I don't think it's a secret that the men around this place have killed people. You don't need to whisper."

I glance at my son gurgling contentedly on the bed and move a little closer to him. "Phoenix Kovalyov," I whisper absent-mindedly, trying his name on for size. "Theo Kovalyov."

"Did you know?" Charity asks gently. She walks over and sits on Theo's other side.

"No," I reply, shaking my head. "I had no idea who he was. I didn't even know his name until the detective mentioned it."

"Fuck."

I flinch.

"Sorry," Charity says. "I thought you'd be over that by now. You did use the word yourself earlier today."

"That was different," I protest. "That was warranted."

She smiles. "For the record, I don't think you have to fear Phoenix Kovalyov."

"Because I have his son?"

"No," she replies. "Because of the way he looks at you."

I stop short. "Huh?"

She smiles. "Oh, honey. You've always been so naïve about the way men look at you. Even when you were pregnant, they still looked at you."

I shake my head. "You're imagining things."

"I can read people," she says proudly. "Especially men. And the one we met today… he's got his eye on you."

"You don't know what you're talking about, Char."

"It must have been intense," she says cautiously. "That night…"

I bite my lip and glance at Theo. Charity is the one who taught me never to trust anyone with your past. She'd stood by her point by never asking me details about that night—or any of the nights that preceded it.

The nights I can't remember. The nights that exist in my head as only a black, shrouded mystery.

Practically my whole life, locked inside my brain with the key left somewhere out in that godforsaken desert.

"It was intense," I agree. "It was… more than I bargained for."

She looks like she wants to keep digging, but true to form, she stops herself. If I'm not offering, I know she won't pry. It's one of the things

I love most about Charity. She may be a little rough around the edges sometimes. But she's all heart.

So instead of interrogating me, she just nods and strokes the back of my hand. We sit that way quietly for a while, both of us lost in our own thoughts.

"Astra Tyrannis," I mutter after a few silent minutes have passed, the name sticking in my memory now. "What is it?"

She sighs. "Elyssa…"

"Please don't treat me like a child, Char," I whisper. "I know I'm not as worldly as you are, but that doesn't mean I don't deserve the truth when I ask for it."

Charity rests her hand on mine. Theo reaches out and tries to join in with his chubby little fingers.

"You're right," she says with a sympathetic nod. "The only reason I didn't tell you is because I didn't want you to worry."

"I'm not worrying. I'm asking."

She hesitates for one beat more before she sighs again and starts to explain. "Astra Tyrannis. It's an… organization, I guess you'd call it. Rumor is they started in Europe, then spread to the East Coast—New York, I think. Then here, sometime in the last ten or twenty years. They sell—or, I guess, trade, or whatever…" She pauses again. Then, in the tiniest, meekest voice I've ever heard from her, she finishes, "…people."

I stare at her in shock. "They sell people," I repeat numbly. "Human beings."

Charity nods. "They abduct girls and women and sell them in the black markets. Auctions and the like."

"To do what with?" I ask.

When she answers with nothing more than a raise of her eyebrows, I feel like a complete imbecile.

"Oh God," I breathe. "Charity! The detective came to the shelter for you. And if he's connected to this organization…"

"This is why I didn't want to tell you, Lys. I don't want you worrying about this."

"Your job lands you in all the wrong places. Today proves that. Your face proves that!"

She waves a hand. "I'm fine."

"Do you wanna take a look in the mirror? You don't look fine! Those bruises don't look fine!"

"They'll heal," she says calmly. "You're the one who told me that."

In a matter of hours, we've switched back to our natural roles. Charity is calm and in control. I'm the nervous wreck who needs consoling.

"Oh God," I say again, shaking my head. "Is that why you insisted we come here with him?"

"From what he said, he seems to be fighting *against* Astra Tyrannis," Charity says. "The cop, on the other hand… Well, I figured it was our best bet to stay at a safe hideaway until this blows over."

She's acting like this is a temporary situation. A stopgap before we move on.

Somehow, I don't think so.

"What do we do?" I ask.

Charity grabs my hand. "We stick together," she says firmly. "We have each other's backs. We'll survive this, Elyssa. Just like we've survived everything else."

Her words were strong, filled with conviction.

But I'm not sure I can see the same sentiment reflected in her good eye. As usual, she's putting on a brave face for my benefit. It makes me feel ashamed. As if I'm the one who constantly needs to be taken care of.

I'm so sick of being the damsel in distress.

"Hey, I'm gonna go take a shower, okay?" Charity says, perking up. "I'll bet the bathroom is the size of the shelter!"

She buries her worry beneath bravado. That's another thing I've always admired about her. I, on the other hand, am ruled by my fear. I have been since the day I left the Sanctuary.

Charity skips into the bathroom and a second later, I hear her high-pitched, sing-song voice. The one she uses only when she's really excited.

"I was right! And it has a freaking jacuzzi!" She pops her head out of the bathroom for a moment. "If you don't see me for a while, don't be alarmed. I've moved in here."

Smiling, I pick Theo up and follow her into the bathroom. She's already half-naked, ready to plunge into the tub.

"Those wounds are gonna sting," I warn her.

"Mama's used to a little pain," she sasses right back.

There's no changing table in the bathroom, but the counters are spacious enough that it doesn't matter. I grab a towel, marveling at how soft and fluffy it is, and spread it out on the bathroom counter. Then I set Theo down on it and get to work cleaning him up.

By the time I've finished, Charity's snoring gently in the bath.

He's starting to get a little whiny and I realize that it's past time to feed him. I would have given him my breast, but my milk dried up months ago. I'd switched to formula when he was only a few weeks old.

Yet another way I've failed him as a mother.

I carry Theo unclothed back into the bedroom—just as the door opens again.

I leap back instinctively, but it's only the stone-faced guard from before. He's carrying several overflowing bags, all of which he sets down next to the door.

"That was fast," I remark.

Without a word, he gives me a nod and leaves.

CLICK. The door locks again.

I look at Theo and sigh. "Well, at least it's a pretty prison."

I set him down on the bed, barricade him with pillows, and head over to examine the bags. Everything I'd asked for is here and then some. There's a plush, luxurious baby seat, pacifiers, a variety of different swaddle cloths, rattles, a soft toy shaped like a monkey. More baby clothes than Theo could possibly wear in a lifetime—and, surprisingly, clothes for Charity and me as well.

When I've finished sorting through everything, I examine the last bag, which the guard set down a little bit away from the others. To my delight, this one is filled with takeout food. It smells absolutely delicious.

I pull out box after box of steaming hot Chinese food. Lo mein noodles, General Tsao chicken, stir fries and fried rice and a pair of eggrolls the size of my arm. I'm salivating already.

But my son needs to eat first. Ignoring the rumbling in my belly, I grab a soft white onesie and head over to the bed to dress Theo. Then I make him a bottle and head out onto the balcony to feed him.

He's just finishing up when Charity emerges from the double doors wrapped in a fluffy white robe with dripping wet hair. She's carrying a couple of the Chinese food cartons, too.

"Didn't expect to see you for a while," I tease.

"Kung pao chicken was just about the only thing on the planet that could've coaxed me out of the tub," she explains. "Did you see the baby seat, by the way?"

"I saw."

"What do you think that cost?"

"More than I earn in three months at the shelter, if I had to guess."

Charity places the food on the table and then goes back inside to get the baby seat. I settle Theo into it, and he looks around in awe, blinking furiously.

"We could get used to this life, huh, T?" Charity laughs at him. But I know she's only half-kidding.

For the first time in a long time, we both feel safe… albeit in the home of one of the most dangerous men in Las Vegas.

What an irony that is.

I set the thought aside for now and we gorge ourselves on Chinese food. Which is, no surprise, absolutely heavenly. When I'm full to bursting, we trek back in and I settle Theo on the bed between Charity and me.

"This has been a crazy day," Charity sighs as she sinks into the soft mattress.

I pull the covers over myself and pat Theo gently. "Charity," I say softly, "you know we can't stay here for long."

"I know. But it is nice to feel safe. For just one night at least."

I glance at her swollen face, the bruises, the fresh scabs, and realize just how risky her life has always been.

Her confidence sometimes fools me into believing that she has complete control. But nothing could be further from the truth. She's at the mercy of powerful men all the time. And if they choose to beat her to a pulp, she's the one who ends up on the run.

Where's the justice in that?

Fear and worry grate at my nerves as I realize that Phoenix Kovalyov is exactly one of those men.

Dangerous.

Powerful.

Handsome as sin.

The last thought makes me feel twisted and dirty. What does it say about me that, after all this time, I still have a visceral reaction every time I look at him?

I look at my sleeping son, and I see so many similarities between the two of them. He kept me safe when I needed it. He gave me Theo. So why do I feel so guilty?

"Hey, Earth to Lys," Charity says, pulling me from my thoughts. "Stop worrying. Just sleep tonight. We'll figure out a plan tomorrow."

I nod. There's nothing to be done tonight anyway. And I am pure exhausted. So when Charity reaches out and smooths my hair, I fall asleep in a minute flat.

But my dreams sag with the lingering weight of my waking thoughts. I start seeing shapes that take on the faces of my demons. One demon in particular.

A tall, lanky man with a calm demeanor, white clothes, and a spindly beard.

A man I accepted.

A man I killed.

When I look down, my hands are covered in his blood. No matter how hard I wash, I can't scrub the sticky crimson off of my fingertips.

Then I look up and see his ghost before me.

His eyes aren't calm in death. They're bright, piercing… accusing. He hates me.

And why shouldn't he? At this point, even I hate me.

So when my dead husband's ghost strides forward and wraps his hands around my throat, I let him. I deserve it.

But when he starts squeezing, I realize I don't want to die. Even my guilt is hollow. Even my shame is a lie.

In the face of death, I cling to life. In the face of punishment, I crave escape.

"Please," I beg. "Let me go."

The ghost shakes his head and squeezes harder and harder, and my breathing slows to a trickle and then to nothing at all, and my lungs are burning, and my eyes are bulging, and everything hurts and hurts and hurts until I reach the edge of the cliff and I fall off, tumbling down into endless shadows below…

⁓

I gasp awake. It's later. The room is dark, and Charity is curled up on the other side of the bed, snoring softly. My eyes go wide with terror as I flail around and search for the one comfort I have left in my life.

"Theo?" I whisper into the dark of the cavernous room. "Theo?"

The center of the bed where I laid him down is empty. Theo's blanket is sprawled messily against the sheets. They're still warm.

"Theo," I gasp, panic turning my voice gravelly with fear. "Theo!"

But he's not here. He's not anywhere.

My son is gone.

14

PHOENIX
PHOENIX'S OFFICE

My office is completely devoid of natural light. A deliberate choice on my part.

I had the windows boarded up about three years ago to make more space for the wall of leads I started days after Aurora and Yuri disappeared.

The paper trail has only grown since then. The boards are now plastered with thousands of documents pinned and connected and highlighted and annotated.

Reports and profiles and detailed bios on every man suspected of being involved in Astra Tyrannis.

News articles on the missing women—and God, there are so fucking many of them. Dozens. Hundreds. Thousands. Countless women and girls ripped from their homes and sold into the shadows of the underworld I call home.

I walk over to my desk and pick up the file lying in the center. Opening it up, I scan the A4-sized image of Detective Jonathan Murray's face.

The file is filled with his details. School records from his youth, hospital forms. Fuck, I even have his goddamn police academy report card. All the things that made him a valuable piece for Astra Tyrannis to recruit.

He's smug in the photo. Proud. Like he thinks that his connections mean he can't be touched. Can't be made to pay for his crimes.

"How very fucking wrong you are, Detective," I murmur to the photograph. I pluck the glossy image from the file and stride over to the wall. Grabbing a pin, I stab it through his forehead and skewer it in place at the end of the lineup of leads I've accumulated over the past five years.

The other men in this section of the lineup have the same look in their eyes that Murray does. Arrogant and cruel. A hardened, greedy glint to their eyes.

Every single one of them is dead now.

I hunted them down one by one. Tortured them into giving up their fellow co-conspirators.

And little by little, I've circled closer to the beating heart of Astra Tyrannis.

I promised those men whatever they wanted to hear in order to coax their confessions. And when flattery didn't work, I made them scream until the cells in my basement rung with their howls.

But every interrogation ended the same way: with the lifeblood of these scum pulsing out of their slit throats as they gurgled at my feet.

Murray will meet the same end if he doesn't cooperate with me.

Well, that's not entirely true. He'll meet the same end no matter what he does.

There's a knock on the door, but before I can answer, Matvei pushes it open and enters. Again, his expression is impassive, but I know him well enough to know that he's concerned.

"He's in the basement cell?" I ask.

"Tied up like a Thanksgiving turkey," Matvei replies with a curt nod. "He's not going anywhere."

"Has he come to?"

"He tried. I put him back to sleep. Should be out for another hour or two."

I smirk as Matvei steps up to the wall beside me. But I can tell he's not really looking at it. He's looking at me.

"Are we gonna talk about it?" he inquires.

"What's to talk about?" I ask. "We've been through this before. First thing tomorrow morning, I start the interrogation."

Matvei turns to me with one arched eyebrow. "Obsessing about Astra Tyrannis isn't going to make them disappear, you know."

I rub my temples. "I don't have the fucking time for this."

"By 'this,' I assume you're referring to your son?" Matvei asks innocently.

I walk back to my desk. I sit down and focus on Murray's file, but I'm not seeing anything other than Elyssa's face. Theo's face.

I've dreamed about her for months.

And then out of nowhere, here she is. With my son in her arms.

I shudder. This is a fucking disaster.

Matvei walks over to the desk and sits down in one of the chairs opposite me. "Is it true?"

"It could be."

"Define 'could.'" I crane my head back to look above. The ceiling overhead is ornate and spotlessly clean. My housekeeper deserves a raise.

"Does this by any chance have something to do with the night of the botched meeting with Ozol?" Matvei asks shrewdly.

Of course he's figured it out. Fucker is sharp.

I nod grimly. "That's the night I met her."

"So she's the one," Matvei murmurs. "I always wondered what happened. You never told me you slept with her."

"Because it should never have happened," I retort with a growl, wrenching my gaze back down to meet Matvei's. "I was reeling from the disappointment of letting Ozol slip through my fingers. And there she was… in a fucking wedding dress with blood caked under her fingernails."

"Jesus. Gruesome."

I shake my head, remembering that night. "There was just something about her. She looked at me like…" I trail off, realizing that I'm speaking out loud now.

"Like what?" Matvei presses.

"She looked at me like she needed saving."

The acknowledgement is heavier than I intended it. And it's more telling once the words are out there in the ether.

I couldn't save my wife or my son. So I've tried to save every other innocent soul who's crossed my path.

It's not absolution I seek. Nothing can redeem me after Aurora, after Yuri. But it's all I have left.

I wouldn't have been able to admit that to anyone else. But Matvei is different. He's the friend I can tell my darkest thoughts to, and he won't judge.

Probably because the same darkness I sense in myself lives in him, too.

"What happened after that?" Matvei asks.

"Ozol set his men on me," I explain. "I told her to run. I told her to meet me at the diner. But when I managed to make my way there, she didn't show. That was that. Until a couple of hours ago, when I followed Murray to this shelter on the edge of town and find her there. With my… my… with the baby."

Matvei's eyes flicker around the room as though he's putting together a mental puzzle. "The math adds up."

"I know."

"And the child looks like you."

I'd noticed that, too. I hadn't realized that Matvei had gotten a good look, but I'm not surprised. The man has an eagle eye. It's all the more impressive because it never appears that he's watching you.

"What's the situation with the two women?"

"I have no fucking clue. Apparently, they don't either. Murray was there for the brunette. Charity."

"And your girl?"

I cringe. "She's not my girl."

Matvei raises his hands, but I notice a tiny smile playing across his lips. "My bad. What would you like me to call her? Your baby mama?"

I glare at him. "You're not funny. Don't try to be," I tell him. "You can call her by her name. Elyssa."

"Elyssa," he repeats solemnly. "Pretty. Just like her."

"She's beautiful," I say before I can stop myself.

"You know, Phoenix, it's okay to want her," Matvei offers gently. "You're not betraying Aurora if you move on."

My hands curl into furious fists. I'm not mad at Matvei, though.

I'm mad at my whole fucking life.

"*Move on?*" I repeat darkly. "There is no 'moving on' for me. Not until I get justice for her death. For my son's death."

"You have another son," Matvei points out. "One that's right here in this house."

I slam my fist down on the table. Matvei doesn't bat an eye. "What are you saying?" I demand. "I have a replacement now, so why bother with the son I lost?"

"You know damn well that's not what I meant."

I turn my head away so he doesn't see the raw emotion on my face. "It doesn't fucking matter," I snarl. "The only thing that matters is the man in the basement."

"Really?" Matvei asks incredulously. "*He's* the one that matters?"

"Nothing has changed. Not a single fucking thing. I'm still taking them down, Matvei. I'm going to make those fuckers pay for all their crimes."

He leans in. "And I support that mission. I've been with you every step of the way, haven't I?"

I give him a grudging nod. "You have."

"But there's a difference between focus and obsession."

"You're starting to sound like my father."

"Only because he's right," Matvei replies rather infuriatingly. "You need more in your life than Astra Tyrannis, Phoenix. The hunt is consuming you."

"If that's the price I need to pay to take them down, I'm okay with it."

"What if I'm not?"

I narrow my eyes. "Then you can walk away. That's not an option for me."

Matvei sighs and slumps back in his seat. "No, it's not an option for me, either."

We stare at each other for a while, neither willing to budge. Two proud men up against a formidable, faceless enemy.

"You have to deal with them at some point, Phoenix," Matvei says at last, breaking the suffocating silence.

"And I will."

I know damn well that he's talking about the girls, not Astra Tyrannis. And he knows that I know that. But it's easier to pretend that this is all business. That the corrupt pig in the basement is the right place to be focusing my attention.

The women's room upstairs might as well be full of demons.

"You want a drink?" Matvei asks suddenly, surprising me with the question.

He knows I do my best to avoid drinking. And he usually isn't the one offering me a drink. But apparently, he thinks the situation is dire enough that it warrants whiskey.

"Yeah. Make it stiff."

"I'll be right back," he says. He gets up and leaves the office.

I grew up with a league of powerful men. All dons in their own right. Each one had an office of their own, exactly like this. And every single one had whiskey within arms' reach

I'd been the first to break tradition and banish the alcohol from my sight. It was a conscientious decision on my part. A result of one too many drunken nights and foggy mornings.

I was determined to be a don that commanded respect. And that meant resisting the temptation to drink.

But fuck, was it hard to stave off the booze. Especially on mornings when I woke up with Aurora's name on my lips, having imagined her death in my nightmares.

Or during nights when I walked past the room that used to be Yuri's nursery and black despair felt like it was choking me out.

Matvei walks back into my office, rescuing me from my thoughts. He's holding two glasses of deep brown-gold whiskey.

He hands me one of the glasses. We clink the rims together out of habit.

When Matvei sits down, I raise the tumbler to my lips and take a bigger sip than necessary. The taste of the whiskey is deep, dark, and rich. Oak hints humming in harmony with dark caramel undertones.

"Fuck, this shit is good," I breathe, letting the golden liquid burn my throat as it goes down.

"The best," Matvei agrees.

"We should do this more often."

"We would if you ever just stopped," Matvei points out.

"Is this where you tell me to stop and smell the roses?"

"Something like that."

I smile. "You're getting sentimental in your old age."

"I won't be old for another fifty years at least," Matvei scoffs. "And I'll still be younger than you."

Smiling, I take another gulp of whiskey. I think I hear a baby cry, but I shake the sound out of my head.

I'm just hearing things again. The same way I'd heard a baby cry for months after my son's funeral.

That whole affair was nothing more than an empty ceremony. There was no body in the tiny miniature coffin we lowered into the ground. I had nothing tangible to grieve. Nothing to say goodbye to.

Just the empty space where my son and wife should've been.

I hear another cry. This time, it's louder. It doesn't feel like a figment of my imagination. It feels so utterly fucking real that I wonder if my own head is finally turning against me. Making a mockery of my pain.

I pull back the glass and finish the rest of the whiskey in two glugs.

Matvei eyes my empty glass, but he doesn't offer to get me a refill. His own is still half-full.

My eyes flicker back to the wall, dripping with pinned pages flickering in the breeze from the fan circling overhead. At the center of it are two side to side images.

One is of Victor Ozol. The second is of Hitoshi Sakamoto. Both big players, as far as I can tell. Both powerful. Both utterly elusive.

"Get some sleep, Phoenix," Matvei says. "It's fucking late."

"I don't need to sleep. I need to sort out the new leads."

He sighs but doesn't argue. "I'll see you tomorrow morning, then."

"Close the door on your way out."

A hush falls over the room the moment Matvei leaves. My own thoughts are always the most dangerous, I've found. But they're a poison I can't resist.

I get to my feet and head over to the wall. As far as I've been able to discern, Ozol and Sakamoto have never actually met face-to-face. But that doesn't mean it hasn't happened. In the underworld I roam in, there are plenty of dark corners where two powerful men can meet in secret.

It's all right here—somewhere. I just need to connect the fucking dots. To find a way to bring Astra Tyrannis to its knees.

And these men are the key to that.

Five years ago, when I started this quest for vengeance, I thought I'd be done before the year was out. That my wife and son wouldn't have to wait long for me to get payback against the people who snatched them from me.

But Astra Tyrannis is a hydra. Every time I cut off a head, two more appear, slithering and foul. It's endlessly frustrating. So much blood spilled and so little gained.

I made a promise to myself, though.

To my dead wife.

To my dead son.

Someone is going to pay for their deaths. I will not die until justice has been served.

Once I've studied the wall into the wee hours of the morning, I find myself back at my desk.

No point in going to bed. I do my best sleeping in this office, anyway. Staring at the enigma protecting my family's murderers.

When I do finally drift off, I see their faces, like always. Aurora and Yuri's. Bright. Loving. Laughing. The way they were before they were taken from me.

But at some point midway through the dream, those faces morph.

And then all I can see is Elyssa and Theo.

When I turn to the side, I hear a hammering noise. It's Aurora. She's on the other side of a strange glass wall, begging to be set free. She stares at me, her eyes wide, blood dripping from them like tears. She bangs her hands against the glass until the skin of her knuckles splits and starts bleeding. Even then, she doesn't stop. Just keeps hammering and hammering until the glass is smeared with blood and I can barely see her past it.

I try and get through to her, but I can't. I can't even get close enough to touch the glass. Something keeps me tethered in place, stretching and striving to reach my wife so I can save her.

But there will be no saving her tonight. Just like there was no saving her five years ago.

There's just the pounding of fists against the barrier and a silent, endless scream.

My eyes fly open as I register that the knocking sound is real. It's coming from the door of my office.

Casting off my grogginess in a moment, I spring to my feet and fly over to the door. When I throw it open, Elyssa's small fist collides with my chest mid-knock.

"What the fuck?" I snarl.

She flinches immediately. "I… my… Theo," she stammers, clearly panicked. "He's gone."

"Gone?"

She nods desperately. "I was sleeping. He was right next to me on bed. And when I woke up, he was gone. The door was unlocked, so I ran out and started looking for him. But this house is too big. And-and-and m-my son… he's missing!"

I doubt she even knows what she's saying at the moment. "Calm down," I tell her.

She gulps back her tears, but her entire body is trembling. A jolt of nostalgia hits me between the eyes. She had been shivering the night we'd met, too.

"Come with me. I'll search with you."

I start moving through the house. She follows behind without a word.

"You didn't hear anything?" I ask.

"No…"

"You just woke up and he was gone?"

"Yes."

"You didn't even hear him cry?"

I'm not looking at her, so I'm not aware of the effect my questions are having. Not until I glance back over my shoulder and see her eyes sparking with hurt.

"You had locked us in!" she cries. She doesn't exactly raise her voice, but given her soft-spoken nature, it feels like she's yelling. "I had no idea someone would sneak in while we were sleeping and steal my child."

I roll my eyes. "No one stole him."

"Then where is he?" she demands. "What've you done with him?"

I'm already on the edge, so when she flings that last statement at me, I can't hold back any longer.

Or maybe I'm just looking for an excuse to touch her.

Either way, I snatch up her arm and use it to shove her back against the nearest wall. She gasps, her eyes going wide with fear as she's confronted with my black stare.

"You are the one that wanted to come here with me," I growl. "And I don't know why. But know this—I don't fucking trust you."

I can practically feel her heartbeat against my own. They seem to be beating in synchronicity. Her breasts are pressed up against my chest and it's impossible not to be aware of that. Or of the heat coming off her.

The fear in her eyes is still there, still evident. But she speaks through it. "Yeah?" she asks, her voice tremoring softly. "Well, I don't trust you either. Why would I?"

I frown. "Why not?"

"I don't know you," she continues. "You may have given me a baby, but you're a stranger to me. So you can judge me all you want for how I'm raising Theo. But I'm doing the best I can. Because you were never there!"

I drop her hands immediately and step back. She glances down at my hands as though she's worried I'm going to strike her. I unclench my fists just to prove I'm not.

But the guilt stays with me.

Her eyes do, too.

And I can't escape either one.

15

ELYSSA

I know I'm dangerously close to hyperventilating, bursting at the seams with fear and exhaustion and tremors I can't control. Tears threaten to spring loose from my eyes and my hands won't stop shaking.

I'm not sure what's causing it—Theo missing? Or Phoenix pinning me against a wall in this dark, empty hallway?

Every cell in me is screaming with fear. But they're vibrating with something else, too. Something I can't quite describe. I feel... alive, in the strangest way.

Maybe that's the wrong word to use. But I stopped understanding how to describe everything happening around me the second Phoenix showed up at the shelter door.

He stares at me without speaking. But his eyes betray the emotion he's trying desperately to hide.

It's a feeling I know well. I've spent my entire life trying to tamp down my emotions. It's what I was taught. How I was raised. Charity is the first person who ever told me I didn't have to do that.

It's okay to cry when you're sad, she always says. *Laugh when you're happy. Rage when you're mad.*

And… *fuck when you're horny.* The last part of her advice flashes across my mind despite myself.

It's the crudest possible way of putting it, which is why I've always omitted it when I repeat her little manifesto to myself at night.

But sometimes, it sneaks into my consciousness all the same. And for the last year, whenever it has, I thought of the man in front of me now.

I remember the way he had pressed himself between my thighs and breathed new life into me on a night when I felt like my world was ending.

The accusation I just threw at him is unfair. He tried to help me that night. He protected me while he could. He told me where to go to stay safe. I was the one who made the choice not to go there and wait for him. The way I see it now, I'm the one at fault here.

But his dark expression prevents me from saying as much.

Something is different about him now. I remembered him being— well, not quite soft or tender—but more… open, more protective. The man in front of me is not that. Not by a long shot. He's a raging inferno of violence. Of darkness. Of pure, seething hate.

It doesn't feel directed at me, though, which is the strangest part of all. I dropped a huge bomb on him. I'd expected the news that he has a son to have a bigger impact. To draw a bigger reaction. Or really, any kind of reaction at all.

"I just… I just want my son," I manage to stammer. "Please."

His eyes rake over my face. "He's here," he says gruffly. "Somewhere."

Phoenix turns and stalks away down the hallway. He doesn't bother to see if I'm following. With a shudder, I scurry along his path and catch up.

We've walked another minute or so when he glances at me. "Where's the other one?"

"Charity? She's searching the other side of the house. It's big."

He doesn't reply to that, except to speed up as though he wants to put as much distance between us as possible.

"Who else is in this house?" I ask, breaking the silence again.

"Many people," Phoenix replies. "Maids, gardeners, chefs, guards, my men."

"Any one of them might have taken Theo!"

"They didn't. He's here."

"How can you be so calm?" I demand, taking offense to just how calm he's being right now.

He glances at me with those molten eyes of his. And I feel my heart constrict painfully.

I never quite know what I'm feeling when he looks at me.

Is it fear?

Nerves?

Desire?

I have no idea.

"Being calm is the only way to get anything done," he tells me harshly. "If you panic, you make stupid mistakes. You say stupid fucking things."

I flinch again, knowing that that was a jab at me.

"Where were you raised?" he asks suddenly. "Some sort of redneck Bible camp?"

I frown. "Excuse me?"

He shrugs. "Every time someone swears, you act like you've been electrocuted."

I try really hard not to blush, but I don't quite succeed. "No, it wasn't a Bible camp," I say softly.

"You're not a Mormon, are you?"

"No."

"In some sort of religious cult?" I shoot him a stare and he shrugs again. "Just curious. It would explain a lot."

I bristle at the statement. But I'm more hurt than angry. Sometimes, hurt feels like my default setting.

And I know it has to do with the place where I was raised. They raised me for a life within their walls. Not for the raw, razor-sharp battle that defines every minute in the real world.

"You don't know me," I manage to choke out, despite my hurt.

"No, you're right about that," he says pointedly, reminding me that I don't know him either.

I don't know why everything he says affects me so deeply. Maybe because I've lived with him in my head for a year. In some ways, I've created a fantasy of who he is. A fantasy that is wholly removed from reality.

I stop short when I realize that I hear the gurgling of a baby. "Theo!" I gasp, rushing towards the sound.

I turn a corner and burst into a room on the right. It's a huge space with arched windows and blinds drawn up high so that you can see the garden. Except that it's still dark outside, so only soft artificial light from the outdoor bulbs floats in.

I survey the room for the source of the noise and spot an older woman sitting in a chair by the window.

She has my son.

I can smell him from here. That unique, supple baby smell I long for whenever I'm away from him for any length of time.

"Theo!" I cry again, rushing forward.

The woman cranes around slowly, her eyes landing on me sheepishly. She's older, silver-haired, and on the heavier side. A cane rests across her lap.

"Shh," she croons delicately. "He just fell back to sleep."

She's got Theo wrapped in a thick cotton blanket. His eyelashes are fluttering slightly, a sure indication that he's only just fallen asleep.

I lower my voice. "Who are you?" I demand, not bothering to sound polite. "And why did you take my son?"

The woman looks like she's in no hurry to answer. But when I feel Phoenix come up behind me, she pushes herself off the sofa with a pained groan and gives him a subservient nod. "Master Phoenix."

"Anna," he says, "what happened?"

Again, he's so calm that I feel like a basket case in comparison. I decide the best way to get a hold of my emotions is to take Theo. I reach out for him and the older woman parts with him reluctantly.

The moment his weight settles into the crook of my arm, I feel my body relax. As though I've spent the last hour separated from a vital organ.

"I'm sorry, Master Phoenix," she says. "I didn't mean to cause any alarm. I was just doing the rounds and I heard the baby cry. The key was in the lock, so I opened it and went inside to check. The girls were sleeping so soundly that they didn't hear the boy, and he just kept crying and crying. So I picked him up and took him out here so they could sleep."

I cringe, realizing that I'd slept through his night feeding. He'd probably needed a diaper change, too.

I check immediately. She notices.

"Don't worry, Miss," she says politely. "I changed him. I fed him, too. He had a bottle about half an hour ago. Six ounces."

I stare at her, trapped between annoyance and gratitude. "You… you could have woken me."

Her eyes are a light, filmy blue. But they're half-hidden behind thick, round spectacles that look decades out of style. "I didn't want to disturb you," she explains. "You looked like you needed the rest."

I take a deep breath as I try to get my bearings. So much has happened in the last few hours.

"Theo!" someone calls. "Where are you?" I jerk to the side the moment I recognize Charity's raised voice.

"Charity!" I shout back. "We're in here."

She runs into the room as though she's trying to put out a fire. But the moment she sees Theo in my arms, she visibly relaxes.

"There he is," she sighs, her eyes flitting to Phoenix and then Anna. "What the fuck happened?"

"It turned out to be just a… misunderstanding," I say, struggling to find the right word.

"This is Anna, my housekeeper," Phoenix says, though he addresses me, not Charity. "She's been with me for years."

I'm surprised by that. The woman certainly has a kindly grandmother vibe about her. But she doesn't strike me as a very capable housekeeper.

For one, she moves slow. The cane in her hand is evidence of that. For another, she looks like she's a few years past retirement age.

"The housekeeper took Theo?" Charity pants in disbelief as she looks between all three of us.

"She heard Theo crying and both of us were dead asleep," I explain.

"Oh," she says. "Well, okay then. He's fine, right? Not hurt or anything?"

"No," I say. "He's fine."

"Great. Then I'm heading back to bed. You coming?"

My heart is still beating a mile a minute. I know I won't be able to sleep anymore. "Actually, I think I'll just walk around a bit with Theo."

Then it strikes me that I might not have the freedom to do that. I turn to Phoenix immediately and he seems to know exactly what I'm thinking.

"You have freedom of the house," he says. "Just… stay clear of the basement."

I nod, barely suppressing a shudder at the thought of what horrors a man like him might be keeping hidden from sight.

His eyes flicker to Theo. They linger there for a moment as if searching for something. Then he turns and leaves the room abruptly.

Charity turns to me and raises her eyes. "Not much of a people person, is he?"

I almost smile. "Go back to bed," I tell her. "Get some rest. I won't be more than an hour or so."

She glances at Anna and then back to me. "You sure? I can wait with you."

"No, I'm good. Thank you, though."

She comes forward and gives Theo a little kiss. "If there's anything…"

"Just yell," I finish for her. "I know."

She gives me a wink and heads out of the room, leaving Theo and me with Anna. The woman's attention is firmly fixed on my son, her expression already painted with maternal fondness.

"He's a beautiful boy," she comments.

"I know," I say with a smile I can't hide. "He's perfect."

"You and your husband must be so proud."

I feel a bizarre spasm of loss at the assumption. I wish I could tell her who I am. Where I came from. I wish I could make her—and everyone else who's ever looked at me with the same pity in their eyes—understand my story.

Even more than that, I wish I didn't have a story that required understanding.

I saw a television show on one of the first nights I stayed at the shelter, not long after my midnight run through the desert. It was something old, I think. Filmed in black-and-white. The opening credits showed a woman waving from behind a white picket fence. She was dressed in a simple, beautiful dress and watering her sunflowers with a gardening can as her husband came out the door, kissed her, and left in his car for work. Her children played in the manicured lawn around her.

What a simple life. What a beautiful life.

It's pathetic how much I want that.

I realize it's been awkwardly long since Anna spoke. "I… I don't have a husband," I tell her, my cheeks coloring at the admission.

"Oh." Her eyes bore into my face. I wonder what she's trying to find. I like her, but as with anyone who tries to figure me out, I feel the need to pull away.

"Anyway, thanks for taking care of Theo," I say. "I'm just gonna take a little walk."

"I'll come with you," she says, botching that particular escape plan. "I can show you around."

"Oh. Right. Er, sure. Thanks."

We leave the airy den and start to meander through the Kovalyov mansion. There's lots of glass, but the rustic painted brick walls keep it from being cold and overly austere. There's also a surprising amount of greenery dotting each crevice and cavity in the house.

Paintings hang on some of the larger, blank walls. Mostly desolate landscapes, with a few colorless abstracts thrown in, all spiky and sharp and violent. That seems very on-brand for Phoenix.

As we walk, I notice darkness seeping out of the house slowly as the early morning sun starts to rise. It illuminates the grass just outside the mansion. It looks almost magical.

"This place is beautiful," I mumble.

Anna nods. "Master Phoenix has exquisite taste."

Something about the way she says that makes me shiver. She's given no indication that she knows all the particulars of my sudden appearance here. But I get a little spooked nonetheless.

I glance at the older woman, noticing that she's limping pretty noticeably. "Are you okay?" I ask.

"Broke a hip a few years ago," she replies. "Now, the limp is part of my walk."

"Oh, no. Does it hurt?"

"Not at all," she says with a chuckle. "Sometimes, I even forget to limp."

I smile, even though the statement strikes me as odd. Nothing about this woman is making sense right now.

"It must be hard for you to work, though, right?" I say, hoping I don't offend her for asking.

"Not at all," she says. "Master Phoenix is always so gracious. He lets me work at my own pace. He calls me a housekeeper, but really, I'm more of a supervisor. I make sure the house runs smoothly and the staff fall in line. I don't do much of the heavy lifting."

That seems oddly benevolent for what little I know about the man. He doesn't seem like the kind of person who tolerates inefficiency.

"You're up really early," I point out.

Anna shrugs. "I've suffered from insomnia for decades now," she says. "So I like to just get my day started the moment I'm awake. Good thing I did, too. The little one was hungry."

She gives Theo another smile, even though his eyes are firmly closed. The fluttering of his eyelashes has stopped, too. He looks still and composed, like a painting.

"I… I usually—I mean, always—feel him stir," I say quickly. "And I definitely hear him cry. It was just, last night…"

"You'd been through something awful, and you were sleeping soundly," Anna says with understanding. "You don't have to feel embarrassed, darling. We've all been there."

"Yeah?"

"One day, when I was a young mother, I fell asleep with my son right next to me. When I woke up, he was gone. I panicked, jumped off the bed, and nearly stepped on him."

My eyes go wide. "He'd fallen?"

"Rolled off the bed in the night," she confirms. "Thankfully, he was so wrapped up in blankets that he wasn't hurt in the slightest. Didn't even notice, the little bugger. But I felt guilty for weeks. Sometimes, I still do."

I smile.

"You're always going to worry that you're doing something wrong," she reassures me. "It's part of being a mother. You're going to make mistakes, too. That's another part of it. But you'll learn."

"Promise?"

Anna laughs and her entire face softens. "Promise."

Sunlight trickles through the glass windows in tiny gold rivulets now. I can see spasms of dust caught in the light. Everything in this house seems not quite real. Or rather, *too* real. Like Technicolor, all saturated and beautiful and breathtaking.

"I usually have a little meeting with the maids at the beginning of each day," Anna tells me when we've circled back to where we started the tour. "I should go get it started."

"Of course! Don't let me keep you."

Anna turns to me, forcing me to a standstill. "If you need anything, don't hesitate to ask me," she says. "And if you ever need a babysitter, I'd be more than happy to look after this little angel for a few hours."

"I'll keep that in mind," I say with a nod.

I don't tell her the truth: *We're leaving this place as soon as we can. It's not safe here for us.*

Anna runs her finger over Theo's cheek and then she ambles off in the opposite direction. I stand there and admire the brightening sunlight before continuing my walk around the house.

I try not to give in to the sense of awe that I feel suffusing me with each new room. There's no point in falling in love with this building or the people who live here. I can't stay. We can't stay.

But the world outside is scary in its own way. So I keep walking, trapped in this in-between space, unwilling to go back to the room just yet.

I'm willing to bet Charity won't be up for a few more hours, anyway. Theo stirs in my arms, so I adjust him and walk into a room I haven't seen yet.

Broad French doors sit in the far wall. Through the panes of glass, I can see glimpses of a veranda of sorts, though there's no patio furniture to mar the sprawling view of the gardens. The predawn sky beyond is washed with gray and silver. The moon still hangs in the sky, bright and pure.

We can't stay here, I think to myself yet again.

But I want to. I want to so, so badly. I want to stay here with this man who can protect me, in this house filled with beautiful things, with gentle people. It's better than the cruel world beyond the walls.

I sigh bitterly and turn to go back to the room—when my peripheral vision catches a flash of movement from one of the corner windows set alongside the French doors.

I turn, expecting to see a bird or squirrel peering within.

But instead, I see the gaunt face of a harrowed man.

We make eye contact. When he sees me, his haunted eyes grow wide. He bangs his fists against the windows so hard that I'm amazed it doesn't shatter.

And his lips form words. I'm not sure whether he's speaking quietly or if the glass is just thick enough to drown out the sound of his voice. Either way, it doesn't really matter.

Because what he's saying is unmistakable. It's the same thought that's been surging through my head since we arrived here.

"It's not safe here," the old man mouths. "Run. Run. Run!"

16

PHOENIX

I hear a scream.

I hear *her* scream.

Despite my show of walking away, I haven't ventured too far. As soon as I recognize the sound, I race down the hallway and into the patio room that precedes the garden veranda.

Elyssa is standing there, clutching the baby, who's started to mewl angrily in her arms. I scan them. Both seem unharmed.

Except that Elyssa's face is white with terror and uncertainty as she turns to me.

"What happened?" I demand, more harshly than I intend.

"I… there… there was a… man," she stammers. "In the window."

I frown. I know all the guards on duty. I know their schedules, too, down to the minute.

No one's supposed to be manning this part of the house right now. The rounds are done four times per hour before each guard returns to a secure position around the compound's inner barricade.

Which means one thing: if there's a man at the window, he does not work for me.

"A man?" I ask. I wonder if she's just seeing things. It certainly wouldn't be a far-fetched assumption. The girl was clearly troubled the first time we crossed paths. God only knows what's happened to her in the year that followed.

Or in the hours since I barged back into her life.

She nods. "He was standing right out there. He slammed his fists against the window and… he… he warned me."

"Warned you?"

She nods. I can tell that she's not sure if she should tell me at all. Apparently, whoever this *mudak* is, he's managed to plant a seed of doubt in her head. And given how fast he's managed to convince her, I'm willing to bet the doubt has always been there, waiting for an excuse to grow.

It bothers me more than I care to admit.

"About what?"

"About you," she stammers. "About this place."

She takes a step back, so I make a point to keep my distance from her. No sense in frightening the little lamb any further.

"What did he look like?"

"I don't know. Older. Receding hairline. He looked… desperate," she says. Then she adds, "And sad."

I frown. No one matching that description comes to mind.

That's when I hear a commotion from the next room. The sound of fists on glass.

"That's him!" Elyssa gasps. "I know it." Her trembling is worse than ever. I can see the baby's chubby cheeks shaking with her terrified motion.

Leaving Elyssa where she is, I run into the next room just in time to catch a glimpse of the mystery man's profile darting past the windows.

So Elyssa hadn't imagined him after all.

I glance back at her over my shoulder. "Go back to your room and wait there. Now!"

I don't stick around to see if she listens or not. I take off after the man, wondering how the fuck anyone has managed to breach my walls. Bursting out into the garden, I see his silhouette racing towards the shrubbery.

"Ostanovis' pryamo tam!" I roar. "Stop right there!"

Caught by the sound of my voice, the man freezes. Turns. And as the predawn glow illuminates his face, I realize something: I know him.

"What the fuck?" I say out loud. "Vitya?"

His eyes go wide, but I register the same desperation that Elyssa mentioned. Coming to his senses, he tries to duck away.

But he's an old man. Certainly not fast enough to escape me. I catch up to him in no time and grab him by the collar, dragging him away from the hydrangea bushes. I don't care if I choke him half to death in the process, either.

I expected a fight. But the moment I grab hold of him, he stops struggling. Just a limp fish, helpless on the line.

He coughs and sputters as I haul him backwards. When he's far from any avenue of escape, I drop his dead weight on the grass and stand over him.

"*Blya radi,* Vitya," I growl. "What the fuck are you doing here?"

My father-in-law looks weathered. He's aged about a hundred years since I last saw him. There are dark circles under his eyes, a patchy beard, and his skin sags in all the places he's lost weight.

It nearly takes me to my knees.

Will I ever escape the guilt? It seems not. It hits me at every fucking angle, reminding me of why I have never been able to rest these last few years.

Vitya looks at me through narrowed eyes. I can tell he's scared. But there's a manic look in his eyes that overtakes the fear. The kind of mania that says he's cast all reason to the wind.

He's given up. Let the grief consume him.

"I had to come," he rasps. "I had to tell them all about you…"

"Tell who all?" I ask in a low, menacing voice. "About what?"

I've known Vitya for many years. At one point, he'd welcomed me into his family and embraced me as his son. He used to look at me with deference. With affection.

Now, all that is gone. He's a shell of a man. And all that's left in his eyes is anger, contempt, and accusation.

"About you," Vitya says again.

He's unsteady on his feet, bobbing from side to side as though he can't stand still. He looks drunk. On vodka, maybe, or perhaps just on misery.

"They deserve to know who you are." His words slur.

"Vitya, *svekor*," I say gently, "you're not well…"

He rears back, clearly insulted by that. "Not well?" he repeats. "How dare you? I am perfectly well. And I'm here to tell the women who work for you the truth."

"And what truth is that?" I ask patiently.

"You get women killed. You promise to protect them and then they end up dead," Vitya spits at me. "Just like my... my... my daughter..."

His voice breaks on the last word. A sob bursts out of his lips and he wraps his arms around his torso to quell the tremors, like he's trying to physically contain the pain threatening to break him apart.

I know exactly how he feels.

"Vitya, I promised you I would avenge her death," I bite out. "And I will."

I notice my men approach from the far corner of the garden, having finally been alerted to the breach in security. One of them is definitely going to answer for the lapse.

At least it's not a serious threat. Vitya, I can handle.

"I will punish all those who had a hand in her disappearance. In her death."

"And what about you?" Vitya crows from where he's still lying sprawled on the lawn. "Who will punish you for what you've done? For what you've failed to do?"

He loved me once. Loved me like his own flesh and blood. Now, he'd cut my throat if he thought he could get away with it.

My men approach slowly, Matvei among them. Surreptitiously, I hold up my hand, letting them know to keep their distance. I don't want Vitya hurt.

"Vitya, you have no idea how much I hate myself for—"

"I told her not to marry you," Vitya interrupts me. "Did she ever tell you that?"

"No," I sigh. "No, she never did."

"Of course she didn't. She'd never have told you anything she thought would upset you," Vitya continues. His eyes range from side to side warily. "But I did. I told her marrying into the Bratva was never a good idea. That the lives of evil men like you have a way of bleeding into the innocence. Poisoning good souls like Aurora. Staining their purity. I didn't want that for her. She deserved better. Far better than you."

His words cut. But I know he needs to say them because if he keeps them to himself, they'll tear him in two.

And I deserve to hear him out. It's the least of the punishment I've earned.

"But she insisted that she would be safe with you," Vitya says. "She told me you would protect her."

My failure twists in my gut, compounded by Vitya's words.

He was right back then.

He's right now.

"So I let her marry you, fool that I am. I gave her my blessing because she seemed so happy with you. What else is a father to do? And then you weren't even married two years before the baby came. Yuri, that sweet, innocent boy... he would have been six years old this year."

"Vitya," I say, cutting him off before he can destroy me further. "Come inside. You need to sit down."

"I'm not going anywhere with you!" he roars, twisting away from my outstretched hand. "You're just going to kill me! Just like you killed her."

I cringe, but I push down the bite of my anger. Vitya's eyes are not focused. The man is not himself right now.

Then again, he hasn't been himself in four years.

"I would never hurt you, Vitya," I tell him. "You are still my father-in-law."

"Bah! I'm nothing to you. That relationship was severed the day you let my daughter die."

I glance past Vitya and nod to Grigori and Alexi, lingering in the shadows. Both men move forward silently. Vitya doesn't notice them until the last minute.

"No!" he screams as they descend on him from both sides. "No! Let me go. Let me go!" He thrashes in their arms, refusing to go quietly.

At another nod from me, Konstantin and Pyotr rush to join their fellow guards in hauling Vitya to his feet.

"Don't hurt him," I order. "Get him up and get him inside. Give him a sedative if you need to."

My men drag Vitya off. The whole time, he rages.

"Do the women in your home know they'll end up dead if they stay here?" he screams back over his shoulder. "Have you told them you can't protect them? She died because of you! She died because of you! She died because of…!"

His voice fades away as they round the corner and disappear into the guesthouse.

My eyes scan the main building, searching for Elyssa's face in one of the windows. Wondering if she's watching. What she's heard. What she thinks.

I don't see her, but my relief is short lived. Something tells me this is far from over.

"Fuck," I growl under my breath.

Matvei approaches me. "The man's coming undone."

"Do you blame him?" I ask. "His daughter was delivered to us in pieces."

"What are you going to do?"

"Call Dr. Roth," I tell Matvei. "I think he needs to be examined before I can decide that. Tell him it's urgent."

With a nod, Matvei starts to walk away.

"Murray?" I ask before he can leave.

"Still tied down in the basement cell," Matvei answers. "Waiting to be interrogated."

"Let's push that back," I say. "I want to deal with Vitya first."

Matvei nods and disappears into the garden. I follow Vitya into the guesthouse.

My men have restrained him against one of the cushioned chairs nestled by the window. His head is drooped low, and his chest rises and falls slowly with every breath. His eyes are closed, and he hasn't noticed me enter, so I stand for a moment and observe.

Again, I'm struck by how much he's aged. I might have noticed the deterioration if I'd kept in touch more in the last few years. But seeing him just reminded me of my own failure.

It was easier to look the other way.

And for most of that period, it seemed he was keen to avoid me as well. But all this time, he's been festering in grief and anger. And it's reached a boiling point. One that's clearly affected his mind.

Konstantin and Alexi back off when I approach. I sit down opposite Vitya, making sure to keep a comfortable distance between us.

Sensing my presence, the older man avoids my eyes completely, but he's fidgeting like a crack addict going through withdrawal.

"Vitya?" I ask gently. "Are you on something?"

He shakes his head from side to side. "I'm not crazy."

"I never said you were."

"I just want my daughter back."

My fists clench. "I know you do."

"For all your power and influence, you can't bring her back, can you?"

"No. No man has that power."

"They say the Bratva can do anything," he scoffs, lowering his head down. "They say you're like a king. Like a god. What a lie. What a fucking lie…"

Before I can think of how to answer, Dr. Roth walks in.

"Doctor," I greet. "Let's step outside."

I pull him out of the guesthouse and explain the situation. "This is Vitya Azarov. My father-in… rather, my late wife's father. Something's wrong with him. He's not himself."

I recruited Dr. Roth shortly after Aurora and Yuri's deaths. He'd never met them, but he knows the history. He's also an accomplished physician and surgeon. And since he works exclusively for the Bratva, he's on call twenty-four-seven.

He turns his dark blue eyes on Vitya, visible through the window, and nods slowly.

"At a cursory glance, the fidgeting and tremors are indicative of some kind of drug," he says. "My first guess is he's been abusing pharmaceuticals."

"What kind of pills?"

"I'll find out," Roth replies. "Will you give me some time with him?"

I nod and gesture for Konstantin and Alexi to accompany me out of the room. Vitya just sits in his chair with his head hanging low.

His hands and legs have been tied to the chair, so I'm confident he won't be a threat to the doctor. I'm more concerned that he's a threat to himself.

Matvei is waiting outside when we exit. I dismiss Konstantin and Alexi first and then turn to him.

"How's Vitya doing?" he asks.

"Roth thinks he's been self-medicating."

"Fuck. The man's really changed."

I grit my teeth. "Haven't we all?"

"Not everything is your fault, Phoenix. You know that, right?"

I turn away from Matvei. The last thing I need right now is to be absolved of my sins.

He sighs, knowing me well enough to know when it's best to change the subject. "I checked with the men to find out how he got in."

"And?"

"Would you fucking believe it? He walked in through the front gate. Liv was the one on duty and he recognized Vitya. The old man told him that he had come to see you and the gates were opened for him."

My anger dissipates somewhat. "Ah, well… the *durak* should have informed me first, but chalk it up to a misunderstanding."

"Liv's shitting his pants right now."

I smirk. "Let him stew a little then. Consider that his punishment."

"Does it trouble you, though?" Matvei asks. "I mean, it's clear that as erratic as Vitya's behavior seems to be, he can be lucid for periods of time."

"I know," I nod. "I don't think it's dementia. I think it's just the grief."

"Doesn't mean he doesn't need help."

"That's what I'm trying to give him."

Matvei nods. He hesitates, then adds, "We can't have him talking either, Phoenix."

"I agree."

"So should we...?"

"We'll do what it takes to protect the Bratva, Matvei. I always do."

A few minutes later, Roth walks out of the room.

"Well?" I ask.

"It's not dementia," Roth confirms. "It's not psychosis, either. The man's just wracked with loss. It's become obsessive. Forced him to make questionable choices."

"Like?"

"Popping anti-depressants like they're Tic-Tacs, for one. I'm pretty sure he's taking other stuff, too, but he wouldn't say."

"What did he say?" Matvei asks.

"That he needs to warn people about you," Roth says. "That you're a danger. That you get innocent women killed."

"Fuck," I growl, running my hand through my hair.

"Listen, he's not insane," Roth says. "But he's not capable of being rational right now, either."

I glance at Matvei, who nods imperceptibly. *Fuck.* I don't like this. But I meant what I said: I will do whatever it takes to protect the Bratva.

And if Vitya is a threat... then he must be handled.

I sigh. "I need you to initiate a seventy-two hour psychiatric hold on Vitya. As long as you can get it extended for. I'll work on getting a district court to arrange something more permanent in the meantime."

"You're going to commit him to a ward?" Roth asks, surprised.

"I don't see that I have any other option. I can't have him out there spewing lies about me. It'll undermine the entire mission."

"If you're sure…"

"I'm sure. Get a couple of the boys in here. And a vehicle."

"Yes, sir." Roth takes Pyotr and Grigori to do as I ordered. When he's gone, I walk back into the room. Vitya glances up at me from the corner of his eyes.

"Vitya," I say patiently as I move to stand in front of him. "I know you think I'm the enemy. I know you're angry. But I really am trying to help."

"Help?" he scoffs. "You don't know what you're doing."

He raises his eyes. In them, I can see the pain of Aurora's loss reflected back at me. It's like no time has passed at all since her death.

For him, it may as well have happened yesterday.

"I'm sorry, you know," I whisper in a harsh rasp. "I wish it hadn't happened. Same as you."

Vitya shakes his head. "You're trying to take them down," he says. "But Astra Tyrannis is a beast with ten heads. You're just one man."

"I'm more than a man," I snarl.

Vitya just laughs. "You are a powerful man, yes. An important man. But still just a man. Still just one man, up against so, so much evil. They're always going to be one step ahead of you. They've got spies everywhere. Even here…"

"Here?" I ask, surprised.

"In your home," Vitya says simply. As if it's something I should know.

He looks stone cold sober. And yet a comment like that forces me to question his state of mind.

My house is in order. I'm certain I can trust every single person under my roof. Wait—I stop short on the heels of that thought, realizing that it's not entirely true.

I can trust every single person under my roof—except for the two women who are currently occupying one of my guest rooms.

A part of me still thinks it's unlikely. That no one who looks at me the way Elyssa does can possibly be working for my enemies.

But I'd be a fool to dismiss it outright. She can't be trusted. I have to remind myself of that.

"Phoenix?"

I turn towards the door. Matvei is standing there with Konstantin and Alexi. I gesture them forward.

"What are you going to do with me?" Vitya asks. "Kill me?"

It irritates me that he thinks that. "Of course not. I'm not going to hurt you, Vitya. I'm just trying to help you."

"My daughter swallowed your lies," he hisses. "I won't be so foolish."

What the fuck am I supposed to say to that? I stand there silently as he's untethered from the chair and marched across the room. He doesn't go quietly. He sends accusations and insults flying in a stream of rapid Russian.

And I just stand there and listen. Swallowing every single one.

~

I'm walking back to the office when I notice a receding shadow on the staircase. I recognize the delicate silhouette instantly.

"Elyssa."

She re-emerges hesitantly, her expression composed but nervous. As she bends forward a little, a tumble of blonde hair falls across her shoulder.

And I'm hit with strange fluttering of déjà vu.

The night I'd met her, her hair had fallen in the exact same way when I'd grabbed her by the hips and set her on the bathroom counter…

Right before I'd fucked a baby into her.

"Where's the baby?" I ask, shaking my head to dislodge the memory.

She takes two steps down the stairs. "His name is Theo, for your information."

I grit my teeth. "Is he okay?"

She looks like she wants to yell at me for something, but at the last moment, I see the fight leave her eyes. She's clearly not comfortable with confrontation.

"Yes," she says instead. "He's sleeping. Charity's with him."

"And why aren't you with him?"

"Because I wanted to make sure everything was alright," she murmurs, taking another step down towards me.

I stand still and watch her. She's so frail. So vulnerable. I want to believe there's no way she could be working against me.

Don't listen to that voice, I snarl to myself. *Don't fucking trust her.*

"Who was he?" she asks timidly. "The man in the window, I mean."

"No one that concerns you." My tone shuts down any further questions, which was exactly my intention.

For some reason, the thought of Elyssa finding out about Aurora—well, it's more than I can handle now.

"He told me to run," she says. "He told me I wasn't safe here. I think I deserve to know who he is and why he said that to me."

I narrow my eyes at her. "In case you forgot, this is my house," I say. "I don't owe you a fucking thing."

Her eyes cloud over. I know instantly I've done it again: said the wrong thing. Hurt her.

But because apologies have never come easy to me, I stand my ground and dig my heels in.

Since Aurora and Yuri, being an asshole is so much easier.

"Now go back to your room," I tell her.

She stares at me as though she's trying to figure me out. For her sake, I hope she fails miserably.

The cost of knowing me is too great. Ask anyone.

Actually, just asking Vitya would be enough.

Instead of turning around and walking up the stairs like I expect, she takes another step down. She's almost at the bottom of the stairs now, which puts her at eye level with me.

She drinks me in with her doe eyes. The same eyes she had used to reel me in that night a year ago. Those fucking liquid honey Bambi eyes that shimmered with an innocence I hadn't seen in a long fucking time.

They're less naïve now. But not by much. Still inexperienced. Still uncertain. Still terrified of the world.

"What?" I ask when she doesn't say anything.

Tension pings off my body like sparks. I wonder if she's aware of that. I wonder if it's happening because of her.

"Nothing," she says, shaking her head. "I was just thinking... No, nothing. Never mind."

She doesn't offer up anything further. And before I can ask, she turns and walks back up the stairs. Her shadow disappears moments after she does.

"Fuck," I growl to myself, feeling her presence long after she's gone. "Fuck."

17

ELYSSA

How can a man be two things at the same time?

I know for certain that Phoenix is more than the cold, brusque don he tries to portray. Because I've also seen kindness and patience in him. I saw it in him the night we first met. In the way he protected me at the risk of his own life. The way he put himself between me and violent men.

Most of all, I saw it in the way he had held me after we made... well, after.

But he's different now. Not because he's changed—but because he's trying to keep me at a distance.

Maybe because putting a barrier up between us is the easiest way he can think of to let me know what he thinks of our night together.

A cosmic fluke.

A cry for help.

A mistake.

I wish I could see it the same way. But when I think of the sweet, button-nosed baby that blossomed in my belly for nine months, I can't. Something tells me that, even without that little angel, I might still hold the same opinion.

Because that night? It saved me. In more ways than I can even begin to count.

Which is why seeing him again, being in his house… it feels wrong. It feels like I've opened up a wound that never had a chance to heal.

When I get back to the room, Charity is stirring and rubbing her eyes. I move to the bed and check on Theo. He's sleeping soundly, his lips puckering softly as though he's trying to find the bottle teat.

Smiling at the sight, I slip into bed next to him, even though sleep is the last thing on my mind.

"Where've you been?" Charity asks.

"Nowhere."

She frowns, stifling a yawn. "You know I can tell when you're lying, right?"

Sighing, I stare at the ceiling. "There was a man I saw earlier. Outside one of the windows of the house…"

"Yeah?"

"He looked… panicked. Terrified, really. Or maybe he was sad. I couldn't tell."

"You sure he was real?" I give her some side eye and she smirks. "Sorry. Continue with your story. Who was he?"

"That's the thing—I don't know," I say. "He… he warned me, I guess you'd call it."

"Warned you about?"

"Phoenix, I assume. This house," I say. "He told me to run. That it isn't safe here."

"Sounds like a nutcase. City is full of 'em."

"He looked like a man who was about to jump off a ledge."

"Proving my point…"

"Sometimes, life is so hard that ending it all feels like the only option," I murmur, in defense of all the broken souls out there who choose to jump rather than live.

I can't blame them. In a way, I did the same thing.

"No. Fuck that. I've had a hard life," Charity says defiantly, eyes blazing. "In fact, I just stared death in the face. And I'm still here. Still determined to keep going. I won't give this awful world the satisfaction of taking me out."

"That's because you're different, Charity. You're strong. Not all of us are."

Charity raises her eyebrows. "I thought we were talking about the crazy man in the window."

"We don't know he's crazy," I point out. "And we are talking about him."

"Sure we're not talking about you?"

I grit my teeth but keep my voice low and even-tempered. "What if his warning was real?" I ask. "Phoenix is Bratva. We already know he's dangerous."

"I'm not disputing that," Charity says. "The man's dangerous, yeah, no doubt about it. One hundred percent."

"Then why—"

"Because he's not dangerous to *you*. Or to Theo," Charity clarifies. "Which is what we should capitalize on."

I stare at her in disbelief. "Charity, what are you saying?"

"I'm saying we should stay here as long as we can."

I blanch. "You want to just live off him?"

"Think of it as living *with* him."

"Charity…"

"What?" she asks defensively. "What other option do we have, Lys?"

"We can go back to the shelter."

Charity scoffs. "No fucking thank you. The moment I could afford to leave that place, I did. No offense."

"You have an apartment in town," I remind her.

"I'm not going back there," she says. "In case you've forgotten, someone is after me. The kind of someone who can keep dirty cops on the payroll."

I bite my lip, trying to think of a way out for us. "We can get a new place. Something small…"

"With what money, Elyssa?" she demands. "I don't exactly have savings. And it's not like I can work with my face the way it is now."

"I have my job at the shelter."

"Which is hardly enough to buy a box of cereal, let alone pay rent in Las Vegas. That's the whole reason you still live in that crappy place, remember?"

Defeated, I feel my mood deflate instantly. Charity realizes a second too late that she went a little far.

"I'm sorry, boo. That was uncalled for."

I'm angry. And hurt. And terrified of the future. But rather than confront those emotions head on, I find myself cowering from them. "It's okay," I reply—even though it's not.

Things are very far from okay.

"This is a good option for us right now, Elyssa," Charity insists. "Phoenix can keep us safe."

"What makes you think we can trust him?"

"He saved you that night, didn't he?" she asks. "At least, that's what you've always told me."

"Yes, but... he's different now."

"Different how?"

"I don't know exactly. He just is. And you can't assume he's trustworthy based on what I told you about one chaotic night that was most definitely a mistake."

"Okay, fine. We don't have to trust him," Charity concedes. "But we can use him, can't we?"

I'm not remotely comfortable with that. But there's a desperation on Charity's face that I'm only just starting to catch up with.

"If we ask to stay, he's going to want to know more about us. He won't want two strange women living in his house without background checks, without interrogations. He's paranoid."

"Okay, so? What have we got to hide?"

I can feel the color drain from my face. Memories start to crop up in my head.

A black metal swan, stained with blood...

White curtains chewed up by flame...

The smell of patchouli in the desert night...

Charity's eyes go wide. "Okay, whoa, you went somewhere just now. Listen, Lys..." She reaches out and clasps my hand between hers. "I've never pressed you on this. I wouldn't ever. Goodness knows there's things in my past I'm not proud of. But I'm only asking now for your own good: is there something in your past you don't want him finding out about?"

Charity is the closest person to me in the world. And even she doesn't know what happened the night I came to Las Vegas for the first time.

She has her assumptions, of course, mostly based on the wedding dress I'd been wearing. But she's never asked me to confirm or deny those theories. In fact, she's pretty much kept them to herself.

"Elyssa? Did you hear me?"

I nod slowly. But she's right—I'm not here right now. I'm drifting off in the past.

The Sanctuary has been the dark shadow hanging over my head the last year. A part of me believes that they're searching for me. Faceless men in white robes, following my bloody tracks through the desert.

If Phoenix were to find out where I'm from, he could use it against me. He could send me back there.

And if he does…

It will be judgement day.

"Elyssa, honey, come back to me. Where'd you go?"

I focus on Charity, but I still see circles of smoke climbing into the dark, open sky above a burning house that was supposed to be my future.

"I went… to my past," I whisper honestly.

She squeezes my fingers tight. "Remember what I told you? Forget the past. It's the future that counts."

"It's the future I'm thinking of, Charity. We don't know Phoenix's motives. We don't know anything about him."

"He's the father of your child. That's kind of all we need to know."

I shake my head. She doesn't understand. Perhaps because she has nothing to lose. But me? I have to think of Theo.

If my past resurfaces and I end up back at the commune, there will be a reckoning for the crimes I committed. What if they take Theo away from me? They'd done as much to women who were guilty of far less.

Thorny memories crop up. Each one hurts like I'm being pricked with a needle.

Girls disappeared sometimes. Vanished into the wind—here one morning and gone the next. It was as if they'd never existed at all. And each of us who lived there went along with the lie. No one ever mentioned their names again. No one raised an eyebrow. We just… accepted it.

I accepted it.

Chills spread through my body. What kind of barbarism is that? What kind of monsters can look at the empty space where a human being used to be and just… carry on?

I feel sick to my stomach and my skin is cold to the touch, prickled up with goosebumps. Just like always. As if my body is rejecting the memories. Banishing them back to that deep, dark chasm in my head where they live. Where the answers to my past, to what really took place in the Sanctuary, reside.

"Elyssa? Elyssa!"

I jerk myself back to the present moment. "There are things in my past I don't want him finding out, Charity."

She tightens her grip on my hands. "Elyssa, your memories are nothing. Just little patterns in your brain. They aren't real. Stop giving them power. Stop giving your past power."

I think of Father Josiah. The way his face looked the night I ran—matted with blood and broken hideously…

"It has power all on its own, Charity," I whisper. "It doesn't need my help. That's why I'm scared."

"It's been a year. Nothing's happened. Your past isn't coming back for you."

I want to believe that. More than anything. But it feels impossible. Can a murderer really get away with a crime so big? So blatant?

And even if that's possible, should she? Should I? Is it fair?

I'm not sure I know what's fair anymore. Or what's right. All I know is that I can't rely on Phoenix Kovalyov.

His whiplash changes in demeanor frighten me. His intensely dark stare makes me feel exposed. Everything about him has me questioning myself. My choices. My perspective. My belief that running is the better alternative to staying and fighting.

"I feel like we're playing with fire, Char," I tell her softly. "If we stay here, we'll get burned."

"We've already jumped into the fire, Elyssa," she points out. "Now, we might as well make the most of it."

I shake my head. "You don't know what you're asking me."

Her stare twists slightly. I can see the pull of emotion tugging at her botched features. She's always so forthright with how she feels. *Cry when you feel like crying.* That's always been her motto. Except I'm starting to realize there's an exception to that rule where Charity is concerned.

Every emotion is acceptable in her eyes—except fear.

Because fear is a liability in a world that only favors the strong. Fear incapacitates you. It makes you vulnerable and weak.

The first time I saw Charity truly afraid was in the minutes after she'd banged on the door of the shelter. Right after she'd almost been beaten to death. And even then, she'd shaken off her fear as easily as removing a jacket.

Or had she? Maybe that was just an act. A lie. A wall she'd put up to hide the fact that, inside, she's still hurting. She's still terrified.

"What about what you're asking of me, Elyssa?" Charity asks, on the brink of tears. "Not only was I almost beaten to death, but he sent a cop after me," she says. "These are powerful men. With connections. What do I have? Nothing. Nothing but hope. I don't think that's going to save me this time. And it's not like I can stay here without you, Elyssa. Phoenix has even less reason to care about me. This place is the only one that gives us some amount of protection. Some safety. If we leave, they can find me. And when they do…"

She trails off, leaving the rest unsaid.

I twist our intertwined hands over so that I'm the one holding her hand. "Oh, Charity…"

"I'm sorry," she says, hanging her head. "I know I'm making my problem your problem right now. That's selfish. I'm sorry."

"No," I say, shaking my head. "It's not. You're not. I should have realized I was only thinking of myself."

"No, you're thinking of Theo. Which is exactly who you should be thinking about. I just… I'm…"

"Scared."

She looks up and I see tears standing in her eyes. "Yes," she says in a small voice.

I'm amazed she's admitting it. "What ever happened to just being scared when you're scared?" I ask, trying to smile through my worry.

Charity offers me a shaky laugh. "Always knew that motto was gonna come back and bite me in the ass."

"You're right, though, Char. About all of it."

"If you really don't want to stay here—"

"I just don't want to rely on a man," I say quickly. "Not a man like him."

"I get that," Charity says. "But, honey, we have nowhere to go. We have no money or resources. We don't have family to turn to or friends we can count on."

"We have each other," I point out.

She smiles. "True. That's something. That's definitely something."

"But I see your point."

"Lys, Phoenix is Theo's father," she says cautiously. "It's not fair that you have to raise him on your own."

"I don't want help raising him."

"No, of course not. But financially…"

I sigh. I don't want to ask Phoenix for anything, especially not money. But the look on Charity's face makes me reconsider. If we had money, we could at least find a safe place to live for a little while. We'd have some sense of freedom, of independence. Something to tide us over until we get on our feet.

And Phoenix has money aplenty.

I don't like it. But sometimes you have to do unpleasant things to survive. I know that better than anyone.

"Okay," I say reluctantly. "I'll ask him."

Charity smiles with relief. "I know this isn't easy for you."

I look at her and then at Theo. I can see only the chubby outline of his little cherub cheek. The rapid rise and fall of his chest.

"If it means we can get by—that *he* can get by—I'll do whatever I have to do."

Charity looks at me for a moment. Then she allows one single tear to fall.

It's the sincerest thanks I've ever received.

18

PHOENIX
PHOENIX'S OFFICE

I'm staring at the wall in my office, but strangely enough, I can't seem to concentrate on it.

That's new. Usually, when I'm here, I'm focused. I'm in the fucking zone. And when I'm not here, I'm thinking about it. Constantly.

I make another attempt at delving in, looking between the picture of Murray and then towards the center where I've taped up images of Sakamoto and Ozol.

I can feel the answers dancing on the fringes of my expansive investigation. But there are still too many question marks. Still too many loose ends.

And the smell tickling my nostrils keeps pulling me out of my thoughts.

What is that? Baby powder and lavender?

...Elyssa.

She'd asked me point blank who Vitya was. And I'd barked at her and dismissed her instead of answering.

I can claim that I don't want her knowing my business. But that's not the truth. The truth is I don't want her knowing about Aurora or Yuri.

Because for some insane fucking reason, I care what she thinks of me.

"Fuck," I growl to the empty room. "Fuck!"

My thoughts are going a million miles an hour. I just want to fucking make it stop. I need some clarity. So I pick up the phone without ever really making a conscious decision to do it.

My fingers move automatically, picking out the second name on speed dial. It rings so long that I'm on the brink of hanging up when he finally answers.

"Well, hello, boy." Almost thirty years in America and his voice still carries the faint edge of an Irish accent. Given that he's the don of the New York branch of the O'Sullivan Clan mafia, however, it's appropriate.

"Uncle Kian."

"This is the first call I've gotten in months. Has someone died? Do you need money? Blink twice if you're in trouble."

I roll my eyes. "You're starting to sound like my mother."

"Your ma would never let you get away with that kind of radio silence."

"That's why she's number one on speed dial."

"And what number am I?"

"Two, believe it or not."

"I can live with that. So long as Cillian isn't ahead of me. That bastard brother of mine is always elbowing his way to the front."

"And then you elbow your way right back past him." I smile. "How are you, old man?"

"Cut the small talk shit, Phoenix," Kian says brusquely. "You called for a fucking reason."

Sighing, I walk around behind my desk and sit down. This is a sit-down kind of talk, anyway. "There's a new development…"

"You have a new lead?"

"No, same leads," I reply. "This isn't about Astra Tyrannis."

"Since when?"

I frown. "What do you mean?"

"Everything for you in the last five years has been about those fucking scoundrels."

Jesus. I'm getting it from all sides lately. "Yeah, well, trust me: if I had my way, I wouldn't be dealing with this shit."

"Which shit is that?"

I bite the bullet and just come out and say it. "A child," I say solemnly. "A baby boy named Theo."

There's silence on the other line. I know Kian is struggling to connect the meager dots I've left him. I'm not quite sure how to tell him the whole story. Hell, I'm not sure how to even admit the whole story to myself. Perhaps that's why my explanation's coming out stilted and unclear.

"A boy named Theo?" Kian repeats. "Is that supposed to mean something to me?"

I sigh. "He's my son. Apparently."

"Jesus, Mary, and Joseph. You got a girl pregnant."

"That's usually how it works," I drawl. "Birds and the bees and all that."

"Spare me the sarcasm, kid. Why don't you start from the beginning?"

Start from the beginning. What a concept. If only I fucking could.

I rub the bridge of my nose and close my eyes. "Remember that night a year ago? The botched meeting with Ozol?"

"Of course."

"I told you what happened."

There's a second of hesitation. "Fucking hell… the girl in the wedding dress?"

"That's the one."

"You found her?"

"Sort of. I stumbled across her," I explain. "While I was tailing Murray."

"The Tyrannis lead? The dirty cop?"

"Yeah. Detective."

This time, the pause on the other line is deliberate and calculated. "She appeared during the meeting with Ozol and then again with Murray. You don't think…?"

"I know how it looks," I interrupt. "It seems too suspicious to be coincidental."

"How much do you know about this woman?"

"Hardly anything," I admit. "Apart from the fact that she was clearly running from something—or someone—the night I met her."

"And then a year later you meet her again… and she has a baby," Kian continues. "That's…"

"Yes."

"How sure are you that the kid is yours?" he asks bluntly.

"He looks like me."

"For fuck's sake, kid, you think that's enough? Is the kid a spitting image or have you just gone soft in the head? Any definitive proof at all?"

"I… well, no," I admit. "He's dark-haired, though."

"And I'm assuming she's not."

"No."

"That doesn't prove a goddamn thing."

"I'm aware."

"And yet you believe the child is yours?" Kian asks.

"Why would she lie?"

"Jesus, nephew, there are a million reasons she would lie! You're Phoenix fucking Kovalyov!" he points out. "Claiming the child is yours definitely comes with strings attached."

He's right. I know he is. But he also hasn't met Elyssa. He hasn't seen the innocence in those amber eyes.

"She doesn't seem like the manipulative type," I say.

"What the fuck does that prove?" Kian bellows. "Christ almighty, I taught you better than this! A talent for deception is the most valuable asset a recruit has. If she's a plant, then you can bet your ass she'll be a good one."

"A plant," I repeat.

"A plant," Kian repeats back to me like I'm dumb. "An Astra Tyrannis plant. You're smarter than this, Phoenix."

I bite down on my tongue, trying to look past my attraction to Elyssa and see things from my uncle's perspective.

But I can't.

Because I keep seeing her fucking doe eyes. I keep seeing the kid. Those dark features. Those long eyelashes.

"He looks like Yuri did," I say softly. "When he was first born."

Despite the fact that we're thousands of miles apart, I can feel the change in my uncle when I say those words. He softens—as much as it's possible for a battle-hardened don like him to soften.

"Fuck, Phoenix, I'm sorry. Temper getting the best of me as always. I never stopped to think what this may mean to you personally."

I clear my throat. "It doesn't mean anything to me personally," I reply harshly. "It's just an inconvenience I need to figure out how to deal with."

"Aye, certainly." I can tell he doesn't believe me. "Where is she, this woman?"

"Elyssa," I tell him. "Her name is Elyssa. She's in the house."

"You brought her home?"

"Yes."

"And…?"

"I've kept my distance," I say, deciding not to tell him about the incident with Vitya this morning.

"And what has she done in response?"

"She seems equally as keen to avoid me," I say. "It's clear she doesn't trust me."

"Okay, well, perhaps it's not as bad as it seemed. Maybe I'm just a paranoid old Irishman. But in case I'm not, some advice: keep her close. Watch her. Stay vigilant."

"I will." I start to hang up, but before I can, he says my name. "Oh, and Phoenix?"

"Yes, Uncle Kian?"

"What if it turns out the kid really is yours? And she has no motive?"

Strangely enough, of everything he's asked, this is the question that really stumps me. "I have no fucking clue."

"Family is family, Phoenix," Kian says ominously. "No matter how they come to be."

"Right. We'll see how this plays out."

"That we will. Does anyone else know?"

"Only Matvei."

"Not your parents?"

"Fuck no," I bark. "And I don't intend to tell them anytime soon. So I'd appreciate it if you don't, either. And don't tell your brother. Uncle Cillian can't keep his goddamn mouth shut."

"Jesus. I feel like I'm back in high school."

"You were never in high school," I point out.

"You're giving me the experience now."

"I don't know why I call you."

He chuckles low. "Don't stop, okay, kid?" he says affectionately. "Any time, day or night. Just ring me. Your secrets are safe with me."

I know I can trust Kian not to share this with his brother or my parents. They're a tight-knit circle, but loyalty is a powerful word in our makeshift little family.

"I know."

"Take care, kid."

I used to hate when he called me kid when I was younger. But I'd grown out of that. Just like I'd grown out of a lot of things.

∼

I head down to the basement cell where Matvei is waiting for me. The door to Murray's cell is hanging open.

"Is he talking?" I ask.

"Nah," Matvei says, wringing his hands together in preparation. "But we haven't really begun yet."

"Do we have any sodium thiopental on hand?"

"A few vials," Matvei replies. "You want to go that route? Truth serum can be a tricky bitch."

"Good. Get one dose ready," I instruct. "If he doesn't talk willingly, I'm going to force the truth from him."

I don't wait for Matvei to return with the drugs before walking into the dark cell. Two weak lights are fastened in the corners of the room. Just enough to sharpen the shadows.

Murray glances up when I enter. His eyes darken and his jaw tightens noticeably, as though he's more determined than ever to keep his secrets hidden.

"Jonathan Murray," I say. "We've never been formally introduced."

"You need no introduction," he snarls.

I smile. "I'm flattered."

"I'm not gonna talk," he continues. "So you're wasting your time."

"I never waste my time." I grab the chair sitting next to the door and drag it in front of Murray. Then I twist it around and straddle it. "This is going to be painful if you don't cooperate."

"I can deal with pain," he scoffs.

The clench of his jaw tells me that he's preparing for agony, but he's still terrified of it. I'm impressed with the bravado he's showing. I expected him to grovel at once. The greedy bastards always break first.

"You're willing to die for Astra Tyrannis?" I ask.

"If I tell you anything, I'm dead anyway."

"Right. So why not at least earn yourself a painless death?" I suggest. "Answer my questions and you won't feel a thing."

He spits on the floor. "No deal."

"Loyalty is a noble trait. But it can also be foolish. Especially if your loyalty is to the wrong people."

Murray looks at me through narrowed eyes. "I have nothing to give you."

"We'll see about that," I say.

I glance over my shoulder as Matvei enters the room. He hands me the large syringe. I hold it up to the dim light and examine it carefully.

"Do you know what this is, Murray?" I muse.

"No."

"Sodium thiopental," I tell him. "Heard of it before?"

His eyes go wide. "Truth serum…"

"Precisely. And this is some next level shit." I shift my gaze to meet his and smile at him. "Now, I'll give you one last chance to come clean on your own."

"Fuck you."

Sighing, I give the syringe back to Matvei. He approaches Murray without hesitation. The detective starts to struggle against his restraints, trying to crane away from the needle's point, but he doesn't have far to go. Matvei ignores him and jabs the needle right into his neck with expert precision.

His veins bulge slightly as the serum is injected. Murray gasps in pain.

"Done," Matvei says, pulling away. "You want a Power Rangers band-aid for that?"

"Fuck!" Murray screams. "You motherfuckers!"

I take to my feet. "We'll give you a few minutes to get acquainted with the drug." I offer him a wink. "Talk to you soon, my friend."

Matvei accompanies me back out into the anteroom. We turn back to watch as Murray struggles against the injection's hold.

"Do you think this will work?" Matvei mutters.

"I don't see why not."

He frowns and looks skeptical but says nothing.

"What?"

"I don't know," he replies. "I just don't know how much this fucker has to give us in the first place."

"We'll see," I say.

The truth is that I'm still clinging to hope. Murray is my last lead. The last string I have to pull. I'm staking all my hopes on this one interrogation.

It's why I skipped the torture part completely and went straight for the truth serum. I don't have the time to fuck around.

I need answers.

Murray's twitches settle down. His jaw goes slack. When he's quieted completely, I check my watch. "Alright. Time to go."

I stride back in the cell and look down at him impatiently.

"Let's start with an easy one. What's your full name?"

Murray shakes sporadically as though he's having a mild fit. His eyes are unfocused, trying desperately not to allow the drug to disorient him. But it's a losing battle.

"What is your full name?" I repeat.

He looks at me through narrowed eyes and the veins on his neck pop again. "Jonathan Claret Joseph Murray."

"Claret?" I repeat. "Damn. That's unfortunate. Born Catholic, eh?"

"Yes."

"Siblings?"

"Three."

"Who's the favorite?"

"My sister, Lillian."

I nod, satisfied that the serum has taken hold. Murray looks furious. But of course, the questions I'd just asked were easy ones. Information he doesn't care about parting with. His rage might help him retain the control he needs to protect the truly important shit.

"You don't know who… who you're fucking with," Murray gasps at me through fat lips.

"I do, actually."

"Astra Tyrannis is bigger than you realize."

"It's a many-headed beast," I admit with a nod. "I'm aware of that. I don't kid myself I can take down the whole organization in one night. But even if I manage to cut off just a few heads… it'll be a start."

"They know you're watching them," Murray blurts.

"I would be surprised if they didn't."

"They'll get you before you get them."

"You forget," I reply. "They may have many heads. But I'm Phoenix fucking Kovalyov. Now, why were you at the shelter?"

"I told you already: I went for the hooker."

"Charity."

"Yeah. Sure."

"And what about the other one?" I ask, reluctant to mention Elyssa's name.

"The blonde with the perky tits?" Murray asks.

It's a throwaway comment—and yet, I react. I punch him in the face so fast that he doesn't even have time to duck or move his face.

Because of that, the impact is strong. His nose cracks under my knuckles and blood starts pouring from both nostrils like a faucet.

"Fuck…!"

Matvei moves forward to help, but I hold up my hand and he stops.

"Fuck, what was that for?" Murray moans.

"Just answer the fucking questions straight."

"I did! What… Does she mean something to you… the blonde…?"

It's my own damn fault. I've made shit worse for myself by reacting like an overprotective boyfriend.

"She means about as much to me as you do right now," I reply harshly. "Which is nothing at all. What were you going to do with Charity?"

"Drop her off at a location."

"Which was?"

"A club downtown," Murray replies. "Some seedy joint called Lady V's."

I roll my eyes at the salacious name. No one in this fucking town is half as clever as they think they are. "And then?"

"And then who the fuck knows? Those were my instructions. I don't ask questions."

I frown. "Who gave you those instructions?"

I clench my fists. Murray definitely notices. The combination of violence and the truth serum is doing wonders to loosen his tongue.

"I don't fucking know."

I frown. "What?"

He shrugs. "Look, Tyrannis knows how to cover its tracks okay? When orders come in, I'm left a burner phone. I pick up the phone and call the one number on it. I get the instructions. Then I chuck the shit down the drain."

"And the voice? Who answers?"

"It's one of those electronically altered voices," he tells me. "It sounds like a fucking robot telling me what to do."

"Where do they send the money?"

"It gets left for me at random places. One day, it was in my laundry basket. Another time it came with a delivery of food. It's how they let me know they're watching me, keeping tabs. It's how they let me know they can get into my house any fucking time they want."

Jesus. These are not amateurs I'm dealing with.

"And what kinds of instructions are you given?" I ask. "What kind of tasks do you carry out?"

"Random bullshit, man. Mostly, it's picking up girls from one location and taking them to another."

"Abducting them, you mean," I snarl.

He shrugs his shoulders. "Yeah, fine, call it what you want. I fucking kidnap who I'm told to. If I say no, I die."

"You deserve to."

Murray stares at me blankly. I can see the effect of the drugs in his eyes.

"What about Victor Ozol?"

"What about him?"

"What do you know about him?"

"He's a powerful man. Can't say I've ever met him, though."

"Where is he?"

"Fuck if I know."

I want to shoot this moron in the face right now. It's a dead end, all of it. Murray's a fucking dead end.

Rather than do something impulsive, I walk out of the cell. Matvei follows behind. "Phoenix…"

"Fuck!" I growl. I ball up a fist and punch a panel on the wall. It crunches beneath my knuckles. The sting of pain is exactly what I needed. It sharpens me. Focuses me.

"He's nothing more than a lackey," Matvei finishes.

I nod. "He ties up loose ends for the organization. If anyone catches him, he gets pinned for all this shit and the organization stays clean. He's useless."

"So now what?" Matvei asks, glancing back over his shoulder where Murray is drooling and moaning nonsense syllables under his breath.

I follow his gaze. The bastard is corrupt. He's pathetic.

And as of now, he's useless to me.

"We kill him," I say grimly. "And we make it fucking hurt."

19

ELYSSA

EARLY IN THE MORNING

Theo blinks his eyes open and yawns in my face. I can't resist leaning in to plant a kiss on his cheek.

After our long early hours chat, Charity fell back to sleep. I'd managed to sleep, too. But not as deeply or as long. And of course, it wasn't restful. It never is. I'd dreamed again. Big, sprawling dreams of desert suffused with patchouli and houses ringed with fire.

Everywhere I turned, I was trapped.

And everywhere I ran, I was followed.

I recognized the faces I saw, but I didn't feel like I knew them anymore. They'd taken on strange characteristics. Inhuman shapes. Monstrous proportions.

But the thing that brought me back to consciousness was my own face. In the dream, I came across a puddle in the desert. An oasis. I leaned over the edge, looked into the reflective surface…

And saw myself.

In the reflection, I was a monster, too.

Blood dripping from my eyes. Teeth pulled back like some sort of banshee. Hair torn off my head in large chunks that left raw scalp on display.

I woke up gasping, scared to even close my eyes again. But Theo calmed me down. He woke up moments after I did, reaching out to stroke my face with his soft fingers.

Like he's saying, *It's okay, Mama. Everything is okay.*

Moving quietly in the early morning stillness, I get out of bed and take my son with me. He fusses a little, but he doesn't start crying until we're in the bathroom. The doors and walls are thick enough that I'm not worried about disturbing Charity. She needs rest to heal.

I prepare the bathtub and strip down. Then I slip into the warm water, taking Theo with me. I stare up into the ceiling as I soak, still afraid to even blink too long lest I see that image of my own face again.

We float around for about twenty minutes before it gets tiring supporting him in the water. Then I get out and towel us both off.

Once he's got a fresh diaper on, I pull out a soft blue onesie with little sharks all over it. Then I slip him into the baby carrier, which has turned out to be a godsend.

The small pile of clothes that Phoenix had sent for Charity and me sits in the corner of the bathroom where I'd moved them earlier. I rifle through and pull out a pair of stylish black jeans and a light grey sweater.

Fully dressed, I grab the baby carrier and slip through the room and towards the door. I probably should just stick to the bedroom, but the idea of being confined to one space makes me feel claustrophobic.

So I just wander around for a while until my arms start to complain. I find myself on the first floor when I smell something cooking. I decide to follow the scent of food.

"Hello, dear," comes a voice as I enter the kitchen.

I snap my head to the side in surprise as Anna shuffles into my view from a door to the side. "Sorry!" I yelp. "Didn't see you there."

"That's alright. I was just in the pantry." She gestures behind her to the pantry, which seems like a wildly insufficient word for the space. It's as big as my room at the shelter and stocked deep with enough food to survive a nuclear holocaust.

Shifting my gaze to the appliances, I notice that two of the six stovetops are currently occupied. I can smell sausages and bacon.

"How about some breakfast?" she offers.

I smile gratefully. "Yes, please."

I heave Theo's baby carrier onto the endless kitchen island. Then I pull out his milk bottle and hold it up to his mouth.

Anna looks at him fondly as she tends to the cooking food. "What a beauty. He looks so much like little Yuri."

"Yuri?" I ask. "Is that your son?"

"Oh, no, no," Anna demurs, her expression faltering a little. "My son's name was Adrian. My daughter was Kara."

"You have two children?"

"Can you say you have two children if you don't know where they are or what they're doing with their lives?" she asks mildly.

I'm lucky I have to concentrate on feeding Theo; otherwise, I might have not known where to look.

"Oh..."

I don't ask for an explanation, but she offers it up easily. "I was stolen when I was in my early twenties."

Her voice is placid. Unbothered. It's as though it happened so long ago that all the emotion has been rubbed from the memory.

"Sold into sex slavery for a period that lasted… well, a long time. I had two children in that time. Both were taken from me once they were weaned."

"Oh my God…" I murmur, looking at Theo as my heart constricts painfully on Anna's behalf. "Anna, I can't imagine what that must have done to you."

"I think about them all the time," she sighs. "At least with my boy, I knew he'd have a chance. But my girl… I worry for her still. Life is so much harder on women."

"That's because the world is run by men," I say.

I think of Father Josiah and I shiver.

She gives me an appreciative smile. "Yes, that's very true. You're a smart girl."

Humming softly under her breath, she turns back to the stove and starts piling food onto a plate for me. When she turns around, I can see sausages, eggs, and a couple of generous curls of bacon.

"I also baked some biscuits," she adds. "Ronda gave me the recipe years ago. She was born in the South."

"A friend of yours?"

"Not so much a friend as a sister in suffering," she says. Again, her voice is weirdly devoid of sympathy. "She died a long time ago. Contracted some horrible disease off one of the men."

"She died from it?" I ask, feeling nauseous.

"Well, when one of us fell sick, we were given basic treatments. But anything extra, well… they'd rather let us die. Many of us did." She pushes the plate towards me. "Eat up."

I stare at the plate, my appetite having completely disintegrated. "Um, after I finish feeding Theo," I tell her, not wanting to be rude.

Anna slides onto a stool opposite me and pours two glasses of fresh orange juice. I can see the juice maker behind her, as well as a few empty orange rinds, so I know she's made the juice herself.

"Anna, can I ask you a personal question?"

"Of course, dear," she says with a fond smile. "Ask away."

"How did you get out?"

"I never truly was freed from sex work," she tells me. "I just aged out. When I hit my late thirties, very few men were interested in paying for me. My fee was slashed, and I ended up sleeping with twice the men for half the money."

It's strange for me to hear a woman like this talk so frankly about the nightmares she's describing. Even up close, her face doesn't betray anything. No trauma. No fear. It's like she's reciting a story that happened to someone else.

"Finally, my owner decided to retire me."

"That's how you got out?"

"Oh, darling," Anna says sadly. "There's no 'getting out' for women like me. I was sold as a domestic maid to a rich man."

My insides roil with horror. Theo burps happily and I pull the bottle from his lips and set it down.

But I still ignore the plate of food in front of me. My own stomach is tied up in knots.

"Was he at least good to you?" I ask hopefully.

The smile she gives me confirms that he was anything but. "He was a brutal man. He lived his life in extremes. When he was happy, he was very happy. When he was angry… he was very angry." She raises the sleeve of her left arm to reveal a horrible, twisting, pink scar that looks decades old. "He gave me this on a weekend morning because I'd forgotten to put sugar in his coffee."

"Oh, Anna…"

Her blue eyes turn foggy for a moment, but there aren't any tears there. Just memories. "I worked for him for years, taking his abuse, cleaning up after his depravity. In some ways it was worse, more degrading than sex work."

I gnaw at my bottom lip. "Why didn't you run?"

"Run?" she repeats, as though the notion never even occurred to her. "Run where? I was a woman in her fifties with no education and no job history. There was nowhere to run. They'd cut off my limbs if they caught me. I had no choice but to stay. To suffer."

She's strong enough to sit there and tell me her story with dry eyes. But I'm not strong enough to hear it without crying. A tear slips down my cheek and she smiles at me. It's an amused smile, of all things.

"Oh, honey, forgive me. I didn't mean to upset you."

"No, you didn't. I'm just… upset for you."

It's pathetic. This woman has suffered through hell and more, and yet, she's the one forced to console me. Sometimes, I hate how damn weak I am.

No—I hate how weak they made me.

"Don't be upset for me," she says softly. "I was delivered from that hell. I was freed."

"How?"

She raises her eyebrows. "Master Phoenix, of course," she says. "Sometimes, life's coincidences can be cruel. Mostly, that's all they are. But sometimes, every so often… they can be miraculous."

"What do you mean?"

"Master Phoenix had been tracking the man I worked for a while. He descended on the house the same night I decided to kill Mr. Gibraltar."

She says it without the slightest bit of inflection. I do a double take. "You… you killed him?"

She nods. "After seven years with him, I'd had enough. I was not in my right mind that night. I was traumatized."

"Of course you were!"

"I did exactly what I'd spent seven years dreaming of doing. And I was standing there with blood on my hands, literally, when Master Phoenix found me."

"Oh my God…" Chills snake down my spine. But not because of the decision that Anna had made that night.

Rather, because I had made the same exact decision a year ago.

Or at least, the old me did. The Elyssa that's still trapped somewhere in my traumatized brain. In the memories I can't access.

All I have is bits and pieces of the night I made the choice to kill Father Josiah. The "why" is a mystery to me.

Then again, I suppose my "why" doesn't really matter. I have blood on my hands, too.

Same as Anna.

She continues, "Master Phoenix pulled me aside, sat me down, had me explain who I was and what had happened. I told him everything. My story came pouring out of me and he listened to every word. It was unfathomable to me that a man like him could exist. Someone powerful but not evil. So when he asked me how he could help, I told him. I didn't have any skills to survive in the real world on my own. I asked if he would hire me to take care of his home."

I wipe away the stray tear, still lost in the few fragments of memory I can recall.

The black swan... the blood...

I'm distantly aware of Anna continuing her story. "... He wasn't sure at first. I could tell he struggled with the idea of bringing a stranger into his home. But in the end, he agreed."

I smile, thankful that Anna has found some peace. I'm also amazed and impressed by the man who had delivered her from her waking nightmare. A man I've always suspected was more than just his bristly façade.

And here is the proof. Sitting in front of me in living color.

So maybe his brusque, disinterested demeanor has nothing to do with him—and everything to do with me.

"Are you okay now?" I ask tremulously. "I'm sorry if that's a stupid question to ask."

She smiles. Her eyes are filled with stories. Most of them too dark to share.

"It's not a stupid question," she reassures me, reaching out to run her hand against Theo's face. "I am okay. I have a purpose now. I know what I have to do. What I'm meant to do."

"Did you ever find your children again?"

She sighs. "No. They are lost to me. I've made my peace with that."

I can't help but glance at Theo. He gives me a big toothless smile, and my heart aches with the injustice of it all. "I'm sorry for everything you went through."

Anna shrugs. "Why? You had nothing to do with it."

"I'm sorry all the same."

I'm on the verge of telling her that I relate to her more than she knows. I may not have had the horrific life she had lived through. But I've lived some of the same moments. I know what it's like to stand over a body and realize you've ended a man's life. Justified or not, that stays with you.

But at the last moment, I hold my tongue. I remember what Charity has always told me: *Don't let people in too deep. It gives them power over you.*

I like Anna, but I only just met her. I need to keep my distance.

"You're not eating," Anna remarks, pushing the plate closer to me. "Come on now, don't be shy. You look like you need the strength."

I almost laugh. She has no idea how much strength I need.

I still don't have much of an appetite, but I pick up the fork and skewer a piece of sausage anyway. I eat almost entirely for her benefit, though after a while, I do start to register the taste.

"Wow," I moan. "This is delicious."

"Thank you, darling. There's more in the pan."

She feeds me like I'm a prodigal child who's come home after a long absence. When I'm stuffed to the brim, I finally push my plate away.

"Everything's been so delicious, but I can't eat another bite."

Anna laughs. "Are you sure?"

"Positive. But I would like to take some food up for Charity, if that's okay?"

"Of course, dear, I'll make a plate for her right now."

I watch Anna move around the kitchen. Her limp seems less pronounced at the moment, but I assume that's because she's distracted.

After a few minutes, she turns around with a plate packed to the brim with sausages, bacon, eggs, and biscuits. It smells heavenly.

"You'll need help carrying everything up," Anna says. "I'll come with you."

"You sure?"

"Of course."

Grateful for her help, I grab Theo's baby carrier. Anna takes the loaded plate. We walk in silence most of the way up to the bedroom.

That is, until I turn to her with an afterthought kind of a question that's not really an afterthought at all.

"Was it hard for you?" I ask. "Adjusting to the outside world when you moved in here?"

I examine her face as she thinks about her answer. There's strength in her eyes. A certain hardness that's bred out of a life that hasn't ever given you room to breathe.

"No, actually," she replies. "It was easy to adjust. Especially because of the staff here. They're all women like me."

"Women like you?" I ask in confusion.

"Women who've been rescued from the sex trade," Anna explains. "Women who've been given second chances to find happiness."

I stare at her in disbelief. "Phoenix brings them here? All of them?"

Anna nods. "He does."

"Wow…" I don't mean to say it out loud, but out it comes anyway.

Anna gives me a knowing smile. Then her eyes flicker to Theo. I wonder if she's putting two and two together. Or maybe she's already deciphered the truth. Still, I'm not going to be the one to confirm anything.

"Such a handsome boy," she coos in a voice laced with sorrow. I wonder if she's thinking about her own little ones.

"You know, I don't mind if you'd like to babysit him sometimes," I offer tentatively.

Her smile gets wider. "Do you mean that?"

I nod. "Definitely."

"Thank you, Elyssa. You're a sweet girl."

Something inside me twists when she says that. I feel like a fraud. A con artist. *Sweet girl?* It sounds good.

But it doesn't fit. Not with me.

I may look like a sweet girl. But sweet girls don't do the things I've done.

I tamp down the guilt and give Anna a half-hearted smile. I let her see what she wants to see.

Or maybe I've just been lying so long that I've forgotten how to tell the truth.

We reach the landing that leads to our room. Anna and I are walking towards the door when I hear it—sharp. Distinct. Unmistakable.

The sound of trouble ahead.

The sound of a gunshot.

20

PHOENIX
FIFTEEN MINUTES EARLIER

I pace back and forth in the anteroom outside the cell. Matvei stands to the side, leaning against the front-facing wall.

"Stop it," I growl.

"Stop what?"

"Watching me."

He smirks. "It's my job to watch you."

"Since when?"

"Since you decided to go after one of the most powerful fucking organizations on the planet."

I stop short and turn to Matvei. My eyes drift towards the closed door of Murray's cell.

"I wasn't the one that started this, you know."

"Of course not. You would never. You're as pure as the driven snow."

"No," I say, knowing he's misunderstood. "I'm not talking about Astra Tyrannis. I'm talking about Kian. Cillian. Artem."

"Your father and your uncles. I'm familiar with them."

I resume pacing. "They made it their mission to dismantle sex trafficking rings in their cities. They extinguished that kind of crime ring from the territories they ruled. But once they started, they realized how deep it went," I continue. "They realized how many women were forced into it. How many men profited off it. It was their cause before it was mine."

I let the words sit for a moment, remembering the early days, when I was just a snot-nosed little kid trying to keep up with the big boys.

Uncle Kian had always been passionate about what we do. It's why he staffed his homes and businesses with women who needed a second chance at life. Women who'd suffered. He gave them freedom.

He used to refer to it as a "cause." He still does. I suppose I caught his passion and ran with it.

"All the rings my father and my uncles put a stop to—they soon realized they were connected to a bigger organization. One that was far more extensive than we ever realized. It was easy to jump on board then. I wanted to prove myself. I never stopped to think about what I would be risking."

Matvei fixes me with his knowing gaze. "You have to forgive yourself, Phoenix," he says quietly. "Aurora and Yuri—their deaths... It wasn't your fault."

"Wasn't it?" I retort. "I failed to protect them."

"The house was secure. Aurora was accompanied by guards wherever she went. What more could you have done?"

"More," I answer. "I could have done more."

"Short of lock her in a room and keep her there indefinitely?" Matvei asks. "She would have been miserable."

"At least she would have been alive."

"That's your grief talking," Matvei says firmly. "A life of captivity isn't worth living. Isn't that what you say to every single woman who comes across your doorstep?"

I grit my teeth and turn away from Matvei. For five years, he's insisted on trying to exonerate me for Aurora and Yuri's deaths. He still doesn't seem to realize that forgiveness is not what I seek.

It's vengeance.

"Phoenix—"

"I'm done talking about them," I snarl. "Don't mention their names again."

"Fine," Matvei snaps back. "Then how about Elyssa and Theo? Are you willing to talk about them?"

He's caught me in a bad moment, and he knows it. But he's trying to force a confrontation with me. Probably because he knows I'll reveal something to him in my anger.

That's the problem with Matvei—he knows me too fucking well.

"No."

"Of course not. Because anything hard, you just choose to ignore."

"Fuck you."

"No, fuck *you*," Matvei throws back at me.

While my chest rises and falls with aggression, Matvei's anger burns slow. You can hardly tell he's enraged at all. All the emotion is contained in his eyes. But right now, they simmer with a dangerous burn.

He never allows it to crack through the surface, though. It always stays just out of sight.

Another trait I find infuriating about him.

Probably because I'm jealous I can't mimic the same type of restraint. Then again, Matvei never lost his wife and child as a result of his own shortsightedness. He hasn't suffered like I've suffered. Suffered in his own way? Yeah, of course. His story is filled with pain.

But you don't know pain until you've seen all the bloodied fragments that remain of the woman you vowed to cherish and protect. Until your son's screams fade from hearing forever.

That's real fucking pain. That's real fucking agony.

"You walk around as though you're the only man in the world fighting against that motherfucking organization," Matvei says, curling his words at the edges. "You act as though you're the only one who cares."

"It's personal for me."

"And you don't think it's personal for me?" Matvei demands. "I loved Aurora like a sister. And I loved that kid, too."

I clench my fists. "I told Aurora once that I thought you were in love with her," I murmur.

Matvei smiles slowly. "What did she say?"

"That you loved the idea of her more."

Matvei's smile grows fond with memory. "I think I could have fallen in love with her… if I'd met her first. Fuck, maybe I was half in love with her. But don't get me wrong—she was yours, brother. From the very beginning. She looked at you like you were a fucking god."

I still, his words piercing through the guilt that's lived inside me for five fucking years. "I know."

"That's why this is so hard for you, isn't it?" Matvei asks. "You think you didn't deserve that love."

I finally sit down on one of the chairs in a corner. "I didn't. I don't. She assumed she was safe with me. She was so sure nothing would ever happen to her. And I'll admit it—I thought the same. I was so fucking cocksure that I was powerful enough to protect her."

"Is that why you avoid Elyssa like the plague?" Matvei asks.

I tense instantly. I hate that I've given him any kind of reaction, but it's too late. And Matvei is too sharp. He doesn't miss anything.

"I'm right, aren't I?"

"Just once in your fucking life, can you try not to be right all the time?" I growl.

He smiles sheepishly. "No can do, brother. I am who I am."

I take a deep, staggering breath. "Elyssa… fuck, I don't know. I don't trust her."

"Is that the reason, then?"

I look up at him, knowing he can see through me. "She reminds me of Aurora," I admit. "Not in looks. Not even in character. It's just…"

"The way she looks at you," Matvei offers.

"You've noticed?"

Stupid question. Of course he's noticed. I'm just surprised that he's paid attention.

"It's impossible not to. She tries to hide it," Matvei says. "But the way she looks at you, it's the same. The same as Aurora."

"Well, I should disabuse her of that notion. She's only going to be disappointed by it. She doesn't know what that look will bring to her doorstep."

"You're a different man now, Phoenix," Matvei points out. "Things will be different this time around."

"*This time around*?" I repeat. The words strike me as suspicious. "There is no 'this time around,' Matvei. Elyssa and that child, they're not mine. I don't want them to be."

He doesn't hesitate. "But what if they could be? What if they're your second chance?"

A second chance? Is that even possible for me?

Out loud, I say, "I don't trust her. I don't know anything about her."

"Then maybe it's time you found out."

I nod. He's right. The woman is in my home. She claims to have my child. She owes me answers. At the very least, she owes me an explanation.

But that will come in due time. Business demands my attention first. I stand slowly and look towards the cell door.

"What are we gonna do about him?" Matvei asks, jerking his head toward Murray.

"Do you think he has anything else to give us?"

"Only one way to find out."

The two of us head back towards the cell. When I push the door open, Murray is sitting against the chair, his chin lolling against his chest.

I slam the door hard against the back wall. It clangs and echoes throughout the basement. He jerks his head up, his eyes unfocusing for a moment before falling on me.

"Please," he begs, his voice shivering. "Please. I have nothing more to give."

"Tell me something," I encourage. "Anything useful. Anything you think might save your pathetic fucking life."

"I don't know anything! I've told you everything, I swear, I swear, I…"

I kneel in front of him. His eyes are liquid fear, frothing and wild. "I'd start to think a little harder if I were you, my friend. What was the last task you carried out for Astra Tyrannis? Before you and I ran into each other."

He tenses, his eyes flitting between Matvei and I.

"I… that's… I…"

I raise my eyebrows. "Murray, it's in your best interests to cooperate with me."

He understands the warning, but I can tell that his fear of Astra Tyrannis is greater than his fear of me. Which is both insulting and illuminating at the same time.

"Speak."

"They expect loyalty," Murray stammers. "Complete loyalty. Do you know what they do to the people that betray them?"

"It can't be any worse than what I'll do to you if you don't answer me now."

He shakes his head, his demeanor growing more and more agitated. He keeps looking around the room as though he's scared of being watched. As though he assumes there's Astra Tyrannis spies hidden in every crack and crevice.

It reminds me of Vitya—and his ridiculous claim that there are spies in my house.

"Murray," I say, forcing him to look at me. "Tell me something: is there a spy in this house?"

He tenses instantly. I can feel Matvei's eyes on the back of my head. "No."

I frown. That answer came too fast. "Are you lying to me?"

"I don't know!" He shakes his head. "They don't tell me anything. I don't have any real information. I just do what I'm told."

He starts sobbing. A cry bursts from his lips, sending flecks of spit everywhere. It looks like he's foaming at the mouth.

He starts rocking back and forth, his chair scraping the hard cement floor with the motion.

"He's losing it," Matvei says, coming forward. "We might've given him too much of the sodium thiopental."

"Murray, stay with me, motherfuck—Oh, goddammit!"

As I'm speaking, he falls back, going down with the chair. It shatters on impact in the most unfortunate way possible—allowing him to get on his feet.

I'm not worried. I know I can take the man.

But as it turns out, that doesn't even factor in. Because Murray doesn't make any attempt to attack either Matvei or me.

Instead, he turns towards the wall and starts bashing his own head against the cracked stones.

"Fuck!" Matvei breathes.

I stare at Murray in shock for a moment, realizing that he's trying to kill himself.

"Stop him!" I command.

Matvei is already moving forward, but Murray's movements are frenzied and desperate now. He looks like he's been possessed.

CRACK! CRACK! CRACK!

His head slams into the jagged stones. I hear the squelch of blood, the cracking of bone.

Matvei grabs him, but Murray swings around, blood dropping off his face and smashes his face into Matvei's chin.

Matvei stumbles back, surprised, and Murray uses the second of disorientation to his advantage.

He snatches the knife hanging from the waistband of Matvei's jeans and stabs my best friend right in the stomach.

I jump forward and grab hold of the manic man. Hurling him back against the wall with all my strength, I expect the force to crack his spine in two.

But even if it does, he doesn't show it. He's too crazed by the demons in his head and the drugs in his system. By his fear of Astra Tyrannis. By the blood on his hands.

Still frothing at the mouth, he bounces off the wall and comes charging towards me. I raise my hands and drop into a defensive crouch, ready to fight.

But he never makes it all the way to me. At the last second, he veers off course and heads for Matvei instead.

Time slows down.

The knife is still clasped tight in Murray's bloodied hands. I know that by the time I get to him, he'll have stabbed my friend again.

Matvei can't protect himself. He's lying on the ground, struggling to contain the rampant bleeding.

My thoughts are warring with each other.

I have to save Matvei.

But I still need Murray.

He's my last lead. And he also knows more than he's letting on. I feel sure of that now. The expression that flickered across his face when I'd asked about spies… it was telling.

Even if he didn't know details, he knew something. And that's more than what I have now.

I have fractions of a second left to decide. Murray is raising the knife above his head. Howling like a wolf, he starts to bring it down, down, down...

BANG.

I pull out my gun and end his fucking life where he stands.

Or at least, I thought I did. But my aim wasn't quite as good as it should've been. Too distracted by all the haunted thoughts running through my head.

Instead of my bullet burying itself between his eyes, it catches him in the chest. He's flopping on the ground and wailing.

I approach him with my gun still raised.

"Matvei!" I roar. "You okay?"

"Fuck," he moans. "Hurts like a bitch."

"Hang in there. I'll get help."

I turn to Murray. And as I do, I realize that the knife is still in his hand. I'm close enough to make a last-ditch swipe at. Maybe he'll get me, maybe he won't.

I raise my gun to fire once more. I won't miss twice.

But he doesn't swing the knife at me.

He brings it to his own throat instead.

"NO!" I bellow.

Before I can stop him, he swipes the knife across his own throat. Blood spurts out in uneven torrents.

One second later, Murray's eyes glaze over.

He's dead. And my last hope for answers just died with him.

21

ELYSSA

I whip around and look towards Anna. "What's happening?"

She clearly has no idea. "Stay here," she says. "I'll go and see."

There's not an ounce of fear or hesitation in her tone. She looks like she's ready to jump into the fray if she needs to.

Where does fearlessness like that come from? From a life like hers, no doubt.

But as brave as she may appear, she's still an old lady in her sixties. She walks with a limp and a cane and honestly, she's been through enough. I can't possibly let her go off on her own into potentially dangerous territory, while I stayed barricaded in my room.

"No," I say firmly. "Stay here with Theo and Charity, okay? I'll go and see what's happening."

Anna's eyes flash with determination. "It might not be safe for you."

"If it's not safe for me, then it's definitely not safe for you," I counter, putting Theo's baby carrier on the floor in front of the door.

At that exact moment, Charity pulls it open. "Oh my God... Elyssa, Theo! Thank God. Did you just hear a gunshot?"

I start jogging down the hall without answering. "Stay in the room," I call back over my shoulder. "Lock the door. I'll be back."

"Elyssa, what the fuck do you think you're doing?" Charity demands.

"Language!" I call back, knowing it'll piss her off. I can hear Anna protesting, too, but I ignore both of them and take off at a run.

I don't know why I'm so adamant to check this out on my own. All I have are the visceral demands of my instincts. And they're scared.

Not for myself.

But for... Phoenix?

The conscious acknowledgement has me reeling for a moment. My interest in him is taking on a new meaning. Now's not the time to parse that.

I follow the sound down towards the basement. The door is closed, but when I push it open, it swings forward, granting me access to the broad staircase.

"NO!"

I freeze. Phoenix's voice.

I race down the staircase, terrified of what I might find when I get there. But I keep going anyway.

The basement is a large, open space with stone walls, cement floors, and low ceilings. The light is poor, but I'm willing to bet that's a conscious choice. The place is clearly intended to intimidate.

A door set in the far wall is hanging open. Shadows move inside it.

I want to call out his name, but it feels too intimate somehow. Like I haven't earned that right. Or maybe my brain is just short-circuiting on adrenaline and fear.

Whatever the cause, I inch forward instead of calling for him. I stop at the threshold.

My eyes spot the dead body in the corner first. I recognize Detective Murray instantly. His vacant eyes stare at the ceiling. There's a jagged red slash across his throat, soaked in blood.

My stomach roils. I turn away from him and notice Phoenix kneeling beside another body.

Unlike Murray, this one is breathing.

I rush forward, recognizing the good-looking man who came to pick us up from the shelter. He's been stabbed in the stomach.

"Move aside!" I order automatically, switching into Nurse Elyssa mode. At least, that's what Charity used to call it when I was attending to injuries in and around the shelter.

Phoenix looks up at me in shock. "What the hell are you doing here?"

"Trying to help," I reply. "Now move. I need to put pressure on the wound so he doesn't lose more blood."

He hesitates for only a second as I drop to my knees. I press my hands on the wound as he gets to his feet.

"What do you need?" he asks quietly.

"Water and clean cloth. Lots of it."

He doesn't question me. Just turns and strides out of the room, leaving me alone with his friend.

The man's eyes flicker towards me. I can tell the drowsiness is setting in. His body is going into shock.

"Hey," I coax. "Stay with me, okay? Stay awake."

He nods slowly. I notice how blue his lips are. Not a good sign.

"What's your name again… Matteo?"

"Matvei," he rasps softly.

"Nice to officially meet you, Matvei."

His face contorts into something that could be a smile. But it fades quickly. He's paling faster with every passing second.

"I need that stuff now!" I yell over my shoulder.

Right on cue, Phoenix shows up with a bucket of water and a bunch of clean cloth and bandages. He sets in down in front of me and I get to work.

First, I put pressure on the wound to stop the bleeding. My hands are drenched in blood, but as the minutes tick past, I notice that the flow of it has slowed.

After five minutes, I notice Matvei's color is improved. Not by much, but it's something.

He's awake, at least. And he can still speak.

"Don't worry, man," Phoenix says. "Dr. Roth is on his way."

"Murray?" Matvei coughs.

"Dead," Phoenix answers with a deadened expression.

"You shot to kill?"

"Not exactly," he says grimly. "He slit his own fucking throat."

It's amazing that they can have a calm conversation in the midst of all this. But neither one seems all that fazed. Now that I think about it, they've probably been in similar situations before.

"Okay," I say. "I think the bleeding has stopped. I'm gonna have to clean the wound now."

"Or we can wait for Dr. Roth."

"The longer we wait, the higher the chance of infection," I tell Phoenix. "But it's your call."

He regards me calmly for a moment and then nods. "Go ahead. Do what you have to."

Taking encouragement from his words, I slowly pull away the cloth to make sure the bleeding has stopped. "This might hurt," I say to prepare him.

He scoffs. "I've been through worse."

I work slowly, taking care to wash well to reduce the chance of later infections. Thankfully, the wound is not overly dirty despite the dirt on the floor and splatters of blood from the dead detective sullying the room.

After a few minutes, I glance at the water to see it swirling red. "I need it changed," I say without addressing Phoenix directly.

Again, he does exactly as I ask without complaint. When I turn back to Matvei, I notice a small smile on his lips.

"What are you grinning at?" I ask self-consciously.

"Nothing, just… very few people get to boss him around," he says. "It's like seeing a dog walk on its hind legs."

I stifle a laugh just as Phoenix walks back into the dark cell with fresh water. He stands back and watches as I rinse out the cloth and continue applying pressure.

"You've been doing the same shit for a while now," Phoenix points out impatiently.

Something tells me that he's just looking for a reason to find fault with me. I don't spare him a glance. "Do you want it to get infected?"

He eyes his best friend. "He's probably done something to deserve it."

"Fuck you, asshole," laughs Matvei, although the laugh quickly curdles into a groan of pain.

"Your doctor's taking a long time," I cut in.

Matvei doesn't say much, but I notice his eyes move back and forth between Phoenix and me. There's something they aren't telling me. Once I've finished cleaning the wound, I apply some of the antiseptic cream Phoenix brought and then bandage him up.

Finished, I look down at my work objectively. "All done," I say, feeling satisfied.

I get to my feet shakily. One leg is so numb with pins and needles that I lose balance and stumble back into a wall. Or rather, into Phoenix.

His hands land on my waist for a moment. That tiny touch, as meaningless as it is, unearths a memory. So visceral, so tangible, that I'm transported back to that night.

The moment he placed me on that bathroom counter...

The seconds leading up to when he had parted my legs and...

"Dr. Roth."

I snap out of the memory and turn to see a man walking towards the room. He definitely doesn't look like a doctor. More like a retired wrestler. I move back, suddenly intimidated that he's going to be examining my work.

"Sorry I'm so late," he says in a rushed voice. "There was traffic on the highway."

He kneels down in front of Matvei and gets to work. I take the opportunity to sneak out of the room.

I can feel Phoenix's eyes on my back as I make my retreat, but I don't turn around. I just keep going until I'm out of the basement.

I take a deep breath once I'm back upstairs. The plan was to return to the bedroom to check on Anna, Charity, and Theo, but for some reason, I find myself going in the opposite direction. I need a moment to breathe, to collect myself.

So I walk outside, noticing the reflection of calm water a few feet away. I walk towards it until I reach the deck. The pool looks beautiful… and so inviting.

If only I weren't so afraid of it.

I don't sense him until he's standing right next to me. And when I do, the hairs on the back of my neck stand on end. Why does my body come alive every time we're in close proximity? It feels like a betrayal.

When he doesn't say anything, I decide to. "What did the doctor say?"

"He'll live," Phoenix replies curtly.

"Good to know."

"Roth said you did a good job."

I'm instantly, pathetically proud. I should be happy that the doctor was impressed with my work. But I'm more thrilled about the fact that he told Phoenix.

Like I said: pathetic.

"Where'd you learn how to do that?" he asks.

This is what I was worried about—questions. If he asks too many, what can I do except lie? Deflect? Deny?

The answer is too ridiculous to believe: *I don't know. I don't know how I know anything.*

At least this time, he's asked me a question I can answer. Not an honest answer. Not completely honest, at least. But it's an answer nonetheless.

"The shelter," I say. "Some of the women who were in and out of there… well, let's just say that they had complicated lives. Some of them needed a refuge from abusive husbands or boyfriends. Some were running from violent fathers. Others were prostitutes who'd pissed off their pimps. Basically, there were a lot of desperate women and a lot of angry men. They came to the shelter. I'd clean them up and tend to their wounds."

He listens quietly, taking that in. "You've learned a lot in a year."

I look at him, but he's not watching me like I suspect. His eyes are trained on the rippling water in front of us. There's a slight breeze in the air. I should be cold, but the heat coming off him is distracting me.

"Why didn't you show up that night?" he asks. "At the diner?"

I freeze. That is the last question I expected. "I… I…"

That's the moment he chooses to swing his eyes to me. They're dark, hooded. Hiding a cavern of secrets.

"I didn't know if I could trust you," I finish.

"That's a lie," he snaps. "You trusted me right away."

I look down. He's right.

"Charity was working at the club that night," I murmur. "She saw me run out and she followed me. She helped me. When I told her about you…"

"She thought you were insane for wanting to meet me," he infers.

"Yes."

He nods. "Smart."

I can't tell if he's angry or relieved. I can't tell anything from his impassive face. I have no idea if he even believes me.

"What were you running from?" he asks. "When you came into the room that night. You looked like you'd just woken up from a nightmare."

And there it is. The one question I absolutely cannot answer.

My jaw tightens. He notices, of course. Those dark eyes notice everything. And when he does, the impassivity gives way to impatience. Annoyance. Suspicion.

"I can't tell you that."

"Why?"

I jerk my chin out. A trait I've learned from Charity. I wish I had her courage for real. I wish I could fight for myself the way she fights for me.

"Because it's not any of your business."

"You made it my business when you asked me for help."

"I didn't ask."

I know that's a lie. A pretty blatant one. But I say it anyway. Because I'm a coward.

"Who are you?" he rasps.

The way he asks the question makes me feel immediately defensive. "What do you mean?"

"You heard me," he says aggressively. "I have a right to know who's living in my house."

"I'm not living here," I shoot back. "I'm just… passing through."

"And what do you want while you're 'just passing through'?"

His question is laced with more questions I can't answer. Questions like, *What do you feel when you look at me? Do you remember what we did the night we met? Do you remember how it felt to be consumed by my kiss, my touch, my body?*

I want to turn on my heel and walk away from him. I want to prove that I don't want or need anything from him.

But that's not true.

It's only what I wish was the truth.

Charity's pleas echo in my ears. I can't go back on my promise to her. Or my son. I can sacrifice my pride if it means saving them.

"I... I..."

"Spit it out," he says harshly.

"I didn't know I was pregnant the night we met. Or, I mean, I didn't know I was going to get pregnant."

He doesn't say a thing. Still as a statue, he watches and waits for me to finish.

"And when I did find out, I had no idea where to find you..."

His expression still doesn't change.

"He is your son, too," I continue, stumbling over my words. I'm pretty sure my cheeks are bright red. "And... and it's been hard this past year... The shelter doesn't pay much..."

I hate the way it's coming out. I stop short, dissatisfied with my own case.

"You want money," he drawls.

The way he says it is a punch to the gut.

"I... It won't be forever. Just until I can get a decent job so that I can support him myself."

He looks at me, utterly unconvinced.

This is not how I imagined a reunion between us. Of course, those fantasies—when I was weak enough to allow them—were always fraught with unrealistic undertones. This is the real world, not a fairy tale.

But then, deep down, I'm the same naïve girl who ran from a place that had secluded itself from the real world. So what do I know about anything?

"Okay."

"Okay?" I repeat, amazed that he is agreeing to this so easily.

"If the child is mine, I will provide for him," Phoenix says quietly.

Wait. "If?"

He raises his eyebrows. "You claim the boy is mine. But I'm going to need more than your word."

"You don't believe me?"

I shouldn't take that so personally. But I do.

"You're a complete stranger to me," he says, his eyes turning cold and distant. "I don't even know your last name. I fucked you once over a year ago, and now I'm supposed to take your word for it that your child is mine?"

I flinch at the crude way he spells it out for me. And that's it—my personal tipping point. Forget what I told Charity. This isn't worth it.

I turn and start walking away from him.

"Stop."

The commanding tone shoots through my body like a bolt of electricity. And despite myself, I do as he orders.

"Turn around."

It's like he's got control of my body. Like he's in my head, controlling me like some sort of expert puppeteer. I turn around, even while hating myself for doing it.

"This conversation is not over."

"I say it is."

"Why?" he presses. "Because it's making you uncomfortable?"

"Yes."

"Tough. Life is fucking uncomfortable," he says. "And you're the one who brought it up."

"Because I thought you'd be a gentleman about it!"

He barks out a harsh laugh. "What the fuck gave you that impression?"

I twitch automatically at his language, but I don't mention it. "You were different with me that night."

He stills momentarily. "Because I thought you needed help."

"I did."

"If that were true, you would have shown up at the diner like I told you to."

"I wanted to!" I say, realizing that I'm actually yelling back. I never yell. "But Charity convinced me—"

"Are you that fucking simple-minded that you can so easily allow other people to manipulate and influence you?"

A sound escapes my mouth. I'm not even sure what it is. A gasp? A sob? Both? Neither? Whatever it is, I find myself staring hard at him, trying to reconcile the dark-eyed protector who gave me my son with the cruel monster in front of me now.

"You don't know anything about me," I finally force out.

The only reason I'm so defensive is because he's cut to the crux of who I am in minutes. He's discovered my fatal flaw. My weakness. He's exposed me in seconds.

And that's forcing me to confront the reality of who I am—or at the very least, who I once was—against the person I've been trying so hard to become.

"No," he rasps. "I don't."

His face may as well be cut from stone. He looks fucking terrifying. And so beautiful.

He takes a step toward me, his square jaw twitching with aggravation. "For all I know, you could be a spy."

He spits the last word at me. It pierces into my chest like a dagger. My vision blurs behind a veil of tears. I spin away because, more than anything, I don't want him to see me cry.

Let him try to tell me to stop again. I won't. Not even for him.

But I can't see straight. I can't even walk straight. I'm so weighed down by hurt that it makes me unsteady on my feet.

And, when I twist around, my foot catches a wet spot near the pool's edge.

I lose my balance. There's a split second of shock, that grappling fear of losing your bearings and falling backwards without anything to hold onto.

Then I fall. As I tumble into the water, my peripheral vision catches his profile. Dark and stoic. Completely unreachable. Like an ancient statue carved from the hardest, coldest marble known to man.

When my body breaks the surface of the pool, all I can register is panic.

On the surface, water looks so beautiful. You expect it to hold you, catch you, float you. But the opposite is true. It swallows you and drags you down into its depths.

Or maybe both things happen at once and I'm just too messed up in the head to make sense of anything. Because when I hit the water, it hurts.

And when I go under, it forces its way into my body, gushing in uninvited. My nose, my eyes, my mouth all fill up with chlorinated water. Choking the air from my lungs, unrelenting and unforgiving. All-consuming.

The only thing I can think is: *Will he save me?*

Then, hot on the heels of that thought: *Maybe I don't deserve to be saved.*

22

PHOENIX

My head is swimming with paranoia.

First, Vitya shows up out of nowhere to warn me of snakes in the grass.

Then, Murray reacts strangely to my question about spies in my home.

It was nothing more than a stutter. But it stuck in my head like a splinter.

When I take stock of all the people in my home, the only two that I can't vouch for are the two women who'd manipulated me into bringing them here. And yet, when I look at Elyssa, the word "spy" doesn't match up with the doe-eyed innocence or the subtle naivete that she tries so hard to overcome.

But perhaps that's exactly why she was recruited. No one would suspect someone like Elyssa. And isn't that the mark of a perfect mole?

"For all I know, you could be a spy."

I hurl the word at her like the lash of a whip. I want to see what she'll do. How she'll react. If my suspicions are right or if my gut knows her better than my head does.

She flinches as though she's been struck. Her face falls and hurt floods her eyes.

I've never been confronted with someone so sensitive that every reprimand is absorbed and internalized. She doesn't even fight back. Her only method of dealing with my accusation is to turn her back on me. To walk away.

She doesn't want me to see how deeply she's hurt by my accusation, but she's not great at hiding. I catch sight of the swirl of tears in her irises as she turns.

Then, like it's all happening in slow motion, she slips. She falls downward in an eerily graceful arc. Not even fighting it. Just accepting that this is how it all ends.

Until the last moment, that is. Right before she breaks the surface of the water, she extends her hands as though she's reaching for something.

Reaching for me.

I stand still, waiting for her to pop up. But she never makes it that far. Instead, she's thrashing around desperately in the water, but her efforts are split in all directions. That's when I realize: she can't swim.

Her head bobs up for one moment. I have only long enough to register her eyes, wide with terror, before the water consumes her again.

A number of thoughts flit through my head in the seconds that follow.

Should I save her? Letting her drown would tie up a loose end. Will I be able to live with it?

I think about the dark-haired child somewhere inside the house right now. I may not know with certainty if I'm his father. But I know for sure that Elyssa is his mother.

Can I rob that baby of the only person he has in the world?

I don't know quite what this woman means to me. She has re-entered my life as strangely and as inexplicably as she had disappeared from it a year ago.

But I do know that, whatever the bizarre connection is between us, watching her die will not resolve it.

That final thought is what sends me into motion.

I coil, spring forward, and dive into the pool, knifing through the water cleanly.

I reach her in one stroke. My arms curl around her slight frame. The moment I have a good hold on her, I kick off the bottom and carry her up towards the surface.

We burst back to the air, but she's still struggling desperately as though she can't trust the rescue.

"Stop," I command. "Calm down. I've got you."

My words have an immediate effect. She stops flailing and melts against me, breathing in huge, ragged gasps. Together, we kick back to the edge of the pool.

I haul her out. The moment she's back on the deck, she splutters out water and coughs. She's shivering badly and her clothes are clinging to her like a second skin. I try not to focus on the fact that the top she's wearing is almost completely see-through, revealing the black bra she's wearing underneath.

Even after she's coughed up a significant amount of water, she stays on the deck, her body trembling uncontrollably. I walk around and squat down in front of her.

"You okay?"

She doesn't answer. Her face is aimed down at the deck. Water drips off her in thin rivulets.

Before I can second-guess the instinct, I scoop her up into my arms and carry her into the house. It feels like she weighs nothing to all, despite her soaked clothes. She doesn't open her eyes or resist at all.

The laundry room is empty when I walk in. Two huge washing machines loom on one side of the room and two dryers on the other.

In the middle, between the machines, is a long wooden table that the maids use for folding and organizing. I set Elyssa down on top of it, fighting the wave of nostalgia that hits me instantly.

We've done this before.

I saved her. Carried her to freedom. And then…

Growling wordlessly, I retreat to the door and close it. I grab two fresh towels off the rack in the corner and head back to her.

The shivering has subsided somewhat, but tremors still run through her body sporadically. She's not making eye contact with me, either.

"We need to get you out of those wet clothes," I tell her.

She doesn't respond. Doesn't even meet my gaze.

Pushing back the guilt, I decide to fall back on anger. It's an easier emotion to process for me. Roughly, I start pulling off her wet top.

I expect her to resist. That's the whole point of trying to undress her myself. I'd hoped for some sign of life.

But she just sits there and lets me strip her.

My growl deepens. Once her top is off, I pull her down off the table and start undoing her jeans. They're harder to take off and she doesn't make any effort to help me.

But in the end, I manage.

I have to squat down again to tug the unforgiving fabric off her ankles. When I look up at her, she's staring down at me with an unknowable expression on her face.

Somehow, it stills me.

I've been moving fast up until this point. I haven't been trying to be patient or gentle. But the look on her face has me slowing down.

I get to my feet and finger the straps of her bra. She trembles again, but this time, I know it has nothing to do with her accident. She lifts her eyes to mine for the first time.

"Phoenix…"

The eye contact is impossibly intense, in contrast to the soft fragility of the way she says my name. It threatens to undo me.

Which is why I break it.

I unhook her bra and rip it off her shoulders. Her breasts spill out and I feast my eyes on them for the first time.

Her pink nipples peak up, hard from the cold water—and maybe from something else, too.

I resist the urge to touch them, to cup them, to suck on them. Instead, I twist my finger into the strap of her panties and pull them off her as well. The whole time, she sits there, allowing me to take liberties with her privacy.

Once she's naked in front of me, I step back.

I look at her body. I don't even pretend that's not what I'm doing.

Then I sweep her wet clothes into my arms and walk over to the washing machine. The moment I've tossed them inside, I start undressing.

I can feel her eyes on me, but I don't turn around. Not until I'm naked, too.

My cock is stiff as a fucking rod, but I make no attempt to hide that fact. I turn around and her eyes fall directly onto my hardness. Her chest rises and falls with faster, deeper breaths. And her legs tighten, as though she's trying to tamp down her lust.

I remember vividly the night we'd fucked. There was something closed off, reserved about her. Every moan and gasp I'd wrested from her mouth felt like a victory.

I wonder if it would feel the same now.

What if I were to bend her over on that table and take her?

What if I forced her to kneel in front of me and take my cock?

Would she moan like she had the first time? Would she allow herself to lose control? Or would I have to fuck that self-consciousness right out of her?

I walk to the wicker cabinet in the corner next to the dryers and look through the small bounty of clothes there. I find a pair of sweatpants with a drawstring. Then I pluck out a dark blue t-shirt and walk back to her.

Her eyes watch me as though I'm some deadly predator. Maybe in her eyes, I am.

But there's new curiosity in her expression now. A thirst to know more.

She's still dripping wet, and she's made no attempt to dry herself, so I put the clothes aside and grab the towel. I'm intensely aware that we're both stark naked. But I'm in no hurry to change that just yet.

Elyssa stiffens as I bring the towel to her body and start wiping her down. Every time she thinks I'm not looking, she watches me unblinkingly.

I can still feel her gaze, though, hot and piercing against my skin. My cock jumps accordingly.

"Enjoying the view?"

She jumps at the first words either of us have spoken in minutes. A blush rips through her cheeks, too bright and sudden for her to hide it.

"I… I…"

I smirk. She just blushes a deeper scarlet.

"You're hard," she points out in a tremulous voice. It's as though she wants to remind me that she's not the only one here who's aroused by the situation.

"I am," I reply without hesitation.

I look at her with raised eyebrows, refusing to be ashamed of my body or my needs. She meets my gaze with another blush, and for the first time, she reaches for the clothes next to her.

I step back and allow her to get dressed. My eyes stay glued to her ass as she lifts one foot into each leg. The pants are so big that they barely stay on her. She has to tie a tight knot to keep them on.

Finally, when she reaches for the t-shirt, I decide to get dressed myself. I pull on my own sweats, but I don't immediately reach for my t-shirt.

Her voice stops me. "Thank you."

It's soft and uncertain, but I can hear the sincerity in her words.

"Swimming is a necessary survival skill, you know," I say. "You need to learn."

"I had no one to teach me."

"That's no excuse."

Her brow knots together, but she doesn't turn away from me. With my nakedness shielded from view, she can focus on other things. Unfortunately, I can't say the same for myself. My cock strains against my sweats, riled up and desperate to bury itself between her legs. I push down the desire, annoyed at my baser instincts.

She seems fascinated by my tattoos. Her eyes linger on one in particular. "That's beautiful," she says, pointing to the intertwined angel wings over my right pec. "What does it mean?"

I freeze. Of all my fucking tattoos, she had to go and ask about that one.

"That's none of your business," I snap harshly.

The atmosphere splinters like glass and her eyes turn distant immediately. And because I don't want to see the hurt in her, I do what I do best: I push more distance between us.

"Go to your room," I order. "And try not to trip and fall down the stairs while you're at it."

She doesn't say a word. I can feel her looking at me, wondering if I'll retract my harshness. If I'll show her the side of me she's so desperate to find again.

I give her nothing.

A moment later, she turns and walks out of the room.

Sighing with frustration, I bring my closed fist down on the table. The swirl of the washing machine masks the sound of the thin wood splintering.

I stand there for a long time after she's gone, listening to the chugging and swish of the machines. My cock is still pulsing with need. And my head is filled with images of Elyssa.

I can't seem to unsee her breasts, taut and perky. I can't seem to push out the image of her glistening pussy.

I free my erection from my pants. My hand falls around the shaft of my cock and I start pumping aggressively.

I try to masturbate the images out of my head. But it has the opposite effect.

With each pump, I can feel her sliding slowly underneath my skin. Lodging herself within me. Refusing to budge.

23

ELYSSA
ONE DAY LATER

It's been almost twenty-four hours and I still haven't told Charity what happened yesterday. Probably because I don't even know how to explain it to myself.

"Why are you dressed like that?" she'd asked the moment I'd walked back into the room.

I'd stalled by reaching for Theo, who was wide awake and irritable. By the time I'd managed to quieten him down, the answer had formulated in my head.

And by "answer," what I mean is "lie."

"I… fell into the pool."

"You did what?" she cackled. "C'mon, you're messing with me."

"I tripped, okay? It's not a big deal."

"You can't swim," Charity pointed out, as if I wasn't aware of that fact.

"I fell into the shallow end," I'd lied. It had come out so smoothly that I surprised even myself. "One of the maids gave me these."

Charity asked me a couple more questions and dropped it. I'd never been more thankful. Putting what had happened between Phoenix and me into words was... impossible, to say the least. The twenty-four hours of overanalyzing that followed did not get me any closer to finding my sense of equilibrium.

"You okay?"

I glance up at Charity as she walks out of the bathroom. She's got a towel tucked around her chest and another one wrapped around her hair like a fluffy turban.

I'm sitting cross-legged on the bed with Theo lying in front of me. His feet pedal in the air. "I'm fine."

"Because you seem a little off." She comes to the bed and sits on the edge, facing me. "Do you think that's his shirt?" she asks abruptly, eyeing the t-shirt I'm still wearing from yesterday.

I never actually took it off. I glance down, pretending to be oblivious. "What do you mean?"

"Come on, Lys. It must be, right?" Charity asks. "It's definitely big enough."

"I have no clue."

"Does it smell like him?"

"How would I know what he smells like?"

Charity gives me a mischievous grin. "'Cause sometimes you look like you want to breathe him in. Like a giant chocolate cake."

I roll my eyes, mostly to cover up the blush racing across my face. "Stop it, for the love of God, I'm begging you."

"Did you speak to him at all yesterday?"

"No. I told you, he was dealing with Murray, and he ordered me to leave. So I did."

It's the version I gave Charity yesterday. I feel horrible for lying to her, but what's the alternative? I can't exactly tell her that Phoenix and I were fighting when I fell into the pool. That he saved me, carried me inside the house, undressed me, stripped naked himself, and wiped me down.

It sounds...

Well, it sounds like a fantasy. Every bit as ridiculous as the ones I've concocted in my head over the last year.

Except that my fantasies were never able to do justice to the near perfection of Phoenix's body. Or the way his V-shaped abs drew my eyes relentlessly down towards...

"Seriously, Elyssa," Charity says, snapping her fingers in front of my dazed face, "are you sure you're okay?"

I try really hard to focus. "I'm okay," I say with a firm nod. "I just... I don't know. I'm worried about us."

"Stop being a mom for five minutes," she complains. "Just enjoy this." She gestures to our luxurious room.

I take the chance to check her out. She hates when I baby or fuss over her. But this time is worse than ever before. Her face is still pretty bruised up. At least she can open her injured eye now and the swelling around the left side of her cheek has gone down. She's starting to resemble herself again.

"As pretty as it is, I'm kinda sick of this room, though," Charity declares. "I wanna go exploring."

I tense immediately. "Maybe we should just stick to the room," I say. "Every time I leave it, something weird happens."

"Like the man in the window telling you to run?"

"Exactly like that."

Before she can keep talking, there's a knock on the door.

I bolt upright and Charity stares at me with raised eyebrows. "Expecting someone?" she asks suspiciously.

"No," I say, cursing my own inability to stay cool. "I'm just jumpy today."

"Understatement of the year," Charity drawls, walking to the door.

I half expect to see Phoenix standing on the other side. But it's only Anna. I definitely feel relief, but there's a fair amount of disappointment, too.

"Good morning, ladies," Anna says with a muted smile. "May I come in?"

"Of course," Charity says, though "unenthusiastic" doesn't even begin to cover it. "What's up?"

"Master Phoenix wanted me to inform you that a car will be waiting outside for you in thirty minutes."

Charity's expression crumples up instantly. I feel my stomach drop. Does this have anything to do with what happened yesterday?

Charity snarls, "If he wants to kick us out, tell him to at least have the decency to come up here and do it himself."

I hastily arrange a bunch of pillows around Theo, barricading him on the bed so he doesn't fall, before running to Charity's side.

"Charity!"

"No, I'm serious. He can't just—"

"He's not kicking you out," Anna interrupts.

"I... what?" Charity falters.

Anna gives us both a patient smile. "He's not kicking you out. He's sending you both on a shopping spree."

Charity and I exchange a dumbfounded look. "Um... can you say that again?" she asks.

Anna nods. "He realizes that you don't have very many personal possessions with you, so he's sending you out—with a security detail, of course—to get whatever you need." When neither of us say anything, she adds, "It's all on him, by the way."

Charity's mouth literally falls open. "Are you fucking kidding me right now?"

"Charity!"

"Oh, come on, Elyssa. A shopping spree! When have you ever been on one of those?"

"Maybe we should just stay here," I suggest.

Charity turns on me with a wild look in her eye. "I've had enough of you dragging your feet on this," she says. "Even if you don't want the gift, I do. So suck it up and come with me."

Sighing, I nod, knowing this is a fight I'm not going to win. "Fine."

"Excellent," Charity says, clapping her hands together. "I'm gonna go get dressed."

She runs into the bathroom, leaving me alone with Anna.

"I'd be happy to take care of the little one while you're out today, Miss Elyssa," the housekeeper says hopefully.

I raise my eyebrows and glance back over my shoulder at Theo. His chubby little legs are still pedaling lazily above the pillow barricade I erected around him.

"I don't know, Anna. I haven't really left him before."

"Well, then, it's about time you did, don't you think?" she suggests. "You need time for yourself, too, darling."

As nerve-wracking as leaving him makes me feel, I do recognize the need for a day of freedom. "Okay," I admit. "Maybe it's not such a bad idea."

"I'll take good care of him."

"But if anything goes wrong, I don't have a cell you can contact me on," I realize.

"Don't worry, dear. I have the numbers of all the men who are accompanying you two," Anna reassures me. "I'll just call one of them."

"All of the men who are accompanying us," Charity repeats, rushing out of the bathroom in jeans and a simple red halter top. "How many are there? And are they cute?"

I roll my eyes. "Just answer the first question."

"Actually, I'd rather you answer the second one. It's way more important."

Anna looks between us with a fond expression. "You'll be accompanied by two guards. Both of whom are reasonably attractive, in this old lady's opinion."

"I can live with that," Charity quips. "Elyssa, can you get a move on, please?"

I head into the bathroom and change into jeans and a tight black t-shirt. I keep my blonde hair loose and forgo makeup entirely. But when I walk out again, I do start to feel the buzz of excitement.

Anna's already got Theo in her arms and she's cooing to him softly.

"Ready for your day out, Mama?" Charity winks at me.

Taking a deep breath, I walk to Anna and plant a soft kiss on Theo's forehead. "You'll let me know if anything comes up?" I ask her.

"Of course, dear."

I nod. "Thanks, Anna."

"Just go and enjoy your day. All will be well with the little one."

Charity hooks her arm with mine and drags me out of the room and down the stairs. When we exit the house through the main door, there's a big black sedan waiting for us.

Two suited security guys stand in front of the vehicle. Both look like Secret Service agents, and true to Anna's word, both are definitely attractive.

"Yummy," Charity mumbles. "Dibs on the blonde."

I giggle. "You can have them both."

"Oh right, I forgot: you've got your eyes on the big dog." I glare at her, and she gives me a carefree giggle. "I'm just kidding. Lighten up, girl. It's not every day we get to be Julia Roberts."

"Julia Roberts? What does she have to do with this?"

"*Pretty Woman*, remember?" Charity reminds me.

"Is that the movie with Hugh Grant?"

"No! That's *Notting Hill*. You are hopeless."

She basically shoves me into the backseat of the vehicle. Just as I'm getting in, I feel eyes on my back. I turn quickly in my seat and stare out the window, but the black tint doesn't really give me much of a view.

I do notice a silhouette in the far-right corner of the house. But before I can roll down the windows, it's gone.

When we're both in the car, the doors lock and one of the guards twists around in his seat to hand Charity a piece of paper.

"Those are the locations we're approved to take you," he says without a hint of emotion in his voice. "Where to first?"

Charity sidles closer to me so I can see the approved list. "Fuck me, there's a bunch of really fancy department stores on here," she says.

"And restaurants. Ooh… and a salon!" Her eyes light up as she looks at the guard in the passenger seat. "The salon first, please," she says, before turning to me. "You're okay with that, right?"

"Do I even have a choice?"

She gives me a wink. "You're a doll. Trust me, we could both use a nice facial. Then we'll be all set to start the shopping spree."

"Does it have to be a spree?" I ask reluctantly.

"Yes, it absolutely does," she snaps. "And stop dragging your feet. You're gonna ruin the whole experience."

I swallow my worries and try to live in the moment. Like Charity. It's amazing how she can be excited about something like shopping after everything she's been through.

Some people might consider it fickle. But I recognize the strength in it.

It's easy to be defeated when you're dealt a bad hand. The harder option is to choose to remain positive after being beaten down time and time again.

So for Charity's sake, I vow to be as bright and cooperative as possible.

For as long as this fever dream lasts.

∼

The salon we're taken to is definitely high-end. It even smells expensive.

I'm intimidated as I walk in behind Charity, but the women behind the black marble counter take one look at our security guards and their expressions transform from snobby to welcoming.

I marvel at the sprawling arrangements of roses dotting the entire salon. They're pure white and almost as big as my face. We're shown to two large comfy black chairs in the middle of the salon. Charity and I sit down side by side. The staff comes swirling forward with trays of hot coffee and a selection of bite-sized biscuits, followed closely by a pair of grinning stylists.

"I could get used to this," Charity murmurs as her hair stylist steps forward. He's a tall, lanky man with bright blue hair that somehow manages to avoid looking tacky. He's wearing a deep V neck shirt that falls to his middle chest, showing off the dozens of silver chains around his neck. He looks too cool for this world. Perfect for Charity.

My stylist isn't nearly as striking, but she does seem friendlier. "Hello, ladies," she greets. "I'm Hannah and this is Louis. What would you ladies like?"

"A cut and color," Charity says immediately. "I want some bronze and blonde highlights. And maybe a couple of inches shorter."

She doesn't hesitate. Neither does her stylist. He starts pulling out instruments from a small cupboard on wheels.

"And you?" Hannah asks.

I stare at my reflection in the mirror. My eyes are wide and uncertain. My body is stiff and uncomfortable. I look like I don't belong. And I feel it keenly.

"I... I'm not really sure."

Hannah studies my hair. "You've got lovely hair, and the color is naturally highlighted. But you've got a lot of split ends."

"Split ends?"

"Nothing a trim won't fix. I can also give you the keratin package. It's a protein-infused treatment that helps revitalize your hair."

I glance towards Charity, silently asking for help, but she's got her eyes closed and her head tilted back.

"I think just a haircut for now."

"Sure. And how about a facial afterwards?" Hannah presses. "You'll feel like Cinderella by the time I'm done with you."

Feeling flustered, I do the only thing I can do: nod and play along.

I spend the next few hours quiet as she works on my hair then my face.

There are moments when I feel relaxed and pampered. But there are equally as many moments when I feel claustrophobic. Like this is all a setup and something terrible is bound to happen at any moment.

When my facial is done, I practically jump out of my chair. "Thanks."

Hannah gives me an appraising smile. "Aren't you a beauty!"

I turn to the mirror and stop short when I see my reflection. The haircut and blow dry has done wonders to frame my face. My hair already looks healthier. And the facial has cleared up my skin quite a bit.

"Damn, girl, that haircut's really working for you."

I turn to Charity as she walks in from the next room where she'd been having her own facial. Her hair is a few inches shorter and bouncier because of it. Her highlights are subtle but effective. Even her face looks so much clearer, just like mine. As if the bruises have been cleaned away.

"You look great."

"I know, right?" she says, with a contented nod. "I didn't actually get the facial."

"Why not?"

"Because my face still hurts like a bitch," she says. "So they gave me a makeover of sorts."

"Is that why I can't really see your bruises anymore?"

"Makeup can work wonders," she says with a wink. She turns to the mirror and checks herself out. "They're covered over with foundation. But at least I can't really see them anymore."

I know what she means—that she's not going to be reminded of them every time she looks in a mirror. That, like me, she can forget the pain of her past.

If only for a little while.

"Okay," Charity says, clapping her hands together. "How about we get breakfast and then start shopping?"

My stomach is definitely in agreement, so I nod. As we exit the salon, I notice one of our guards handing Hannah a black credit card.

"Damn," Charity mutters, grabbing my arm.

"What?"

"I've seen those cards before. They're freaking amazing. They don't even have limits. This is going to be a great day."

I'm not sure how I feel about spending Phoenix's money. I have no claim to it. And it feels wrong to pretend like I do.

But maybe, for once in my life, I've actually gotten lucky. I ought to try to enjoy it.

Once we're in the car again, Charity picks a bistro from the approved list of restaurants on our list. We're whisked away, and what feels like moments later, we're being seated at the best table and served endless dishes. One of everything—stuffed croissants, towering stacks of French toast dripping with syrup and dusted with white sugar, benedicts, quiches, and a frittata the size of Theo. I eat until I feel like a beached whale.

After that, it's a blur of department stores and stylists and more clothes than I've ever seen in my life. The guards accompanying us stagger out of each boutique and load dozens of bags into the trunk of the car.

Hours later, I'm both exhausted and missing my son. But Charity's in no hurry to go back.

She's got twice as many bags as I have, and I only have that many because she basically threatened me until I'd made some purchases.

"I don't know where I'd wear some of these things," I had argued.

"Not the point. Just buy them."

So I did. Because I'm a pushover, I guess. And apparently, shopping takes the fight right out of me.

At six-thirty, Charity finally turns to me and nods. "I think we should call it a day."

"Thank God," I breathe.

We head back towards our ride, only to find another identical black jeep parked right behind it.

"What's going on?" I ask, looking at our driver. "Why are there two cars now?"

"We've been sent instructions to take Miss Charity back to the mansion," he replies. "And you, Miss Elyssa, are to be driven to a restaurant downtown."

Charity and I exchange a glance. "By whose orders?" she asks.

But I already know.

"The boss," the driver answers curtly. "Let's go."

"Wow," Charity remarks. "Looks like you're getting the deluxe princess treatment."

I turn to the guards, who are waiting anxiously for us to get into the jeeps. "I'm not interested in going anywhere else today."

Charity grabs my arm. "Elyssa, don't be silly. You should go."

"But…"

"No buts. Just do it. I'll go back and take care of Theo."

Sighing, I glance back at the driver. He looks right back at me as if to say, *You don't have much of a choice in this anyway.* But then, I knew that already.

Sighing, I give Charity a hug and climb into the second jeep.

∼

It's a lonely drive to the restaurant. But when the vehicle comes to a stop, I gasp in shock.

The name above the marquee is written in a flowing gold script. The place is elegance personified. Gold and velvet everywhere, plate-glass windows polished to within an inch of their life. It screams class.

And when I catch sight of my reflection, I realize I'm screaming "tired and poor."

Gulping, I look down at my jeans and t-shirt combo, feeling intensely out of place as I walk forward uncertainly. I should've changed into one of my new outfits. Too late for that now.

At the guard's gesture, I enter the restaurant. Apart from the maître d' and the waitresses—all of whom are dressed in fancy black coats—I'm the only other customer in there.

"Good evening, madam," the maître d' says, bowing low. "We are delighted to host you this evening."

"Oh, uh, thanks…"

"I am obligated to inform you, however, that we do have a dress code."

My cheeks blaze with embarrassment. "I'm sorry. I wasn't prepared. I didn't know I was coming here tonight. I'll just go—"

"I assume you bought clothes while you were out today?" comes a familiar voice from behind me.

I whirl around.

Phoenix is standing in the high archway that leads to the main restaurant. He's wearing black dress pants and a crisp white shirt with an open collar.

He looks… incredible.

"Did you?" he asks again.

"Uh, yes…"

"Then I suggest you pick something and change into an appropriate dress," he says. It's not really a suggestion. "There are rooms you can use in the back. William?"

"I will assist her, sir," the maître d' says with another low bow.

Phoenix is about to turn away when I call out to him. "Wait! I don't understand. What is this?"

He raises his eyebrows as though the answer is painfully obvious. "This?" he repeats. "This is exactly what it looks like, Elyssa. We're having dinner."

24

PHOENIX

Even in jeans and a fucking t-shirt, she looks beautiful.

A little annoyed. Very tired.

But beautiful, nonetheless.

Which is probably going to make this night a lot harder. It doesn't matter to me, though. I'm determined to figure her out either way.

There's something she's not telling me. Maybe lots of things. And I need to know what. Especially with the child hanging in the balance.

I take a seat at the table they've arranged especially for us. The restaurant is empty, as per my instructions, and we're seated at the glass windows overlooking the koi pond. A few white swans swim languidly on the dark, glistening water.

I've kept my distance from the boy all this time. He looks like me. Too much like me.

And far too much like Yuri.

The last thing I need is to grow attached. Especially if it turns out that Elyssa is just a beautiful and convincing con artist. It ended in disaster last time, and I swore an oath to myself: never again.

No attachments. No love. No feeling.

Just cold and ruthless vengeance. That's all I live for. That's all I'll ever live for.

She emerges ten minutes later from a door to the side. I try and control my expression, but I feel my pulse rise the moment I lay eyes on her.

She's… fucking gorgeous.

The dress she's wearing is a simple silver slip with thin spaghetti straps. The neckline descends in a smooth V that shows off a hint of cleavage. The hemline is modest, falling to mid-calf.

But there's nothing modest about the shoes she's got on. High heeled stilettos in a luxurious black leather.

Only her shoulders are bare for me to see. And yet, she manages to look like sex walking.

Her blonde hair floats buoyantly as she makes her way toward the table with William walking behind her like he's escorting a princess.

I stand when she approaches. Her eyebrows hit the ceiling. The fact that she thinks chivalry is beneath me is somewhat amusing, so I shrug off the implied insult.

Let her think I'm a brute. I don't give a fuck what she thinks of me, really.

It's what I think of her that determines what happens next.

William pulls out the opposite chair and she slips into it gracefully. I notice that she's trying very hard to avoid my eyes.

"I'll bring the menus in a moment, sir," William says graciously.

"*Spasibo*, William," I growl in Russian.

As soon as he walks away, I turn my attention on Elyssa. She's wringing her hands together nervously and biting her lip at the same time.

She doesn't just look out of place in this luxurious restaurant. She looks out of place in her own skin.

"What would you like to drink?" I ask.

She jumps at the rasp of my voice, though she tries not to let me see it. "Water's fine."

"Water it is. I like your dress."

Instantly, her cheeks blush red. "Charity forced me to get it. I thought it was… too much."

"It's exactly enough."

The blush gets deeper. "I don't have any place to wear it."

"You're wearing it now," I point out.

"This is the first and last time I'll ever be in a restaurant this fancy," she says, her gaze flickering over the swans outside the window.

"Never say never."

When she takes a breath, I realize how hard she's trying to compose herself. "What is this?" she blurts, cutting to the chase. "And don't just say 'dinner.'"

"But that's precisely what it is."

She eyes me suspiciously. But I don't miss the fascination in her gaze. She's curious about me. More so than she wants to be.

"No," she retorts, her voice getting less shaky. "It's something else. There's an ulterior motive here."

I smile and spread my hands. "You're looking for something that's not there, *krasotka*."

"I know what you think of me," she continues.

I chuckle. "Somehow, I doubt that, little lamb. I doubt that very much." I wave my hand at her and add, "But go on. Tell me what you think I'm thinking. Tell me everything."

She shivers, the blond hairs on her arms prickling up despite the warmth in the room. She eyes me warily for a moment, then sets her jaw and straightens up.

Brave little kiska, I think. *You've got fire in you after all.*

"You think I'm some naïve, empty-headed idiot. Or you think I'm a lying, scheming spy. Honestly, I don't know which is worse."

It's the closest she's come to a full-on outburst. This time, I'm the one who's fascinated. I have to bite back my grin.

When I say nothing, she says, "Well? Are you going to answer me?"

"I didn't hear a question in there."

"Fine. Why did you invite me here?"

"Because yesterday, things got out of hand."

She tenses. "Yesterday…"

"But," I continue, "it's nothing that can't be solved with a simple, honest conversation."

She flinches subtly at the word "honest." My intrigue only grows.

William reappears with a flourish before she can figure out how to reply. "Two menus for the master and the young lady. Can I interest either of you in some wine? We have a wonderful selection this evening."

"No wine tonight," I answer without ever taking my eyes off Elyssa. "But some champagne would be lovely."

William bows, then walks away. Elyssa watches him go in disbelief. "You come here often?" she asks when we're alone again.

I shrug. "Not as often as I'd like."

"What does that mean?"

"It means I'm busy."

"Busy doing what?"

"Busy running an empire." I jut my chin at her menu. "They have an extensive selection. You should start deciding now."

She shakes her head. "Places like this... I wouldn't know what to order."

Something about her voice catches my attention. It's not just inexperience or intimidation, although both of those things are definitely present. It's a kind of untouched purity I've never seen in my entire life.

I lean forward and prop my elbows up on the table. "Where are you from, *krasotka*?"

"I'm from Washington. A little town outside of—"

"*Fignya*." My word slices through her rehearsed jumble.

She blinks in confusion. "What?"

"Bullshit. Lies. Tell me the truth, Elyssa. I won't settle for anything less."

I watch as the knot in her throat rides up and down with a nervous swallow. She has her hands clasped tightly in front of her, as if to stop them from shaking.

Then, to my surprise, she closes her eyes and shudders. When she opens them again, she's got a stony look. Like she exposed herself for a moment, but she's now retreated back to safety behind her castle walls.

"I'd like you to order for both of us, please," she says quietly. "If you don't mind."

I study her expression for a long moment. So many mysteries here. I want to crack them all open with my bare hands.

In due time, I tell myself. *It'll come.*

William reappears a moment later with a bottle of Dom Perignon Rose Gold.

"The seafood prix fixe, William," I request as he uncorks the bottle and fills our glasses. "All five courses."

"Of course, sir. Right away." He smiles, bows, and disappears again.

"Five courses?" Elyssa balks. "Isn't that a little… extravagant?"

I stare at her without blinking. "Precisely."

She breaks off the intense eye contact and looks out the window. I notice her light up a little as a swan glides by. She's trying hard to hide her enthusiasm every time she notices something new, something unfamiliar, something dazzling.

But she's failing miserably.

It's hard to believe that this woman could be a spy. She wears her heart on her sleeve.

When she turns and catches me still staring, she drops her gaze as her cheeks go red yet again. I wonder if she's this affected by every man's attention—or if it's just mine that rattles her.

"Why do you keep looking at me?" she asks meekly.

"Because you keep trying to disappear," I answer. "But if that's your goal, you should have picked a different dress."

She controls the blush this time, to my mild disappointment. But I don't miss the flicker of worry that shadows her eyes.

The first course arrives quickly. It's the beginning of one of the best tasting menus I've ever eaten. An army of servers comes bearing gilded plates that emanate mouth-watering scents like nothing else in this world.

Crab and oyster bisque to start. Rich, truffle-accented, but smooth enough to guzzle straight from a glass if I wanted to.

Then comes butterflied avocados, stuffed with butter-poached prawns in a light, savory cream sauce.

The main course is lobster with foie gras and caviar. William informs us that it was caught that morning off the coast of Maine and flown directly to the restaurant by private jet. Elyssa looks at him like he's speaking an alien language.

When the fourth course hits the table, Elyssa looks at the rich chocolate mousse with reluctant longing.

"What's that on top?" she asks, poking at it tentatively with a fork.

"Gold leaf."

"It's… it's not actual gold, is it?"

The moment she asks the question, I can tell she regrets it. I don't laugh, though. I don't want to humiliate her—not like this. What I want is to crack her open like an eggshell and see what secrets are lying inside.

"Never mind," she mutters. "That was a stupid question."

It's fucking annoying how damn endearing she is. How pure.

She picks up her spoon, hesitates, and then sets it down again.

"What's wrong?" I ask.

"I try not to eat too many desserts," she admits. She seems embarrassed as soon as the words leave her mouth.

"Why?"

She shrugs her delicate shoulders. I have the urge to hurl the table aside and run my lips down her neck and all the way down to her breasts.

"Um, well… I don't want to gain weight."

I almost choke on a bite of mousse. "Come again?"

"I want—or, I mean, I was taught—to keep my figure for…"

She trails off. I'm immediately invested in her answer. "Please don't tell me that sentence ends with 'husband,'" I drawl.

She looks incredibly embarrassed, but she doesn't deny it. "I know it sounds crazy. It was just… how I was raised."

Interesting.

"That's a ridiculous notion," I tell her. "Life is short for damn near everyone. And even if you're lucky enough to get a long way, it's a fucking shit show."

I get the predictable flinch I'm expecting.

"Let me guess: you were raised not to swear, either."

She narrows her eyes at me. "Why am I here, Phoenix?" she asks in a tone that finally has a little more fight in it.

There we go, krasotka. *Push back. Show me your cards.*

"I've been thinking about your request that I help support you with your son."

Her expression crumples. "He's your son, too."

I tighten my fist in my lap. "That remains to be seen."

"Why would I lie?"

I raise one eyebrow. "For exactly this," I say, gesturing around the restaurant.

Her spoon hits the plate with a clatter. She pushes herself away from the table instantly. "You're accusing me of extortion? You think I'm some… some… gold digger?" She says the word like it's poison.

"Not if the child is really mine."

"You're a brute."

I can't help but smile at the conservative word. "Oh, *krasotka*…" I murmur.

"Stop it!" she snaps, raising her voice for the first time all evening.

"Stop what?"

"Stop calling me that. Stop looking at me like… like I'm broken."

That gives me pause. An unexpected answer. "That's what you think I'm doing?"

"That's exactly what you're doing. I'm not stupid. It's how the whole world has looked at me ever since I left home. It's almost enough to make me wish I never left."

"You don't mean that."

"How do you know?" she asks defensively.

"Because you're not a good liar."

"Oh? Then why are you so convinced I'm a spy?"

I smile. "Touché."

"Are we done here?" she asks. She sounds bitter, angry. Desperate to be anywhere but here.

Too bad I have no intention of letting her go.

"Not quite." I gesture for one of my security guards to come forward from where he's standing in the shadows.

Elyssa glances back over her shoulder as Mika approaches with a huge duffel bag. He sets it down next to me and walks back to his spot without saying a word.

"What's that?" she asks, looking nervously back and forth between the bag and Mika's retreating form.

"A game," I say simply. "Look at me."

She does, and I feel a sharp pang of tension shoot through my cock at the way she obeys me so automatically—and then how she stiffens up when she realizes what she's done. What she's revealed.

"I don't want to play a game," she mutters.

I ignore that. "Let's start easy. What is your name?"

She frowns. "I said I don't want to play."

I bend down and unzip the duffel. Then I pull out a thin stack of cash and set it down on the table between us.

Her eyes go wide with shock as she stares at the money. Then her gaze moves slowly to meet mine. "What are you doing?"

"The question is, what are you going to do?" I ask. "Answering my questions will earn you what's in this duffel. Refuse, and the money goes back in."

She shakes her head. "You're trying to buy answers from me."

"Wrong. I want answers. You want to care for your son. What we have here is simply an exchange of desires. Money lets that happen."

She grits her teeth. I can see the conflict rage in her eyes. She wants to be able to be able to flip me off and walk out of here.

But she needs what I have to offer.

On some level, I know this is cruel. I've never made anyone else jump through these hoops when they needed help. But this woman... she's different. I want to help her. But I also want to make her squirm.

"Fine," she says at last. "My name is Elyssa Jane Redmond."

I slide the wad of cash across the tablecloth towards her. She doesn't glance at it, though. She keeps her eyes fixed on me.

"Next question. Do you have any siblings?"

"No. I'm an only child."

I offer her another wad of cash. "Where did you grow up?"

"In the middle of the desert, just outside Las Vegas."

That gives me pause. "Right outside Las Vegas."

"That's what I just said."

"And the night we met, was that the first time you've ever been in the city?"

She sighs. "Yes."

"Why?"

"Because I couldn't stay at home anymore."

"Why not?"

She has the body language of a trapped animal. Knee bouncing, hands twitching, eyes darting around the restaurant as though she's expecting someone to burst through the glass at any moment.

Finally, her gaze settles back on me. "It wasn't the life I wanted anymore," she offers quietly.

She's holding back—that much is obvious. Her answers are deliberately vague, as if she's practiced how much she can say without saying anything at all. That's not good enough for me. Not by a long shot.

"Why were you in a wedding dress?"

Her mouth falls open for a moment, before snapping shut again. She gives a tiny shake of her head. As if to say, *No, you can't ask that.*

It makes me want to pin her against the wall by her throat and show her that I can do anything I fucking want.

I raise another wad of dollar bills. "Are you done playing?"

She eyes the money sadly. Like she knows she can't refuse it no matter how badly she wants to do exactly that. "I can't fully remember what happened that night."

I search her face but can't quite suss out a lie. Maybe there isn't one to catch. I decide not to interrupt her because she's still talking.

"… Everything is hazy. All I remember is that I needed to run. If I stayed, I'd be trapped."

Trapped. The word carries weight. Carries stories. Something tells me they're not the kind of stories that come with a happy ending.

"Who was the man who you were meant to be marrying?" I ask.

She cringes and her eyes fall into her lap. "His name was Josiah," she says softly.

"You ran because you didn't want to marry him?"

She looks down at her chocolate mousse, still untouched except for the tiny divot her fork left when she scratched at the gold leaf. Her eyes are shimmery. But with what—tears? Memories? Both? Neither?

"Maybe once upon a time, I thought I did," she says.

I let those words hang between us. We've gone around and around in circles without progressing much of anywhere.

"Why do you even care?" she snaps suddenly before I can settle on my next move. "Why do you care who my parents are or if I have siblings? Why do you care where I'm from? Who I was or wasn't supposed to marry? Why do you care about anything?"

"Information is power," I answer simply.

She nods sadly. "Charity told me that, too. The night we met, actually."

"She was right. Tell me about your parents."

She frowns again, confused by the sudden lurch from topic to topic. "What do you want to know?"

"Whatever you decide to tell me," I say with a shrug. "But I want real information. Not this evasive shit you've been doing all night. Give me something I can believe in, Elyssa Jane Redmond."

She lets that sink in for a moment. Then she starts to speak. Though she still refuses to look at me.

"My father was a quiet man. He never spoke much. He was always in some corner of the house, whittling away at any scrap of wood he could find. Mama was the same. Quiet. Obedient. We went to… to church a lot. And school. And… and…"

I'm surprised to hear her voice catch and notice a single tear splash down to muddle the gold leaf on top of her dessert. She raises her eyes to look at me finally. More tears cling to her eyelashes stubbornly.

"I haven't thought about them in so long," she whispers. "I've forced myself to forget so much."

"Forget what?"

She shrugs. "The way they lived their lives. The way they taught me to live mine."

"They wanted you to get married and be a good, obedient wife?"

Elyssa nods.

"And what did you want?"

She hesitates. "I wanted what they wanted. I couldn't fathom anything different. It was how life was with them. With everyone there."

This place Elyssa grew up in, it's starting to sound less like a town and more like a cult. The desert is full of them. Creepy communes of deluded people who think they can purify their way to salvation.

They're wrong, every last one of them.

Salvation doesn't fucking exist.

I'm reluctant to use the word "cult" out loud, though. She's finally talking, and I don't want to do anything that will shut her down again.

"The man you mentioned you were going to marry, Josiah… Was this an arranged marriage?"

The words sound strange coming out of my mouth, but I have a strong feeling I'm right on this one.

She looks at me guiltily. "I agreed to it."

Fucking hell. "Why?"

"Because he was a good man. And because he'd helped my family out so many times. And because… because I was told it was what was best for me."

"Clearly, you disagreed," I point out.

I notice a tremor run along her body.

"You know, it can be hard to change behavior after a lifetime of conformity," I tell her. "But there's no time like the present to start."

I glance down at her dessert pointedly. She does the same.

After a quiet moment of contemplation, she picks her spoon up and takes a mouthful of the silky chocolate mousse.

"Oh my God…" she sighs as it hits her tongue.

"Good?"

"That's the best thing I've ever put in my mouth."

I have a sudden image of my cock sliding slowly down her throat. I tense as I try to stop my erection in its tracks. But it's a fucking lost cause. One look at Elyssa's full pink lips and all I want to do is take her right here on this table.

Somehow, I manage to control myself. It helps that one bite of the mousse is all she takes.

It's enough, though. It's progress.

I don't throw any more questions at her. She deserves this moment to enjoy a piece of something that had been denied her for so long.

When our meal is over, everything is cleared away by silent waiters. My erection is still throbbing painfully behind my zipper.

Which is exactly why I need to end the night now.

I scrape my chair backwards as I rise. She watches me with curious eyes. "We're leaving?"

"Yes."

"But I never got to ask you any questions."

"This night wasn't meant to be about me."

"Did you get what you wanted?" she asks.

I stare at those big brown doe eyes as my body aches with desire. Then I shake my head. "No, *krasotka*. Not even close."

25

PHOENIX

She's quiet on the ride back to the mansion. Her hands are resting on her lap, though I notice her fingertips twitching nervously every few seconds.

I could have pushed our little game. I could have gotten more from her.

But something in her face made me stop.

It's not in my nature to stop, especially when I know I'm making headway. But with Elyssa, I find myself ignoring my usual way of doing things.

Slowly, her head turns towards me, and I feel her gaze searching my face. "Who are you?" she asks suddenly, as though it's only just occurred to her to ask.

"Me?"

"No, the other guy in the car with us," she retorts sarcastically. "Yes, you."

I turn and look at her somberly. "I'm the guy bad guys are afraid of."

She holds my gaze for a second before she looks down. "And what about me? Should I be scared of you?"

"If you're smart."

She looks out at the windshield but I can tell she's not actually watching the road. There's something melancholy about her demeanor now.

Hearing her talk about her parents was illuminating. The fact that she's not as worldly as other women her age also makes sense. She's lived her life in seclusion, in a controlled environment that never gave her the chance to discover what she wanted in life. She doesn't know who she was, who she is, who she might one day want to become.

All she knows is what they taught her.

"You've never gotten in touch with your parents since leaving?" I ask.

She stiffens but doesn't look back at me. I half-expect her to dodge the question. "No. Never."

"Not even when you found out you were pregnant?"

"I thought about it once," she admits. "But… no. Even if the circumstances had been different, they would have been disappointed in me."

"What circumstances are those?" I ask.

She shrugs. "Just… the way I left."

"You didn't say goodbye?"

"Not exactly."

I keep thinking about the blood caked under her fingernails the night we'd met. Whose blood was it?

"My mama always wanted to be a grandmother. But not this way."

"Which way is that?"

"I had a child out of wedlock," Elyssa says like it's self-explanatory. "And up until recently, I didn't even know your name. How could I have called and told my mother that?"

"What would she have thought?"

"Nothing good," Elyssa says with a shudder. "Nothing good at all."

"And what did *you* think?" I press.

She clears her throat as if she's fighting the urge to cry. "Honestly? Charity helped me through it. I cried for days when I found out. I didn't think I was ready. I didn't want to have a baby, much less a baby without a husband."

"So what changed your mind?" I ask.

Elyssa gets very still. "I didn't want to be alone," she admits. She glances up at me. "Is that a horrible thing to say? Am I a horrible person for saying it?"

I don't know what to say to her. I certainly don't expect her to look to me for validation. God knows I don't have any fucking answers about what it means to be a parent.

"But that was at the beginning. Everything changed when I felt him kick for the first time. It was like he was trying to comfort me. Every time I got sad or scared, he'd kick inside me, and I'd be reminded that…"

"That you weren't alone," I finish for her.

"Yes. Exactly."

The rest of the drive is silent. When we get back to the mansion, I leave the car parked outside the main door and walk Elyssa into the house. She's got her arms wrapped around her body as though she's trying to comfort herself.

She turns to me when I offer her the small bag of cash that she won tonight. She stares at it, but she makes no attempt to take it. Almost like she thinks I'm about to snatch it away and laugh in her face for being so stupid as to think I'd ever make good on my promise.

"Go on," I urge. "You won it."

"It feels... strange to take it," she admits. She bites her lower lip—another endearing gesture that I refuse to be distracted by.

"Why?"

"Because it feels like you're paying me off."

"I'm not. If I was, there'd be less than half this much money in the bag. Silence is cheap."

She shakes her head. "You have no idea how hard it was for me to ask you for money," she says. "But for my son, for Charity... I'm willing to swallow my pride and ask."

"For Charity?"

"We're more than just friends," Elyssa replies proudly, lovingly. "She's my family. The only family I have left."

"You talk as though you'll never see your family again."

"I don't plan on it."

"Why?"

She looks down at the bag in my hand. "The game is over," she tells me. "And I'm tired."

"Take the money," I say, thrusting it into her arms.

She accepts it without a fight. But there's obvious reluctance in her hazel eyes. Melancholy in there, too—then again, that's been there since the moment I met her.

"Thank you for dinner," she whispers. "For the entire day, actually. I felt like I was someone else today."

"Someone else?"

"Someone normal."

Before I can unpack the weight of that sentence, she turns and walks up the stairs. I can't take my eyes off her ass. The silk of her dress hugs it beautifully. Every switch of her hips makes my cock jump.

Even after she's disappeared around the corner, I still stand there, feeling her presence.

"Fuck," I growl at myself when I'm alone again. "Phoenix, you need to get a fucking grip."

∼

It's late but I know Matvei will be awake.

First, though, I head back to my office. I need to scour through my investigation, try and get my head back in the game. I've been out of focus lately. And I have only Elyssa to blame.

But the moment I enter my office, I know something is not right.

Someone is in here.

"Hi, there."

I turn to find a dark-haired woman standing against my investigative wall. She's wearing shorts and a strappy blouse. And she looks perfectly at home.

"Charity," I growl, relaxing slightly—but not completely.

"Were you about to kill me?" she muses.

"I still might."

She smiles as though the threat means nothing to her. "Before you do, I'd like to talk to you."

"How'd you get in?" I ask, ignoring her previous statement.

She shrugs. "Isn't it obvious? I picked the lock. It's not that elaborate a skill to learn. Comes in handy."

I give the room a quick scan. Nothing seems out of place but that is meaningless. All my files on Astra Tyrannis are right here, in this one room. And I have no idea how long she's been in here snooping.

"This is quite the investigation you've got going," she says, gesturing to the wall behind her without actually looking at it.

Her face is looking much better now. The bruises are well on their way to healing and she's got two functioning eyes. Apparently, it's done wonders to restore her confidence.

"Maybe a tad bit creepy. Definitely obsessive. But thorough."

"I'd watch how you proceed," I tell her, sitting back against my desk as I regard her with cool detachment. "You're on shaky ground."

"So are you," she counters.

I raise my eyebrows. "Is that right?"

Her expression hardens and her eyes turn to flint. I sense a threat coming. But what she says instead takes me by surprise.

"Elyssa is a good person," she says quietly. "And she doesn't deserve to be fucked with."

I narrow my eyes. "What exactly are you trying to tell me?"

"I'm telling you that, if you hurt her, you'll have to deal with me."

"What makes you think I'm going to hurt her?"

"Because that's what men like you do," she says. "You use and discard. But she's not some random hooker. She's not like me. She's... better."

"Better," I repeat. "In what way?"

"In every way! She's the best person I know. And she's a lot stronger than she seems. So I wouldn't be fooled by the big brown eyes if I were you. Don't say I didn't warn you."

"You broke into my office to threaten me about Elyssa?"

"There's no better reason," she says.

"Is that the real reason?" I ask, looking around. "Or just a convenient cover?"

"Listen, I know you don't think much of me," she says with a shrug. "But I don't care. Think of me what you will. I just want Elyssa to be okay."

"You have nothing to worry about as far as I'm concerned."

She looks at me skeptically. A lifetime of distrusting men is swirling in her eyes. I can't really blame her—I'm sure she's seen the worst behavior the male species has to offer.

"What happened yesterday?" she asks abruptly.

"Yesterday?"

"Elyssa came back to the room with wet hair, wearing clothes that clearly belong to you," Charity explains. "She told me she fell into the pool and a maid gave her those clothes. That you had nothing to do with it. But I know Elyssa. I know when she's lying. And I definitely know when she's not telling me something."

I cock my head to the side. "If she hasn't told you, she doesn't want you to know."

"She's got a weird fascination with you," Charity says, as though she's disappointed with Elyssa's short-sightedness. "And I get it. You were the handsome stranger who saved her on the most transformative night of her life. But I think her—let's be nice and call it a 'preoccupation'—is dangerous."

"Why do you think that?"

"Because *you're* dangerous."

"Do I need to remind you that you're the one who wanted to come here with me?"

Her jaw clenches. I realize how scared she must have felt that day to have seized upon me as her lifeline.

"You're Theo's father. I was hoping that might mean something to you. Maybe I was wrong, though."

"What are you saying?"

"That you don't seem very interested in Theo at all. And he deserves better. So does Elyssa. So if you don't want them in your life, give them the means to survive on their own."

"Ah, so that's the real reason you're here. Money."

Her expression darkens, but she doesn't deny it. "Money is security," she says simply. "And this is a man's world. I've done what I could but it never seems to be enough. The deck is stacked against women like Elyssa and me. So yeah, it forces me to break into your office and ask you for money. But surviving is more important than pride. If you'd ever suffered in your life, you'd know that."

Her words are rife with emotion, with sorrow, despite the fact that her face is devoid of it. She's learned to hide her scars from the rest of the world. But men like me know where to look.

"What makes you think I haven't suffered?" I ask, flipping the conversation around.

She looks around melodramatically, gesturing to the walls of the mansion as if it's self-explanatory. "Seriously?"

"Money doesn't equal happiness."

"Says the man with the money," she sighs. "Anyway, I think I've made my point. I'm going back to bed."

"How long were you in my office for?"

"About an hour," she replies. "And yes, I snooped. But don't worry—I have no interest in getting involved in anything that's in this room."

"And I'm just supposed to take your word for it?"

She looks me dead in the eye. "That's exactly what you're supposed to do."

"Give me one good reason why."

She shrugs. "Because I'm not a liar."

I bark out a laugh. "How the hell would I know that?"

"Use your instincts," she says as she sashays to the door. "Trust me: I'm aware that every face on that wall is dangerous. I speak from experience."

"Wait," I command, forcing her to stop in her tracks. "What do you mean?"

"I mean, I've seen some of these guys around Wild Night Blossom. They always use the VIP rooms and when they come to play, the nightclub is closed to everyone else."

Her words set my heartbeat to pounding. I move towards her urgently. "Have you spoken to any of them?"

She looks a little wary now, but she answers. "Just one. That dick over there."

She points squarely at the center of my wall. I feel my breath shorten immediately.

"Hitoshi Sakamoto?" I ask. "Is that who you're pointing to?"

"The Chinese dude?"

"He's Japanese, and yes."

"Then yeah, that's who I'm pointing to."

"Fuck," I growl. *"Khrenoten!"*

"What?" Charity asks. "Have I just helped you crack your case? Because if that's true, I feel like I should be compensated for helping." She gives me a sheepish grin.

I glare at her. "You can go now."

Her eyes flit back to the wall. "How bad is he?" she asks carefully.

My eyes rove over her face, drinking in the fading bruises. "You tell me."

She nods softly like that settles it. Then she turns to leave.

The fact that she's had direct contact with Sakamoto gives me pause. It's just too fucking convenient. Too many coincidences in a row. In my world, there's no such thing as coincidences. There's fate and there's death. Nothing in between.

I walk out of my office, leaving it unlocked for now. I'll improve the lock situation later. Right now, I'm more concerned with this new information.

I head straight to Matvei's room. Dr. Roth prescribed bedrest as the quickest means of recovery. It's only been a few days, but I know Matvei and I know for damn sure he isn't keen on staying still for long.

When I open his door and walk in, relief flushes across his face. "Thank God. I'm bored out of my fucking mind in here."

"You should be sleeping."

"If I were, you wouldn't be able to unload all your problems on me," Matvei points out. "What the fuck has been happening?"

"Like you don't know?"

"I hate getting reports. I'm usually the one doing the reporting."

I smirk, sitting down by his bedside. "Should I have brought you a teddy bear or something? A bouquet of pretty flowers?"

He flips me off. "*Ya sru na tvayu mat*," he snaps.

"Balloons, then?"

"Asshole, tell me why you're here."

He's desperate for news. Desperate to be anywhere other than this room. Desperate to do what he was born to do: crack skulls and make bad men bleed.

"I walked into my office just now. Charity was in there. She picked the lock."

"Fuck me. She's the brunette with the busted-in face?"

I nod. "And the attitude to match."

"If she got into your office, she knows too much."

"I agree."

"Then I'm assuming you took care of her?"

"No."

"No?"

"I can use her."

"For fucking what?" Matvei asks impatiently.

"She recognized Hitoshi Sakamoto from the wall," I tell him. "Apparently, the bruises on her face are courtesy of him."

He whistles. "No fucking way."

"Like I said, she might have information we can use."

He's got his skeptical frown on. "Why was she even with the man?"

"I'll find out. But chances are, she was just working a job. She is a hooker."

"A hooker who found herself with one of the most powerful allies to Astra Tyrannis. That's convenient."

"We don't have proof," I remind him.

"The bastard nearly beat her to death," Matvei argues. "Then, when she escaped, he sent out a stooge in blue to bring her to him. It all checks out."

"It brings us one step closer to finding someone deep into the organization," I say, feeling optimistic for the first time in a while. "Apparently, Wild Night Blossom closes for the public every time high profile mob bosses frequent it. Which means…"

"Sakamoto is part of the crowd those nights."

"Exactly. Or Ozol is."

"You really think Ozol would go back to that club after what happened the last time?"

"Hubris is one trait every mob boss has in common."

"Including you?"

I narrow my eyes at him. "There's a difference between men like him and men like me."

"Forgive me, oh great and fearless don. Mortals like myself cannot possibly grasp the limits of your magnanimity."

I lean in and jab a finger against his wound.

"Oh, fucking hell," he roars. "You bastard!"

Smiling, I get up and turn towards the door. "I know you've got a few more days of bedrest to go. Which is why you're the perfect person to do the grunt work. I'll bring in a bunch of computers for you. I want you to try and see if Sakamoto's movements are trackable."

"Aye aye, Captain Dickhead," he grumbles.

"That's the spirit. Glad you're on the mend, Matvei. The Bratva needs you."

I'm at the door when Matvei calls to me. "Hey, Phoenix?"

"Yeah?"

"Where'd you go dressed up so nice?"

"I…" It's not a question I'm expecting. I'm flustered for just long enough that Matvei notices.

"If you're about to lie to me, don't."

Sighing, I shrug and concede the truth. "I had dinner with Elyssa."

"No shit?!"

"It's not what you think," I snap, before he can imply anything. "I just wanted to get her talking."

"And did she?"

"I laid the groundwork."

"Groundwork for what?"

"For trust," I reply.

Then I walk out the door.

26

ELYSSA

THE BEDROOM IN THE KOVALYOV MANSION

"Elyssa, calm down," Charity cautions.

But I can't calm down. Because none of it makes sense.

I was stupid enough to think that, after last night, we'd made some progress. Sure, Phoenix hadn't revealed much about himself. But I still thought I'd felt something shift between us. As though maybe we were becoming less combative. More open with each other.

Then this morning, I'd woken up to find two things. Breakfast laid out for us by the window…

And a locked door.

"Why would he lock us in again?" I cry out.

Charity sighs and bounces Theo on her hip as she walks over the path I've been pacing back and forth since I discovered the situation.

"I think I might know."

It strikes me that she wasn't in the room when I'd come back to the room last night. Theo had been asleep, and Anna was reading a book by the window. I was so wrapped up in my own thoughts, I hadn't even questioned it. I just figured she needed a late-night walk or something equally innocent.

But in my preoccupation, I'd forgotten that Charity doesn't do "innocent."

"What did you do, Char?"

"Why do you assume it's something I did?" she asks defensively.

"Charity!"

"Fine," she huffs immediately. "Just keep in mind, I'm holding your son."

"Is that supposed to make me feel better?"

"Well, no, I guess not."

"Just tell me."

"I went for a walk last night and, oh, y'know… stumbled across Phoenix's personal office."

My eyes go wide. "Tell me you didn't go in."

"Curiosity got the better of me. I may or may not have picked his lock and gone inside."

"You snooped around his office?" I practically screech.

Theo bobs his head in my direction, clearly tickled by the sound. But I can't even enjoy his entertained expression because my mouth is hanging open as I stare at Charity in disbelief.

"Oh, God." I close my eyes as if I can make all this go away. "He found you in there, didn't he?"

"Well, yeah, but it's not a big deal. I made my presence known. I was waiting for him."

"Why?"

"I was planning on seducing him."

My eyes fly open. An emotion squeezes the life out of my stomach. I guess you'd call it fear. Or jealousy, maybe? Whatever it is, it's hot and ugly and I don't like it one bit.

Charity takes one look at my expression and bursts out laughing. "Oh, goodness gracious! Don't worry, my little rabbit. I'm only kidding. I wouldn't do that to you."

Another feeling surges through me. I'm pretty sure this one is relief.

"Just tell me why you were really waiting for him, Charity," I whisper, suddenly exhausted.

She coos at Theo for a few seconds before turning to me again. "Because I wanted to warn him."

"Warn him? About what?"

"About me," she says with a proud chin. "I told him that if he hurt you, he'd have to deal with me."

I'm at a loss for words. "I... I... Are you serious?"

"Cross my heart. That's the God's honest truth."

I shake my head, feeling laughter and shock compete for dominance. "I can't believe you."

"Had to be done."

"Charity, you said it yourself: he's a dangerous man. There's probably a lot in his office that he doesn't want anyone to see."

Charity's expression shifts somewhat. Is there more she's not telling me?

"What?" I ask urgently. "'Fess up."

"The Astra Tyrannis thing," she says. "He's in a lot deeper than either one of us realized."

"Deeper? Meaning…?"

"He's been tracking the organization's movements for years. Like, literal years! And as far as I can tell, he's just been hitting dead end after dead end."

Charity's eyes shine with interest. It's the dangerous kind of curious look I've seen her display countless times before—usually right before she does something very, very stupid.

"Charity, this organization… It sounds not good."

"You're right about that. Very not good."

"As in, deadly not good."

"Exactly like that."

"Then you should stay far from Astro Whatever and everything to do with it."

"That kinda includes the dark, sexy don we're currently bunking with, don't you think?" she muses with a chuckle.

"Which is why we should have left a long time ago!" I say. "We have money now. We have options."

I gesture to the large wardrobe where I've hidden the money I "won" last night. Charity and I had counted it this morning in utter disbelief.

Ten thousand dollars. Neither one of us had ever held that much money in our hands at one time. It's oddly humbling—and extremely frightening.

Frightening to me, at least. Charity veered more towards giddy excitement.

"Ten thousand dollars is nothing," she points out. "We'll need more before we can think of leaving. And you have a good chance of getting more now that you and the big boss are practically an item."

I stiffen instantly. "I don't—"

Before I can finish my sentence, there comes a strong knock on the door.

Theo squeals with surprise and starts bawling immediately. I pluck him out of Charity's arms and turn towards the door just as it opens.

Anna is on the other side in a floral blouse with bright buttons down the front. She adjusts her weight onto her good leg and gives me a smile.

"Elyssa, dear, you're wanted down in the main living room on the first floor."

"Who wants her?" Charity asks before I can.

"Master Phoenix, of course."

Charity glances at me. "Heard that, Lys? He *wants* you." She waggles her eyebrows suggestively.

I ignore that and turn to Anna. "Now?"

"Now," she confirms with a pleasant nod.

"Oh. Okay."

She moves forward with her hands out and I switch Theo over to her. "How about we go for a little walk, sweet boy?" she coos.

"Great plan. I'll come with," Charity says immediately.

"Ah, I'm sorry, Miss Charity," Anna says, her eyes turning flinty. "My instructions are to make sure you stay in the room."

Charity's face falls. "But... but..."

"I'm sorry," Anna says.

She follows me out the door and I watch as she shuts the door on Charity and twists the key in the lock.

I bite my lip, feeling guilty about leaving my friend behind. But I can't deny that I'm a little annoyed with her, too. It was a risky move, breaking into Phoenix's personal space to make a point. Actually, to make a threat.

Still, I can't be completely mad at her. She did it for me. Out of love—which is in short supply in my life these days.

"Can't you just take her with you?" I ask Anna.

"Master Phoenix's instructions were clear, Elyssa," she says gently. "She abused her freedom in this house."

Unable to argue with that, I sigh in defeat and head towards the staircase. Anna walks with me as far as the living room and then gestures for me to go inside. I plant a kiss on Theo's forehead, take a deep breath, and walk inside to whatever's awaiting me.

27

ELYSSA

Phoenix is standing by the sliding glass doors, looking out at the pool.

I stop a few feet away from him but he doesn't even acknowledge my presence until I clear my throat. Only then does he slowly turn to face me.

"Our room was locked this morning," I tell him.

"A result of your friend's late-night visit to my office. My *locked*, private office."

I sigh. "Charity can be impulsive, but she doesn't mean any harm."

A wry smile plays across his lips. Lips that I'd dreamed about last night, as a matter of fact. Lips that kissed down my spine, up my thighs, between my…

I push away the thought immediately. I don't want Phoenix to know how deep in my head he's gotten.

"'Doesn't mean any harm'?" he repeats. "She personally threatened me."

"Empty threats," I say. "She's just… protective."

"There's no such thing as an empty threat."

"Maybe not in your world," I say. "But what power does she really have? She has her looks and her wits."

"And those things have gotten her into very important places with very important men," he says darkly. "Anything is a weapon in the right hands, Elyssa."

A burst of adrenaline rushes through me the moment he says my name. But I cast it aside and balk at the insinuation in his tone. "She has nothing to do with those men! Apart from…"

"Fucking them?"

I cringe. "Well, yes. She did what she had to do to survive."

"I'm not judging her life choices, Elyssa. Merely telling you what I have to do in response to who she's become. More than that, I'm just pointing out certain… coincidences that have popped up since you and your friend entered the picture."

I narrow my eyes at him. "Are you accusing me of being a spy again? We've been down this road already."

I try to say it strong and bold. To let him know I'm not afraid of him. But somehow, it has the opposite effect. I sound like a petrified little girl asking for approval.

He doesn't answer me. Instead, he reaches behind him and pulls out a small bag. "Here."

I take it but I don't look inside. "What is this?"

"Your first lesson," he tells me coolly. "And you'll need that."

I open the bag and reach for whatever's inside. To my surprise, I draw out a black one-piece with a daring V neckline and a scooped back.

I stare at Phoenix in confusion. "This is a swimsuit."

"Very astute. Put it on."

"Why?"

"I just told you: you're about to have your first lesson."

I glance towards the pool, realizing what he's trying to do. "You're going to teach me to swim?"

"Would you rather drown?"

I'm dumbfounded as I look down at the elegant swimsuit. I've never actually worn one before. I've never needed to. Back on the compound, there was no body of water big enough to require it.

"I… I…"

"I don't have a lot of time," Phoenix snaps. "So get changed. There's a bathroom down the hall you can use. Meet me by the pool when you're decent."

Before I can say another word, he opens the sliding doors and walks out towards the pool. I stand there gaping at him for a few seconds. Then, as though on autopilot, I turn and head for the bathroom down the hall.

The bathroom, like everything else in Phoenix's mansion, is massive and ornate. All gleaming marble and fluffy white towels, with a faint scent of lavender floating through the air.

With trembling fingers, I strip out of my clothes and step into the bathing suit. Once it's on, I turn to my reflection in the mirror.

Immediately, my cheeks flame. I've never felt so on display. The cut rides high over my hips, making my legs look supermodel-long, and the plunging neckline presses my breasts up while barely covering my nipples.

For a one-piece, it's awfully revealing.

It's also pretty sexy.

But am I the kind of woman who wears something like this? No, not by a long shot. I've seen billboards in the city, advertisements in the magazine, those kinds of things, where women wear bathing suits like this. And those women are never anything like me.

They're always laughing and sipping some fruity drink. Flaunting their tans and their happiness and their freedom.

But I'm not free. I've never been free.

What choice do I have, though? I'm in Phoenix's house, playing by Phoenix's rules. So I swallow down my self-consciousness, wrap myself in a huge white towel, and head for the pool.

Phoenix is already in the water when I arrive. He's discarded his clothes for a pair of swimming trunks in a deep, sea green.

The first thing I notice is his chiseled chest. His abs are shielded by the water, but I can still see definition and a bronze tan. Droplets of water cling to his chest hair.

He looks like something out of a dream.

He raises his eyebrows when I approach. "You'll need to remove the towel before you get in," he drawls as if I'm stupid.

I glare at him. "Couldn't you have gotten me a different swimsuit?"

I regret it the moment the words are out of my mouth. Now, I've gone and drawn attention to what I'm wearing. I'm positive he'd have noticed either way, though. I swear I catch him looking at me almost as much as I look at him.

"What's wrong with it?" he asks.

"It's… revealing."

"It's a one-piece," he replies.

"Bikinis aren't the only swimwear that can be sexy, you realize."

He smirks. "Do you have a problem with looking sexy, little lamb?"

This conversation is looking more and more like a mistake. "Never mind. Can we just get this over with?"

"Sure. Just get rid of the towel and we'll begin."

I turn my back on him, gritting my teeth and trying to steel my courage. My heart is hammering hard, and I can practically hear it.

I'm aware that it's ridiculous to be so self-conscious. He's seen me naked. He's been inside me, for God's sake!

But somehow, the new dynamic between us has me feeling incredibly insecure. I bite down and decide to just rip the Band-Aid off.

Tossing the towel aside, I hurry towards the little steps that descend into the pool. I can feel his eyes on me, but I pointedly ignore them.

Thankfully, the water's warm, so I submerge myself as quickly as possible. Once I'm in the water, I feel tons better.

That is, until he glides over to me.

"It suits you," he murmurs.

"Thanks. What excellent taste you have." He chuckles. I just roll my eyes. "Are you here to teach me or laugh at me?" I snap.

"Okay, first lesson: stop being afraid of the water."

"Easy for you to say."

"Elyssa."

"What?"

"Look at me."

I wish I had the power to resist him. I wish I had the power to look at him without feeling tremors running riot inside me.

But I don't have that power. Because when Phoenix Kovalyov speaks, all I can do is listen.

I drag my eyes up to his face. "I'm looking," I whisper in a tiny voice.

"There's nothing to fear. I'm right here with you, and I'll never let anything happen to you. Do you understand that?"

I swallow back a strange taste in my mouth. "Okay," I say. "Okay."

"Good. Now come here."

"Come where?"

He holds out his hands. "We're going to practice floating."

"Why do I need to be over there for that to happen?"

"You need to get comfortable in the water," he explains. "You need to let it hold you. Carry you. Support you."

"Sounds like a lot to ask. We just met," I say woodenly. The joke falls extremely flat.

He still smiles. A pity smile, most probably, but I take it. "You're nervous."

"What gave me away?"

"Because of the water?"

I'm not expecting the question which is the only reason I answer honestly. "Mostly because of you."

He tilts his head to the side as if to look at me from a new angle. "Why?"

I shake my head, refusing to answer.

"Fine. Keep your secrets. But you have to listen to my instructions. Now come here."

Doing my best to hide my trembling, I do as he says.

"Push your legs up and fall back against the water," he instructs me. "Face the sky. Let the water carry you."

"I'll sink," I say, slightly panicked.

"You will because your fear will sink you," he says calmly. "But I'm going to support you while you get used to this."

He puts his palm on the small of my back and tilts me back. I go down, guided by his hands.

I face the sky as I float, extremely aware of his touch underneath me. Five points of fire against my exposed skin.

"Relax, Elyssa."

"I am!"

"No, you're not. Remember what I said: fear will sink you."

"I—I don't think I can…"

"I'm not going to let you go, okay?" He moves a little closer so that he's looking down directly at me. "I'll never let you go."

"Okay," I whisper.

"You trust me?"

"I… yes."

He nods. "Then close your eyes and take a deep breath."

I do as he says, and I feel the weight on my chest ease.

Just a little, but it's enough. And just like that…

I float.

∽

We spend the next hour going through different things. Phoenix teaches me to submerge myself in water and open my eyes. He teaches me to float without his hand supporting me.

Once I can float with my head in the water, I start gaining confidence and enthusiasm.

By the end of the second hour, I can swim a few feet in a straight line. It's not amazing, but it's more than I could do two hours ago. And it's a heady feeling.

"Wow! I can swim!" I exclaim when Phoenix declares it's time for a break.

"I wouldn't go that far," he chuckles. "But you've made a lot of progress in a short amount of time. I'm impressed."

"I've impressed you?" I snort. "High praise."

We're both leaning against the edge of the pool. There are only a few inches between us, but he's taken care not to touch me unless he absolutely has to.

Still, the energy between us is as calm as it's ever been. Which is why I decide to take a chance.

"Phoenix?"

"Yes?"

"Charity's my best friend. She's the only family I have."

He glances at me, his expression cautious. "I'm aware of that."

"She's also a good person. She just… she doesn't trust easily. And she's worried about me and Theo."

He sighs. "You want me to give her freedom of the house."

"Please?"

"I'll think about it," he says gruffly.

Then, before I can thank him, he turns around and pulls himself out of the pool, splashing me in the process.

"Where are you going?" I ask, staring up at him.

He's haloed by a circle of sunlight. A living, breathing Greek god that's taken form right in front of me.

My body quivers and I'm forced to clench my legs.

"I have work to do," he says curtly. "I've been here too long."

His whiplash about-face in demeanor is jarring. But the only cause for it has to be the fact that I spoke up for Charity. What else could have brought on such a stark and sudden change?

"You're leaving?" I ask, knowing how disappointed I sound and hating myself for it.

His phone starts ringing, preventing him from answering me. He turns to the deck chair and answers the call. "Yes?"

A moment passes as he listens to whoever's on the other end. His expression is screwed up in concentration.

Then: "What!?" He sounds pissed. "No. No. I did not authorize that! ... For fuck's sake. I'll be there in half an hour."

He doesn't even grab a towel as he heads back into the house. I watch him go…

Hoping that he'll turn back.

Knowing that he won't.

28

PHOENIX

I head straight to the hospital. I don't stop to consult with Matvei. I don't take any of my men with me, either.

All I know is that I need to put as much distance between Elyssa and myself as possible. So, as infuriated as I am with the call I just received, a part of me is relieved for the slap in the face from reality.

This has been the longest I've gone in years without thinking about Astra Tyrannis. About my purpose.

And I'm starting to feel very fucking guilty about it.

The world is still turning, and bad men are still out there doing fucked-up shit to innocent people. And where have I been? Oh, nowhere important—just giving fucking swimming lessons to a naïve little wallflower who shouldn't even be in my house in the first place.

"Fuck," I growl, slamming the palm of my hand on the steering wheel of the Rolls Royce. "Fuck!"

Another call comes in on my cell from the same area code as the first one. But since I'm only a few minutes from the hospital, I ignore it.

I tear into the parking lot, screech to a halt right out front, and leap out of the car. I don't give two flying fucks about the security guard screeching at me that I'm not allowed to park there.

"You're gonna get towed, buddy!" he warns.

I stop, whirl around, and get up in his face. "Lay one fucking finger on my car and you won't live to see morning," I snarl.

He goes ghost-white and backs away without another word.

"That's what I fucking thought."

Then I'm back on my warpath, blowing through the main doors of the psychiatric ward. Several nurses and doctors are congregated at the front desk. Every one of them turns to look at who the hell is barging into their hospital like a fucking tornado. They look for a moment like they're about to scold me.

Then they see my face and realize that's a very bad idea.

"Where's Dr. Pendergast?" I demand.

The crowd seems to melt away almost immediately. From its fraying edges emerges a young doctor in a crisp white coat. His bouncy blond hair and ready-made smile annoy me immediately.

"He's not available right now," he says in a cool, measured voice. "Can I help you with something?"

"What the fuck happened?"

"I'm sorry?"

"My name is Phoenix Kovalyov, and I just asked you what the fuck happened. Stop apologizing and start explaining."

The smile on his face falters for a moment in the face of my wrath. "Listen, Mr.—uh, Mr. Kyovoloyavov…"

He butchers my last name. That's the second strike.

"Well, we're not quite sure, sir," he says, quickly switching over to a form of addressing me that he can actually pronounce. "We're trying to figure that out."

"You're telling me that my father-in-law was discharged from this fucking facility without my consent and you still don't know how? Or why? Or where?"

His face pales. "I… Well, I…"

"Enough with this shit. Where is Dr. Pendergast?"

"In his office." He points down the hall.

"Take me there," I snap. "Now."

The blond fuck doesn't say another word. He turns in the direction of the massive arched corridors adjacent to the main desk and starts striding away. He's got his shoulders squared and chin high like he thinks presenting a brave front will save him from me.

It won't.

That's strike three.

The glass-walled corridors hug a courtyard awash in greenery. Patients walk the grounds slowly, nurses at their sides. It's peaceful, even beautiful, but there's something depressing about it all the same. Maybe it has something to do with all the half-mad people that call this place a home.

Dr. Pendergast's office is at the end of the corridor. The blond idiot knocks but I push him aside and strongarm my way in.

The moment I'm inside, I slam the door on Blondie's face. Then I turn to the tall, bald man sitting behind his dark mahogany desk.

"Mr. Kovalyov," he greets as he scrambles to get to his feet. "I—"

"Where is my father-in-law?" I demand, walking right up to his desk and slamming my hands down on it.

"Mr. Kovalyov, I wasn't here this morning. When I arrived, I was told that… that *you* discharged your father-in-law."

"I did not discharge Vitya Azarov," I say, enunciating every single word.

Pendergast takes the book in front of him and twists it around to face me. "See?"

I look down at the name next to Vitya's. It's definitely my name. But the handwriting is all wrong.

"Are you serious?" I growl. "This is supposed to be the best fucking psychiatric ward in the state."

"And it is—"

"If you're having breaches like this, then no, it's not!" I snap. "This is not my handwriting. A mistake that could have been easily avoided if you'd bothered to check this signature against the papers I signed when I admitted Vitya."

"I… I…"

"You're trying to figure out what happened?" I say, beating him to the punch.

"Well, yes, of course…"

"If you weren't here when Vitya was discharged, then who was? Who authorized his release? And who was stupid enough to mistake a stranger for me? Hasn't this fucking place heard of asking for identification?"

"Mr. Kovalyov, I can assure that we operate with the highest measures of security. All patients are required to be…"

His voice fades into the background. I don't even hear him blabbing. Because it just struck me—this isn't a breach.

It's a fucking inside job.

Someone with reach, someone with power, someone with the money to make things happen—that's behind this shit. And there's only one organization that has operatives in every single place of note in the city.

"Fuck," I growl as realization floods through me like ice water.

Pendergast gives me an odd look. "… Mr. Kovalyov?"

"Who checked Vitya out of here?" I ask. "A nurse?"

"No, of course not. Only doctors have the authority to discharge patients."

"Then bring me the doctor who authorized Vitya's release. Now."

Pendergast doesn't argue with me. He clears his seat and heads straight for the door. The moment he vacates his seat, I take it.

I notice the panicked expression on his face as he rushes out into the hallway. He's scared. That's a good thing. Fear is a good motivator, and I need fucking answers.

Because this proves what I've believed from the beginning: Astra Tyrannis hasn't forgotten about me.

Not even close.

I pull my phone out to discover three missed calls from Matvei. He's probably going crazy cooped up in his room, but I can't deal with explaining anything to him right now. Especially since I don't have any of the answers.

I put my phone on silent and look around the office. Everything's neat and tidy. There are a bunch of patient files stacked onto tall shelves that take up an entire wall. Everything feels sterile. Aloof.

A few minutes later, Pendergast re-enters the office looking predictably terrified.

"Well?" I ask.

He approaches his own desk with increasing weariness. "Mr. Kovalyov—"

"Spare me. Just give it to me straight."

"The staff member that signed him out—well…"

"Let me guess: they aren't where they're supposed to be."

"No, sir, they're not."

"Round up your staff," I order. "We'll handle this my way."

"Mr. Kovalyov, some are on duty and—"

"I don't give a flying fuck. You fucked up, and now I'm here to clean up your mess, Pendergast. Have them gather in the courtyard."

When I rise, Pendergast takes a step back as though he's terrified I'm going to make a move towards him. If I weren't so pissed off, I might have laughed. The man looks like he's about to shit himself.

"Do I need to repeat myself, Doctor?" I ask.

"N—no. I'll round up the staff," he stammers, backing out of the door again.

I follow him out into the wide corridor that overlooks the courtyard. A bunch of ravens are circling overhead. It reminds me of an old Irish saying that Uncle Kian used to spout all the time: an unkindness of ravens signifies trouble ahead.

Fucking Old World bullshit. But the sight unsettles me anyway.

I walk down the corridor and stop where Pendergast is ushering his staff to herd up. Some look confused. Others impatient. And a few look like they're about to piss themselves.

The last group are the smart ones, apparently.

"Is this everyone?" I ask him.

"We have a few doctors on leave today," Pendergast replies. Blondie comes up to him and hands over a clipboard with a list of names on it. He passes it to me immediately. "Here's everyone who signed in today."

"Look at those names," I tell him. "Who's on this list but not in front of us right now?"

Pendergast scours over the list for a moment. I know the exact moment when he realizes that someone is missing from the lineup because he stiffens immediately.

"The name?" I ask calmly.

"Avery Michaels," he says softly, looking up. "Where's Avery?"

The other doctors look around as though they've only just noticed that one of their own has gone missing.

"Tell me about Avery," I say.

"Uh, well, he is new to our staff here."

"Of course he is. How new?"

"A week, I believe?"

"Almost two," the blond man interjects, clearly the teacher's pet.

I ignore him and look at Pendergast. "I had my father-in-law committed here eight days ago," I tell him. "And you hired this new doctor seven days ago. Is that right?"

"I suppose it was something like that," Pendergast says, looking positively terrified now. "Mr. Kovalyov, I assure you there must be some explanation. This is all just a big misunderstanding. No one working for me would ever—"

"This doctor of yours was never working for you. He was working for someone else entirely."

"He came highly recommended," Pendergast protests, trying desperately to defend himself. "He had a wealth of experience. We did a background check..."

"It came out clean as a whistle?"

I snort. I have the urge to pull out my gun and shoot this fucker in the face. But I know that's just my anger talking. In truth, the man isn't to blame. He hired a doctor that impressed him. He had no idea that the doctor in question had ulterior motives.

But the question remains: what motive could that be?

I'm not sure what purpose abducting Vitya serves.

My best guesses: either they think taking Vitya will serve as leverage in the future. Or else, they're scared of what he knows. What he's discovered.

He told me there were spies in my home. At the time, I dismissed his warning as ravings. Now, I'm starting to think that he wasn't quite as mad as he came across.

"Someone dial Avery Michaels," I command.

Several doctors rush to pull out their phones while others look around helplessly at their colleagues. Tensions are running high. None of these people are accustomed to being in a scenario like this. They have no idea if they're in direct danger or not.

In my experience, that puts me in a good position. No one cracks faster than a panicked person without a clue.

"Put it on speaker," I instruct the first person who dials.

A younger female doctor listens immediately. I hear a dial tone for two seconds and then dead air. A second later, an automated message rolls through. "This line has been disconnected."

I snarl in distaste. *Fucking predictable.*

"You've been had, Doctor," I tell Pendergast. "And apparently, so have I."

"Mr. Kovalyov…"

"Save it," I snap. "There is nothing more to be said here."

I turn to leave as Pendergast scurries behind me. "Mr. Kovalyov, I can assure you this has never happened before in the history of my—"

"What the fuck does it matter that it's never happened before?" I ask, turning on him. "It happened now. And it only has to happen once."

"But my license…"

"I don't give a fuck about your license. This is the last you'll be seeing of me," I tell him. "If I were you, I'd clean house."

Before he can respond, I turn and head towards the door. I'm walking from the massive white building towards the parking lot when I sense eyes on me.

A second after I've even registered that I'm being targeted, I catch movement from my peripheral vision.

Then I hear the bullet.

The sound breaks through the calm of the day. I leap out of the way but it's too late—the bullet makes contact, grazing my calf.

I buckle under the shooting pain that sears up my leg and drop to one knee on the unforgiving tarmac.

But the bullet has done nothing to blunt my skill. I pull out my gun as fast as I can and open fire. Three gunshots in quick succession.

The first one misses.

The second one doesn't.

The third one is just out of spite.

The shooter's body hits the ground but he's far enough away that I'm not able to pick out any distinguishable features. I see only the dull black of the shirt he's wearing.

His hair might be brown. But it might be blond, too, for all the details I'm able to absorb in the heat of the moment. I'll get all the details I need once I've stopped the bleeding on my leg.

I pull off my belt and use it to apply a tourniquet. I move fast, working sloppily in order to get through it faster. I can hear the commotion at my back, and I know the doctors will have heard the gunshot, too.

"Mr. Kovalyov…!"

I don't even glance behind at Pendergast.

"Go back inside, Doctor," I tell him through gritted teeth. "I've got this."

"You're hurt!"

Wincing, I force myself back onto my feet. "Don't concern yourself," I say, walking towards the parking lot in the direction of the shooter's body.

I limp around the corner where he fell—and come to a screeching halt.

"What the fuck?" I breathe.

The barrel of my gun is still fucking warm.

I saw a body hit the ground.

And yet…

There's no one there.

I quicken my pace, my eyes darting from side to side. I know I'm being impulsive and reckless. I shouldn't be out in the open like this. Especially in my current condition.

God only knows who the fuck else is out there right now, waiting to gun me down. Every nook and cranny, every shadow and crevice could contain a man who's come to end my life.

But nothing happens.

And, as I slowly pivot, I see no trace of the one man I know for sure was sent to kill me.

He was here literally a minute ago.

Now, he's gone.

29

ELYSSA
THE KOVALYOV MANSION

"And he didn't ask you anything else?"

"No!" I say for at least the tenth time in the last half hour.

Theo grabs my finger and tries to stuff it in his mouth. Charity and I are sitting on the sprawling carpet in one of the living rooms on the first floor. It's one of the more frustrating conversations I've had in a while.

"Geez," she mutters. "Just asking."

"You've been asking the same question for ages now. I don't know what else to tell you."

She eyes me suspiciously. "Hm."

"What?" I ask.

"I don't know," she admits. "It's just that, sometimes, when it comes to him, I feel like you don't tell me everything."

I don't have a leg to stand on. Her instincts are totally right. But I can't bring myself to admit that to her.

"I'm telling you everything, Charity," I insist. "Promise."

"Just tell me you're not catching feelings for the man."

"Of course not!" I can feel my face heating up and I busy myself combing Theo's hair with my fingers so Charity can't see them trembling.

"That was a quick answer."

"Which should convince you that it's true."

She taps a finger on her bottom lip. "So then why am I not convinced?"

I shake my head in frustration and choose to focus on my baby. He's just started rolling onto his chest now. Another tiny little milestone in his life, flashing before my eyes. I just wish I was in the headspace where I could enjoy it.

"I don't know what you want from me, Charity," I say. "You were the one who wanted to come here. Then you wanted me to talk to him and ask for money."

"Yes—because we need a means to survive."

"And I have a bag of money upstairs in our room that'll hold us over for a while."

"This is Las Vegas, Elyssa," Charity snaps impatiently. "That money won't last us more than a couple of months."

I'm not used to anger. Back in the Sanctuary, only men were permitted to feel it. To express it. Women like me were taught that giving into rage was giving into sin: utterly unforgivable.

So even now, free of all those rules, I'm still unsure of how to process my anger which is probably why it turns to tears. They swim across my eyes, but I blink them back.

"So you're implying I should get more money from him, right? But every time I spend time with him, you treat me like I'm some... some... some *criminal* you don't trust."

Seeing my raw emotion, Charity's face slowly transforms from indignation to regret. "Jesus, babe, I'm sorry," she sighs, reaching out to pat the back of my hand. "I know I'm being a bitch right now. I'm just worried."

"Why?" I demand.

And that's when I realize—she knows something I don't.

"What aren't you telling me, Char?"

"Nothing! Nothing. I just... I'm worried about you, Lys. Back before we knew Phoenix was Phoenix, the way you spoke about him..."

"What?" I ask self-consciously.

"I don't know. Sometimes, I think you caught feelings that night... when you two cooked up this little tyke." She pokes Theo's jelly rolls affectionately.

"That's ridiculous. It was one night. Not even a night—just an hour or two. He was a stranger. Still is."

"But the way you used to talk about him—"

"I constructed a fantasy for myself," I admit. "But mostly, for my son. I wanted to be able to tell him something about his father one day. And honestly, I never expected to see Phoenix again."

"Okay. But—"

"I don't have feelings for him," I interrupt. "End of story."

"Okay, because if you did... Elyssa, that would be bad," Charity warns. "He might be a powerful don but knowing what I know now about his involvement in Astra Tyrannis—"

"His involvement?" I interrupt immediately. "What involvement? You said he was trying to bring them down."

"He is," she says. "But that's exactly why that makes him more dangerous for us."

I frown. "What do you mean?"

"I've worked the nightlife long enough to know about these things, Elyssa," she says, lowering her voice. "Astra Tyrannis… they're bad. Really fucking bad. And if Phoenix is trying to bring them down, you can bet your ass they'll hit back. I don't want us to be caught in the crossfire when that happens."

My heart is beating fast now. Panic is slowly clamping down on my throat.

I don't want my son in danger. But my protective instincts are warring hard against my desire to stay with Phoenix.

He does something to me. Something for me. Something I can't explain or describe or even fully process.

When those dark eyes land on mine, it's like my soul shivers.

Charity reaches out and puts her hand on mine again. "I'm sorry. I don't mean to worry you. I didn't even want to bring this up unless I absolutely had to. But we've got to look out for ourselves, babe. More importantly, we've got to look out for each other."

"We're family," I whisper, repeating the very same words Charity had said to me what felt like a lifetime ago now.

"Exactly," she nods, giving me a reassuring smile. "We're family. Us and Theo. The only family we've got. Everyone else? They don't matter."

I know Charity's right. It's been the two of us for a year now. The two of us and Theo, that is. We have to stick together.

"Okay. I'll work on getting us more money," I say, buying myself a little more time. "And once we have enough, we'll get out of here. Start over someplace else."

Charity smiles. "Maybe we can even leave Las Vegas. Go somewhere peaceful. Quiet. Cheap."

I force myself to smile. She seems to recognize the conflict waging inside my head because she gives my hand a reassuring squeeze. Before I can delve deeper into the depth of my feelings for Phoenix, I hear a door slam.

Then I hear a deep voice. And I know immediately it's him.

"Boss?" someone asks—one of the maids, probably.

"Get me some fucking bandages!" Phoenix roars.

Theo starts wailing at once. I almost want to join in with him. Instead, I shout, "Stay with Theo!" to Charity as I get to my feet and race out of the living room.

I turn out of the door and see Phoenix standing by the staircase. "Standing" might be the wrong word, actually—more like he's bent over it, holding the banister as if he's going to collapse to the ground if he loosens his grip for even a second.

There's a clumsy tourniquet applied to his leg, but the blood has still soaked through the leg of his pants.

"Oh my God!" I gasp. "What happened?"

"It's nothing," he grunts.

"It doesn't look like nothing. Let me take a look."

"Not necessary."

"Are you really so proud you won't even let me look at it?" Apparently, his latest mood swing is still fighting fit. But given the state of his leg,

I ignore it. "You're gonna bleed out onto the floor if you don't see to that wound right now."

He growls unintelligibly but I sense the note of concession in it.

"Great," I drawl. "Wonderful. Fantastic. Glad you're on board. Let's go to the kitchen."

He limps off to the right and I start to follow him until I sense Charity behind me. She's standing in the threshold of the door with Theo in her arms.

"What happened?" she mouths to me.

"He's hurt," I respond. "Stay here."

I leave her in the living room and follow Phoenix into the kitchen. Anna is clearing up the lunch plates.

"Master Phoenix!" she exclaims when she catches sight of him.

"It's not that serious," he says with some extremely predictable male bravado.

"I'll be the judge of that," I intervene. "Anna, Theo will need a bottle soon. Would you mind?"

"Of course not," she says, her eyes flashing with worry. "Do you…?"

"If I need help, I'll let you know," I tell her.

Before Anna leaves, she places the first aid box on the bar stool next to me. Then she takes a full bottle to Theo.

"The woman's a godsend," I say as I crack open the box and start hauling out supplies.

Phoenix doesn't respond. He seems to be lost in thought. His eyes are barely focused as they stare out at the glass panel windows that overlook the lake in the distance.

"The bullet?" Him getting shot at is just a guess, but I have a feeling I'm right.

"It only grazed me," he replies stiffly.

I fall into silence as I clean the wound. His flesh has parted slightly where the bullet kissed his skin.

"I'll need to give you a few stitches," I tell him. "Unless you'd rather wait for your doctor."

"Just get it done," he says with a dismissive wave of his hand.

"This might hurt a little."

He looks at me with clear insult in his eyes. "I assure you I've had worse."

Sighing, I give him four stitches quickly, then pull back to look at my work. The stitches are clean and neatly constructed. I'm satisfied. Phoenix hasn't made a single peep.

"There," I say proudly. "You're good to go."

He only grunts in acknowledgement. I can tell he's pissed. He's trying to claw himself out of the web he's found himself in. Either that or he's busy trying to weave a web to catch someone else.

"Phoenix."

His eyes focus on me, and this time, I can tell he's really looking at me. "Yeah?"

"What happened?"

"It's a long fucking story."

"What else do I have to do?" I ask. "To get you to talk to me."

I expect him to dismiss me like he did a moment ago but instead, he looks at me contemplatively. His dark eyes are filled with conflict. I wonder how much of that conflict has to do with me.

"My father-in-law was abducted from his psychiatric facility today," he says without inflection.

I freeze for a moment, stumbling over the phrase "father-in-law."

"Your… father-in-law?" My heartrate is rising again.

"Yes."

"You… you're married?"

Why had he never mentioned it before? Why had no one in this house mentioned it before? And also… where is she?

"I was," Phoenix replies.

"You're divorced."

"Not quite."

It takes me a long time to put the pieces together. But when they finally fall into place, I get it: *she's dead.*

I feel instantly horrible for asking. His expression is impassive, though. He looks detached from the conversation, but I think I'm beginning to understand him a little better now. It makes so much sense.

The cool façade is just that—a façade. A false construct to mask the raw edge of his pain. Hiding a loss that clearly has something to do with the organization he's hell bent on destroying.

I understand more now than I have since I first set foot in this house.

And what I understand terrifies me.

"Phoenix, I'm so sorry."

Our eyes meet and he allows me in past the façade for the briefest flash. Just enough that I see his pain. Recognize it.

It runs deep. And in that moment, I don't want to leave him alone with his grief. I've felt alone before, and it may just be the worst feeling in the world.

Instinctively, I reach out and cup his face with my hand. And to my shock, he lets me. I can feel the rough growth of stubble coming in. He doesn't lean his face into my palm but he doesn't cringe away from it, either.

"I'm sorry," I say again, just so he understands how much I feel what he feels.

"I know."

For one wild moment, he lets me linger there. Past the walls. Past the defenses. Just two human beings, raw and real and vulnerable.

And then I see it again—the whiplash change in his mood. I feel myself being ejected from that dangerous space, hurled out back in the direction I came from.

Something dark ripples across his eyes, and he pulls away from me.

He pushes himself off the chair and walks around the counter so that we have the kitchen island between us now. Sighing, I try and shake off my disappointment. But my façade isn't as good as his is at the moment.

"How'd you get shot?" I ask, trying to salvage the conversation.

"That's a good fucking question!" someone interrupts.

Both Phoenix and I turn in the direction of the person who spoke. Matvei's standing in the doorway, stomach wrapped in thick gauze, staring between the two of us.

Phoenix grimaces. "You should be in bed."

"The hospital called me. You went in alone, didn't you?" he accuses.

"I didn't think—"

"Who else would pull Vitya out?"

There's something about Matvei. Something almost boyish about him when he's relaxed and content. But when he's angry… well, everything about him shifts. The angel becomes a beast.

"I made a decision," Phoenix says.

"You make all the decisions," Matvei retorts. "And lately, they've been the wrong ones."

"You questioning my judgement, old friend?" Phoenix asks dangerously.

I shiver, caught between the testosterone-fueled heat of two alpha males.

"You're goddamn right I am," Matvei says without mincing his words. "You could have been killed."

"It's only a flesh wound, and Elyssa's already stitched me up. I'll recover faster than you will."

Matvei limps forward, jabbing an accusatory finger in the air. "You should have taken backup."

"I didn't think I needed it."

"I would have told you that you did if you'd just spoken to me before you left."

"I don't take my orders from you, Matvei."

"No, you don't take orders from anyone. You don't take advice from anyone, either. You used to."

Phoenix's eyes flutter to me for a moment. Then he sighs. "We should talk in private. Not here."

The two of them head out of the kitchen. On his way out, Phoenix turns to me. He doesn't say anything but his eyes linger on my face for a few seconds. Searching for something. God only knows what it is, though.

Then he disappears around the corner. When they're gone, I head back to the living room.

Anna is sitting on the carpet with Theo in front of her. "Where's Charity?" I ask, looking around.

"She said she needed to use the bathroom," Anna says without taking her eyes off Theo. "She's been gone for a while, poor thing."

I sit down next to Anna and pat Theo but my focus is split. I'm worried about Charity and what she's up to. I just barely managed to convince Phoenix to allow her freedom of the house. If she abuses that right again, I know no amount of pleading on my part will move him the second time around. She'll be a prisoner here for as long as he keeps us.

"You okay, dear?" Anna asks, eyeing me warily.

"Oh, sure, yeah. I'm just worried."

"About Master Phoenix?"

I blush. *Am I really that transparent?* "About Charity," I lie smoothly.

"Probably just something she ate," Anna says with an oblivious smile.

"Right," I say. "I'm sure that's it."

Anna looks around and sighs. "Where could it be...?"

"What's wrong?"

"Nothing important, dear. Just misplaced my phone again. I'm getting old. I'm half-scared I'll be put out to pasture soon."

"Don't be ridiculous. You've got tons of good years left."

She smiles warmly. "I hope so."

I want to be able to distract Anna but I'm overly distracted myself. Theo is content to absorb fifteen minutes of my time, though. Anna and I play with him, chuckling as he flips around again and again.

I'm just about to go look for Charity when she appears as if by magic at the threshold.

"Elyssa," she says, "can I talk to you for a second?"

I jump to my feet and follow her out of the living room. "Where were you all this time?" I hiss when we reach the hallway.

"Calm down. No one caught me."

I close my eyes with frustration. "What did you do?"

Charity looks around conspiratorially. "I was just doing a little eavesdropping outside Phoenix's office. He's in there with the hot second-in-command."

"I beg and plead Phoenix to convince him to let you out and this is how you—"

Charity grabs my arm, cutting off what I was about to say. "Lys, things aren't looking so good."

I frown. "What do you mean?"

"From what I heard, the organization is closing in. Why else would they have abducted this person from the psychiatric ward? He's obviously close to Phoenix."

"Father-in-law," I mutter.

"What?!"

"Yeah," I say. "He was married. His wife died."

"Fuck," Charity says, her brows knitting together. "Oh my God!"

"What?"

"Of course. It makes so much sense now. Clearly, his wife was killed by Astra Tyrannis. That's what's driving all this."

"All what?"

"This vendetta! This war we're trying like hell to stay out of!"

"Charity," I say, trying to get her to refocus, "what did you hear?"

"Enough to tell me that being close to Phoenix is getting more and more dangerous by the second," she says. "Which means we need a backup plan."

The more she talks, the less I like the sound of anything she's saying. "Charity—"

"And the backup plan is get out sooner rather than later."

"Do you really think—"

She ignores me and keeps rattling on. "Listen, I think we should think long-term. We could maybe collect info on the Bratva operations before we leave. That way, we can sell the information if we need to."

"*Sell his information?*" I yelp. "Are you crazy?"

"Yeah! To the cops. Or the feds. They'd pay for it."

"Charity, that's…"

"We need to think about ourselves here, Elyssa."

"I get that. But we don't have to screw over Phoenix in the process."

She raises her eyebrows and for the first time, she stops her frantic planning to really look at me. "You're worried about *him*?"

"He took us in even though he didn't have to."

"Because I forced his hand!" she points out. "We don't know what his motives are. Men like him always have a motive, Elyssa."

"I think his motive was trying to help us."

"I thought you didn't have feelings for him," she says, flipping it back around on me.

"I don't!"

"You could have fooled me."

"He's still Theo's father," I tell her, falling back on another truth.

"He's shown no interest in being Theo's father," Charity retorts bluntly. I wince at the cold truth. She grabs my hand. "I'm sorry. I know I'm pushing right now. I know I'm crossing the line. But sometimes, it takes a bitch to survive."

"I'm not one," I say shakily.

"I know," Charity replies with a nod. "But you don't have to be. I'll be the bitch for both of us. But we just need to stick together, okay?"

I look down, unable to commit, unable to justify betraying Phoenix like this.

Taking a deep breath, Charity pulls out a phone that looks slightly familiar.

"Where'd you get that?" I ask.

"Anna's," Charity explains unapologetically. "I swiped it when she was busy with Theo."

"Charity!"

"I needed to know what was going on in the outside world," she says.

I tense instantly as she pulls up an internet page and starts searching. Her fingers move fast against the keyboard on screen.

"Here," she says, shoving the clip into my face. "I didn't want to have to show you this. But I think it's necessary now. Just watch it."

So I do.

The reporter standing in the center of the shot is a well-manicured redhead with light makeup and a smart blue pantsuit. As attractive as she is, my eye goes straight to the backdrop she's standing against.

"Oh my God," I gasp. "That's the shelter!"

"… I'm standing outside the Las Vegas Women's Shelter. This is the site at which decorated police detective Jonathan Murray was last seen. A distress call was made from Detective Murray's phone to his department on the seventeenth of May. The exact time of the call was not disclosed. However, our source in the police department did say they are on the lookout for a woman by the name of Elyssa Redmond who is believed to be connected with his disappearance."

At the mention of my name, my fingers shiver so violently that I drop the phone. It clatters to the ground.

I fall to my knees in time to hear the reporter finish, "…The young woman is believed to have lived and worked in the shelter for the past year. Since Detective Murray's disappearance, her whereabouts are unknown. It is believed she vanished shortly after Murray visited the shelter. The police department of Las Vegas hopes that Ms. Redmond will come forward in the following days to make a statement."

The clip stalls and buffers but I swipe away and hand it back to Charity.

"Oh my God. They want me for questioning…"

Charity tightens her hold on my arm. "Breathe. Remember what I told you. We'll get through this. We just gotta stick together. Right?"

I take a deep breath and try to be as brave as the situation calls for. To be the bitch I need to be to survive.

Not just for myself—but for my son.

"Right," I tell her. "Right."

30

PHOENIX
MATVEI'S RECOVERY ROOM

"How bad is it?" Matvei asks, his gaze flickering to my leg.

"A graze. Nothing more."

"She fixed you up?"

"Yes."

We turn to each other and face off as though we're gearing up for a Wild West gunfight.

It strikes me that Matvei should be a don in his own right. He was never meant to follow. He's as much a leader as I am. And yet here he is, taking orders from me. It takes a strong man to be able to do that when he knows he's destined for greater things.

Not for the first time, I'm glad Matvei chose to pledge his allegiance to me. But I'm fully aware that his fealty is a mark of respect, not subservience.

At any moment, he can walk away. And I know if that happens, I won't stop him.

"You do realize we're on the same side, right?" Matvei asks with one raised eyebrow.

"Matvei…"

"Don't," he snaps. "You asked me a lifetime ago to work with you. And I vowed that together we would bring down that fucking organization, once and for all."

"It's personal for me, Matvei."

"It's personal for both of us. I want these motherfuckers dead as bad as you do. I just want to do it right."

"And I don't?"

"You should have consulted with me before you went, Phoenix. That's all I'm saying."

"What would that have served?" I ask, irritation bleeding into my tone.

"You would have understood more about what you were walking into."

I frown, waiting for him to continue.

"After I was stabbed by that cop fucker, you gave me a job," he reminds me.

"Yes. I told you to try and track Sakamoto's movements."

Matvei nods. "Precisely. I haven't just been sitting on my ass watching Netflix this whole time. I've been doing my job."

I tense with anticipation. "You found something?"

"Only that he seems to be tracking someone himself," Matvei tells me. "And from what I can tell, the person he's tracking is…"

"Spit it out, brother."

He sighs and raises his gaze to meet mine. "You."

"Sakamoto's tracking me?" I repeat. *"Blyat'."*

I turn to face my wall, dripping with printouts and photos and scrawled notes. Matvei wants his news to shock me. To scare me.

But it's doing the exact opposite—it's proving I'm on the right track. That's got me fucking giddy.

"You very nearly died today, in case you forgot," Matvei points out. "Only reason you're still standing here is dumb fucking luck. They've clocked you, Phoenix. They're coming for you. For us."

"Let them come," I snarl. "I've been preparing for this my whole fucking life."

"It still requires planning—"

I barely hear his cautionary words. "You said you've been tracking him?"

"Yes, but—"

"So where's he going to be next?"

Matvei eyes me warily but he answers anyway. "He's got a fundraising gala he's attending tonight."

"Tonight? Hm." It's sooner than I expected but I'm not about to postpone my plans for a more convenient date. "Tonight works."

"Phoenix, hold the fuck on. You're not seriously thinking about going after him tonight?" Matvei asks incredulously.

"You should know better than to ask."

"Phoenix, it's too soon. We're not prepared."

"I've been prepared for years. Since I held my wife's dead body in my arms. It's not too soon, brother. It's five years too late."

"Sakamoto is not going to be an easy target," Matvei argues. "He's going to be surrounded by security. Not to mention he's going to be at a gala for every rich bastard in the metro area. The place is going to be crawling with armed goons."

"Your point?"

"You have no strategy and no time to come up with one!" Matvei yelps, grinding his teeth together. "This gala is less than five hours from now."

I smirk. "I've always liked a challenge."

"Apparently, you like death wishes, too."

"I like revenge, Matvei. That's why I'm doing this. To make things right again."

He screws up his face in distaste. "I'm coming with you."

"You're in no condition for a field mission," I snort. "You've got enough bandages around your torso to pass for the Michelin Man."

Matvei grits his teeth. "I'll manage."

"It wasn't a question. You're staying put. In any case, I need you to run interference and coordinate with me from here."

He growls in wordless anger. But I know him well enough to know that he understands I'm right. His ego just doesn't like being left behind. Even if there's a perfectly good reason for it.

"Okay, I'll humor you. Let's say you somehow manage to get into the gala," Matvei says. "Then what?"

"Then I hone in on Sakamoto, get him alone, and beat some answers out of him before I kill him."

"That's a lot to accomplish in one night."

"You doubt my abilities?"

"No, but I do question your logic. What if he doesn't talk?"

"I'll make him talk."

"What if he gets the upper hand on you?"

"Then I deserve to die."

"Jesus, Mary, and Joseph," Matvei says, throwing his hands up in frustration. "You're not going to back down, are you?"

"Not in the least."

"Phoenix, this plan is reckless, even by your absurdly reckless standards."

"Yes, it is—which is exactly why it'll work."

Matvei narrows his eyes at me. "What does that mean?"

I take a breath. "I'm starting to think that Vitya was right when he warned me of spies among my men."

Matvei frowns, but he doesn't say anything.

I continue, "If there is a mole in our midst, then any plans I make are at risk of being discovered and passed on. But if I act off the cuff, then there's no time and no opportunity for the mole to inform on me to his superiors."

"Or *her* superiors," Matvei amends.

"You suspect Elyssa?" I ask, trying not to sound affronted by that fact.

"Not necessarily. It could just as easily be the other one."

I nod begrudgingly. In my world, everyone is guilty until proven innocent. Even doe-eyed Elyssa. "Fine. But until we know for sure, this is the way I'm going to do things."

Matvei sighs. "I still think it's too hasty."

I smile, knowing I've won this conversation. Matvei growls at me with annoyance and turns to the door. "If you insist on doing this, I'm going to need to get shit sorted out."

"You're a shining star amongst men, Matvei. A credit to humankind. A hero we don't deserve."

"Yeah, and you're a fucking pain in my ass."

Grinning, I watch Matvei leave my office. His weight is shifted to one side because of the stab wound but I can tell he's recovering fast. I hate that he can't accompany me tonight. But I won't risk him, either. He's too important to the Kovalyov Bratva. And he's also one of the few souls on this earth that I trust without reservation.

I'm high off the euphoric feeling of having a plan and an immediate mission. I leave my office and make my way to my weapons vault. I'm halfway there when I notice a shadow emerging from one of the rooms to the side. A second later, Elyssa walks out and nearly runs into me.

She's carrying the baby. He giggles as she jerks to a stop before she hits my chest.

"Goodness, where'd you come from?" she gasps. "I didn't even see you."

"I could ask you the same question."

"Theo got restless, so I decided to take him for a walk," she says, popping a kiss on his forehead.

This is the closest I've come to the child in a while. He turns his face to regard me with curious eyes.

And all I see in them is… Yuri.

I take a step back as my demons rush around me, stealing away the euphoria of action and replacing it with the same creeping dread that's marked every waking second since my family was snatched away from me.

"Phoenix," Elyssa says, her face screwed up with concern, "are you okay? Is it your leg?"

"No, I… it's fine. I'm fine."

Her forehead is scrunched with worry. A worry that feels weirdly intimate.

"I need to go," I blurt.

"Where are you going?" she asks. "You need to rest. You just got shot!"

"This is nothing," I say gruffly. "I've had worse."

"Let me check it again."

"No."

She flinches at my curt tone but she doesn't let up. "It'll only take a few seconds—"

"I said no."

She sighs heavily and ignores me in the same breath.

"Here." Before I can protest, she's shoved the baby into my arms and let go. I stand there, frozen in place, holding a baby for the first time in five years.

And fuck if it isn't the most triggering thing that's happened to me in a while.

"Elyssa…"

She squats down in front of me. Without permission, she raises the cuff of my pants and examines my wounded leg.

My cock isn't quite sure how to process the sight of her on her knees.

My heart doesn't know how to process the comforting weight of the child in my arms.

The result is a painful erection and a burst of temper.

"Get on your goddamn feet," I hiss.

She glances up at me from her knees. "What's wrong?" she asks, soundly truly mystified as to why I might be angry now. The baby looks at me, too, as if to ask why I'm shouting at his mother.

Guilt and desire course through my veins, reminding me of a time when I'd had everything in the palm of my hands.

Kind of like I do right now. Except I'd fucked it up back then. I'm at serious risk of making the same mistake again.

"Phoenix?"

I step back without an answer. After a moment's hesitation, she rises slowly to her feet. She glances between me and the baby.

For a second, I think she's nervous. Then she smiles.

It's a slow, beautiful smile that makes me realize just how young she is.

"You look good holding a baby," she murmurs dreamily. A blush colors her cheeks moments after the words leave her mouth. "Or what I meant was… was…"

"I know what you meant." The words come out harsh but I can't hold back the smirk that follows.

Somehow, she's managed to completely dissipate my anger with just a soft smile and a blush.

"You're a natural," she clarifies, her eyes fixed on the baby in my arms. I can see the love there. That unconditional, all-consuming feeling that swallows you whole the moment they grab your finger for the first time. I know it well.

"You should take him back," I say, holding out the infant.

She shakes her head. "He looks comfortable."

"That makes one of us."

For the first time since I've known her, her eyes go cold. The effect is strange. Jarring. And extremely unwelcome.

"Then why don't you just—"

"Holding him reminds me of everything I've lost," I explain in a sudden outburst. The words gush out of me before I have a chance to re-think them.

She stops short, her eyes traversing my expression, searching for any hint of a lie. She doesn't find it. "Oh."

The baby boy is still staring at my face as though he recognizes me. Then he reaches up and tries to grab my nose. I stare down at him, remembering a time when I had been high on the excitement of new fatherhood. A tremor of the same kind of emotion simmers just beneath my skin. But I refuse to let it crack through the surface.

I buried that part of me forever when I put my wife in the ground.

"I know you think that I'm just here for money," Elyssa says softly. "But maybe what I'm really here for is… you."

I'm not expecting that. Our eyes snap together and she realizes that her words haven't come out quite like she wanted them to.

"I'm just trying to say that, like… what I mean is… Theo needs a father. Every boy needs a father."

"There's no point in getting attached, Elyssa," I say vaguely. "This life? My life? It's built on unpredictability."

She frowns, a ripple of fear coursing through her eyes. "What does that mean?"

"It means that tomorrow is not promised. Especially not for me."

"I don't understand."

I push the baby back into her arms. This time, she takes him without protest. But she never takes her eyes off me.

"You know what I do. Who I'm fighting. Don't you?"

She doesn't pretend like this is news. "Yes."

I nod. "I'm not naïve enough to think that I'm invincible. Yes, I am powerful. But so are they. In fact, they've been powerful for much longer."

She shakes her head. "Then maybe you should stop," she says.

"Stop?"

"Stop going after them," she says urgently. "Just end the mission. Live your life."

I frown. "This is my life. This is the only thing I know how to do. Even if I wanted to—which I don't—I wouldn't even know how to stop."

She looks as though she's trapped suddenly.

I can't look at her anymore. If I do, I might be forced to pull her to me. Comfort her. And if I do that, it'll break down the carefully constructed barrier I've managed to maintain so far.

I've come so close to bringing it down several times before.

That time after she'd fallen into the pool remains the closest call we've had. But even then, I'd retained some crucial sense of distance. A part of myself I've refused to show her.

I need to keep that now.

"I have to go," I tell her, taking a step back.

"Where?"

"That's my business."

"Phoenix," she says softly, "are you about to do something dangerous?"

I can see the worry in her eyes. Too familiar. It's all too fucking familiar.

"Go back to your room," I say gruffly. "And take care of that kid."

Then I do the best thing I can do for her and my son: I walk away.

31

PHOENIX
THE WEAPONS VAULT

"What do you think you're doing?" I ask as Matvei shuffles into the weapons vault.

"Picking out a gun," he replies. "Same as you."

I shift my gun to my dominant arm and turn to him. "Maybe Murray knocked you in the head, too, because you clearly misunderstood what I said upstairs: you're not coming with me tonight. I thought I made that clear."

"Fine, I don't have to be on the field. But I can still help onsite. In fact, I can help better if I'm close."

"Is this going to be another agonizingly drawn-out argument?" I snap.

"Probably. I'm as stubborn as you are when I set my mind on something."

I ignore the jibe and shrug my shoulders. "Fine, but if some asshole starts shooting at you, I'm not gonna step in."

Matvei smiles. "Don't worry. I know you're no hero."

He walks up next to me and the two of us face the weapons wall. Rack after rack of rifles stare back at us.

"A rifle? Little ostentatious, don't you think?"

I roll my eyes. "I'm not going to the gala with a fucking rifle," I say. "I just like looking at them. They calm me."

"You're a fucking head case, Phoenix Kovalyov."

"Don't I know it?" Smirking, I turn towards the door. "Gotta go get ready."

"I'll meet you in the car in fifteen minutes. Unless you need longer to primp?"

"Careful. I can still leave you behind."

Matvei laughs. "You wouldn't dare."

The change in him is stark. It's amazing what the promise of action can do to a man like Matvei Tereshkova. He was born for this life. For the violence, the danger, the chaos of it all.

Just like I was.

Of course, I'd gone and ruined it all by getting married and pulling an innocent woman into my world. If I'd been smarter, I might have realized that this world was not conducive to a family, to normality, to happiness. I'd just been misled. I'd grown up surrounded by happy couples.

My parents. Cillian and Saoirse. Kian and Renata.

Is it any wonder that I'd fallen into the trap of believing that you could build both an empire and a family?

But I've long since realized that not every marriage ends well. Not every ending is happy. I should have done instead what Matvei did: embraced a life of eternal bachelorhood and said good fucking riddance to the things that normal people cherish. I'm not normal and

I never will be. No one can change that.

I head to my room and swap my everyday clothes for a Brioni charcoal gray suit, Tom Gray loafers, and a crisp white button-down.

Satisfied with my reflection, I hide my guns and head downstairs where the car I'd requested has been pulled up front. A second later, Matvei appears.

"I thought you'd be here before me," I remark. "Did you get mascara in your eye?"

Matvei gives me the finger. "I was preparing, asshole. We've got eyes on Sakamoto."

"Good. 'Bout time you started pulling your weight around here."

He grins and gives me the finger again. One of my black jeeps roll up behind the BMW, and I give Konstantin and Alexi a salute where they're sitting up in the front of the vehicle.

"Let's get this show on the road," I say grimly.

Matvei and I get into the BMW, and we set off towards the gala. According to my navigator, we should be there in twenty minutes.

"You sticking with your off-the-cuff plan?" Matvei asks as we drive, regarding me coolly. His expression gives nothing away but I know him well enough to know he's worried.

I nod. "I told you—those are always the best ones."

"The women?" he asks. "Elyssa and Charity…?"

"What about them?"

"Where are they?"

"In the house. Where else would they be?"

"They didn't see you leave, did they?" he asks.

I know why he's asking. And where Charity's concerned, I don't care about the suspicion. But with Elyssa, I feel defensive. Another bad sign.

"I knew it," he says before I can even formulate an answer.

"Knew what?" I snap.

"You care about the girl," Matvei says. But he's not accusatory. Not as much as I'd expected him to be, at least.

"I don't care," I reply brusquely. "I've seen women like her all my life. Marginalized, controlled, and abused since the day they were born. It's in my nature to feel sympathy for her. It doesn't mean anything."

"Yeah? Then how come you don't seem to feel the same kind of sympathy for the brunette?"

I shoot him a side glare. "She's just annoying."

Matvei laughs. "It's not a sin to admit that you might have feelings for another woman, you know. You're allowed to move on."

"Are you trying to convince me that she's a spy? Or that she's a good lay?" I demand impatiently.

Matvei chuckles. "I was just making a general statement. I don't care who you move on with. As long as you move on."

"You know, if I wanted a shrink, I'd get one."

"It's a question of need, not want," Matvei says smugly.

"Jesus Christ, you're a prick."

Matvei grins at me like a fucking Cheshire cat. I can tell he's excited about the mission tonight. The opportunity to get back into the field is probably the only thing that's making him overlook the riskiness of this non-plan of mine.

I sure fucking hope it works out.

The gala is on the fortieth floor of the Waldorf Astoria, in the ballroom overlooking the city. I know the space reasonably well from prior events, but I'd had Matvei go over the floorplan with me just to be sure.

The ballroom itself is just one open space. But it sprawls out into more intimate nooks and crannies. Small, shadowy verandas stud the perimeter. Quiet places to talk—or to kill.

Valets try to direct me to the queue of cars but I ignore them and find a patch of shadows in a distant corner of the lot to park in. Konstantin pulls the jeep up a few feet behind us.

"Okay," Matvei says, jumping into focus mode. "I'm going to get in the back of the jeep. My computers and shit are in there, and I can keep you informed."

"Where's my earpiece?"

"Right here," Matvei says, passing it to me.

I secure it into my ear and turn to him. "Can you see it?"

"No, you're good. James fucking Bond."

"James Bond wishes he looked this good," I say with a grin.

Matvei rolls his eyes. "Let me correct myself—you look like James Bond... if he fell out of an ugly tree and hit every branch on the way down."

It's my turn to give him the finger. Then, laughing, we get out of the car. Konstantin and Alexi do the same. Matvei gives them both a nod and clambers into the back of the jeep.

"I need you two to do a sweep of the place and report back to Matvei," I tell them. "He'll keep me informed. Stay discreet."

The two of them nod and slip off towards the hotel.

I arch my neck back and take in the building. It's grand and opulent, like a glowing diamond in the middle of the desert. Everything looks perfect from where I stand now. But I know that when I get close enough, I'll start to see all the scars. The flaws. The chinks in the armor.

"Phoenix, come in," Matvei says in my earpiece. "Can you hear me?"

"I hear you loud and clear," I inform Matvei.

"Good. I'll be your fairy godmother for the evening."

"Then for my first wish, I want you to shut the fuck up."

"No can do, brother. Wishes are for genies. Fairy godmothers do whatever the hell they want."

I shake my head and laugh. But it's time to be serious now. So with a sigh, I crack my neck and slip into my persona for the evening. *Phoenix Kovalyov. Don of the Kovalyov Bratva. Stone-cold killer.*

Matvei says in my ear, "Alright, you're good to go. The boys have eyes on the entrance elevators that lead to the ballroom floor. Sakamoto still isn't here."

"Where is he?"

"No more than fifteen minutes away."

"And so it begins," I mutter to myself. I hope to fucking God this ends how I want.

I take one step towards the glistening hotel when I hear a noise that sounds like it's coming from… the trunk of my BMW.

"What the fuck?" I growl. I pause, turn, and approach the car slowly.

"Phoenix?" says Matvei in the earpiece. "What's wrong?"

I pop open the trunk and whip my gun out in the same motion. My finger is on the trigger and I'm ready to start blasting…

Until I see a waterfall of blonde hair.

Then Elyssa pops upright and swings her legs out of the trunk.

"Phoenix? All good? Do I need to come out there?" Matvei asks.

I check the angles. From where he's situated in the back seat of the jeep, Matvei won't be able to see us. And for some reason, I'm not ready to hear his thoughts on this development just yet.

"No, everything's good," I lie. "Just waiting for the right opportunity to move in."

"Right. Okay."

I turn a furious gaze onto Elyssa but she just stares at me sheepishly. When she opens her mouth to speak, I force my hand over her lips. Her eyes go wide.

I drag her down the road and make a left behind a catering van. Once we're out of sight of the jeep, I pull out my earpiece without jostling it too much.

"What the fuck are you doing here?" I hiss.

Elyssa cringes back from my anger but she still stands her ground. "I knew you were going to do something dangerous. And… I came to stop you," she stammers out.

"Are you fucking serious?"

"I'm right, aren't I?"

"You're insane is what you are. You can't be here."

"You shouldn't be here, either."

I narrow my eyes at her. "You're going back right now."

She reaches out and seizes my hands. There are several people walking by, and every one of them glances at us as they walk past.

"Please, Phoenix, I'm begging you: don't go in there."

"Elyssa—"

"If you insist on sending me back or going in there on your own, I'm going to scream so loudly that it'll ruin all your plans anyway."

I blink as I process what she's saying. For someone who looks like a shy wallflower and flinches every time I say "fuck," she's pretty goddamn stubborn right now.

Perhaps I've underestimated her. The girl's got some guts.

"I can't stop this, Elyssa," I say to her. "These men, this organization—they're the ones responsible for killing my wife. And my…"

I shake my head as the words die on my lips.

"I can't rest until I've taken them down."

"You could die trying."

"I'm willing to."

She looks at me with desperate eyes. "Let me come with you then."

"That's out of the question."

"Don't make me scream."

"You're seriously threatening me right now?"

She looks uncertain but then she nods, her chin jutting out stubbornly. "Yes, that's exactly what I'm doing."

"Jesus." I look around, contemplating my next move. "Come back to the car with me. We'll figure something out."

"I can be naïve," she retorts. "But that doesn't mean I'm stupid. If I walk back there with you, you're going to lock me in there and leave me behind."

Goddammit. "Fair enough. Why do you even want to come?"

She looks at me helplessly for a moment. "Because I want a chance to be useful."

Well, fuck. What am I supposed to do with that?

"You can't go in dressed like that," I point out. "This is a gala. You need a gown."

"Let's go find me one then."

I frown. "Where the fuck are we supposed to find you a gown at…" I trail off as a middle-aged couple walk past.

They're clearly made of money, judging by the designer clothes they're wearing. His tux is Gucci and the watch he's wearing is set with black diamonds. Her dress is brilliant, too. A one-shouldered gown in a deep emerald green.

Two things cement my selection.

One, she looks to be the same size as Elyssa.

And two, despite their obvious wealth, she and her husband are clearly not important enough to warrant bodyguards.

Sitting fucking ducks.

"Come on," I say, gripping Elyssa's arm and towing her down the street behind the couple.

I turn on my earpiece again, and after a moment of static, I hear Matvei's shallow breathing.

"Phoenix?" he asks. "Are you back? Everything okay?"

"There's a crowd. Gonna turn this thing off. It's distracting."

"Since when? Wait, hold up, don't—"

I turn it off and pick up the speed. There are too many pieces in play for me to jeopardize this plan by backing out now. I don't know when I'll have another crack at Sakamoto.

It's too late to back down now.

The moment we enter the hotel lobby, the woman in the emerald dress heads for the elevators with her husband.

"What's the plan?" Elyssa asks nervously.

I don't answer. But I do snatch a glass of sparkling water from a tray sitting in the foyer of the hotel and hand it to her.

"You're gonna have to spill this on her," I say, gesturing to the woman in the green dress.

"What?"

"We're taking her dress."

Understanding dawns in her eyes and she goes pale as a ghost. Then, seeing I'm deadly serious, she nods.

Again, I can't help being impressed. I didn't think she had this in her. Maybe there's more to Elyssa than meets the eye.

We ride up in the spacious elevators with the older couple. The woman gives me an appreciative glance and I realize that she has no real interest in being at this event with her husband.

Elyssa sidles a little closer to me and the smile drops from the woman's face. They hurry off the elevator as soon as the doors open.

I linger back for a few steps to give them enough of a lead. Then I jut my chin after them.

"You wanna play with the big dogs, little pup?" I ask. "Well, go on then. You're up."

Her expression falters, but she moves forward. For a moment, I wonder if she's willing to go as far as this. She's a nobody who's never done anything of the sort before. A few days in my world and I'm giving her just a taste of what it's like to be me. To do the things I must do.

Will she falter?

Or will she succeed?

In the end, it's maybe a little of both. Her trip looks so real that I'm convinced it wasn't staged at all. She careens into the woman's back and the water in the glass she's holding splashes everywhere.

"Dear Lord!" the woman cries, literally clutching her pearls.

"Oh God! I'm so sorry," Elyssa gasps. "I wasn't looking, and I tripped and... I'm just so sorry. Please, can I help you clean up?"

The woman gives Elyssa an impatient glance and turns to her husband. "I'll meet you inside," she snaps. "I need to visit the ladies' room first." She heads towards the restrooms, Elyssa trailing in her wake.

I give them a head start.

Then I follow.

32

PHOENIX

The older woman turns with a start when she sees me enter behind Elyssa. "You can't be in here!" she snaps. "This is a women's—"

"I'm sorry," I say, striding forward fast. "We just need to take care of one quick little thing."

Before she can react, I pull out the handkerchief in my back pocket and press it to her face.

Her eyes go wide with shock and then flutter hopelessly. She struggles—for an old woman, she's got plenty of fight left in her—but it's a useless fight. As her eyelids finally drift closed, the rest of her sinks into limp unconsciousness. I ease her to a seated position on the floor, back against the wall.

When I turn and stand, I notice Elyssa frozen to her place in horror. "What are we doing?" Elyssa murmurs. "Is she… is she…?"

"She'll be fine."

"How'd you do that?"

I hold up the handkerchief in my hand. "Chloroform."

She looks slightly relieved. "So she'll be okay?"

"Of course. She'll wake up in an hour or so," I tell her. "Now undress her. We may not have much time."

I move immediately to the locked storage closet. Snapping off the handle with the butt of my gun, the door swings open. Inside, I find exactly what I'm looking for—an "Out of Order" sign. Moving to the main restroom entrance, I hang it up on the door and then lock the handle, just to be safe.

I turn around to see Elyssa struggling to turn the woman on her back so she can access the zipper. She looks like she is trying to do it without touching the woman at all.

I go hunch down beside her. "Move," I bark gruffly. I make quick work of it, rolling the woman onto her belly, then grabbing hold of the zip and tugging it down.

She's wearing two layers of spanks over a bright set of red lace lingerie. Not bad for an old broad. Her husband doesn't know what he's missing. The old son of a bitch is so oblivious, it'll take him hours to realize his old ball and chain is MIA.

With my help, Elyssa manages to pull off the dress. But I can still feel the guilt wafting off her.

"You're the one who asked for this," I point out, though she hasn't said a word.

I expect her to fire back at me but she accepts the guilt and drops her head. "I know."

I feel the bitter tang of my own guilt on my tongue. This is my world and I know it; I understand it, I've accepted it. But for Elyssa, this is all shocking and violent.

"She'll be okay," I reassure her again.

She nods but her eyes are pasted on the woman's face. She shakes it off—or tries to, at least. Once we've got the dress off her, I carry the woman into one of the stalls and set her down on the closed toilet seat. With her forehead resting against the stall, she looks like she's sleeping.

"You'll have more fun in here than you would have out there," I murmur to her.

Then I shut the door and leave her behind me.

I enter back into the area in front of the sinks to find Elyssa pulling off her t-shirt. Her back is to me so she doesn't see me enter. I have a sliver of time to look at her.

She's wearing a plain white bra. It's the kind of bra you wear when you think no one's going to be seeing you in it. And yet, she still manages to look sexy. Though her body is pale and skinny, she's still got subtle cords of muscle in her arms.

She looks in the mirror and her eyes meet mine. She blushes at once and tries to cover herself up.

"Keep going," I order. "We don't have time for you to get embarrassed."

She sets her t-shirt aside and starts unbuttoning her jeans. I don't make any secret of the fact that I'm watching her closely. My dick springs to life the moment she pulls the jeans down over her taut ass.

She pirouettes slowly. I can practically see her heart beating from here.

"You can't wear a bra with this dress," I tell her.

She glances towards the dress and then back to me. "I don't think—"

"I've seen you naked before."

"That was different."

"Why?"

"Because I was in shock then," she says. "I didn't really know what was happening."

"Is that what you've been telling yourself?" I ask, unable to hide my smirk.

Her eyes narrow. My smile gets broader. For someone as passive and soft-spoken as she is, seeing the spark in her only makes me harder.

"Take off your bra."

Her body stiffens. But not in anger. If I'm not mistaken, that's arousal I'm sensing from her.

I know I'm letting her distract me yet again. I know I'm putting my preoccupation with her above everything else—including the obsession I've nursed for the last five years.

It's like a car crash. I see it coming. I hear it coming.

But I can't stop it. I cannot fucking stop it.

I feel possessed. "Maybe you need some help," I growl, stepping forward until there's only an inch of space between us.

I know we don't have time for this. But fuck it—I'll make time.

She keeps her eyes fixed on mine and her hands limp at her sides as I reach behind and unhook her bra. It snaps apart and she shudders as my fingers graze her naked back.

The way she's looking at me feels like an invitation. Her chest rises and falls fiercely, and I can see her eyes dilate.

"Careful, little lamb," I warn her—or maybe it's myself I'm warning. "You're in too deep."

I see a flash of pride run across her eyes. "You don't know what I'm capable of."

"No? Then maybe you should tell me. Or better yet, show me."

The effect of those words is immediate. Her eyes shut down and she pulls away from me. "People say that," she murmurs. "But they don't mean it."

"I'm not like everyone else," I say. "I've done much worse on my best day than you'll ever dream about on your worst."

She shudders again. "I believe you."

"Then why aren't you running from me?"

She avoids my eyes and reaches for the dress. She pulls off the silver brooch pinned to the front. It's absurdly huge, absurdly glitzy, the point big enough to stab someone with. This old lady didn't do anything halfway, apparently.

Elyssa sets the brooch on the bathroom counter and raises the dress in her arms. "I'll need your help putting this on," she says. She's still not looking at me.

"You didn't answer my question."

"Well, maybe I don't have an answer."

I'd love to be able to press her for one. Or at the very least, press up against her for one. But now's not the time.

I watch as she steps into the dress and turns her back to me. She's hugging herself and goosebumps prickle up and down her spine. She sucks in a breath involuntarily when my fingers brush her shoulder blades as I zip her up, one tooth of the zipper at a time.

But when she spins in place, it's my turn to shiver.

She genuinely takes my breath away. Even with her unkempt hair and the complete lack of makeup on her face, she's fucking beautiful. Too fucking beautiful to die.

"You are lovely," I murmur.

I mean that. I truly do. She's exquisite and fragile, like a piece of handcrafted porcelain. But the words are more like an apology for what I'm about to do.

She notices something in my demeanor. "Phoenix?" she balks. "Phoenix, what are you—"

I grab her by the forearm and shove her back into one of the stalls.

For a moment, she grips my arms as though she thinks I'm taking her in there to fuck the life out of her—and then she realizes what I'm going to do.

"No…!"

She crashes into the stall. The toilet strikes her in the back of the knees and she plops down into a seat on the closed lid.

I stand in the stall threshold blocking her. She stares up at me, the betrayal clear in her eyes. "You said I could come with you!"

"I lied."

Then I slam the door in her face and grab her discarded t-shirt from the bathroom counter.

I hook it around the door and tie a firm knot.

"Phoenix, please!" she cries, hitting the stall hard. "Please don't do this. It's too dangerous."

"I know. Which is exactly why you're not coming with me."

"Phoenix—"

"I let you distract me once before. It's not happening again."

I pull out my phone as I exit the bathroom. I make sure the Out of Order sign is still hanging off the front as I screw the earpiece back into place and switch it on.

"Phoenix, what the fuck? Where are you? Konstantin and Alexi are inside. They have eyes on Sakamoto, but not you."

"It's all good," I say. "Walking into the ballroom right now."

"What happened?"

I sigh, but I can't avoid it any longer. "Elyssa," I explain.

"Seriously? You're thinking about her now?"

"No—I mean, yes—What I mean is, she followed us here."

"What the hell are you talking about?"

"We had a stowaway in the trunk," I tell him. "She's currently in the bathroom just outside the gala ballroom, northwest corner of the floor. Get someone to her and get her out of here."

"Fucking hell, Phoenix!"

If he says anything else, I ignore it.

The gala is in full swing. Men and women glide around the room, sipping champagne and discussing shit that only rich people care about. Everyone is in their finest, their glitziest and glammiest. Trying to impress one another with how much they spend and how little they care.

I spot Sakamoto immediately. He's the only one with a full security detail surrounding him. I have to resist the urge not to roll my eyes. The surest way to make yourself a target is to arrive with a fucking entourage.

I then catch sight of Konstantin and Alexi on one side of the ballroom. I give them a nod. The two of them will have to run interference if my impromptu meeting with Sakamoto is disturbed.

As I adjust to my surroundings, I become vaguely aware of Matvei in my ear again. "*...ty khudshiy grebanyy slushatel'!*"

"I know, I know," I interrupt. "It's inconvenient."

"Inconvenient?" Matvei repeats. "Or fucking suspicious?"

I stop short, realizing what he's thinking. "You think she's the spy?"

"Why else would she follow you here? Why else would she want to be involved?"

I grit my teeth. "It doesn't matter. I've removed her from the equation."

"Is she still breathing?"

"Yes."

"Then you haven't removed her from anything. I'll deal with her."

The fury that courses through my body is so violent that I see red spots for a moment. I distantly notice Konstantin squinting at me before I lose him behind my own anger.

"Matvei, you are not to touch her. Your orders are clear. Take her safely from the bathroom back down to the jeep and keep her there. She is not to be hurt under any circumstances."

There's a second of silence on the other line. He can tell I mean business.

"Yes, boss."

Then the line goes dead.

"Fuck," I mutter as I circle around to where Alexi is standing.

Sakamoto is a few meters away. Neither one of us is facing him or his entourage, but we both have one eye on the lot of them.

"Well?" I say out of the side of my mouth.

"I don't know how we're going to get him away from that group," Alexi says.

"He'll move from them during the course of the night," I say confidently. "Look, he's already got his eye on one of the hostesses. He's going to want to get her alone."

Sure enough, we both notice Sakamoto's eyes drinking in the hostess's ass every time he thinks she's not looking.

"So, what do you want to do?" Alexi asks.

"We wait," I reply. "We wait for our chance to end this shit."

The pieces are all in motion tonight. We'll see which king ends up on top.

∽

Ten minutes later, it's like the gods are shining down on me and my mission.

Sakamoto removes himself from his entourage and makes his way across the ballroom. The doors to the pool patio have been thrown open now and people are milling in and out.

I look to Alexi. "Keep an eye on his men," I say before slipping out after Sakamoto.

It appears as if he's heading towards the bathroom but then he turns to the side and heads to one of the private rooms that accompany each balcony.

Apparently, he can't wait until the end of the night to fuck the hostess of his choice.

The moment he disappears behind one of the large jade green doors, the young hostess I'd seen him talking to emerges in his wake.

She's dark-haired, buxom—and she looks wary. Which works perfectly for me.

I intercept her before she can get her hand on the door. "I wouldn't," I advise.

She frowns. "What do you mean?"

"Get out of here. Claim you're coming down with something and leave."

Her frown deepens. "If I do that, I could lose my job."

"If you stay, you might lose a whole lot more."

Her light hazel eyes wrinkle with understanding. She gives the door a glance and then she spins on her heel and starts walking away fast.

I smirk. *Smart girl.*

I slip into the room through the jade green door. It's empty but the balcony door is open. The white marble on the floor gleams with flecks of silver. I can see Sakamoto's shadow cast along the balcony.

His back is to me. We're alone. Far from the party.

It's a perfect fucking setup.

… Too perfect.

As I take the final step towards him, he whirls around. The gun in his hand is aimed directly between my eyes.

"You were not the company I was expecting," he says, his accent slight but elegant.

"Why don't I believe you?"

He smirks. "A man like me is always prepared. I may travel with a circus but I can take care of myself."

This time, I do believe him.

"You've been keeping tabs on me," I guess.

He smiles. "I could say the same about you."

"Vitya Azarov. Where is he?"

His smile gets wider. "Somewhere safe. Don't you worry."

"Are you being ironic?"

"Just giving you some friendly advice."

"What do you want with him?"

"Him? Nothing. You, on the other hand…"

I'm itching to pull out my gun but I know if I so much as flinch, he'll shoot. I have no doubt his reflexes are razor-sharp.

"You have me now," I point out. Probably not the smartest move, considering he's the one who's armed and I'm currently a sitting duck. But my pride is working overtime here.

"Indeed. It's fitting we should meet like this."

"Is it?"

"I have more advice for you, young man," he says.

There's something intensely polite about the man. He's been bred well, that much I can tell. But he's no less deadly because of it.

"I'm all ears," I drawl.

"Give up on your mad quest. If you value your life, give up now."

I narrow my eyes. "Is that a threat?"

"A statement of fact," he shrugs. "You're messing with the wrong people."

"Do you mean Victor Ozol?"

Sakamoto stiffens. "I don't know that name." An obvious lie. One that's so obvious that he doesn't even bother trying to make it convincing.

"Forgive me if I call bullshit," I say. "Why are you working with him?"

"Why ask questions?" he asks. "You're about to die."

"You've got that backwards," I tell him. "You're the one who's going to die tonight."

He doesn't give himself away. Nothing about his body language or his expression betrays him. But my superpower has always been my instinct.

And it doesn't fail me now.

I lurch to the left in the second before he fires. The bullet passes so close beside my face that I feel the pressure of air just next to my cheek. My ears are ringing.

By the time I pivot around, my gun is out and raised. I fire twice, forcing him to retreat against the corner of the balcony and reposition.

He tries to duck back into the room but I shoot again, forcing him to stay on the balcony. One more squeeze of the trigger, and this time, my bullet strikes gold. It buries itself in his arm. His gun drops immediately, and before he can grab it again, I lunge forward and kick it out of his reach. It goes skittering to the edge of the balcony and falls over, forty stories down.

I take the opening to pistol-whip him in the jaw with my weapon. He crumbles to the floor, but he recovers quickly. From the marble floors, he looks up at me, though there's not a drop of fear in his expression.

At least, not yet.

"You've underestimated me," I tell him.

"No, we haven't," he replies. "Why do you think we're working to take you down? We don't go after small fish."

"Well, consider me flattered."

He shakes his head. "Killing me won't change anything. They will destroy you and everything you hold dear—again."

The threat hits me harder than I expect. Elyssa's face flashes across my eyes. Then the boy's.

"Not if you start answering my questions."

He spits blood onto the white marble. "Torture will not make me talk."

"We'll see about that."

Before I can ask my next question, he kicks my legs, causing me to stumble back and land hard on my spine. Even with his wounded arm gushing blood, the man moves with a speed and power that I can't help but be impressed with.

He pounces on top of me and attempts to wrestle the gun out of my hand. I bring my elbow up and hit him in the face. He shakes off the hit and goes for my gun again.

The scrabble sends my weapon flying back towards the interior of the hotel. So now I'm weaponless and in a terrible position. The blood from Sakamoto's wound is dripping into my face, blinding me. At the same time, he's raining swift elbows down on my face and throat.

I swing recklessly, hoping to make contact. But he blocks or dodges every punch.

And then his hands find my throat. For such a slender man, his grip is powerful.

He bears down, putting his entire body weight into the strangulation. But I'm still confident I can fight him off. I just need a little more time.

I just need to—

I see the hand at the last moment.

The blinding shine of a sharp edge as it slashes his neck.

Sakamoto's eyes go wide as a spurt of blood soaks the edge of his collar. His hands loosen around my neck.

Not the loosening of defeat—but the loosening of death.

He falls back against the marble. By the time I sit up, he's already dead.

I turn to the side and stare up at the person who stabbed him.

She's standing there in her emerald dress, clutching the brooch pin in her bloodied hand. She's trembling like a leaf.

But when Elyssa's gaze meets mine, her expression is iron and steel.

33

ELYSSA

That's two now.

Two men I've killed.

Two lives I've ended.

Two crippling pangs of guilt that I have to carry around for the rest of my life.

How has it even come to this? I was supposed to get married, have children, keep a house, and take care of my family. That was always how it was supposed to be.

And yet, here I sit, staring down at my bloodstained fingers…

Again.

A sickening sense of déjà vu wraps its ghostly hands around my throat and squeezes. I cough instinctively.

Phoenix's eyes snap to mine. "You okay?"

Am I okay? What a question. I have no idea. I should be feeling… something, right?

But all I can feel are the iron shackles of the life I'd thought I'd thrown off a year ago. I can feel it catching up to me. And with every passing second, it gets harder and harder to breathe.

How is it possible that this has happened again?

The first time, I could claim it was an accident. A horrible misunderstanding.

But this time? This time, I knew what I was doing.

When I managed to break out of the bathroom stall by kicking as hard as I could until the door gave way, I stumbled out, saw the brooch lying on the bathroom counter, grabbed it, and left.

I don't know if it was fate or sheer dumb luck that I emerged into the ballroom just in time to see Phoenix slipping out. And I don't know if it was bravery or stupidity that made me follow him through the beautiful jade green door.

But I do know that when I emerged from the shadows onto the veranda and saw the other man strangling the life from Phoenix's throat, it felt like the simplest decision in the world.

I had the brooch in my hand. And I didn't hesitate.

Why not? Wouldn't another person—a moral, sane, normal person—have hesitated before taking a life?

What have I become?

The better question: have I become like *him*?

I can feel tears starting to prick at the outer corners of my eyes. I blink them aside impatiently. No, I don't deserve to cry. Once was a mistake. Twice...

Well, that makes me a murderer.

"Elyssa?"

I jump in my seat when he says my name. Phoenix is here, too. The man I sacrificed my soul for. *If you even had a soul to begin with,* says a nasty voice in my head.

Whose voice is that? It can't be mine. My mother's, maybe. Or my father's?

No. I know whose it is. A voice I'll never hear again.

Father Josiah.

It's been so long since I allowed myself to think of him. To think of that night. But it's all coming back now.

Not the moments leading up to it—but everything that came after I woke up with a splitting headache and a cast iron paperweight in my bloody hands.

One year later and nothing has changed.

I'm still wearing a dress that doesn't belong to me.

My hands are still bloody.

And I'm still running from the darkness of a world that just won't let me go.

"Elyssa!"

I turn to Phoenix, but I don't really see him. Not truly. His features are blurry behind my guilt.

He takes one look at my face and swerves the car to a stop onto a lonely stretch along the side of the road. Two cars whizz past us as Phoenix turns to me.

"You need to breathe," he says in an even voice.

He looks so strong and in control. It's like nothing has fazed him. He was the one who took my hand and walked me out of that hotel as though everything was fine. Even now, he seemed completely unaffected by everything that has come to pass.

"Breathe, *krasotka*," he says again.

This time, I hear him.

This time, I see him.

This time, I listen.

I suck in a huge, gasping breath, as big as I can. It relieves some of the pressure on my chest but not all of it.

"You're shaking."

I look down at my hands and I realize he's right. My body feels like it's a few shivers away from spasming out of control. He pulls open the center console between us and takes out a small bottle of water.

"Here," he orders. "Drink."

I don't accept the water immediately but when he continues to glare at me, I take it and down a few sips. That helps, too.

"Feel better?"

"No."

"Why?"

I gawk at him in shock. "*Why?*"

"That's what I asked."

"I... I killed a man."

His eyebrows rise. "You didn't mean to?"

"I just... I wanted to get him off you," I tell him. I blink and my tears fall free onto my cheeks. "I didn't mean..."

"You're telling me you didn't mean to kill him?" Phoenix asks.

The edge to his tone has me pausing. I can see suspicion. Uncertainty. Distrust. I just risked everything to save his life, so why is he looking at me like I could be the enemy?

"What are you asking me?" I ask sharply.

As I speak, I feel the skin of who I once was start to shed. I'm not that girl anymore—the good girl, who listened to the elders and followed the wisdom of the people who knew best. That hasn't worked out for me once in my entire life.

So yes—Elyssa from the Sanctuary is as good as dead.

"Nothing."

"No," I insist. "Say what you want to say."

His expression turns cold. "I needed him alive."

"I just told you I didn't mean to kill him."

"And I'm supposed to believe you?"

I stare at him, trying to make sense of the accusation in his tone. *One step forward, two steps back.*

"You think I meant to take his life?"

"I needed answers from Sakamoto. Now, a key figure in the Astra Tyrannis hierarchy is dead. And dead men don't talk much, in case you haven't noticed."

All the pieces click into place at once. "You still think I'm a spy, don't you? You think I'm working for…"

His expression ripples and I realize that I've hit the nail on the head. I turn to the door and fumble around with the handle. It's locked. I yank at the lock but it refuses to budge.

"Let me out," I say. "Let me out!"

"No."

"I can't breathe… I need… I need to get out!"

The lock snaps back. I thrust open the door and fumble onto my feet. I stumble forward, putting as much distance between Phoenix and me as possible.

I just risked everything for a man who thinks I'm the enemy. He believes I'm working for a horrible organization that traffics in women. Is that what he sees when he looks at me? Not just a killer but a monster? A liar?

Horror and hurt battle inside me as I keep walking. I gulp in huge bursts of air, but it doesn't help. Not this time.

"Elyssa. Stop!"

For the first time, I don't listen. I can feel him closing in on me but I'm too rattled and too tired to speed up. Even if I do, I know it won't make a difference. He'll catch me. One way or another, the house always wins. Isn't that what they say in Vegas?

Phoenix grabs my arm and twists me around to face him. I tear myself away. "Don't touch me!"

"You can't blame me for thinking that," he says—as though he expects me to understand.

"I saved your life!" I cry out, anger momentarily overtaking the hurt. "If it weren't for me…"

"I would have won that fight."

"That's your pride talking," I snap. "He had his hands around your neck. He was going to strangle you. He would have, too, if I hadn't stopped him." I pull up my hands and shove them in his face. "Look at my hands! That's blood. *His* blood. I did it for you."

He hasn't said anything. But I can see that he's still not convinced.

I shake my head. "Why are you letting me stay in your house if you really believe I'm a spy?" I demand. "What's the point of all this?"

He exhales slowly. "Elyssa, just get back into the car."

"No."

"Elyssa—"

"I'm not going anywhere with you."

He looks surprised by my raised voice, my rage. It's strange for me, too. But part of it feels shockingly good. Like I've repressed this aspect of myself for so long that it's finally getting to relish its time in the spotlight.

"You have to come with me."

"Why?"

"Because I have your son."

My anger deflates almost immediately.

My son.

Theo.

And Charity…

My complete and utter helplessness slaps me across the face. I was a fool to have followed him tonight. I should have left well enough alone and stayed put. Stayed with Theo and Charity—the only people in this world who truly matter to me.

"Hey…" His hand brushes against my arm and I flinch but he doesn't pull back. "It's been a difficult night. Let's get you back to the mansion."

I raise my eyes to meet his. I so desperately want to trust him. But now, I'm not so sure I should. If he thinks of me as a threat, how much longer before he takes measures to make sure I'm taken care of?

"Elyssa, Hitoshi Sakamoto leads the Yakuza. They're going to be thrown into disarray after tonight. And they're going to want revenge. We have to get back to the mansion. It'll be safe there."

I nod slowly as he takes my arm and leads me back to the car.

The drive back to the mansion is silent. Phoenix parks in the garage and comes around to open my door. "Come on," he says impatiently, gesturing for me to follow him.

"Where are we going?"

"Just hurry up."

The exit of the garage opens onto a meandering cobblestone pathway that feeds into the gardens that surround the mansion. The mansion looms silent and intimidating in the night, a block of glass and shadow.

Phoenix strides ahead of me. I don't bother trying to catch up to him. The part of the garden he leads me to is shrouded in darkness. But I notice the dark fire pit sitting in the center of the space.

He sets to work quickly. Within minutes, Phoenix has a roaring fire going. Warmth spreads across my limbs and I move a little closer.

But when Phoenix approaches me, I back away from him. "Are you going to kill me?" I ask.

He looks startled by the question. "No," he says at last. He doesn't bother giving me any other reassurance.

"Okay," I whisper. I can't decide whether or not I believe him.

"Take off the dress."

"What?"

"You heard me. Take off the dress. It's covered in his blood, and we can't have anyone finding evidence that we had anything to do with the murder."

You would think that the word "murder" would stand out to me. But strangely, it doesn't.

It's the "we" that gets me.

Maybe that's why I don't argue as I try to reach back and unzip myself. After struggling for a few seconds, Phoenix walks closer to me.

"Let me," he says harshly. "Turn."

I spin slowly away. I feel his hands graze up my sides before he unzips me.

I shimmy out of the dress, and he immediately flings it onto the firepit. The flames roar as it consumes the silky fabric.

"What about you?" I ask.

"My coat is clean," he says, shrugging it off his shoulders and handing it to me. "You're going to be cold once we're away from the fire."

I look down, realizing that I'm naked except for the white panties I'd pulled on that morning. I take his coat and slip it on. It swallows me whole. It smells of him.

Phoenix pulls off his shirt. There's only a little blood on the collar and sleeves, but he throws it into the firepit anyway. That leaves him standing there in the firelight, naked from the waist up.

The shadows reflect off his perfectly sculpted torso. He looks like a statue come to life, all hard lines and brutally sharp edges. It's unreal.

When I raise my eyes, I realize that he's watching me watching him. The blush is inevitable but I don't avert my gaze. I hold his as though I have something to prove.

He walks right up to me until we're practically nose to nose. Red flames dance around in his dark irises. Hot flames. Dangerous flames. Flames that want to consume me—and they will, if I give them the chance.

"How bad is it?" I ask when the silence gets so heavy that I can't bear it any longer.

He waits a while before answering. "If even one person saw you tonight, they're going to connect you to me."

"The woman whose dress we stole..." I mumble.

"Yes, she'll most likely give us up. Identifying us is all it would take."

"The police are already after me."

"How do you know that?" Phoenix asks sharply.

I raise my eyebrows. "You know?"

"Of course I know," he says impatiently. "I make it my business to know everything that involves me or my house."

"Why didn't you tell me?"

"What purpose would that have served?" he says.

He had kept it from me to... protect me? Spare my feelings? Keep me from worrying? All those reasons suggest that he cares about me.

One step forward.

"Elyssa," he begins. The heat I'm feeling is coming off him now, not the fire.

"Yes?"

"Why did you follow me tonight?"

"It was a mistake," I say at once. "I shouldn't have done it. I'm sorry."

He nods. "That doesn't change the fact that you did. I want to know why."

I bite my lip. "I knew that wherever you were going was dangerous," I say, stumbling over my words a little. Already, it's coming out all wrong. "I guess I didn't want you to be hurt. I thought that maybe if I followed you, I could convince you not to put yourself in danger."

"That has always been my life."

"I know but I just couldn't bear it."

I don't say anything else, and he doesn't ask more of me. We just stand there, staring at each other in the firelight. The moment feels heightened but I'm not sure why. My feelings are complicated enough. I can't even begin to try to decipher what Phoenix might be feeling.

"Come on," he says.

"Where are we going?"

"Inside," he replies. "We've got to wash the blood off."

I look down at my fingers to notice them trembling. He grabs my hand, holding it tight in his.

"Stop," he orders gently. "Stop re-living it."

"I can't."

"Then remember this: Hitoshi Sakamoto was evil in every sense of the word. He trafficked in girls and women. He stole them and forced them into a life of sexual slavery. He deserved to die."

I drink in the comfort he's giving me. I take the absolution and try to absorb it. "But… you needed him alive."

"Yes," Phoenix agrees. "I did."

Those words sit between us for a moment. But our hands are linked and that makes the silence less harsh.

"But if I couldn't take him alive, I'd rather he be dead."

The firelight flickers discreetly against Phoenix's face. The embers are dying out slightly now that they've gorged themselves on fine silks. Without the crackling, the night is calm and peaceful.

The atmosphere has shifted considerably. It's still tentative. Nothing has been decided; nothing has been resolved.

But at least for the moment…

It feels like a truce.

34

ELYSSA

He never lets go of my hand. I don't question it and I don't try to pull away—mainly because the pressure of his touch feels like the only thing that's keeping me sane right now.

He leads me upstairs but he doesn't take me towards my room. Instead, he makes a right. When we walk into a large, dark room, I realize why everything in here looks so spartan in its minimalism.

This is *his* room.

He guides me into the bathroom. A jacuzzi rests in front of floor-to-ceiling windows looking out onto the lush garden. On the opposite side next to the double sinks is a glass-walled shower the size of my room back at the shelter. Gleaming silver showerheads dot the walls with one huge one hanging from the ceiling like a chandelier. Everything is silver-onyx tile that refracts and bends the light into otherworldly shimmers.

I feel like I'm becoming untethered from reality. The luxury, the touch of everything—and the smell.

It smells like him.

I turn around slowly. Phoenix is standing by the bathroom door, regarding me with an unknowable gaze. I want to ask him what he's thinking, but I'm not confident I'll get an answer. I'm not confident that words exist for what's going through his mind right now.

He walks forward and teases his suit jacket off me. I shiver when the fabric comes free from my skin, but it has nothing to do with the cold. His eyes drop to my breasts and linger there for a long time.

He discards his coat in the hamper thrown to the side. Then he strips down himself. Slowly and smoothly. Undoes his belt and tosses it over his shoulder. Unbuttons and unzips his pants and steps out of them.

Shivering and moving on pure autopilot, I slip off my panties and cast them to the side. He nods like I did precisely what he wanted. He doesn't say anything but I can almost hear the thought running through his head: *Good girl.*

He strips off his boxers. I try to avoid looking at his cock but my eyes have a mind of their own. And once I take one look, I can't stop. He's half-erect already. Thick and powerful, like a weapon between his legs.

I look up at him through my eyelashes. "Phoenix?"

"Yes?"

"I want... I want you to touch me. I want you to make me feel safe."

He doesn't so much as flinch. All the reaction is contained to his eyes. I see the desire in them.

He reaches out and rests his hand against my neck. Then he moves down until he's fondling my breast.

I close my eyes, marveling in the sensation of his touch. It's been so long... As though I've been holding my breath for a year, and I'm finally allowed to release it.

Is this what I've been waiting for?

Not absolution.

Not vindication.

But… him?

I take a clumsy step forward, moving so fast that I step on his toes. He doesn't seem to notice or care, and I take my cue and push myself up to reach my lips to his.

When our lips come together, there's a strange harmony that spreads through my body. I wonder if I'm the only one feeling it.

Probably. But in this moment, I don't care.

I want him. Even if I have to face the consequences later, I want him now.

When he parts my lips with his tongue, I moan into his mouth, inviting him in. His hands run down my back and land on my ass. In one smooth move, he grips my ass cheeks and lifts me up so that I'm straddling his waist.

Then he walks me into his shower. He doesn't put me down, though. He just pins me up against the cool, tiled wall. I gasp as the prick of chill claws at my back. It doesn't last long. Moments later, the heat of his kiss consumes me.

His cock is pressed against my thigh, and I moan again, aching to touch him there. It's strange—he's the father of my child. He's been inside me. He's changed my life in so many ways. And yet there are still so many firsts we haven't crossed yet. I've never truly touched him between the legs before. I've never kissed him quite like this— hungry and desperate and eager for more.

But as those firsts fall away one by one, so do the last remnants of my old life. The last ripped pieces of the veil I was born with.

There was a lot I was told was right and appropriate and acceptable behavior for a girl like me. I'm only just starting to realize that I was force-fed a book of arbitrary rules that don't apply to the real world.

It's time to write my own rules.

I slide my hand down between us and wrap it around his massive shaft. I'm clumsy and inexperienced but I recognize a certain instinct that I didn't realize I've always had.

A hunger that I was always told to hide.

A desire that I was told to be ashamed of.

A wantonness I was told to bury down and forget.

My body knew it long before my mind has come to understand. It knows how to act, how to move, how to feel. It knows what to do next. My center is slick with desire and his cock keeps nudging my entrance. I moan as I rub myself against his tip.

"Ah, please… please…"

"Tell me what you want, little lamb," he growls in my ear.

A shudder rips through my body like a lightning bolt. I wrap both arms around his neck, trying to pull him as close to me as possible.

"I want you inside me. I want you to feel you again…"

He doesn't need to be asked twice.

I can feel his own desire topple over and collide with mine. Two stars combusting side-by-side, each one consuming the other.

He lines his cock with my opening and thrusts into me. He does it so slowly that my eyes go wide and my mouth forms a perfect O shape as I stare into his dark, sinful eyes.

The scream is caught in my throat but the moment he sinks all the way into, I feel it release as a babbling groan.

"Yes, yes… oh God…"

He tears both my hands from around his neck and forces them against the wall. His fingers are vise grips around my wrists but it's the most titillating form of bondage I've ever experienced.

Unable to do anything more than grip his hips with my legs, I throw my head back and cry out as he thrusts into me again.

He still takes it slow. So slow that it verges on torture. It's only halfway through that I realize he's doing it on purpose. He wants me to be the one to ask for more.

Lucky for him, I'm more than willing.

"Phoenix," I whisper, my words coming out in short, exhausted bursts, "harder, please. Faster."

He doesn't ease me into anything. He goes from zero to a hundred in less than no time.

And God, I want it so bad.

Suddenly, he's slamming his hips into me, driving his cock in so deep and so hard that my back hits the wall over and over again. Pain and pleasure wind together and I lose all sense of myself.

In this moment, I'm just one raw nerve ending. And I'm firing off pleasure in all its different incantations.

The fact that I can't hold on to anything, the fact that he's got my hands restrained against the wall, only heightens the experience. I'm helpless—and I'm free.

And when the orgasm tears through me, I come completely untethered.

My legs clench, my core throbs, and my walls feel like they're about to split open. But he never stops. He keeps going until he's wrenched the orgasm from me and turned me into a limp puddle in his arms.

He pulls out suddenly, and I hope he's not going to step back because I know with certainty that I'll collapse without his support.

He doesn't. But he doesn't let me go, either. Instead of setting me on my feet, he places me on the little marble seat jutting out from the wall.

His left hand finds my throat. I gasp from the shock of it as he pins me against the tile surface but I don't push him away or fight.

This is how it should be, I tell myself. *You're a killer. He's a killer. Your love should be as violent as you are.*

With his right hand, Phoenix grabs his cock and starts stroking. He's already glistening with sweat, and his cock is dripping with my juices. He uses it as lubricant to push himself over the edge.

I sit there and look up at him, sucking in tiny breaths against the pressure of his hand and watching as pleasure ripples across his face.

And then he erupts.

He drenches me in him. My face, my breasts, little droplets of it falling onto my bare thighs.

I sit there and take it, feeling myself start to throb all over again. Apparently, my body has been starving this whole time, and I've finally given her permission to ask for what she wants.

And what she wants is *this*.

He rumbles low as he finishes emptying himself onto me. And when he's done, he exhales with relief. Like he's finally exorcised demons he's been carrying for a long, long time.

His eyes meet mine for a moment before he goes to the nozzle on the front-facing wall and turns it on.

Water descends from the showerhead onto both of us. I flinch, expecting it to be cold—the showers at the women's shelter are always frigid—but it's refreshingly warm.

Phoenix turns away from me and tilts his head up under the stream. I stare at the powerful muscles on his back, admiring all the rippling lines and knotted scars. His tattoos are elaborate and beautiful. But I remember what happened the last time I asked about one of them—he shut down completely and pushed me away. I'm not about to make that mistake a second time.

He turns slowly to face me once more, water running down his darkly seductive features. I'm aware that I'm staring. Probably drooling, too. But I've made my desire for him pretty transparent now. There's no walking back certain revelations.

His cock still looks hard and it's making my body come alive again. I didn't even think it was possible to want him again so soon after the way he had just taken me up against the wall.

But apparently, when it comes to sex, there's a lot left that I have to learn.

I'm aware that his seed is still all over me… but I'm content to let it sit there for a little while longer.

That is, until he stretches his hand out to me. I lace my fingers into his and he pulls me up to my feet. My legs wobble dangerously but he wraps an arm around my waist and holds me close against him.

He washes himself off me without a word. His touch is tender. Delicate. He dabs with a washcloth and wipes away all evidence that this ever happened. The only proof is in the ache between my legs. The fire in my belly. The weakness in my trembling thighs.

I'm aware that neither one of us has really said much since we were down at the firepit. But somehow, I can't bring myself to break the silence between us.

Once the blood, sweat, and seed has been washed off both of us, we step out of the shower. My center is still throbbing. But it's a happy, hungry ache.

I stand awkwardly in front of the sink, unsure of what I'm supposed to do now. Then I see Phoenix come up to stand directly behind me. He's so tall and so huge that his shoulders stick out above my head. He dwarfs me completely in every way. I've never felt so small, so helpless—and I've never loved it so much.

His hands land on my hips and he pushes me forward.

I feel his hard cock slide between my butt cheeks, and I get wet all over again. With rough, unruly hands, he bends me over the bathroom counter and enters me again without ceremony.

I keep my eyes on the mirror in front of us, watching his every thrust, drinking in every flicker of expression that crosses his face.

His muscles expand and contract with each savage twitch of his hips. I just gaze at him, both mystified and enthralled by his dominance, his strength.

He's ruined me for every other man. I understand that much, if nothing else, as he takes me for the second time.

Our eyes are fixed on one another, connected through the mirror that records the fragile union we've formed for tonight. He slams into me with unrelenting aggressiveness.

And I welcome it. I didn't think I'd like this kind of lovemaking, if you can even call it that. But I've surprised myself countless times already. The good girl I thought I was died a long time ago. She died in the desert a year ago.

So who am I now?

Someone darker.

Someone bolder.

Someone far more terrifying.

35

PHOENIX

PHOENIX'S BEDROOM

I wake up with her arm draped across my chest. She sought me out in the night without ever waking up, as though her body craved my warmth. I wasn't sure whether to hold her close or throw her out altogether.

It's been years since I slept next to someone. With Aurora, I had been a restless and selfish sleeper. I kept to my side of the bed, and she kept to hers.

But Elyssa... she's different. Everything feels different with her. I'm still trying to decide if that's a good thing or a bad one.

Her eyes are shut tight. Her lips flush pink against the dim sunlight filtering in through my blinds. I look at her and wonder just what the fuck she is doing here—not just in my bed but in my life. In my world.

Her blonde hair is strewn across her shoulders and down her naked back. The kind of hair that's begging to be used. Handled. Last night, when I'd taken her from the back, I'd been itching to grab fistfuls of it, yank it backwards, use it to break her.

But I'd held back—because I could sense the surge of emotions she was drowning in. She's meek in sex, just like she's meek in life. There are moments, though, when she breaks through her shell. When I feel her deepest nature come out. The fight against those restraints rages in her all the time.

Apparently, someone somewhere told her that taking what you wanted just isn't acceptable.

Who told you that, little lamb? I ponder silently. *Who warped your brain to make you so afraid of what you are inside?*

She sighs and nudges a little closer to me. Instinctively, I try to move out from under her. Sharing a bed with a woman after so long—it brings guilt.

Not that I spent much time wallowing in my guilt last night. No, when she was bared before me, lust was all I gave a flying fuck about. I took her again and again, and then twice more for good measure.

Once I allowed myself to acknowledge my desire for her, I couldn't be sated. And the fire in me lit the fire in her. She let herself be consumed like it was fucking salvation.

Maybe she doesn't realize just how dangerous that can be.

Determined to get out of here now, I push out from under her and take to my feet. She gives another sigh and turns over. I see the round peaks of her nipples and my cock springs to life once more like it didn't get plenty of Elyssa last night.

I have the urge to get on top of her and slip my cock between her lips but I resist it. In the light of a new day, I've also been cursed with perspective.

I can see now that last night was inevitable. Doesn't make it any less of a mistake, though.

The tension between us was there from the beginning. In some ways, it's been building since the first fucking night we met. That kind of chemistry was bound to have come to a head at some point.

Now, I've got her out of my system, I can—

I break my resolve and look down at her again. It's just a quick glance and the sheets are pulled up around her chest. But the material is still flimsy enough that I can make out the shapes of her breasts. The hard nubs of her nipples. The sleek lines of her collar bones.

And it all proves one thing: apparently, I haven't gotten her out of my system at all. Not if the throbbing of my erection is anything to go by.

Maybe *I'm* the one who doesn't realize how dangerous this can be.

From here on out, I'm going to have to exhibit some willpower. Some sense of control over myself. For both our sakes.

I pick up my phone and glance at the screen. It's glowing with notifications.

A missed call from Konstantin. Two from Alexi. Four from Matvei.

"Fuck," I mutter.

I stride into the bathroom and change. Then I slip out of the room towards my study. When I walk in, Matvei is sitting at my desk. Apparently, he's been waiting for me.

"Enjoyed your night?" he asks. He's clearly annoyed but there's a hint of disbelief combined with amusement in his tone.

"You're in my seat, wiseass."

He narrows his eyes at me but the smile stays on his face. "Is this your seat?" he asks, feigning innocence. "I had no idea."

"What are you rambling on about?"

"You don't seem that interested in the mission anymore," Matvei shrugs. "That's all."

"Careful," I warn.

Matvei leans in. "What happened last night?"

I curb my anger. He has a right to be pissed. Especially given that I'd essentially left the building without so much as an explanation. And then I hadn't checked in with him or the boys afterwards. If any of my guys had pulled that shit, I'd have come down on them for it. Hard.

"I… was dealing with something," I reply vaguely.

"And by something, do you mean Elyssa?"

I grit my teeth. "Perhaps."

"Okay, so I'm going to assume one of two things: either she's buried somewhere in the backyard or else she's lying naked in your bed as we speak. Which of the two is it, brother?"

"Get out of my seat."

He smiles as he rises to his feet. "How was it?" His tone has shifted. It's gentler now. I don't like it any more than I did when he was annoyed.

We cross each other as we switch positions. I ignore his question.

"Is she going to be a problem?" Matvei presses.

"No."

"Why am I not reassured?"

"Because you're a distrustful bastard."

"It's necessary to be one in this world. You used to be the same."

"I haven't changed," I argue. "But—"

"Don't tell me she's different."

I hesitate. "Fine. I won't."

"What happened?" Matvei asks again.

So I tell him. I don't pull any punches. I don't sugar coat anything that transpired. I give him a complete play-by-play, including and up until the moment that Elyssa had lodged the brooch pin in Sakamoto's throat.

His eyebrows leap up into his hairline. "She killed him?"

"Skewered him like a fucking rat."

"Before he told you anything significant?"

"Yes. Hard to confess your sins with a four-inch brooch in your throat."

"And you trust her?"

"I haven't spent a lot of time thinking about it."

"Clearly."

I narrow my eyes at him. "Your turn."

He sighs like he's still mulling over everything I've just told him. "After you left, it took about ten minutes for all hell to break loose. That's when they found Sakamoto's body on the balcony. Minutes later, hotel security also found a half-naked old lady locked into a bathroom stall."

I chuckle, remembering the look on the woman's face. Not quite the glamorous night she was expecting to have.

Matvei frowns. "What about this is funny? She sang like a goddamn bird as soon as the cops showed up."

"She ID'd us?"

"She sure as hell did. And there are pictures of both you and Elyssa, placing you at the event last night. Only two snapshots, the two of you in the background, walking towards the elevators. Your face is almost completely hidden from view. But…"

I look up, frowning. "But what?"

"But Elyssa wasn't so lucky." Matvei seems suddenly very interested in a loose thread at the hem of his shirt.

Fuck. "How clear is the picture?"

"Not very but Elyssa's face is pretty recognizable. It doesn't help that the police are looking for her anyway in connection with Murray."

Fuck again.

"You know the cops are the least of our worries, right?" Matvei reminds me. "The Yakuza are going to be on our asses now."

"Fuck the Yakuza."

"Phoenix, you and I… we've been brothers-in-arms for a long time now," he says. He sounds almost tired now. "And even if you drop the 'in-arms,' we'd still be brothers in spirit. Which is why I'm comfortable saying this to you. This girl… best case scenario, she's a distraction. Worse-case scenario? She's a spy."

Everything he's saying is one-hundred-percent true. I'm trying to fight it but the evidence is overwhelming stacked against Elyssa and her troublesome friend.

"The child…"

"You don't know if the child is yours," Matvei interrupts. "You've taken her at her word. And even if the child is yours, you don't know if that was part of the plan."

I freeze as I weigh those implications. "*Blyat!* You think she was sent to me?"

"She materialized out of thin air the moment before your meeting with Ozol, right?" Matvei asks skeptically. "You can't deny that her showing up completely botched the meeting."

Again, he's right. Again, I hate it.

"She fucked you the same night and disappeared for a year. When she does pop up again, it's in connection with the shady cop dealing with Astra Tyrannis."

I close my eyes. "Enough."

"And then, when you've finally got someone who knows something in a position to give you new intel, she stabs him? It's—"

"Enough!"

Matvei sighs. "You don't want to hear it because you know I'm right."

I get to my feet and head for the door. "You may very well be right," I concede. "But my instincts are telling me something different."

"Don't confuse your instincts with your cock, Phoenix," Matvei snaps back at me. "Stronger men than you have lost bigger battles to their lust."

I glare at Matvei from the door. "There is no battle bigger than the one I'm fighting. And there is no man stronger than me. You'd do well to remember that, *brother*."

I slam the door on him as hard as I can, leaving him in my office with the sound reverberating through the corridor.

I don't know where I'm going—I just need to walk. I need to breathe, calm down, to fucking *think*.

I've been warned about spies in my home, haven't I? And God knows I've run into enough dead ends to suspect that someone on the inside might be betraying me.

But Elyssa showed up long after that started happening.

Is she innocent?

Or am I a blind fool?

I hear a gurgle of contentment and I stop in my tracks. I keep forgetting there's a baby in the house. And every time I remember, it's like being stabbed in the chest with an icepick.

I hear footsteps coming. I brace myself, ready to see the face that's thrown my world into chaos…

And then Charity walks out of the living room, holding the baby in her arms.

Her expression goes cold when she sees me standing there. "Where is Elyssa?" she demands.

"In my bed."

Shock ripples through her eyes for a moment. Clearly, Elyssa left her out of the decision when she decided to hop in my trunk last night.

"You didn't know, did you?" I ask.

"No," she confesses. "I didn't."

"That surprises you?"

"It shouldn't," Charity replies. "Elyssa's both naïve and easily manipulated."

"Is that right? And you think I'm the manipulator in this scenario?"

"Oh, come on! Elyssa's not used to the kind of mind games that you dabble in."

This girl has got balls, I'll give her that. But I wonder: does she have answers to the questions running rampant through my head?

"Has she told you about the night she came to Las Vegas?" I ask bluntly.

"I never asked."

"Scared of what she might say?"

"No," she says firmly. "I just knew it wouldn't matter either way. She suffered some trauma; she ran from it. She was brave enough and strong enough to get herself out of a bad situation."

"And yet you think she's too weak and simple to resist climbing into bed with me."

"That's different."

"Why?"

"Because when it comes to men, women can be stupid. Blind. And when it comes to you, Elyssa can be…" She trails off, probably realizing that she's said way too much.

"Elyssa can be what?"

"Nothing," she says quickly, bouncing the baby on her hip. He's started to fuss a little. He keeps craning his head from side to side as though he's looking for his mother.

"Hey now, little one," Charity says soothingly. "You're okay. You're okay."

"Maybe he needs to be changed."

"He doesn't," Charity snaps. "I just changed him. He's hungry."

"Anna's probably in the kitchen," I tell her. "She'll help you make him a bottle."

Charity stares daggers at me. "I know how to make him a bottle all on my own," she snaps. "I'm the one who's helping Elyssa raise him."

"What a saint you are," I quip back sarcastically.

Her eyes go cold. "You better not have got her into trouble last night," Charity says. "You might be able to walk away from everything unscathed but women aren't that lucky. Especially not women like Elyssa and me."

I remember what Matvei told me only moments ago, about the picture of the two of us walking towards the elevators in the hotel.

My face is hidden. Hers is not.

"Maybe you should have thought of that before coming here with me."

Her face falls a moment, and she looks at the baby. "I wasn't just thinking of myself, you know," she says. "I was thinking of Elyssa. And mostly… of Theo."

I'm trying not to look at the child, but it's hard. He's a beautiful baby. Just like his mother. He turns towards me and breaks out into a cry.

"Here," Charity says, pushing him into my arms. "I think you should be the one to feed him. You are his father, after all."

"I—"

"Anna's in the kitchen," she says, throwing my own words back in my face. "She can help you make a bottle for him."

Then, before I can protest, she turns on her heel and heads toward the staircase. Just like that, she's gone.

I stare down at the baby. He's looking at me with a slight frown, as though he's trying to place me. I see a flash of Yuri for a moment. It's gone as quick as it came but the nauseating feeling it brought with it, like getting punched in the gut, lingers.

His weight fits snugly in my arm. It all feels so natural. So familiar. Even his smell pulls me back years into the past.

I swallow past the bitter knot in my throat and stride towards the kitchen.

When I step through the threshold, though, Anna's not there like I expect her to be. Then I remember that I don't need any help. I've done this before.

I've changed diapers, made bottles. I may have lost my son but I never stopped being a father. It's not the kind of thing a man could stop even if he tried.

And believe me—I've fucking tried.

Balancing Theo with one hand, I make him a bottle of milk. I sway from side to side, the same way I used to handle Yuri.

He looks confused for a moment and then he starts giggling. By the time I give him his milk, his mood has considerably improved.

We go to sit by the window. Theo is drinking his milk, and I'm trying furiously not to let the old loss invade this moment when Anna walks in.

"Master Phoenix?" She steps close and observes the two of us together. "Well, isn't this a beautiful sight!"

"He was hungry," I say gruffly.

"You always were a natural," she remarks.

I expect her to move away but she keeps standing there, staring. After the first few minutes, I start to get uncomfortable. "Was there something else, Anna?"

"Oh, no, nothing," she says, shaking her head. "I just… It's been a long time since I saw you this… content."

Something flickers across her wizened features. Then she turns and goes about her business in the kitchen.

I try not to let her words strike me. But it's too late.

They've already made their mark.

36

ELYSSA

"Why did you go, Elyssa?" Charity says, blocking my path to the door. "Why?"

"It's… it's complicated, Charity."

That's the understatement of the year. But it's as good as I can explain it right now. I can't even explain my own actions to myself.

"Complicated?" she yelps. "We discussed this! It's too dangerous here. We need to get out, not get more involved."

"You made that decision for me."

"You agreed to it!"

"Because you wouldn't allow me enough room to think!" I snap.

I try to move past her, but she blocks me again. "You're not leaving until we figure this out."

"I want to see my son."

"He's fine," she says impatiently. "He's with Phoenix."

I frown. "He is?"

"Why?" she asks. "Are you nervous?"

Am I? I'm not quite sure. There's definitely a strong feeling in my chest. But I don't know if it's nerves—or something else I can't quite put a finger on.

"Maybe that should be the litmus test," she says harshly when I don't answer. "If you don't trust the man with Theo, maybe you shouldn't trust him at all."

I shake my head at her and throw my hands up in frustration. "You're being unbelievably unfair right now, you know."

"Me?"

"Yes," I say, refusing to back down. "You're the one who wanted to come here in the first place."

"Because I thought he was strong enough to protect us!"

"He is!"

"You just want to believe that because you're fucking him."

I cringe at her crude phrasing but I don't bother denying it. She knows I slept in his bed last night. It's not hard to connect the dots.

"You yourself told me that he was one of the most powerful dons in Las Vegas."

"Not compared with Astra Tyrannis!" Charity practically yells. "Elyssa, Phoenix is one man who controls one Bratva. Astra Tyrannis controls so much more."

"Why didn't you tell me all this before?"

"Because I didn't want to upset or panic you."

"Or maybe you just wanted to control me."

She stops short, staring at me with her mouth open. I feel horrible but I don't take back the words.

"Is that what you think I'm doing?" she asks finally.

"Think about it, Charity. In the past year, you're the one who calls the shots. And yeah, I go along with it. But maybe that needs to change."

"And *this* is the time you choose to take a stand? Lys, you don't know what we're messing with here! These people are more serious than you could ever imagine."

"We can't just leave now," I say. "It's too dangerous. The cops are looking for me, Charity. Leaving his protection will leave us exposed."

"We can disappear."

"Where?"

"Anywhere. Someplace far."

"And have what kind of life?"

"A better one. A safer one."

I look down, unable to properly explain to her just how I feel about the idea of leaving.

"Ah. I see."

I look up. "What?"

Charity's looking at me now with a hopeless expression in her eyes. "You're falling for him, aren't you?"

I rear back. "I don't know him well enough for that."

"Why'd you risk your life going after him last night?"

"Because I didn't want Theo losing his father."

Charity shakes her head at me. "You know, there's a reason people say love is blind. It clouds your judgement, Elyssa. It makes you do dumb things. And if you—"

I shove past her before she can finish, unwilling to be lectured to anymore.

When I'm out in the hallway, I turn to her, trying to fight the angry emotion coursing through me. "You treat me like I'm some idiot who doesn't know anything," I say. "I may not have experienced as much as you have but that doesn't make me stupid."

Then I walk away fast. She doesn't follow me.

It hurts for a moment before I shove that pain aside.

∼

I've calmed down considerably when I walk into the kitchen a few minutes later. Phoenix is standing by the windows with Theo in his arms.

Phoenix looks even more beautiful with Theo in his arms. And my boy looks pretty comfortable.

I hold out my hands. Phoenix passes him to me—a little reluctantly, by my observation. I raise him up in the air and turn him on the spot slowly like I'm checking for imperfections.

Theo giggles and tries to grab my hair. Smiling, I plop him into the crook of my arm and look up at Phoenix. "Thanks for taking care of him."

"It was only for a little while," he replies. "It's not a big deal."

He's trying to act nonchalant about it, but I can sense that this last half hour with Theo has meant more than he's willing to let on.

I give him a tentative smile. After a few seconds, he returns it. It's not exactly fully realized, but it's… something.

"Are you ready?" he asks suddenly.

"Ready?"

"For your second swimming lesson?"

Hope and happiness burgeon inside me so fast that it's pathetic. I try not to look too eager as I nod. "I'd love that."

Anna takes Theo happily, and twenty minutes later, I'm back in the pool with Phoenix.

"How long do you think it'll take me to learn to swim on my own?" I ask as we go through another set of drills.

He laughs. "Impatient already?"

I nod and twirl around in the water. "I never thought I'd enjoy it so much," I admit. "Being in the water…"

I do wonder if my enjoyment has more to do with Phoenix than with the lessons themselves, but I decide not to overanalyze that part.

"Surely you had a pool where you lived?" he asks.

I know we're entering dangerous territory, but somehow, I'm less nervous about it than I ever have been before. "We did," I admit. "But it was mostly reserved for the boys."

"Did people think girls have gills?"

I laugh and splash water in his face. "No, of course not. Don't be ridiculous. Girls just have a lot to learn."

"Like what?"

I shrug. "Like how to be a good wife."

Phoenix freezes on the spot like I electrocuted him. "*Chto za khernya,*" he mutters. "What kind of fucking cult raised you?"

A strange bolt zips through me the moment he uses the word "cult." I'm immediately defensive and horrified all at the same time.

"It was just… different."

"No wonder you ran away."

I twirl around in the water again, mostly to hide the guilt on my face. I feel as though if I stay still for too long, he'll see the truth.

I didn't choose to run. I was forced to.

A second later, I feel his hand on my face, smoothing the wet hair away from my eyes.

My heart is beating hard. His body is almost pasted up against mine. His lips are only inches away. It would take the smallest lean on my part to reach him. To kiss him again, like I've been dreaming of doing since the second I woke up alone in his bed.

Smelling like him.

Aching from him.

Dying for him.

"Are you trying to avoid looking at me?" he rasps.

I shake my head. "No."

"You've got to get better at lying."

I frown. "I'm a better liar than you think."

Probably not the right thing to say to him under any circumstances. But sometimes, I worry that all people see when they look at me is a naïve little idiot who'll believe anything she's told.

Maybe that's who I was once. But not anymore. Not ever again.

"Is that right?"

I turn away from him. "Well, no. I just mean—I don't know why I said that…"

He grabs my arm and twists me back around so that I'm facing him. He hasn't acknowledged last night at all, and I'm not brave enough to bring it up on my own.

So we've danced around it all morning, pretending as though this is just a swimming lesson.

Instead of what it really is—an excuse to touch each other.

But, standing here in the water, I realize that there's no reason to acknowledge something that's so obvious. The connection between us feels almost visceral. It eats up all the open space we've allowed. Words would just clutter the last little distances left here.

Phoenix stares down at me for a moment. Then he raises his hand and cups my jaw. His expression is contemplative. Haunted, almost.

"What are you thinking?" I ask, hoping that the question won't cause the whiplash change in mood that I've come to expect from him.

"You don't want to be inside my head, *krasotka*."

"What if I do?"

Something ripples across his eyes. It's gone before I can catch it. "You're so fucking young," he sighs.

My brow ripples. "What does that mean?"

"Exactly that. You're young."

"It's not code?" I ask.

"What would it be code for?"

"Naïve. Gullible. Inexperienced."

He smiles. "You think too much."

Then, like we both knew it was coming all along, his lips come down on mine. My hand catches the side of his neck as the kiss deepens and I feel my body fuse against his.

It's the kind of body that's made to be objectified. Pure masculinity, marbled muscle, and a light smattering of dark chest hair. I run my hands down Phoenix's torso until I land on his perfectly carved abs. My hips are grinding up against his and I can feel his hardening—

"Ahem."

We spring apart and look to the pool deck, where Anna is standing and holding a little black box with a gold ribbon tied around it.

"Sorry to interrupt," she adds sheepishly.

"What is it, Anna?" he asks.

"Something arrived for Elyssa," she says vaguely.

I blush furiously as I head to the edge of the pool. When I glance back at Phoenix, he looks completely unaffected by the interruption. In fact, he looks a little annoyed. Shrugging, he turns away and starts doing laps up and down the pool.

He's a brilliant swimmer. Even when his arms and legs break through the surface, he hardly displaces any water at all. Just knifes through it like a dolphin, all elegant, glistening lines and efficient motion.

I eye the package in Anna's hands as I get out of the pool and towel off.

"This was left at the main gate for you, dear," Anna says, offering up the package. "Be careful—it's a bit heavy."

Frowning, I take the package and examine it. "For me? Are you sure?"

"Yes."

"There must be some mistake. No one knows I'm here."

"Clearly, someone does," Anna says with a shrug and a smile.

A nasty feeling is brewing in my stomach. I only hope that I can hide it fast enough.

"Something wrong, dear?"

I force a smile and nod. "No, thank you, Anna. Where's Theo, by the way?"

"He's inside with Charity."

She gives me another smile and heads back inside.

The sinking feeling is only getting worse. I don't want to open it but I feel as though the longer I wait, the more painful this will be.

I sit down on one of the pool chairs and untie the gold ribbon. It falls away easily. The only thing left for me to do is lift the lid. Or maybe I should just throw this away. Don't look at it, don't fret over it. Just put it out of sight and out of mind.

But I knew even before Anna handed it to me that that wasn't an option. This is destiny in a box. I have no choice but to open it.

My hands tremble as I pop open the top. I'm praying to God that whatever's inside will be innocent. I'm hoping that there'll be a simple explanation for the package as well as its' sender.

But I'm wrong about that.

I'm so, so wrong.

Because what's sitting in the box is the physical reminder of the crime I committed to steal my new life and disappear from my old one.

Even more than that, it's the terrifying reality that I haven't succeeded in disappearing.

I'm not free.

I never was.

They haven't forgotten me.

And this is their way of letting me know.

You can run, but you can't hide. We're coming for you. No one ever truly leaves.

I stare down at my gift, fighting back terrified tears. I don't want it to be true, but there's no escaping it: my past has finally caught up to me.

Because nestled amidst decorative tissue paper is a cast iron paperweight.

Shaped like a swan…

And covered in blood.

37

PHOENIX

I pause at the edge of the pool and look over at Elyssa. She hasn't moved since she opened whatever box Anna handed her. And maybe it's just a trick of the eye but I could swear her fingers are trembling.

"Someone sent you a gift?" I ask, sounding casual as I pull myself out of the pool.

She nods slowly. "Sort of. It's just... I don't know how they knew I was here."

My mind jumps to the photos Matvei mentioned. The pictures of Elyssa and me at the gala. The evidence linking us to the crime. Someone has it—the cops. The media. My enemies.

And they want us to know that.

Matvei sounded confident that my face was unrecognizable but whoever saw it clearly knew where to send the package.

The question remains... what else do they know?

"What is it?"

I sit down opposite her, drenching the pool chair in water. She hesitates for a moment before she pulls it out.

I frown. "What is that?"

"It's a… um, paperweight," she says. "I think." She stares at it before popping it back in the box with the slightest of shudders and clamping the lid back on top like she's trying to stop Pandora's demons from escaping.

"A paperweight?"

She nods. "Yeah. It used to… belong to me."

I can't tell if she's lying or not. Her body is tense, her eyes furrowed together. There's more to this hunk of metal than she's letting on.

"Who do you think sent it?"

She keeps her eyes averted. "Someone from my home, I guess."

"I thought you haven't been in contact with your family."

"I haven't. Which is why I'm surprised to have received it at all," she admits. "It's strange."

"I'm assuming it has some sentimental value to you?" I ask.

"No," she replies with another subtle shiver. "Not exactly."

"Then why send it at all?"

"I don't know." She shrugs. But the gesture lacks conviction, and her expression is riddled with muted panic.

That warm feeling of contentment that's engulfed me these past few days turns to ash. I feel the bitterness spread through my limbs like poison.

Elyssa is hiding something from me.

And she's lying about it.

Too many people have implied that there's a snake in the grass in my home.

Vitya.

Matvei.

Murray.

Sakamoto.

I'm starting to think that my desire for Elyssa is a luxury I can no longer afford. There's more at stake here.

"Is there anything else you'd like to tell me?" I ask point blank.

She looks up at me, startled for a moment. I can see the battle in her eyes.

Prove me wrong, little lamb, I whisper in my head. *Tell me the truth.*

"No," she says. "No, there's nothing."

I clench my teeth together. *So be it. Then your fate is sealed. Time to do what I should've done a long time ago.*

Disappointment and anger burn together but I keep my expression neutral.

"Where are you going?" Elyssa asks as I rise to my feet.

"Inside. I have things I need to deal with. The lesson is over." I say it with a finality that makes her flinch.

I'm walking away when she calls out to me. "Phoenix!" I pause, weighing whether to turn and face her. Before I can make up my mind, she runs to stand in front of me, her blonde hair swinging in the wind behind her.

She looks like a fucking dream in her sexy black swimsuit, water droplets refracting the sun on her shoulders.

"Phoenix," she says, putting her hand on my arm. I look down at the point of contact but she refuses to remove it. "I never did thank you."

"For what?"

"For saving me," she says.

"Which time?" I ask bluntly.

She smiles softly. "All of them."

"Why say this to me now?" I ask, curious about her motives.

She looks off to the side but her hand stays on my arm. "I don't know," she replies. "I was trying not to overthink it."

She gives me a smile that makes me want to forget all the doubt raging inside my head. But all I can think is, *I need to get away from her. I need to be able to think clearly.*

"I have to go," I say brusquely.

She looks disappointed but she nods. "Okay." Then, unexpectedly, she reaches up on her tip-toes and kisses my cheek.

She races away before I have time to react. I stand there for a long time, savoring the feeling of her lips on my skin. Not knowing if it's a mark of hope—or a kiss of death.

∼

Eventually, I wrench myself back to the present moment and head back into the house.

I need to talk to Matvei but I'm also equally wary of the inevitable conversation. I already know where he stands where Elyssa is concerned. Do I need to hear more of the same shit?

Right on cue, my phone starts to ring and I pick it up swiftly. It's Matvei's number on the screen. *Speak of the devil.*

Just as I answer, though, the line goes dead. Before I can call him back, a text from him pops up on my screen.

Come quick. Shit is going dopgkgld;lptrpoip-4 W4oyu[ning.

Great. Just what I need.

I rush into the downstairs bathroom and change into dry clothes. Within minutes, I'm in the garage, getting into the Wrangler parked up front. I speed through the gates and onto the broad roads in the direction of our closest warehouse, where Matvei was doing a security inventory this morning.

The GPS says it's only seven minutes away. But I know better than anyone: a lot can happen in seven minutes.

A part of me questions if I should be leaving Elyssa at the mansion alone. At the very least, she should be supervised. At least until I can figure out what she's hiding and how much of a threat she really is.

I decide to deal with her after whatever's going down at the warehouse.

The warehouse gates are hanging wide open. I zoom inside, the jeep screeches to a halt in a cloud of dust, and I jump out practically before it's stopped moving.

Two of my men are standing out front. "Ilya," I bark. "What's happening?"

"Vitya," he replies.

I stop short. "What did you just say?"

Ilya nods darkly. "The man's going off the deep end, boss," he says. "We haven't managed to contain him."

"Contain him?" I repeat. "The man's pushing seventy. There's at least ten of you here."

"The problem is not subduing him," Ilya explains, following me as I stride into the warehouse. "The problem is getting our hands on him."

I look around urgently but I can't see Vitya. In fact, I can't see anyone.

"Where the fuck is everyone?"

"Out back," Ilya tells me. "They're trying to make sure he doesn't jump."

Jump? Fucking hell.

I start running at a dead sprint. I only stop when I come out the other side of the long warehouse building and see what's happening.

Matvei is standing in the center of the small group of my men. They're all looking up at the roof of the warehouse.

I turn around and catch sight of my father-in-law. He's somehow managed to scale the wall and get right up to the apex of the warehouse roof. It's at least a forty-foot drop from there onto nothing but pure concrete.

"How the fuck did he get up there?" I roar.

Matvei turns to face me. "There was a ladder on the side, the one we use to maintain the gutters. He got up there and pushed the ladder out. Broke the fucking thing, too."

"We have other ladders. Why the hell is everyone standing down here?"

"Every time anyone even attempts to get up there, he threatens to jump."

"Maybe we should let him," Ilya says darkly.

I twist around and fix him with my most scathing glare. "That man up there is my wife's father," I tell him. "I'm not about to let him die. Even if he wants to."

Ilya crumbles underneath my stare. "Right. Sorry, boss."

I look up. At the same time, Vitya spots me. Even from this distance, I see his eyes go wide and his nostrils flare.

So his little stint at the psychiatric ward hasn't exactly helped improve his impression of me. Either that or something happened since my enemies freed him that has soured his thoughts even further.

"Vitya!" I call, holding up my arms. "Listen, you need to—"

"No!" he wails. His voice is wracked with grief and madness. "Not you! You're the murderer. The monster who took my daughter."

"For fuck's sake, Vitya," I say, "you used to refer to me as your son. Do you remember that?"

"I remember everything," he seethes. "And I'm sick of remembering. I want to forget now."

"Vitya, please. I can get you help."

"There's no one that can help me. Least of all you. You're the reason she's dead."

"I know," I say.

I don't have to take the blame on—I already have it in spades. I've been carrying it with me since the moment she died. Since the moment she and my boy were taken from me.

"She begged you not to go through with the operation at Primm. She knew it was dangerous. You did it anyway…"

I stop short. As far as I know, Vitya hadn't been privy to the operation at Primm.

But what he's saying was true. She had begged me not to do it. Not to leave the house that night. Not to fight the war against Astra Tyrannis that my family has been fighting for a long, long time.

"They took their revenge," Vitya sobs. He's dangerously close to the edge of the roof, teetering with his eyes closed in the whipping breeze.

"They took their revenge on you because of what you did. That's why my baby had to die. They were trying to teach you a lesson."

My blood goes cold. I've never heard him speak like this before.

"Vitya, how do you know that?"

"He… he told me," Vitya cries. "The man who came to see me, he told me everything. That's why they killed Aurora. That's why they took my grandson away from you. They're dead because of *you!*"

Matvei's looking at me with alarm but I can't take my eyes off Vitya. The man is coming undone. I'm dangerously close to coming undone as well.

"Vitya!" I yell. "Who told you that?"

"The man! The man!"

He's a slip away from falling. One toe in the wrong place and we'll watch him die here and now.

But the things he's saying are horrifying me. "What man, Vitya? Was he Japanese?"

He shakes his head frantically.

No? Fuck. I'd been so sure that Sakamoto was the one who'd abducted Vitya from the psychiatric ward. If it wasn't him, who did it?

"Vitya, it's important you tell me what the man told you. Did he give you a name?"

"Yes," Vitya replies, through tears. "But not the name you want. He gave me the name of the next person on their kill list. I saw my daughter's name on that list. And my grandson's… Both crossed out."

A chill spreads through me. I haven't felt anger like this in a long time. Those fucking bastards. They make war as if it's a fucking game. They kill for sport, for pleasure, for the sheer fucking thrill of it.

"Whose name did he give you, Vitya?"

But I already know the answer. Even before he says it, I know.

"Your name," Vitya replies, so softly I can barely hear it. "He gave me your name."

And then he jumps.

I know the moment I see the trajectory of his fall that this is the end for him. It's not just the way he gives himself up freely to gravity—it's the hopeless expression on his face.

He has no intention of surviving.

I look away. I hear it, though—the sound that will haunt me for the rest of my days.

It's an undignified sound to end a life.

The silence that follows is a void big enough to swallow me whole. Same with the thoughts and memories surging through my head.

Primm. Aurora begged me not to go out on the mission. She held my forearm, clung to my clothes, wailed and wailed and wailed.

"I have a bad feeling," she'd sobbed. "You won't come home." She cried so hard her tears stained my shirt. But I'd pushed her aside and left anyway.

She was wrong—I did come home.

But she wasn't there when I did.

The mission was a success, as far as the original objectives. I'd killed three Astra Tyrannis operatives, freed a dozen helpless women and children, destabilized an entire region of human trafficking.

But now I know—in cutting off Astra Tyrannis's arm, I had unknowingly left myself open and vulnerable.

They'd come for my heart that very same night.

And they'd ripped it right out of my chest.

38

ELYSSA

"What's that?" Charity asks, eyeing the box in my hands as I walk into the bedroom.

My first instinct is to get rid of it so that I never have to lay eyes on it again. But I know that won't change the fact that someone from the Sanctuary knows I'm here. Someone who wants me to know that they can find me whenever they want.

"It's… a long story."

Charity narrows her eyes. "Spill."

I ignore her and instead walk to the bed, where Theo's lying on his back. He's only just started learning to roll over and it takes everything in my power to resist the urge to help when I see him struggling. He gurgles at me, and I set the box aside and pepper him with kisses.

It makes me feel just a little bit better. But the panic lingers just a hair's breadth from the surface.

"Elyssa?"

I exhale violently and meet her eyes. "Someone sent that to me earlier today," I explain.

"With a love note?" she teases.

I shake my head. "There was no need. I know who sent it."

"Oh God," Charity mumbles, reading my face. "It's not a decapitated head, is it?"

I give her a weary glance. "I probably would've reacted a little more dramatically if that was the case, Char."

"You're not really a screamer," she points out. "You just go quiet and pale—which, coincidentally, is what's happening right now."

"They found me," I blurt out.

She wrinkles her nose. "Who did?"

"My... family. My home."

Charity knows bits and pieces of my past. She knows that I lived in a secluded little community that believed some things not many other people saw eye-to-eye on. She knows that it was tight-knit, heavily controlled.

She knows that I ran away from a man and a marriage and left a fire in my wake. She knows I don't remember much.

But she's never pressed me for details, and I've never been keen on sharing them.

Especially one tiny detail—the body I'd left behind. The body of the man who was supposed to be my husband.

"Fuck," she says, her eyes widening. "Well, it's not so bad."

"Not so bad?" I repeat incredulously. "How on earth do you figure that?"

"I mean, maybe your parents just want to… reconnect. Make amends. That sorta thing."

I realize that she doesn't know what's in the package they sent me. And she certainly doesn't know what it signifies.

She notices the direction of my gaze and she looks curiously at the package. "What's in it, by the way?"

"It's a cast iron paperweight," I explain, knowing I can't hide the truth anymore. "In the shape of a swan."

"Weird. Is it expensive?"

"It's not a peace offering, Charity. It's… a message. They're telling me they know what I did."

Charity stills for a moment and looks at me with a searching gaze. "I've never asked you…."

"I know," I say. "And I always appreciated that because—well, I guess I never wanted to face the truth of what I did that night."

Charity frowns. "Lys, hon, you're talking as though you're the criminal. But you aren't. You were the victim."

"No," I say, shaking my head. "You just assumed I was and I… I let you believe that."

She glances at Theo, who's rolled over again, then back to me. "I don't understand."

"I told you that I was married off to the… the man in charge," I say. "Josiah."

She looks a little startled.

"What?"

"Nothing," she says. "It's just, you've never mentioned his name before."

I look down. "That was his name." I don't add that it tastes foul and bitter on my tongue. "He was the center of our entire community. When it was announced that we were engaged—well, it was considered the ultimate honor."

"Honor?"

"That he chose me."

"*Chose* you?" Charity balks. "You mean, he picked you. Like you were an object on a shelf?"

I hate the way she says it. But I can't refute a single word.

"Yes," I tell her. "And I agreed. In fact, I was flattered." I avoid Charity's face, scared of what I may see there, and charge ahead with my story. "You assumed that he was abusive. That he tried to rape me."

"What about it, Lys? We don't have to do this. We don't have to re-live your—"

"I don't know if that's true," I interrupt.

"What do you mean?"

"I don't remember much from the night it all happened," I stammer as tears of helplessness surface in my eyes. "The only thing I remember is waking up with a horrible headache. And… something heavy in my hand."

I glance over at the paperweight.

"That, to be exact."

Charity is blinking fast as she processes what I'm saying. "You were holding the paperweight? What does that have to do with anything?"

"It was all bloody, Char. And when I forced myself back to my feet, I discovered Father Josiah on the floor—with a crater on the side of his head…"

A stunned silence ensues.

Charity's jaw drops. "Fuck me," she breathes.

"I… I didn't run from him, Charity," I confess. "Not exactly. I killed him. At least, I think I did. And then I ran because I was scared of what they would do to me if I stayed."

I close my eyes and brace myself for what comes next. For her to call me a killer. A liar. A criminal.

For her to say she's turning me into the cops or to the commune or to anyone who might want to make me atone for my sins.

I expect this to be the end.

Instead, she reaches out and grabs my hand.

"Elyssa, you would never do something like that without a reason," she says with complete conviction. "Now, I wasn't there that night. I don't know what happened exactly. But I do know that you wouldn't have done anything that violent unless he deserved it."

I stare at her in disbelief. "I murdered a man, Charity."

She shrugs. "One less misogynistic fucker that we have to deal with."

"But… you don't think less of me?"

She laughs, much to my surprise. "Actually, I think more of you. You're right—I have underestimated you all this time. You've got fucking balls, babe."

It'd be a lie to say I feel completely relieved. There's still too much fear and suppressed memory left in me for that to be true. It's more like I've spent a year living in pitch black darkness—and Charity's proud grin is the first crack of light I've seen in all that time.

"I don't know what I did to deserve a friend like you," I say with complete sincerity.

Charity laughs. "Something sinful, clearly."

Her chuckle fades away, lapsing the room back into silence.

And it takes with it that little spark of joy.

The truth is that this isn't over like I thought it was. As a matter of fact, it's just beginning.

I take a deep, shuddering breath. "I thought they'd forget me. I thought they *had* forgotten me," I continue. "But I've just been fooling myself this entire time."

Charity squeezes my arm. "What are you gonna do? Scratch that—what are *we* gonna do?"

"I don't know yet," I say, shaking my head. "But I do know that I can't hide anymore. And I certainly can't run."

"What are you saying?"

"I'm saying I need to deal with this, Charity. I need to deal with them. Otherwise, I'll never be free."

"This isn't like 'the prodigal daughter returneth,' Elyssa. If what you're saying is true, you killed a man. I understand you had good reasons. But not everyone else will appreciate that nuance. Stay with me. Stay with Theo."

"My parents won't turn me in, Charity."

"How do you know? They gave you away to a psychopath."

"It wasn't like that," I protest. "Charity, I… I chose him, too. I accepted him."

"Because you were brainwashed into believing he was the ultimate catch! Clearly, he wasn't."

She sounds so sure. But how can she be? She has no idea what the Sanctuary was like. What my parents or Josiah or my life were like. She's just making assumptions.

No—I'm the only one who knows what it was like to be raised in that community.

Except that at the moment, I can't trust my own feelings. Or my recollections. Over the past year, I've questioned certain habits, certain ingrained perspectives. But I never allowed myself to delve too deep into the ifs and whys.

I didn't want to understand—I wanted to forget.

But now, I understand how foolish and naïve I've been.

Because you can't outrun the kind of demons I fled from. They're inside me, screaming to be set free.

"I need to figure out why they made contact," I say softly. "I have to find out what they want."

Charity looks skeptical. "Elyssa, I don't like the sound of that. How are you going to find them?"

I laugh without humor. "Finding them was never the problem. They'll be in the same place they've been for the last several decades. The Sanctuary doesn't move."

"The Sanctuary?" Charity says. "That's what the place is called?"

I nod. "I haven't said that name out loud in a long time."

"How does it feel?"

"Weird," I admit.

She smiles. "I'll come with you."

"No!" I blurt immediately. "No, this is something I have to do on my own."

"Jesus, give me a break," Charity protests. "That's the kind of bullshit line you hear in movies."

I sigh. "My life has kinda been like a movie so far. So maybe it's fitting."

Charity reaches out and grabs my hand. "You don't have to do this alone, Elyssa."

"You don't understand, Charity. My family, the whole community… they're not exactly welcoming to strangers."

"I don't give a fuck," she snaps. "I don't need a fucking red carpet. I just want to make sure they know that there's someone who has your back."

I can't help but smile sadly. What would I do without Charity? She's been more of a family to me in a year than my own family was for the first two decades of my life.

"I appreciate that, but—"

"Maybe you should tell Phoenix about this," Charity interrupts.

"Phoenix?"

"Yeah. Since you've decided to throw your hat into the ring with him, you may as well. At least we know he can protect you from your… people."

It's probably a good idea. But my pride refuses to admit it out loud. I feel as though I've spent my entire life relying on other people. This one thing I should do alone.

It's time I faced the truth of what I'd left behind.

I pick Theo up and cradle him in my arms. He twists around and tries to grab at my face. I pepper his face with kisses and breathe him in.

"Will you keep him safe until I get back?" I ask, knowing that she will.

"I don't like that you're going alone," Charity insists. "I still think I should come with you."

"Someone needs to stay with Theo. I don't want to take him back there."

"Anna will stay with him."

"I like Anna," I reply. "But I don't know her at all. And I certainly don't trust her like I trust you."

I can see Charity's eyes go filmy with emotion but she manages to compose herself in time. "Fine. We'll do it your way. But I'm not happy about it."

I smile. "Noted."

I hug her tightly and she returns the hug after a few seconds. Theo whimpers, annoyed to be stuck between us.

The embrace lasts longer than I expected. Like we're both finding solace and comfort in it.

"You're my rock, Char," I whisper in her ear.

"Forever and always," she whispers right back.

Then we break apart. I kiss Theo's soft head one more time. The splash of my tear on his fine hair surprises me. The Sanctuary is still miles away and I'm already getting emotional. I need to get my head on straight before I wade back into the burning hell I left behind.

I hand Theo over to Charity before I completely break down. Then I pick up the package with the cast iron swan.

"I'll see you soon."

"I don't mean to be dramatic, but if you're not back before the sun sets, I'm calling in the big guns."

"Don't let Phoenix hear you calling him that," I tease. "It'll go right to his head."

"Lord knows his head is big enough already," she retorts, rolling her eyes.

I grin. "Don't worry, though. I'll be back."

"You better be."

Then it's time to go. Before I get cold feet. I head out of the room and down the stairs, hoping that I won't run into Phoenix. I'm pretty sure he's not in the house at all but I can't be sure.

As I pass the massive mirror hanging off the wall in the living room, I slow down and take a look at my reflection. I'm wearing jeans and a tight white t-shirt. It's perfectly normal, utterly nondescript—and yet I look so different from the girl who ran into Las Vegas from the desert that I almost don't recognize myself. My hair is shorter; my features have matured. I even hold myself differently. If I notice the changes, I'm certain they will, too.

The question is, who is "they" nowadays? Who will have taken over for Father Josiah? Faces and names I haven't thought of in twelve long months ripple past my mind's eye. Hamath and Lionel and Eliezer and Rajnesh.

I turned my back on the Sanctuary and more or less assumed that it vanished from existence. But that was a mistake. The world kept spinning, the Sanctuary along with it.

I've changed. Have they?

It occurs to me about ten steps shy of the mansion gates that I don't even know if I'll be let off the grounds. But by now, it's too late to turn back. One way or another, I'll get out of here. I feel like something is tugging me towards the desert like a fish caught on a lure. Call it destiny or stupidity, I'm not sure which. Whatever it is, I can't resist.

Right on cue, one of the men on guard duty steps out of the little side shed that flanks the gates.

"Whoa, going somewhere?" he asks.

"Um, yeah," I mumble. "I just need to run an... errand."

"An errand?"

I show him the box in my hands. "I need to take this back to my parents."

He eyes me and the box suspiciously. "Is this authorized?"

"I didn't realize I needed authorization to go see my parents," I tell him confidently. "I'm not a prisoner."

"Hold on," the guard says, slipping back into the shed. I watch him dial a number and hold for a long time before he finally gives up.

"Okay, the boss isn't answering. And neither is Matvei."

I roll my eyes. "What's the problem?" I ask. "I've left my son here. I'm not going to run off."

That seems to get through to him, but he still seems hesitant. "If you have to go, you'll go in one of the cars," he says. "With a driver."

"That's not necessary—"

"It's the only way I'm letting you out of here," he says. "If you're not happy with that, you can wait for the boss to get back and ask him."

I exhale dramatically. "Fine. Actually, a car and driver would be useful."

He nods and makes another call. Less than two minutes later, a sleek silver car pulls up beside me just as the gates start to crank open.

The driver is a beefy, dark-haired man with tinted shades that completely hide his eyes. He's deliberately scary-looking. Ironically, that makes me feel a little better.

I get into the backseat. The car rolls smoothly out of the private driveway and onto the broad road.

"Where to?" the driver asks in a thick, husky voice that suits him perfectly.

"South," I order. "Towards the desert. I'll guide you."

He doesn't react at all. Just presses the gas pedal down and pilots us off into the burning distance.

I didn't think I'd ever have to go back there. And yet, deep down, maybe a part of me always knew that I hadn't quite escaped for good.

Because, in this life, consequences always find you.

No matter how far you run.

39

ELYSSA
SOMEWHERE IN THE DESERT OF NEVADA

To serve is to find peace.

To obey is to find happiness.

To listen is to find truth.

I haven't prayed in over a year.

But the words are there. They never left.

It seems a lot is coming rushing back to me the closer we drive to the Sanctuary. I keep leaning in towards the driver so that I can see over his shoulder. The last of the city buildings faded out half an hour ago, giving way to scrubby brush, craggy rock, hardened dirt.

It's not as dead as it looks. I lived out here long enough to know that, as barren as it might seem, it's teaming with life just beneath the surface.

A desert is deceptive that way. It hides its most precious secrets. It doesn't let anyone in.

The sand dunes grow taller and broader with every passing mile. Even in the air-conditioned capsule of the car, I can feel the searing heat.

Every cell in my body senses it, too. Like magnetic vibrations are surging through me.

My legs bounce. My hands shake. My eyelids spasm.

The driver has ignored me the entirety of the trip, but I'm reaching a place where the silence is starting to twist my thoughts into unwelcome shapes. I need to hear myself speak or else I'm going to go insane before I even get the answers I came for.

"Um, you never told me your name," I say.

"I did not."

I roll my eyes. These mafia men are all the same. "What is your name?" I grit, like a teacher who makes you rephrase your question when you say, *Can I go to the bathroom?*

"Vlad."

"Short for Vladimir?"

"Yes."

"That's a scary name," I mumble like an idiot.

He doesn't respond.

"I mean, uh, it's a nice name. Just, it's very Russian and Russians are… scary."

I'm making it worse. Maybe I should have stuck to the silence.

"I'm sorry," I blurt. "I barely know what I'm saying. I'm just nervous. I haven't seen my parents in a long time."

I expect more gruff silence so he surprises me by speaking. "Why are you seeing them now?"

I lean in a little and rest my chin on the back of his seat. "Because I've got to stop being a coward. I left without saying goodbye. Without giving them an explanation."

"Do they deserve one?"

The question takes me by surprise. Maybe I shouldn't have judged a book by its cover—or a mobster by his sunglasses. "I… I don't know. But maybe this is less about owing them an explanation, actually. Maybe they owe me one."

He nods. We fall into silence again.

"I don't know how long I'll take."

"My job is to wait."

"Er, okay. Right. That'll work."

I glance out through the front windshield again. And when I do, a sight in the distance takes my breath away.

At first, it looks like a mirage. Just another shimmering bit of nothing in the desolate heat of the Nevada desert.

Then I see the high wooden spike that marks the corner of the barrier that separates the Sanctuary from the sinful world around it.

The fear comes right on its heels.

"Oh God…" I breathe.

Vlad stops the car at once, screeching to a dusty halt in the middle of the road. He turns to me and raises his sunglasses. His eyes are a light gray, and maybe I'm just projecting, but I could swear they're the friendliest eyes I've ever seen. Maybe he wears the sunglasses so no one sees how kind his gaze really is.

His voice is as gruff as ever when he says to me, "You're gonna be okay."

I gulp. "How do you know?"

"Instinct."

I smile. "Thanks, Vlad."

He nods and lowers the shades once more, and just like that, the moment is broken.

Turning back to the wheel, he crosses the last quarter mile, then stops just short of the gate. He doesn't say anything or look back at me. Just puts the car in park and stares straight ahead.

My move.

I get out of the car with the package tucked under my arm. I'm shaking like a leaf and my mind is racing with half-forgotten memories:

Mama saying to me, "Why would I ever leave? The whole world is inside these walls."

Father Josiah pointing that long, skinny finger at me. Of all the girls, he chose me.

Miriam as they dragged her away, screaming, "Not my—!"

I convulse involuntarily. The name "Miriam" is like poison in my blood. I cast it out of my head as if ridding myself of a virus.

Then I focus my attention back on the gate. It's open, as it always was. No security in sight. The desert was the only protection we ever needed. Not many people could wade through the deadly heat and come hurt us even if they wanted to.

And the gates? Well, those were meant to keep us in far more than they were to keep others out.

I feel strange to be here in my jeans and tight t-shirt. It looked normal back in the mirror at Phoenix's mansion, but out here, I'm practically in another dimension. I almost wish I'd changed before coming.

But it's too late for that. No point in denying that the real world has morphed me forever.

I keep my head down as I slip down the backroads into the west side of the commune where my parents' house sits.

Everything looks familiar and yet, it's like I'm seeing everything with new eyes.

The modest houses are fenced in. It's merely a land marker because the fences are so low that they don't keep anything out. Every single property has an elaborate vegetable garden. Some have chicken coops. The other livestock is run by the farmers whose homes are located in the east wing of the commune.

Long clotheslines dripping with pure white garments string along the sides of the houses, swaying in the wind. I use them like camouflage as I pick my way towards the only home I ever really knew.

But even though I'm careful, even though I wait long enough between every sprint to make sure there are no unwelcome witnesses, I still can't help feeling like there are eyes on me. Eyes expecting me. Eyes waiting for me to cross the final distance.

I pause at the corner of one house. Motion through the window catches my eye. I shouldn't be surprised to recognize the person—after all, I grew up here, there aren't that many of us living in the Sanctuary, and I haven't been gone that long—but I do.

Macy Grey. She and I had been friends, what feels like a lifetime ago. We were born only days apart and spent our entire lives growing up two doors down from one another.

We'd drifted apart after she'd gotten married five years earlier to one of the junior pastors. Sixteen years old and she was already desperate to "start her life." To be a mother, a wife. To take her place in the fabric of the community.

She'd visited me the week before my wedding with a basket of handmade sugar cookies and told me I was the luckiest girl in the world.

Father Josiah will bring you much happiness, she'd murmured. *And many sons, I'm sure.*

I shudder at the suddenly recalled memory. How much else have I allowed myself to forget?

I stand there, caught in the past, for a long time. Too long. Macy turns suddenly. I leap out of sight but I wonder if she caught me.

Shivering, I turn and continue down the gravel path. Then, when I round the corner, I see it…

The house I grew up in.

The house of my parents.

The house with answers to the questions that have been burning in my brain since the night I ran.

How could you? How could we?

It looks terrible. I notice the patchy roof and broken windowsills as I walk up to the porch and knock on the door three times.

"Hold on!" My father's voice. Brusque and gravelly, filled with preemptive impatience.

I'm barely able to take a calming breath before the door's thrown open and I'm confronted with the man himself.

He's lost a lot of weight. And that's saying something, considering he had always been a lean, wiry man. His cheeks and nose stand out all the more prominently.

He's lost almost all his hair, too. The last few faint threads of salt-and-pepper that wisp to the sides of his temples.

"Heavens protect us," he whispers. Then he raises his voice. "Mary!"

I flinch when I hear my mother's footsteps hurrying towards the door. "If it's Jedediah Collins coming to collect, tell him we—"

She stops short when she sees me standing on the threshold. Her palm lands over her heart and her skin goes ghostly pale like she's about to faint.

The whole time, I just stand there silently.

Mom has changed, too. But she's gone the opposite of Dad. Where he's wasting away, she's thickening, mostly around her hips and ankles. She looks like the extra weight is a burden on her soul. At least her blonde hair is mostly intact, still curly and bright. Everything else about her looks worn-down and gray.

"Elyssa…?" she whispers, coming forward. "Is that you?"

I nod and raise the package in my hands. "I got your gift."

My parents exchange a glance. "Come in here," Papa orders, slowly gaining back his composure.

I step inside. The house is completely unchanged but I know I'm looking at it differently. Where once I saw it in color, there's now only black and white.

They walk me into the living room, and I take a seat on one of the handcrafted chairs. I perch on its edge, wary and trying not to let the nostalgia drown me.

"What are you doing here?" Papa asks, looking at me with pure exhaustion coloring his gaze.

I frown. "Like I said, I got your package."

They both stare at the box as I set it on the heavy wooden center table.

"We didn't send you that," Mama says. "Why would we send you anything? And how? We didn't know where you'd gone."

I flinch at that, even though I probably deserve it. "You didn't send me this box?"

"No," Papa says impatiently. "What's in it?"

"A… a paperweight," I say dumbly.

"That's ridiculous," Mama says, anger flashing across her eyes. "Why would we send you that?"

I'd been so sure it was my parents. But if not them, then who? I stare back and forth between the two of them, feeling completely lost.

"I... I... need to know if anyone else in the commune is trying to... to... threaten me?" I ask, tripping over my words.

My parents exchange another look.

"We don't know anything," Papa replies carefully. "But if someone is trying to threaten you, it's probably deserved."

My fingers have started to tremble. "Mama, Papa—"

"How could you!?" Mama explodes without warning, as though she can't hold in her hurt any longer. "You had the world in your palm! You were to be married to the shepherd of our community! You would have had comfort and security and... and a *life*."

"I have a life now."

"A life?" Mama repeats. "You abandoned the Sanctuary. You turned your back on your family. You are condemned, Elyssa Redmond."

That word: *family*. Why does it feel wrong coming out of her mouth?

"Mama, what ever happened to Miriam?"

"Who?"

Other names come flooding back to me. "Miriam," I repeat. "Or Rebekah. Or Beulah. Or..."

I can see all their faces in my memory. Eyes studded with tears. Cheeks reddened with rage and sorrow. Each of them dragged away one by one and sent... where? Where were they sent? Why were they taken?

Her eyes go wide. "What? Why are you asking about them? They were exiled from the Sanctuary. Just as you were. You shouldn't be here, Elyssa."

Papa must see me flinch at the harshness of the word *exile*. "Are you shocked by that?" he asks with condescension. He shakes his head. "You humiliated us all. We are paupers now because of what you've done. Cursed. Marked."

I stiffen. I want to fight back, defend myself. But I can feel the old ways slipping back through my pores.

You never spoke back to your elders, especially not your parents. A part of me is still trapped in the girl they molded me to be.

"I… I'm sorry, Papa," I say, looking down. "I don't know what happened that night. I can't remember—"

"That's convenient," Mama snaps without any sympathy.

Neither one of them has asked me for my story. Not that I'd be able to tell them, but still.

Shouldn't they want to know?

Shouldn't they care?

"I am sorry," I tell them. "I never meant to do what I did. I was just scared and… and—"

"You have to go," Mama says, cutting me off. "You're not welcome here anymore."

"Here in the Sanctuary?" I ask. "Or in your house?"

"Both," Papa intones with finality.

"People must have seen you come here," Mama says, glancing around fretfully. "We can't be associated with you…"

It's what I expected. But it still hurts more than I ever could have known.

This was a mistake. I thought it would be worth the pain in order to get answers, to get closure, to seal the door on this part of my life forever. But it was wrong.

It hurt everything and explained nothing.

Mama's right. I should leave.

I stand to do just that. But at the very same time, there's a loud, confident knock on the door. Both my parents fly to their feet in panic.

"You can leave through the back door," Mama says urgently. "Run!"

"Mary, Solomon," comes the deep baritone from the threshold. "It's okay. You don't have to hide her. I just want to talk to our wayward sheep."

All three of us freeze. I hear the front door creak open. Footsteps thud.

And then a man walks into the living room. He's tall and graceful. But the first thing my eyes go to are the hideous burn scars running down his right arm.

Oh God...

"Elyssa," Father Josiah says with a sickly-sweet smile that traps me under his gaze. "It's been a long time. But I'm glad you're here. It's about time we talked... don't you agree?"

40

PHOENIX
THE WAREHOUSE

"Fuck," I growl as I stand over Vitya's broken body.

He's a patchwork mess of blood and shattered limbs that bend at all the wrong angles. It's grotesque. Haunting. An image that will be burned into my retinas forever.

But his eyes? His eyes are peaceful. They gaze up at the sky with fondness.

He was prepared for death. He was ready for it.

Matvei's hand lands on my shoulder. "I'm sorry, brother," he rumbles. "I know you wanted to save him, for Aurora's sake."

"No. No, he would never have been happy in this world," I reply somberly. "He was too far gone. Maybe this way, he'll find some peace."

"And what about you?"

"I said goodbye to peace a long time ago, Matvei," I grit. "I made my hell. Now I'm going to have to live in it."

Matvei shakes his head. "Your problem is that you believe all that shit Vitya was spewing. None of it was true."

I smile without a trace of warmth in it. "Thanks for the pardon but I don't want it."

"That's your other problem."

As Konstantin comes forward for my orders, I gesture towards Vitya. "Get him ready," I instruct. "We'll bury him this evening. I want to lay him to rest next to Aurora."

"Yes, sir," Konstantin replies.

I happen to own the piece of land that Aurora's buried on which is why my men can organize the funeral on such short notice. There's no need for priests or anything of the sort.

I'm not religious. Neither was Vitya nor Aurora. If there's a God in this universe, he's a sick fucking bastard and I'd never want to meet him. So all the pomp and circumstance can get fucked.

It's all bullshit anyway. Just a simple coffin and Vitya will finally be able to sleep.

I head towards the front of the warehouse with Matvei close behind me. "This is the part where you explain to me how the fuck this happened," I snarl.

Matvei shakes his head, still in shock and disbelief. "He appeared out of nowhere," he admits. "Just walked into the warehouse off the street."

"Someone dropped him off," I infer.

He nods. "The men are scouring the surrounding area and reviewing the security footage as we speak. There's no sign of anyone."

"So they dumped him near here and hit the road?"

"Seems like it."

"But they knew enough to stay out of range of cameras and security patrol."

"Correct."

"Sakamoto is dead," I grimace. "Which means we're dealing with someone else entirely."

"Ozol?" Matvei ponders.

I shake my head. "That fucker would never concern himself with petty, mind-fuck shit like this. This is a trivial play. Ozol only concerns himself with big stakes."

"Or maybe he's playing the long game."

"Our intel puts him in Europe at the moment," I remind Matvei.

"Our intel could be wrong. Besides, Ozol is one slippery motherfucker. Maybe he just wants us to believe that's where he is."

"No," I say, shaking my head. "I feel it in my gut. This isn't Ozol we're dealing with."

I don't have a good reason for my stance. I just know that my instincts are telling me something totally different. And in this business, you either trust your instincts or you won't live long enough to regret it.

I get into my car as Matvei heads for the passenger seat. I've just started the engine when my phone buzzes in my pocket to remind me of a notification. Only then do I realize that I have a missed call from Gunther. He's the head of my home security detail. I chose him for the job specifically because he doesn't talk, doesn't call, doesn't ever bother me.

"What's wrong?" Matvei asks, reading my expression.

"I have a feeling I'm about to find out."

I return Gunther's call. He picks up almost immediately. "Boss?"

"What happened?" I snap impatiently.

He hesitates—very unlike him. "I've been trying to reach you, sir. So the situation is, that the, uh—"

I don't like where this is headed. "Spit it out, Gunther. I have shit I need to do."

"The girl—er, Miss Elyssa—she walked out of here a few hours ago," he says, trying to speak past his nerves. "She said she wanted to go see her parents."

I tense, aware that Matvei is straining his ears to hear Gunther's side of the conversation.

"*Walked out of here...*" I echo in disbelief. "And you just... let her go?"

"She made some good points, sir. Told me she wasn't a prisoner and that she was leaving her kid behind and everything. Made sense, ya know? So I said okay. But I didn't let her go off alone neither if that makes a difference. Vlad went with her."

That makes me feel better but only slightly. "Vlad's with her now?"

"Yeah. They're not back yet."

I grind my teeth together. "Alright, Gunther. Alert me the second she's back within range of the mansion."

I hang up and search for Vlad's number.

"What's going on?" Matvei asks. "Is it the girl again?"

I ignore him and hit call on Vlad's number. He answers immediately.

"Where are you?"

"With Miss Elyssa, boss," he replies. "In the desert."

"The desert?" I repeat. "Be a little more specific."

"It's hard to say for sure, Don. Pretty much the middle of fucking nowhere. She directed me here. We went southwest. About two hours from the mansion. We got here a few minutes ago."

"And where is she?"

"Inside."

"Inside what?"

"Inside the walls," he explains. "Some kind of compound, like one of those crazy cults that live out here. I saw some sign that said, *'This way to the Sanctuary,'* so I guess that's what it's called. She said she needed to speak to her parents."

"She gets one hour," I say firmly. "If she's not out by then, go get her and drag her out."

"Got it, boss."

I hang up and drop the phone onto the dashboard. "The Sanctuary," I mutter under my breath. "What the fuck is that?"

Matvei whips out his phone and starts searching. It doesn't take him long.

"There's not much. Best I can find is a small article written a couple of years ago. Apparently, they're supposed to be this fundamentalist group that live off the land. Not friendly to outsiders, it seems."

"That's it?"

He nods grimly. "Whoever these bastards are, they don't leave much of a footprint. Guess you'll have to ask Elyssa yourself to find out why she went there in the first place. And this time, I wouldn't take no for an answer."

༄

It takes another twenty minutes before we get to the private cemetery.

It's a lush, verdant meadow set in the middle of the desert. Trees dot the acreage and stir in the hot breeze. The irrigation needed to keep it growing like this must cost a fucking fortune. Actually, I know it does—because I'm the one who pays the bills.

I bought the land years ago. Not for myself—but for Aurora.

"Let's retire here, Phoenix," she'd told me once. "We can build a big house and live our golden years gazing out at a meadow of green. We can spend forever here."

So when I'd been confronted with her mutilated body, this was the only place I could think of to lay her to rest.

She's spending forever here, indeed. Just not the way we planned.

Once we park, Matvei and I head in the direction of Aurora's grave. It's a grove of trees that stand guard around two white marble headstones.

One for my wife.

One for my son.

But there's only a single body buried in the plots. Yuri's name might be etched into the marble but his body rests somewhere else entirely. No matter how far and wide I've searched, I've never been able to find a trace of him.

"You okay?" Matvei asks quietly as we approach.

"Fine."

"When's the last time you came here?"

"Been a while," I admit. "Too long."

"You know, I can bury Vitya on my own. You don't need to—"

I shoot him a vicious glare. "I can do this, Matvei."

"I know you can," he says. "I'm just saying that you don't have to."

"I'm good."

Matvei drops it.

When we reach the two headstones nestled between the cluster of trees, my men are already there. Vitya's body has been prepared and his grave is almost halfway done.

"Boss," Konstantin says, looking up over his shovel, "I spoke to our guy in the funeral parlor. The headstone's gonna take a few weeks."

"That's fine," I reply. "We'll add it later."

"You need to let me know what you want it to say."

For a moment, I'm stumped. And then I realize how obvious the answer is.

"Vitya Azarov—*He Never Stopped Searching.*"

"You got it, boss. Would you mind writing that one down for me?"

"Jesus, Konstantin," Matvei cuts in with an eyeroll. "Just keep digging. I'll fucking write it down for you later, dumbass."

Konstantin throws Matvei a dirty look but he keeps digging.

For a second, I'm pulled into the man I was several years ago. That man would have laughed at the exchange. That man would have been amused by it.

I'd stopped finding the humor in such petty things a long time ago.

I feel something foreign twist inside me: a longing for lighter days. Things hadn't always felt quite so heavy, quite so doomed. But I buried all the light I'd ever been given right here, five years ago.

I'm never going to get it back.

"Grave's just about ready, boss," Konstantin notes, stepping back and letting the others finish the job.

Matvei and I move forward. I squat down in front of Vitya's body.

The boys have cleaned him up as much as possible and wrapped him in a white cloth nestled inside the coffin. It's better like this—we don't have to see how broken he is.

I put my hand on his chest and sigh. "Goodbye, Vitya," I say. "I will remember as you used to be: laughing with your daughter, holding your grandson."

Then I stand and direct my men to lower him into his grave.

They work quickly and silently. Once he's been laid to rest, they start shoveling the soil back on top of him.

I listen to the sound of shovels scraping through dirt. The grunts of the men working. The breeze whispering through the treetops. It's almost meditative, in a strange way. I find myself just starting to drift off into memories better left forgotten…

Until someone in the distance catches my eye.

My gun is out and up in seconds. Trained on the target—a man emerging from between the broad trunks of two trees.

For a moment, I think I'm going mad.

His features are so similar that I actually believe that Hitoshi Sakamoto has risen from the dead.

"Do you see him, too?" I whisper to Matvei, who's standing right beside me.

"Yes," he growls.

The man moves closer. He's alone and unarmed. "I merely came to pay my respects," he says in a quiet Japanese accent.

Despite the fact that there are half a dozen Bratva guns aimed at his skull, he's remarkably relaxed. Not with arrogance but the quiet confidence of a man who knows that it's not yet his time to die.

And then it comes to me. Who he is. Why he's here. The name rolls off my tongue.

"Eiko Sakamoto."

He smiles in acknowledgment but it's ice cold. His eyes appear dead. Completely devoid of emotion.

Well, no. That's not quite true. More like his eyes are filled with the promise of death.

"You killed my brother, Mr. Kovalyov," he says, the courteous smile still plastered onto his flawless face.

I hear a barrage of guns cock in unison.

I glance to the left. Then to the right.

Eiko's men surround us.

"It wasn't personal," I tell him.

"Haven't you learned by now, Mr. Kovalyov?" Eiko says. "In this life… everything is personal."

41

ELYSSA

MARY AND SOLOMON'S HOUSE—THE SANCTUARY

"Father Josiah."

Those two little words feel unbelievably heavy as they pass my lips.

I feel like I'm hallucinating. Like my head has been stuffed full of made-up memories that don't match reality the way I thought they did.

Because the truth of the matter is that he looks… good.

His features are the same as I remember. Calm. Stoic. Wise. So assured of himself and his mission that it would be impossible to ever doubt him. That's why my parents and all the others followed him out to this patch of desert to begin with.

His blue eyes seem muted in the strangest way but I can't quite figure out why. I suppose it doesn't matter. Even with the crow's feet stamped at the corners of his eyes and more silver threaded through his hair than I remember, he looks supremely confident.

I can spy only one jarring difference to confirm that I'm not crazy. That the things I remember actually happened.

A huge, knotted scar on the side of his face. Ripped white flesh like candlewax melted along his jaw and over his ear.

But if it pains him or hurts his vanity, he doesn't show it. There's not a trace of self-consciousness as he looks at me with all apparent fondness, a mysterious smile dancing along his lips.

"Now, now, Elyssa… *Father Josiah* is so formal, isn't it? Please—my first name is all that's necessary."

I feel an old memory ping at the forefront of my consciousness but it doesn't quite manage to break through. There's too much else going on.

I glance at my parents. Both are standing off to the side, looking completely horrified. I'm sure I look the same. Father Josiah is the only one at ease.

He must notice the discomfort tightening the air because he says, "Mary, Solomon, please— there's no need to worry. I just want to talk."

"We were just telling her that she needed to leave," my mother says immediately. "She shouldn't be here. It isn't right."

She takes a step back to punctuate her sentence as though to set as much distance between us as possible. She doesn't want my reputation to taint hers. Given the state of the house and the sullen gloom that lingers over my parents, I'm guessing it's too late for that, though.

"Leave?" Josiah says, looking mildly surprised. "Why on earth should she leave?"

"She doesn't belong here anymore," Papa speaks up, his tone prickly with anger. "She left. She abandoned the Sanctuary and its principles. She's a shame to our family name. We renounce her!"

I feel the heat of his words but I'm numb to them right now. I'm still reeling from the knowledge that Josiah is alive.

Not just alive—thriving, by the looks of it.

For a full year, I've believed I killed him the night I fled. This is like seeing a dead man come back to life. Like the rules of reality are melting away right before my eyes.

"A shame?" Josiah murmurs, looking between my parents and me. "No, I wouldn't say that."

"She's a lost cause, Father Josiah," my mother says respectfully.

"No one is a lost cause, Mary," he says simply. "Not one wayward sheep from the flock. And what am I if not her shepherd? Now, if you don't mind, I'd like to talk to Elyssa alone for a few moments."

I stiffen. I can't speak, can't move. My eyes flit to the door, to the window, to every possible avenue of escape. But my feet are rooted down. I can't stop looking at Josiah's scars.

I did that to you, I think silently. *You should be dead. How are you here?*

More importantly, why am I here?

This was a mistake.

This was a mistake.

This was a mistake.

"Are you sure, Father Josiah?" Papa asks him, eyeing me cagily.

"Of course," Josiah croons. "Elyssa, will you walk with me to the backyard?"

How can I say no? Since the day I was born, he's ruled over my life. His word is gospel behind these walls. A year in the real world hasn't been enough to cure me of the hold he has on me. The hold he's always had on me.

I thought I was done with him. And maybe I was.

But the husband I killed doesn't seem to quite be done with me.

So I nod. Robotically and automatically.

Like I never, ever had a choice.

He gives me a calming smile and gestures for me to lead the way. It's wild how that one simple sweep of the hand frees me to move again. As if he cast a spell to keep me rooted in place the moment he entered.

I shudder and pick through the house. As I walk through, my eyes dart from side to side, noticing the subtle degradations that have taken hold like rot since I left.

This place is falling apart. Did I do this to my parents? Did my crime stain them like it stained me?

I find the back door, step through, and walk down the porch steps into the big backyard that I used to play in when I was a child. In my memory, it was endless and perfect. Now, I see it for what it is: a barren patch of earth, sunbaked and dying in the middle of nowhere.

"It must be strange for you to be back."

I turn to face Josiah.

He's kept a good few feet between us. I'm grateful for that. Any closer and the panic would have choked me out completely.

I notice my parents' faces clustered at the kitchen window. They make no secret of the fact that they're watching this exchange. I wish I could lie to myself and say it's because they want to make sure I'm safe.

But I know well that it's because they want to keep Father Josiah safe from me.

"Elyssa?"

I look back at Josiah. He's gazing with me with what seems to be genuine concern.

"Are you okay?"

"I… I'm sorry," I stammer. "Yes, it's strange to be back."

He nods with understanding. I want to believe in it. In his sympathy, in his compassion. And by all appearances, it's real.

But I can't let myself do that.

Maybe I'm just hard-wired to believe it. Maybe I've never truly shaken off the programming that this place and this man built into me. Maybe I never will.

I just know that every cell in my body is screaming at me that something here is so, so wrong.

But I do know that you wouldn't have done anything that violent unless he deserved it. That's what Charity told me.

She wasn't there that night; she doesn't know for sure. But then again, I don't know for sure why I did those things either, do I? Those memories are locked away in the broken part of my brain. I may not ever get them back.

I know one thing, though: I didn't kill him.

He's here in front of me, alive and breathing and exuding the same holy confidence he's always had.

I'm not a murderer. I don't have to carry that guilt with me anymore.

"Of course," Josiah sympathizes. "Of course it is strange. But I'm glad you came back."

"You are?" I can't keep the shock from my voice. I mean, he has to know what happened that night…

Right?

Unless he's forgotten as much as I have.

The thought feels illogical but why else would he be standing in front of me now, looking as though he's genuinely glad to see me? Nothing's adding up. Maybe I'm the one who got hit in the head, not him.

"Elyssa," he says tenderly, "you know how I care for you. How much I always cared for you."

I shake my head. "I'm sorry."

I don't quite know what I'm apologizing for. I'm just so confused. Everything about Josiah—his kind eyes, his soft smile, even the friendly clasp of his hands behind his back—has the look of the man who raised all of us here in the Sanctuary. Our shepherd. Our leader. The one who taught us right from wrong, good from evil, holy from sinful.

So why do I want to run from him?

The answers are locked away somewhere inside my head. And they refuse to step into the light.

"Don't be sorry, Elyssa," Josiah says, taking a step towards me. "There's nothing to apologize for."

My eyes linger on the burn marks racing up and down his arm like pale vines.

He sees me looking. "They don't hurt, if that's what you're wondering," he offers. "Nothing hurts anymore. The powers that be took all my pain away."

I nod, trembling. "That's good."

He seems to be inching closer to me. My body rails against the proximity. I could run; I *should* run.

But I can't. I have so many questions.

How are you alive?

What happened that night?

Who sent me the swan and why?

I glance towards the sun-bleached wall behind me, the one that separates the Sanctuary from the rest of the sin-riddled world. I wonder if Vlad would be able to hear me if I screamed.

"Elyssa, my little doe, you seem upset," Josiah croons. "Is there something I can do or say to put your mind at ease? Or perhaps I could just listen. If we share our burdens, they no longer feel quite so heavy."

I try and steady myself against the onslaught of dizziness. And then, out of nowhere, a new question pops into my head. Different from all the rest.

What would Phoenix do?

He wouldn't do what I was right on the verge of doing: spilling everything, showing my whole hand, believing in the goodness of people and the purity of Father Josiah's soul.

He would say that men are evil. Powerful men doubly so.

He would say to trust no one.

And he would be right.

I search for a lie. A way out of here, this unreal place I never should have returned to. "I... I came back..."

Why did I come back?

Closure. That's what I'd told Vlad in the car. It was true then. It's true now.

"I came back to say goodbye," I finish.

The words come out in a huge exhale. It's taken me a long time to find the strength to recognize certain things about this place. But I'm not that naïve girl anymore. I'm not willing to believe everything I'm told, everything I'm shown.

I've seen enough out in the real world to know now that things are not always what they seem. There's an underbelly to everything in life.

And you can't allow yourself to be fooled by the surface.

"Goodbye?" Josiah asks with raised eyebrows.

I nod. "I shouldn't have left the way I did."

"Oh, Elyssa," Josiah sighs. "You have nothing to mend. This is where you belong. Where you've always belonged."

"No," I say with absolute certainty, despite the anxiety creeping around in my gut. "Maybe I did once. But not anymore. I've changed."

He smiles sagely. "Why, of course you have! Change is the natural order of things. And change is the only way we can evolve. Look around you, my lost lamb." He turns and sweeps his arm to encompass my parents' decaying little hovel. "Your mother and father have suffered in your absence."

I stiffen. All I can do is nod. The more I look, the more I see. The missing roof tiles. The cracks in the sagging windowsill. Paint peeling away, desperate to be replenished in its fight against the Nevada sun.

His gaze comes and settles back on me. "Come back home to them, my dear. Take your place among us once more. Continue the trajectory you were always meant to complete. I will always be your shepherd, Elyssa Redmond."

I flinch at each word. It's like a barrage of heavy hands trying to press me back into the cookie-cutter mold I broke free of a year ago.

I see an image in my mind of the blood-stained wedding dress I was wearing the night I ran. I remember the feel of it, wrapped around me like a vice. I remember how it smelled when Charity and I burned it that same night.

I shake my head and take a step back from him. "Father Josiah…"

"Josiah," he corrects. "Please."

"Josiah," I repeat numbly. "…no. I can't. I won't."

I let my eyes flutter closed and wait for his anger. A line from a sermon he gave years ago strikes through my head like a lightning bolt: "God has a righteous fury, and as men made in his image, it is good and just to be angry. Women are a nurturing kind but wrath is how men shape the world to our liking."

Anger would make sense. I hurt him. Ran from him. Abandoned a night, a marriage, a future.

This kindness he's showing just does not compute. So I tense and wait for the fury.

But it never comes.

When my eyes open again, Josiah is right where I left him. Tall and graceful and composed. He simply looks… disappointed.

"You may think your life is outside these walls," Josiah murmurs. "But you're wrong. This is where you belong."

It's the second time he's said that to me. And now, I can sense something underneath the words. A promise I don't want to keep. A memory I refuse to acknowledge.

"No," I say softly. "It's not."

With that, I turn tail and run. Back to Vlad. Back to the real world. Back to Phoenix and Theo and Charity.

No one stops me.

42

PHOENIX
THE GRAVEYARD

"You were tracking us?"

Eiko is more diminutive in stature than his brother. His features are finer, too. But the same dark gleam lives in his eyes.

"Of course we were. We didn't just deposit Vitya outside your warehouse and leave," he says solemnly.

He glances around at my men. "I must say, I'd expected more. They told me to be careful. But really, the warning seems rather unnecessary."

My men bristle at the insult but they know damn well we're badly outnumbered and outgunned.

Matvei stands a few feet away from me. His sharp eyes have been tracking the Yakuza men. He's looking for weak links.

"Maybe they know more than you do," I say pointedly.

"Or maybe they just severely overestimated you."

I grit my teeth but this line of conversation is a dead end. I have too many other questions in need of answering.

"Why take Vitya?" I ask.

Eiko looks distastefully at the partially filled-in grave. "He was useful while he lasted," he replies. "But unfortunately, he was too broken to be useful for long. I have you to thank for that."

"Me?" I snap. "Actually, you and your bosses are the ones responsible for that."

"Are you referring to the dead daughter he couldn't stop whining about?"

My hands roll into fists. I'd give anything to unleash them on the cocky prick right now. I can feel Matvei's eyes on the side of my face, though. *Calm down,* he's telling me. *We've got to be smart.*

He's right. I take a deep breath and rein in my temper.

"She had a name."

"So did my brother."

"He'd been following my movements for a long time now," I counter. "I had to answer in kind."

Eiko's eyes grow cold. "So it seems. And here I am: answering back."

"I see," I say, with a nod. "So it all ends here, is that it?"

"Precisely. I kill two birds with one stone."

"And which two birds would that be?"

"I take care of an irritant—that would be you. And at the same time, I gain the favor of the men behind the curtain. I prove myself loyal. Useful."

I laugh. "So this is an initiation to the big boys' club, then? How nice. Gold star for Eiko. Or does Astra Tyrannis prefer stickers with smiley faces on them?"

Eiko's eyes narrow into slits. He looks deadly. "Watch yourself, Mr. Kovalyov."

"While I have you here," I add, "mind answering a few other questions for me?"

I chance a glance towards Matvei. No one is paying attention to him, and I don't want to pull their focus. So I keep my eyes trained on Eiko but I have a hard time hiding my smirk.

Because we've been brothers-in-arms for so long that I know exactly what he's doing: the one-button speed dial.

It was a safety precaution we put in place years ago. One button sends a pre-generated text to a pre-programmed hotline—*Code Red. Back-up needed urgently*—along with a set of GPS coordinates.

It's monitored constantly by men across my empire. That means fifteen minutes or less until backup arrives.

The only issue with the plan is we have to survive at least that long. Good thing Eiko Sakamoto seems to love the sound of his own voice.

"You have questions?" Eiko asks with amusement. "Let's see if I can oblige you. The floor is yours, Mr. Kovalyov."

"How did you know where to find Vitya?" I begin.

Eiko smiles with delight, like a teacher whose student asks precisely the right question. "You still don't know," he says in amazement. "I wonder, do you even suspect?"

A sense of dread spreads through my extremities slowly. And my instincts ping with new warnings.

There are spies in your house, Phoenix! Vitya himself roared those words in my face.

I clench my jaw and wait. Eiko will talk. I know it. Men like him can't help themselves.

"Do you know when Astra Tyrannis first started?" Eiko asks.

It takes everything in me not to roll my eyes in the pompous fucker's face. "Is there a point you're trying to make?" I growl.

"1901 is the answer. Born in Amsterdam, it flourished on the continent until it had outgrown its home. And then it came here."

The Japanese don certainly has a flair for the dramatic. Which is probably why he didn't just ambush us at the warehouse. Too straightforward. No, a guy like Eiko lives for the art of the chase. For cat-and-mouse games, for overdrawn soliloquies.

Most of all, he lives for a captive audience. He's got one now and he isn't keen on letting it go just yet.

"I'm sorry, is this supposed to be an ambush or a history lecture?"

Eiko's eyes narrow further. "There's nothing wrong with knowing history. It keeps you from repeating it."

"Fucking spare me," I snap. "I'd rather swallow the bullet than the sermon."

"My point is that Astra Tyrannis plays the long game. They stay in power because they can see into the future. They can plan twenty steps ahead because they know their enemies' next ten steps."

I'm close to bursting now. Not just because of the fucker in front of me but because of the truth he's implying.

I can't avoid it any longer. I give him the answer he's giddy about.

"They planted a spy."

He looks mildly irritated that I cut to the chase but he recovers quickly. "Ah, so you *do* suspect?"

"I have for a while now," I say. "And since it seems as though I won't leave here alive, you might as well tell me who the spy is. For closure. A favor from one don to another."

"Where's the fun in that?" he chuckles. When he laughs like that, he seems like a nasty little boy, lighting ants on fire with a magnifying glass. Sick fucking pup. "Tell you what: I'll give you three guesses."

"I don't have time for this shit," I snarl.

He laughs again, clearly enjoying himself. "Oh, don't be such a spoilsport. You don't have time for anything anymore, Mr. Kovalyov. I'll give you a clue. The spy in question is unassuming as a bird, innocent as a fawn—and yet, underneath all that naivete, there's a siren singing her death song."

I shake my head. Refusing to believe it, even when it's staring me right in the face.

"You invited her into your home," he whispers hoarsely. "And she's betrayed you over and over again."

I can feel Matvei staring at me but I ignore him. I'm trying to reconcile what I feel with the truth that's now staring me in the face.

Elyssa. This whole time, it was her. Of course it was her—and I knew it. The signs were all there, plain as day.

She was there that day at Wild Night Blossom when she never should've been anywhere near that place. She intercepted the meeting with Ozol. She created the distraction so that he could flee.

Then, a year later, she enters my life again… with a child she claims is mine.

Maybe he really is mine. But she used him as a bargaining chip. A way to gain access to my life.

To my home.

To my fucking head.

"Oh, dear! Don't tell me you went and caught feelings for the spy?" Eiko asks with condescension. "How very unfortunate."

"Shut the fuck up," I spit.

Eiko grins at me as though I've just given him a compliment. "The woman was well-placed and well-used," he continues. It's almost like he wants to take credit for her role in this master plan. "She turned out to be much more valuable than any of us expected."

I see Matvei's nod from my peripheral vision. The subtle clench of his fist.

But I'm not the only one who notices. One of Eiko's men starts to smell a rat.

"Hey, wait…"

Before he can get the rest of his sentence out, a hail of gunfire slices through the grove. Several of Eiko's men drop instantly.

Eiko lets out a very unflattering shriek but he's spared a quick death as his remaining men group around him to shield him from fire.

All hell breaks loose from there.

I'm firing and running and ducking. All around me, my men and Eiko's are doing the same.

It's a cacophony of blood and bullets.

Men scream.

Men cry.

Men die.

Then, as if the sea is parting, I raise my gun just in time for one of Eiko's bodyguards to crumple to the ground with a Bratva bullet in his gut. It's the perfect window. The Yakuza don's eyes meet mine and bulge out.

"I can see into the future, too, motherfucker," I tell him. "And today's not the day I die."

I start to pull the trigger. But before I can, a branch from a tree overhead comes crashing down on top of me. A stray shot must've severed it from the trunk.

Either that, or a cruel god is looking out for the last living Sakamoto.

It's the lapse that Eiko needs to get away. Konstantin and a few of my other men come sprinting over to heave the bough off of me but I can only watch helplessly as Eiko and a few of his last guards retreat to a sleek black SUV that comes screeching up just in time.

The door slams shut. The car roars away.

And just like that, Eiko is gone.

But he left a few of his troops behind. With their leader gone, they've all dropped their weapons and are holding their hands high overhead.

My men look to me as Konstantin helps me to my feet. Waiting for orders. For me to decide: mercy or murder?

I don't hesitate for even a moment.

Every man tainted by the Astra Tyrannis poison is going to die.

Starting now.

I nod. A chorus of gunfire rings out at once. The remaining Yakuza slump to the floor as the grass drinks up their spilled blood.

Konstantin turns to me. "What now, don?" he asks quietly as the silence steals back over us.

"Burn their bodies," I instruct as I spit blood onto the ground. "And finish Vitya's grave."

Then I turn and head in the opposite direction, towards my vehicle.

"Phoenix!"

I don't stop so Matvei is forced to run to catch up to me. I can sense the concern radiating off him but I don't have the patience for it now.

"Where are you going?" he pants, grabbing at his stitches.

"Back to the house," I reply. "I have business I need to take care of."

He knows exactly what I mean.

"You don't have to do it yourself, you know," Matvei warns.

My feet hit the ground hard as I stride to the vehicle. I'm seething, and it has nothing to do with Eiko getting away.

I reach for the car handle. But before I can clasp it, Matvei's hand shoots out and closes around my wrist. He forces me to look at him.

"I mean it," he says again. "I know what she means to you. You don't have to do this yourself."

I look my best friend in the eye. "I'm the only one who can do it," I snarl.

Then I shake him off and get into the car. Matvei steps back as I fire up the engine and careen back onto the road. I glance into my rearview mirror to watch him disappear.

Along with the last fuck I had left to give.

∼

The vehicle chews up highway at breakneck speed. I know I'm driving recklessly but I can't help it. Adrenaline is bursting through my veins, and it's only being fueled by my anger.

I've been such a fucking fool.

Was fucking me part of the whole damn scheme? Or was that just a cruel twist of the knife?

I should never have brought those two back to the mansion.

The child, though… The child is what forced me to change my mind. The perfect fucking bait.

She'd spread her legs for me, had never once mentioned protection. From the very beginning, I was nothing but a mark.

And now… the tables are about to be turned.

I flash my lights at the gate the moment I see it in the distance. They slowly crank open and I race through, just shy of barreling into them.

I come to a screeching halt in the private driveway. Then I jump out of my car and rush inside.

"Elyssa!" I roar like a fucking Viking. "Elyssa!"

The echo of my scream reverberates through the house but I don't receive an answer.

And then I remember—she took a car to the desert hours ago. *To visit her parents,* Gunther said. Was that a lie, too? Was she just being recalled by her masters?

My thoughts are flying in a hundred different directions as I rush towards my office. I stop short when I realize the door is half-open.

I'd had new locks installed after Charity's little intrusion, a new security system in place so that I'd be alerted if anyone so much as tried to open my office door. I wasn't going to let that lapse happen again. My secrets are mine and mine alone.

I glance at my phone but I have no alerts. No indication that anything has been broken into.

"Fuck," I growl.

I pull out my gun and creep the last few steps to the open threshold. At first glance, it seems as if it's empty. Am I wrong? Am I paranoid?

I can see my men doing their normal rounds outside in the garden. As if everything is fine. And why wouldn't it be?

As far as they know, any threat would come from beyond the property boundaries.

As far as they know, there's no security breach—because the spy was always inside the house.

I'd fucking invited her in.

Then I smell it—blood, rich and tangy. I walk around the desk.

The baby is nowhere to be seen.

But her body is there, sprawled on the floor, hands stretched out as though she's trying to catch someone's attention. Her eyes are glazed over, staring unseeingly at the ceiling. The bullet in her chest has caused her to bleed out onto my carpets. The stain is crusted dry.

By my guess, she's been dead for at least half an hour.

I walk forward and stand over Charity's cold corpse. She doesn't look like a spy.

But then again, isn't that the whole fucking point?

43

ELYSSA
THE KOVALYOV MANSION

"We're here."

I open my eyes and look out at the mansion. Is it right to call it home? I don't really know what that word means anymore.

Vlad turns and looks at me over his shoulder. His sunglasses are off now. Those gray eyes are seeing things in me that I'm afraid to see in myself.

"I don't like to ask people about themselves," he begins in a gruff rumble, "but I'm gonna make an exception just this once. Are you okay?"

I take a deep, shuddering breath that doesn't really help. "I honestly don't know."

He nods slowly like that's a good enough answer, even though it's a little ridiculous.

It's funny how intense situations can compress time. I feel like I've known Vlad for a lifetime, despite having said maybe two dozen words to him ever.

I think back over the last year and realize that's true of all my new relationships. They're like diamonds—horrible things squeezed by intensity into something beautiful and rare. There's something weird about that, and also something perfectly normal.

It's not weird to be craving Charity's comfort—she's the one who saved me from tumbling over the edge, after all. My first friend in the real world.

It's not weird to miss my son, either. He's my baby boy. The silver lining to the darkest cloud I've ever faced.

What's weird is longing for Phoenix.

It's not just my body that craves the proximity of his. I want to see his face, speak to him, be as close to him as he'll allow.

I want him to kiss me so I know I'm safe.

I want him to touch me so I know I'm loved.

"Did you find what you were looking for?" Vlad asks, wrenching me back to the present. "Back there?"

I weigh my answer. "I suppose in one sense, I got exactly what I expected."

He nods again. "Nothing quite like going home to break your heart, eh?"

I blink and look at him in a new light. For some reason, it's strange to think of him as having parents or a home. Men like him—brutal, gruff men, rough around the edges—seem like they ought to just spring from the ground fully-formed.

But he did have parents, and a home, and a childhood, and dreams of what his life might one day become. I wonder if he's happy. I wonder if he's ever even asked himself that question—*Am I happy? Did I do the right thing?*

When I don't answer, he clears his throat. "I haven't been home in twenty years. Folks weren't happy with my choice of work."

I can't help but smile. "What did they want you to be?"

"An engineer, if you can fucking believe it," he replies. "Never had the head for books, though."

"No," I laugh bitterly, "me neither."

"Somehow, I find that hard to believe."

A bubble of laughter escapes through my lips. I relax just a little. I allow myself to be distracted.

"Well, maybe a little bit," I admit. "I used to read. But, like, silly stuff. Kid stuff. Fairy tales and adventure books, things like that. Whatever I could get my hands on, really. The library in the Sanctuary was… limited."

"Let me guess—they didn't let you girls have much choice, did they?" he asks.

He says it kind of flippantly but I realize that he's moving towards a point. Or maybe he's nudging me towards one. One that's been staring me in the face for longer than I'd care to admit.

I wasn't raised—not really.

More like I was *groomed*. Born into a cage and told that it was everything I could ever expect to have.

And whether I like to admit it or not, no matter how hard I've tried to cast off the chains that still tie me to that place, to those people, to that man…

They all still have a hold on me.

"Not really," I admit softly. "They monitored everything."

"Well, then, maybe it's a good thing you did whatever you did. At least it got you out of there."

My features harden, fighting a smile. It feels a little too convenient to justify my crimes that way. If blood is truly the price of freedom, is it even worth it?

"I don't know," I whisper. "You don't know what I did."

"I don't need to."

I bark out another sarcastic laugh. "Believe me—if you knew, you'd think differently."

"No," he retorts bluntly, "I wouldn't."

"Oh yeah? What makes you so sure?"

He settles back in his seat and looks at me in the rearview mirror. Those eyes, full of depth and life, swallow me whole.

"I've seen a lot of bad shit in my lifetime. Sins of every shape and color. You know what I've never seen?"

I take the bait with hesitation. "What?"

"The men who did those things apologizing. They don't feel remorse. They don't feel guilt."

"So you're saying I shouldn't either?"

"I'm saying it makes you more human than most to feel what you're feeling."

I take that in. But it doesn't fit right. Doesn't feel true the way he seems to believe it is.

"I don't know what I am," I whisper. "They tried to make me something, and maybe I was that thing for a while. But I'm trying to be something different now. Is that even possible? Can people really just… change?"

Vlad is quiet for so long that I wonder if he's even going to answer. It's getting dark outside the car. The exterior of the mansion is glowing with the garden floodlights. I see a shadow pass across the window of

Phoenix's office and wonder what he'll say when he sees me again. I wonder what I'll say to him.

"No one is just one thing," he murmurs. "We've all got a little darkness in us and a little light. A little bit of bad and a little bit of good. You choose what comes out."

It's so poetic and out of character for the driver that I almost laugh. "Did you come up with that yourself?" I ask. "It's kind of beautiful."

"Nah. Stole it from a self-help book. Stole the book from the store, too, now that I think about it."

I chuckle then fall silent. The shadow passes over the window again.

"What about Phoenix?" I muse, more to myself than to Vlad. "Does he have light in him?"

"He did," Vlad says with the utmost certainty. "As for now? That's above my paygrade."

I nod. "I think I may be in trouble, Vlad."

"Then I suggest you get yourself out of it," he replies calmly.

"And if I can't?"

"Then ask for help," he says. "Simple as that."

Ask for help. A few months ago, there was only one person I trusted implicitly in this world—Charity. That was it.

But now, I realize that I have one more name to add to the list. The problem is… I'm not sure he feels the same way about me.

"Okay," I say quietly, mostly to myself. "I'll ask."

And the moment I say the words, I realize something else—subconsciously, I've made the decision already.

A decision to throw my hat in the ring with Phoenix. Even when Charity had suggested the idea of leaving with intel on his Bratva, I'd rebelled against the idea. Because I knew: I'm his now. For better or for worse.

"Miss Elyssa?" Vlad gives me a reassuring smile when I jump at the sound of his voice. "Go rest. Sleep does a soul good."

"Thank you," I whisper as I get out of the car.

Once I'm out, I turn and give him a wave. He nods curtly and drives towards the garage. I stand there and watch his taillights flash for a second before they disappear around the corner.

I don't have an excuse to linger any longer. I turn and head into the house.

I have no idea how I'm going to start this story. I have no idea if Phoenix will understand. But I don't have many options left. My parents had denied it. Josiah had denied it.

Which means one of them was lying. Or someone else had sent me that package. And whichever the case, I'm in over my head. I do need help, so I'll swallow my pride in order to ask for it.

∼

The house is empty when I walk in. And quiet—spookily quiet. Something is off.

I peer around, a strange sense of foreboding overcoming me as I walk quietly through the halls. Normally, Anna or one of the other maids are working on something or other around the mansion.

But tonight, everything is dark and silent.

The ground floor is empty so I mount the stairs. A long hallway beckons from the landing. I turn to go to my room when I notice a triangle of light emerging from a doorway at the far end of the corridor.

Phoenix's office.

For some reason, I tiptoe down. Don't ask me why—just a feeling that this is the kind of silence I shouldn't break. Moving forward, I peek around the corner.

Phoenix is standing at the corner of his desk with his back to me. His eyes are cast down at his feet. I follow his gaze down…

And my breath catches in my throat.

It hurts how bad I want to scream, to cry. Is this how it feels to have your world torn apart?

Charity.

Charity.

Charity…

I keep saying her name in my head. That's all I'm capable of processing at the moment.

The blood pooling around her is unmistakable. The devastating proof that I am now undeniably, completely, and wholly on my own.

My knees start to shake. I know I'm seconds away from hitting the ground. Seconds away from releasing my grief in a wail that will alert him to my presence.

And then what—he'll kill me like he killed her?

I consider just letting him do exactly that for just a moment. It would end my pain, my suffering, my guilt.

But Theo needs me. I can't leave him here, in this house, with this man.

I'm a fool. A damn fool.

Maybe I always have been. I back out of the room before he notices me, tears blurring my vision. I head through the house, searching for signs of my son.

Instinct takes me to the room I once shared with Charity. I walk through the door, and relief floods me when I see my baby lying in his crib. At the foot of it is a hurriedly packed duffel bag. Clothes have been strewn in willy-nilly, both mine and Charity's, with Theo's thrown on top for good measure.

Frowning, I race over to Theo and scoop him up. He gurgles softly but otherwise doesn't make a sound. I run my touch over his fingers, his toes, checking him for any sign that he's been hurt.

But I find nothing. He's okay. *Thank God.*

Still running on pure survival instinct, I throw the bag over one shoulder and tuck Theo into my arm as I sneak out of the room.

I don't know where I'm going. I don't have any place to go. I don't have anyone to turn to.

All I know is I have to get my boy as far away from this place as possible. And for him, I'm willing to be as brave as I need to be.

I'm willing to run through the desert once more.

44

PHOENIX
PHOENIX'S OFFICE

Who killed her?

Even as my mind runs through the possibilities, I raise my gun. The killer might still be in the house.

It is possible that Elyssa pulled the trigger?

Perhaps the sisterly bond between them was bullshit. Another ruse. Another cover. Another lie.

I start to turn towards the door. I don't hear the gunshot. But I feel the air ripple as the bullet escapes a chamber just a few feet behind my head.

I swear I have just long enough to think, *So this is how it ends.*

But I'm wrong. Narrowly missing my hand, the shot hits my weapon instead. It rips it out of my hand and sends it skittering across the floor, into the gap underneath the leather sofa.

My ears are blistering as I pivot slowly. I can't hear anything besides the scream of remnant white noise.

When I turn, though, I see.

And when I see, I understand.

"Anna?"

She's standing in the doorway, pointing a pistol straight at me. The barrel of her gun is smoking slightly.

"Hello, Phoenix," she says in a tone I've never heard before. It sounds so strange for a moment—and then I realize why.

This is the first time she hasn't called me "Master." From the very beginning of her time in my employ, she'd insisted on it.

It seems things have changed.

She walks into the room, and I'm shocked at the sure-footed, confident gait she exhibits.

There's no limp.

There's no fucking limp.

But there is a fresh wound on her arm and scrapes that look like claw marks on the side of her face.

My eyes immediately zip down to Charity. I can only make out one hand, but the blood underneath her fingernails is unmistakable.

"You killed her?"

Anna glances at Charity with mild irritation. "She put up more of a fight than I expected."

She takes a seat in an armchair in front of me and gestures with her gun for me to do the same. "Please," she adds politely.

I stay where I am. Staring at her, trying to figure out where I'd gone so wrong.

I'd found her in the home of an enemy, enslaved and mistreated. She was the one that pulled the trigger that killed her owner's life. Mario Gibraltar. A known agent of Astra Tyrannis.

I'd walked in on the scene moments after it happened. Soon enough to see the bastard's body still twitching and bleeding out. But now, in light of this new revelation, the timing seems rather convenient.

"Everything you told me was a lie," I say. "Wasn't it?"

She sighs. "Sit down, Phoenix. Please. This may be a long conversation and I'd hate for you to be uncomfortable."

For the first time since I'd known her, she's showing me her true face. Gone is the warm, affectionate grandmother who's tended to my home for years. In her place is a cold-blooded assassin who shot my gun out of my hand from across the room without batting an eye.

"I could break your kneecaps," she muses. "That would force you to sit. But I'd much prefer not to go to the trouble."

I have to resist the urge to launch myself at her and throttle her with my bare hands. One look at her casual grip on the gun, though, and I know that I'd have half a dozen holes in me before I made it one step in that direction.

So instead, I lower myself down to the couch just behind me.

She gives me an approving nod, as though she's disciplining an errant child. "Thank you."

"What's your real name?" I ask.

"I was born Martha Blackwell," she says. "But I've had many incarnations. Many lives. I've also been Alison Nathanson. Diana Adison. Grace Copper. Susan Lewis. Joanna Robinson. I've been so many different women. They all start to blend together eventually."

"And you've worked for Astra Tyrannis the whole time?"

"Since I was fourteen years old."

"Where did they find you?"

"In an orphanage in northern France," she says with a wry smile, as if recalling a fond memory.

"So they steal away little girls with no family and turn them into weapons."

"I had no purpose," Anna corrects haughtily. "They gave me one."

"You call this a purpose?" I ask with disgust. "You help Astra Tyrannis steal and enslave thousands upon thousands of women."

She shrugs as though those crimes are removed from her. "They created me," she replies. "Who am I to question my creators?"

"And you feel no guilt?"

A flash of surprise runs through her eyes. "Should I?" she asks. "No, I feel no guilt. This was always what I was meant to be."

The glint in her eyes tells me all I need to know—she's a fucking psychopath.

The complete lack of conscience.

The unyielding belief in a monstrous cause.

The bloodlust that she can't quite hide anymore now that her veil has been ripped away.

"It must have been torture for you," I remark. "To play the part of the aging housekeeper."

I notice the flicker of irritation in her expression. "As it turns out, everything and everyone has an expiry date," she says. "There was talk of retiring me. Once I hit my late forties, I could no longer function how they wanted. They wanted their spies vibrant and beautiful. But I made them see that a spy didn't have to be beautiful or young to get information. In fact, the most unsuspecting spies were the women you never really saw, never really noticed. The women who creep around you every single day and every single night of your life, watching you as you look right through them."

I shudder. "They positioned you in Gibraltar's house, didn't they?" I surmise. "They put you there so that I would find you."

"You frightened them, Phoenix. You had the force of the Bratva. You also had the Irish mafia to call upon. They knew that you needed to be… handled."

I bristle at the word. She's doing it purposefully—trying to goad me, trying to reduce me down to a child. I resist the urge to react.

"So they concocted a plan."

"And they sacrificed Mario Gibraltar in the process?" I ask.

She smiles and shakes her head. "Gibraltar was useful once upon a time. For many decades, actually. But he'd been slipping a lot in those days. He was also starting to get cold feet. Maybe he was just growing a conscience. Either way, the powers that be decided that he needed to be taken out. No one knew this, of course. Astra Tyrannis business always stays within the family. As far as the world was concerned, Gibraltar was still a powerful man, working for a powerful organization. One who had his back at every turn."

I close my eyes for a second. *How fucking perfect.*

"Two birds with one stone," I say quietly.

"Precisely." Anna smiles. "Poetic, isn't it?"

Her face is transformed by the manic glint in her eye. The fact that she's so controlled only makes her depravity all the worse.

"I was sent to Gibraltar's home that night under the pretense of coordinating a new mission to deal with you," she tells me. She leans forward, the gun dangling in her grip. She's getting more and more enthusiastic about her story. "Astra Tyrannis had been monitoring you for months. They planted clues. Left you a trail of breadcrumbs."

"They wanted me to attack Gibraltar's home that night."

She nods, pleased that I'm following along so well. "They wanted you to walk in on the exact moment I killed Gibraltar. It would be hard to question my allegiance after that."

And it had been. She'd fed me a story and I'd believed every word. She'd just killed a high-ranking member of Astra Tyrannis. How could I not believe her story was legitimate?

They play the long game. Eiko had said as much to me only a few hours ago.

"You're the spy Vitya warned me about," I say, mostly to myself.

Which means something else. Elyssa and Charity? They were innocent all along.

I'm a fucking fool.

"Vitya Azarov was another tool in the organization's belt. It was easy to do, considering how poorly you protect those closest to you."

She's just poured acid on an open wound. It hurts like a motherfucker —and there's not a damn thing I can do about it.

Because she's right. Vitya was right, too.

I failed them all. Aurora. Yuri. Vitya. Charity.

My eyes go wide as I remember all those mornings I'd walked into the kitchen to find Anna holding Yuri as Aurora drank her coffee.

"My wife," I choke out. "My son."

She smiles, as though she's been waiting for this particular question. "What about them?"

"You... you spent so much time with them. You cared for Aurora. You looked after Yuri."

"I did," she replies.

Her eyes go filmy for a moment. And for that single moment, it's as though she shares my pain. It's as though she can feel their loss as keenly as I can.

"Aurora was a trusting girl. She wasn't used to this world. You did her a disservice by bringing her into it. And the baby… he was a lovely boy. As beautiful as you are. He would have grown into a handsome man."

"You loved them," I breathe. "You had to have loved them."

"You shouldn't have gotten involved!" Anna hisses, her tone dripping with venom. "You should have known that if you play with a viper, you're going to get bit."

I'm twitching like a live wire. Bursting with the need to move, to act. But I have to resist. I need to hear how this story ends.

I need to know what happened to them.

"How?" I ask. "Who did it?"

She raises her eyebrows at me. "You were a fool," she tells me. "You should have protected them better."

"I know that," I reply softly. "And I will always carry that guilt around with me. It'll kill me before anything else does."

"Oh, I highly doubt that." She admires her gun for a moment. "She trusted me so implicitly," Anna continues. "She used to confide in me. Did you know that?"

"No," I whisper. "I didn't."

"She was terrified from the beginning. Not for herself—it never even crossed her mind that she might be in danger. She was scared for *you*. For your son."

I grind my teeth and squeeze the arms of the armchair so hard I wonder if they'll disintegrate in my fists. But I stay still. I have to stay fucking still.

"There were nights you didn't come home," Anna says. "There were days you disappeared with only a text or two to hold her over. She used to come to my room then and cry. It was so easy to do it, in the end. Too easy."

"No... no..."

The loss and pain on her face wilts away when she makes eye contact with me. She smiles—and I feel the chill bone deep.

There's no soul in those eyes. Whatever Astra Tyrannis did to her, they did it well.

"I was given the order minutes after you left on a mission. Aurora came to my room with the child. She was so distraught, so worried for you that she didn't even see it coming. While she was unconscious, I bound and gagged her. I hid her in my wardrobe."

I always assumed that finding out how they died would give me some clarity. Some closure.

But I was wrong.

This is like watching them die in front of me.

"The boy was crying," Anna continues. "I killed him right away."

My body convulses and she gives me a sympathetic smile.

"I was gentle with him," she adds, as though it's the saving grace I've need. "A pillow to the face. He suffocated quickly."

That's the final straw. There's no more sitting still here. Not when I'm staring my enemy in the face and hearing that bone-chilling laugh.

I react instantly. I lunge off the sofa towards her, intent on choking the life out of her.

But I'm not fast enough.

Anna raises her gun. Pulls the trigger.

As before, her aim is perfect. It's not a kill shot. The bullet buries itself in my arm and I fall back against the sofa, gasping in agony as blood squirts between my fingers.

"Now, now," she chastises. "I wasn't done with my story yet."

"What did you do with his body?" I ask through gritted teeth. The world is swimming at the edges. But after the initial shock, the pain recedes to the background. I barely feel a thing anymore.

All I'm capable of feeling in this moment is white-hot rage.

"Buried him in the backyard," she replies, gesturing towards the window. "He's been right here on the property this whole time."

"Am I supposed to thank you for that?"

"I would. It was kind of me," she replies. "As for Aurora… you looked everywhere for her. But she was right here, too. The entire time, she was in my room. Hidden away in my wardrobe."

"You kept her caged?" I snarl. "Like a fucking animal?"

"You're the one that caged her!" Anna retorts angrily. "You caged her when you married her. Don't you understand, Phoenix? She was dying long before I killed her. She started dying the moment you married her. You picked the wrong woman to drag into this underworld."

"Several times, it would seem." I laugh bitterly.

She smiles at the joke. "The plan was to move her out of these walls," Anna continues. "Hand her over to the men in the shadows. But she was too weak in the end. She died before I could get her out."

"So you dumped her body on the grounds and made it seem like she was thrown over the wall."

Anna's smile makes her blue eyes come alive.

"I thought my best days were behind me the day they brought me in and told me I was to be retired as an assassin. But as it turns out, I'm so much better suited to be a spy. It takes a certain skillset that the young don't always have. It takes grit, patience, and a—"

"Complete lack of morality?"

She snorts with laughter. "Morality?" she asks. "Men always expect more of women than they themselves are willing to give. None of the men I've ever come across apologize for making hard decisions. So why should I?"

"I may not be a saint," I growl. "But I'm no monster, either."

"Why? Because you're saving women? Rescuing them from the real monsters? Give me a fucking break," she scoffs. "It's nothing more than an ego trip for you. It was never about the women themselves—it was about your reputation. Your legacy. It only became personal when they killed your wife and son."

"When *you* killed my wife and son."

She shrugs as though the detail is irrelevant. "I was following orders," she explains. "They'd still be alive if the powers that be had decided otherwise. You want revenge, Phoenix? Well, guess what? They did, too. It will never end."

"I plan on ending it."

She smiles. This time, her lips curl upwards. "No, I'm afraid I'm the one who will end it," she says, raising her gun. "Our conversation is almost at an end, Phoenix. I must admit, you were a good boss. I almost feel bad about what I have to do."

"No, you don't."

She laughs. "You're right. I don't."

She cocks it. As she does, I realize how beautifully she's played her cards all this time. After I'm dead, she'll simply sound the alarm and play up the tears. I'm not sure what story she'll spin to my men but I have no doubt it'll be airtight.

I hope Matvei will see through it. But my hopes are slim. I never saw through her. Why would anyone else?

"Any last words?" she asks.

"Fuck you."

"Disappointing," she sighs. "Aurora said so much more."

45

ELYSSA

SOMEWHERE IN LAS VEGAS

I walk until my legs hurt and my back aches. Theo has been quiet since we left but now he's starting to stir and whimper.

"Sorry, my boy," I say, my voice shaking badly. "We just need to be brave a little while longer."

He blinks at me and lets out a loud wail.

Instinctively, I glance back over my shoulder but no one's following me. It's just paranoia talking.

The one good thing about Las Vegas is that no matter how late it gets, it's never truly dark on the streets. Then again, as Charity always said, *"The road to hell is paved in neon."* She was right—it is a little spooky.

My heart throbs at the mere thought of her name.

I shake my head and focus on my surroundings. I'm waiting to cross a busy intersection when a tall prostitute in silver boots approaches me.

"Having some trouble, honey?"

"Um, I... I..."

Her face ripples with sympathy. Beneath the caked-on layers of makeup, I see the kinds of worn lines that suggest a hard life.

"It's okay," she says kindly. "Take a deep breath. You in some kinda trouble, baby?"

I nod after a moment. Theo's still crying and I can't seem to get him to stop.

She starts to say, "There's a shelter a few miles—"

"No!" I blurt, cutting her off on accident. "No shelters."

"Ohhhkay then," she concedes. She gives me a funny look. "Whatever you want, doll. What do you need then?"

"A... a car," I decide.

I want to get as far away from this town as possible. I have the cash I won from Phoenix tucked away in the duffel bag. God only knows how long it'll last but that's a problem for future Elyssa to worry about.

"A car," she says, raising one eyebrow. "Even a shitty car don't come cheap, honey."

"I have money. Some money," I add hastily.

She smiles. "There's a used auto shop a few blocks up from here. It's called Lowell's. Go over and say Roni sent you. They'll give you a good deal on a second-hander."

I blink at her, overcome with emotion. "Thank you," I murmur. "Thank you so much."

"Go get your car, honey," she smiles. "And then put that child to bed. He needs a bottle and a good night's sleep."

I give her a tearful nod then head off in the direction of the dealership. Every step hurts but I try to keep my chin held high, even when I desperately want to sit down and rest my legs. I'm also afraid of what'll happen if I stop for even a moment.

What thoughts will catch up to me. What memories. What monsters.

I keep seeing Charity's body in my mind's eye. I keep seeing him standing over her. And every time, I want to throw up.

How could he?

How could he?

~

Ten minutes later, I find myself standing in front of the shop. It's hardly the fanciest dealership I've ever seen, but I don't need fancy. I just need functional.

Lowell turns out to be a handsome older man with dark, simmering eyes and an easy smile. "Didja say Roni sent you?" he asks.

I nod, not trusting my voice.

"You been crying, girl?" he asks.

"It's nothing."

"You and your boy both, huh?"

I wipe the tears off Theo's face. "We're fine."

"It's okay," he says, hands held up to calm me down. "You don't gotta tell me the whole story. You just gotta tell me what you need."

"A car," I say firmly. "One that'll get me out of Las Vegas."

He nods. "And I'm guessing you're looking for cheap, too?"

"If you have anything like that."

"Lowell's got everything, baby. Come on back."

He walks me out into the open-air dealership. The floodlights overhead highlight every pockmark and rusted scar in the rows of cars we pass. I'd guess the average vehicle is older than me.

Lowell stops at the last line and gestures towards two cars in the back. "Got two choices. The blue one's been through quite a few hands but she's got a low mileage on her," Lowell explains. "Marked at three thousand, but I'll let it go for twenty-six hundred."

"And the other one?"

"Hi Ho Silver over here. She's been dinged up once or twice—haven't we all?—but she runs just fine. And those little stains won't bother you much."

"Stains?" I ask.

"Old feller bled out in the back," he replies bluntly. "Tell you what—I'll let her go at two grand flat."

I shudder. "I'll take the blue." I've had my fill of blood and violence. I don't need a constant reminder of it on what is very likely going to be my bed for the foreseeable future.

I fork over the cash, trying not to think about how little I have left, and take the keys from Lowell.

"Best of luck, darling!" he says as he saunters off whistling. "Ride her 'til the wheels fall off!"

"As if I have a choice," I mutter to myself.

I hold my remaining cash in my hand. It's such a thin stack. I'm confident I can make it last for a few weeks at least.

I'm far less confident about everything else, though.

I sink into the back seat with Theo and prepare a quick bottle of formula for him. While he eats, I gaze up at the night sky. The floodlights wash out any trace of stars, so it's just a big sheet of blackness.

I remember how bright the constellations were when I lived on the Sanctuary. How close the whole sky felt. As if you could reach out and run your fingers through the stars like glitter.

Nothing about those days feels real now. Like my whole world has been lit up with harsh neon, and all the things I once thought were beautiful have been exposed as used, rusted trash.

∼

Half an hour later, I'm piloting the car through Las Vegas. I stopped by a store and bought the cheapest car seat I could find for Theo. That plus the milk put him to sleep, thank goodness.

But I'm wired. The lights and sounds of the city don't help. It's all surreal and glaring and overwhelming. I feel the same way I felt the first night I arrived here.

I didn't think I could survive in a place like this. How can I now... without Charity?

The thought of her name threatens to destroy the dam I've been using to pen back my emotions.

"No," I whisper. I can feel it cracking. Threatening to give way. "Please... not now."

But I lose my vision behind a veil of tears, and I know I need to find somewhere to stop.

I keep it together long enough to leave the city behind and pull off onto the shoulder of a dark highway. Then, falling out of the car, I drop to my knees and start to sob.

It's a fresh wave of pain that feels so damn raw that I wonder for a moment if I'm going to survive it or if it'll swallow me whole.

Charity was my hero. My best friend. My mentor. The sister I never had.

She had taught me that it was okay to feel what you were feeling. To rage when you were angry, to laugh when you were happy, to cry when you were sad.

"To fuck when you were horny," I say out loud, looking up at the sparse stars above me.

Who knew that you could laugh at the same time you cried or that both of those things would hurt so badly?

"I'll make sure Theo knows about you, Charity," I whisper up to the dark sky above. "I'll make sure he knows about his beautiful, brave, fearless aunt. I'm sorry, my friend. I'm so sorry. You deserved a better ending. A happy ending. I'll miss you. I love you."

I take a deep breath and let the words settle. A few cars zoom by. I don't feel any better, though.

Because I can't feel Charity with me.

People always say that when their loved ones die: *I know they're with me, watching over me. I can feel them.*

But even if that's true for some people, it's not for me. Charity's gone. She's gone somewhere she can't hear me.

The words I speak are for me and me alone.

I turn back to the car and get into the backseat, next to Theo. He's still sleeping soundly.

I kiss his upturned cheek, drinking in his pure scent, thanking God for the fact that he's safe and alive and with me now. Then I put the overhead light on and pick up the duffel bag that Charity packed.

I root around inside to see what's inside. The money. Theo's formula, his clothes, one lone stuffed toy. Some of her clothes, some of mine.

I root around a little more and realize there's a hard object hidden in the side compartment of the duffel. I open the zip and squeeze my hand inside to find…

A gun.

I have to stifle my scream so I don't wake Theo. Dropping the gun back on top of the pile of folded clothes, I breathe and compose myself.

My fingers had brushed against something else in the side pocket. Trembling, I pull the zipper wider open and peer inside.

It's... a phone?

Even weirder, I recognize it. But why would Charity have stolen Anna's phone?

I try to guess the passcode, wondering if there's anything on here that'll shed some light on what happened in the last moments of Charity's life.

But after five wrong attempts, the screen informs me that I've been locked out for ten minutes. Sighing, I run my hand through the corners of the side compartment, hoping for something else.

My fingers hit nothing more than the crinkle of paper. I pull out a crumpled-up receipt. I'm about to discard it when I notice a familiar scrawl on the back.

Lys, in case we miss each other: Remember Little Red Riding Hood? The bad guy is not always the obvious one. Sometimes, the grandmother is the monster.

It makes no sense. "Charity," I whisper. "Who were you trying to warn me about?"

I glance at the phone next to me—and then it hits me like a bolt of lightning.

I read the note again. *The bad guy is not always the obvious one. Sometimes, the grandmother is the monster.*

"It's Anna," I whisper out loud. "Oh, God."

I stare out ahead at the empty stretch of road that promises to take me far away. If I keep going, I'll have a chance at a fresh start. Theo deserves that. So do I, after all we've been through.

But going back… Well, I don't know what it would mean. What it would hold. Who or what is waiting for me back at Phoenix's mansion.

But I can't keep driving. Not now. Not knowing what I know.

I have to tell Phoenix.

So I get into the driver's seat and turn the car around. I ran once before, and it didn't stop my demons from catching up to me.

So maybe it's time to stop running.

Maybe it's time to fight.

46

PHOENIX
PHOENIX'S OFFICE

As I stare at the barrel of the gun, I can almost swear that it's staring right back at me.

Odd, though, how I'm looking death in the face and thinking instead about life. About my life in particular. Have I made the most of it? Have I done everything I set out to do?

The answer is obvious: of course not.

I've always been a greedy beast—I just hid it behind a veil of nobility.

I've always been a monster—I just stayed out of the light so no one could see.

Aurora and Yuri were the last pure things in my world and look how that turned out. I should have realized that the only way to keep them pure was to keep them far away from me.

"What are you going to tell my men?" I ask.

She shrugs. "That Charity was a spy. That you found out. You fought. You killed each other."

"Clean."

"Isn't it?" She smirks. "That's why I'm the best."

There's real pride in her voice. And it strikes me that she's been waiting a long time to have this conversation with me. She must have hated playing the part of the aging housekeeper, the tottering old woman who'd been put out to pasture.

She must have hated the way people looked at her. The way they spoke to her.

"I proved my worth to the powers that be," she continues, "time and time again. When I retire, I will live like a queen."

"But you'd be bored."

She shrugs. "I'll make my own fun."

"I have no doubt."

"I understand why you're stalling," she says. "But it won't stop the inevitable."

"I'm not afraid of death."

She eyes me carefully, then nods. "I believe you. Shame, really. You would have done well in the organization."

I scowl and spit at her feet. "I'll take that bullet now."

She laughs. Shrugs. Takes aim.

But the gunshot seems to come prematurely. Like time broke for one bizarre instant.

Except that I don't feel a thing.

And then…

Anna screams. Her arm buckles and I realize that blood is blossoming on her chest, more and more with every passing second, like a rose blooming in fast forward.

She stares at me, her eyes wide with shock. A dribble of blood spills from her lips. "H-h-how…?"

I don't have the answer.

Until I turn and see Elyssa step into the room.

"I… I came back," she gasps when her eyes meet mine.

Her cheeks are wet with tears but she keeps her gun raised.

"You… little wh-whore…!" Anna wheezes.

She lunches forward, ignoring the blood still spreading across her chest. Startled, Elyssa screams and rears back. She fires again, but her panic makes her shoot blindly. The bullet whizzes past Anna and destroys the window behind us, shattering it in a hail of glass. Tiny shards pepper my face and draw blood.

Anna stumbles into Elyssa and the two women tumble to the ground in a mess of blood and hair and flailing limbs.

Elyssa is panicking, her arms flailing wildly as Anna tries to claw at her face. I swallow past my shock, stride forward, and yank the old bitch up by the roots of her hair.

She groans in my grasp as I twist her towards me. I want to look her in the eyes for this last part.

Her expression is bleak. Mute. Accepting. She knows she's halfway to death.

And I'm about to help her cross the final distance.

"Did you enjoy it?" I snarl. "Killing them?"

Blood gushes from her mouth from somewhere deep within but she still manages to speak. "I… followed orders."

I hurl her down and bring my foot down hard on her knee. She screams but the blood in her throat is starting to choke her. The screams turn to strangled gurgles.

"Phoenix!" Elyssa cries. "What are you doing?!"

I ignore her. I've held my rage in for long enough. For five long years, I've wondered what I'd do if I caught the people who killed my family.

Now, I know.

"You finally have your limp," I growl at Anna.

I break her other leg. Her body jerks, but there's no scream this time.

She's going to die soon. She has a minute, maybe two, no more than that.

But it's all happening too fast. I want so desperately to save her—just so I can draw out her death for the next several months. She deserves no less.

I kneel in front of her, grabbing her face and forcing her eyes to mine. I need her to look at me when she goes.

"This is for Aurora," I say as I draw the knife from my boot sheath and hold it up under her jaw. "This is for Yuri."

Anna tries to spit in my face but she doesn't have the strength. It turns into a dribble of blood and saliva on her chin. "F-fuck… y—"

I laugh mirthlessly. "Tell the devil I said hello."

Then I cut her throat like the animal she is.

Elyssa cries out, turns to the side, and dry heaves. But there's nothing in her stomach to come up. I'm distantly aware of her crawling away from Anna's twitching corpse.

I'm dripping in the traitor's blood. I have everything I wanted. Revenge, hot and bloody and complete. I finally got her.

And yet…

It feels like nothing.

I don't feel relief. Or happiness. Or satisfaction.

I just feel empty.

Anna may have been a monster. But she worked for worse ones. And they were the ones pulling her strings. Handing down their orders while they sat in their castles, removed from the bloodshed and devastation they cause.

My masters, she called them. *The powers that be. The men in the shadows.*

All synonyms for one thing: monsters too cowardly to do the dirty work themselves.

A cry in the hallway draws my attention. I look through the open door to see a car seat set on the ground. In it, I can see the top of Theo's downy dark hair.

So like Yuri's.

He's buried somewhere on this property, she said. But until I find his remains, I refuse to believe that Anna was telling the truth. She spewed lie after lie. Who knows what was true, what was false? What was intended to explain and what was intended to hurt?

Elyssa is still on her hands and knees, retching out nothing more than air. Her eyes are wild with panic and her body is trembling like a leaf.

Now, I have her to deal with. She may or may not be another spy. But I was right about one thing: she's a weakness.

"Get a hold of yourself," I say coldly.

It's a curious feeling, the seeping cold that's frosting over my limbs and making me feel nothing but anger. But it also makes me feel in control.

She glances back at me. I can see the helplessness in her eyes. She's trying not to look at Anna's body but her eyes keep flitting to it anyway. Then, with a show of willpower, she wrenches her gaze away and looks instead at Theo.

"He's sleeping," I tell her. "Babies can sleep through anything. Yuri was like that, too."

She opens her mouth, but nothing comes out. She's still in shock, her body convulsing in sharp, involuntary waves.

"Take a deep breath," I instruct her.

She tries—at least, it looks like it—but the panicked spasming only gets worse.

I pull her onto her feet and toss her into the seat that Anna had been sitting on. When I release her, my bloody fingerprints are imprinted against her fair skin.

She stares at me through her tears. "I… I came back…"

"You went to see your parents?" I interrupt.

Confusion ripples across her shell-shocked face. She doesn't understand why I'm being so cold. So cruel.

Too bad I no longer care what she thinks. She may have saved my life just now but my days of trusting innocent faces are dead and gone now.

"Yes."

"Why?"

"I… I…"

"Fucking speak!"

She gasps but the gasp is drowned out by the sound of rushing footsteps. My men burst onto the scene with their weapons drawn. The first shot must have alerted them.

Ilya stands in the threshold, staring between Elyssa and me.

"Fucking hell…" he murmurs when he sees Anna's corpse. "Anna?"

"She was an Astra Tyrannis spy," I inform my men.

There's immediate exclamations of shock and outrage. But mostly disbelief. I can't wait for them to catch up, though. I need to deal with Elyssa.

"Take the baby," I tell Ilya. "Make sure he's comfortable."

"Where are you taking him?" Elyssa asks, finding her voice instantly.

"He'll be fine," I say harshly.

"Let me have him!"

"No," I retort. "You and I need to talk. Ilya, now."

Elyssa's eyes go wide with terror but she knows better than to argue. Ilya and the men grab Theo and slip out without another word.

"Explain yourself," I say when we're alone again.

"I was leaving Las Vegas."

"You were running?"

Her brows knot together. "I walked in here and saw you standing over Charity's body." She sobs over Charity's name. "I... I thought you killed her. So I grabbed Theo and ran."

"Why did you come back?"

"Because I found something in the duffel bag that Charity packed."

"Besides the gun?"

She flinches, staring at the handgun that's now lying discarded on the carpet. "Yes," she says softly. "It was a note that Charity left for me."

"A note?"

"She found out something about Anna. She was trying to warn me. But obviously..."

"Anna got to her first."

"Charity is—she was—so smart. She must have known that Anna suspected she was onto her. Which is why she left me the note. But I was too late. When I realized, I had to come back to warn you."

"And I'm supposed to be flattered?"

She flinches again. Always fucking flinching. I used to think it was proof of her innocence. Now, I just wonder if it's another tactic meant to deceive and disguise.

"Why are you looking at me like that?" she whispers.

"Like what?"

"Like I'm the enemy."

"I haven't decided if you are or not yet."

She stares at me in shock. "I just saved your life."

"A surefire way to earn my trust," I reply. "Just like Anna killing an Astra Tyrannis underboss was a way to earn my trust. We both know how that turned out."

"You really believe I'm a spy?" she asks, hurt suffusing her amber eyes.

I ignore that question. "Why did you go back to see your parents?"

She looks down.

"Fucking answer me."

"I thought they were trying to send me a message. Maybe even threaten me. I went back to find out which."

"The gift you were sent earlier in the day. That's what drew you."

"Yes."

"What was inside?"

She hesitates for a moment, but then she replies. "A cast iron black swan."

"Excuse me?"

"It was a paperweight."

"And it means something to you?"

Her eyes go back down to her hands. "It involves a part of my past I'd rather forget."

"You don't have the option of forgetting now," I tell her. "Tell me what you're hiding."

"I... I can only tell you parts."

"What does that mean?"

"It means that I can't remember everything," she says, her voice flaring up for the first time tonight. "It means that I've lost huge chunks of time. There are whole parts of my childhood, my adolescence, that I can't really remember."

"How convenient."

"I know it seems that way, but it's the truth!"

I laugh without humor. "I'm not fucking playing around anymore, Elyssa. I've been far too tolerant with you. I want some goddamn answers. And I want them now."

47

ELYSSA

"I'm not the enemy!" I cry out.

"Yeah?" he hisses. "Prove it."

It hurts the way he's looking at me now. Everything hurts. Charity's body is only feet away from me but I can't really see her behind the desk.

Anna, on the other hand, is on full display. The sight of all that blood and gore is making my guts churn with discomfort.

I know she deserved what she got. But seeing a human body splayed open like that... it's a reminder of just how fragile we all are. We're all one knife's edge away from death.

"Elyssa," Phoenix growls. Even the way he says my name is a threat. "Start talking. Now."

I shudder and swallow back the billions of feelings threatening to overwhelm me. It's hard to look him in his eyes after what he just did to Anna. It's hard to look at his hands, too—the hands that just tore her apart. Her blood drips from his fingertips.

He's a fucking savage.

The question remains, though... what will those hands do to me now?

So I start my story. What I can remember of it, at least.

"The night I ran from the Sanctuary, I... I woke up, I guess you'd say. I was confused. Didn't know where I was or what was happening. I was wearing the wedding dress and there was something in my hand."

"The paperweight?"

I nod. "Yeah. The paperweight... covered in blood."

He doesn't say a thing, so I continue. Even when the fear running through my veins burns like battery acid.

"It wasn't my blood—that much I knew. I got to my feet, and I realized that I was in someone else's home. Someone else's room. I turned and saw there was a body by the side of the bed. Father Josiah's body. And he was..."

"Dead?"

I nod, not trusting my voice.

"You killed him?"

I flinch. "Honestly, until today, I thought I had."

Phoenix's eyes darken. "What do you mean?"

"When I went back to the Sanctuary today, he was there. Josiah. He wasn't dead at all. He survived." I drag my eyes up to meet his. "Phoenix, I'm... I'm scared. I don't remember the weeks leading up to that night. In fact, I don't remember years leading up to that night."

He's staring at me like he doesn't know who I am. Which is fair—at this point, I don't know who I am, either.

Am I Elyssa Redmond, daughter of the Sanctuary, betrothed of Father Josiah?

Am I Theo's mother?

Am I Phoenix's lover?

Am I a runaway, a killer, a monster, a mistake?

"The last thing I remember really clearly," I continue in a low, hollow voice, "is my fourteenth birthday. A few snippets here and there. My best friend getting married. Feeling lonely, isolated. A job I can't remember very well. But the rest of it… it's all blurry. It makes my head hurt just trying to think about it."

His eyes narrow. "And I'm supposed to believe that?"

"It's the truth."

"What would you know about the truth?"

He's being purposefully cruel. But I have no retort. No leg to stand on.

"I don't know," I whisper. "I can't remember anything."

"You don't remember attacking him?" he asks.

"No."

"You don't remember putting on the wedding dress?"

"No."

He leans forward and grabs my arm. His fingers are sticky with Anna's blood but he seems not to even notice. He pulls me upright, towards him. My body hits his chest with a dull slam and I ripple with anxiety.

He's so beautiful. Is it twisted that even now, even when he's leering over me threateningly, even when I'm fully aware that this man could be my end…

I still can't quite extinguish my feelings for him?

"Please, Phoenix," I beg, hoping he can see past my flaws, my sins. "Please believe me. I don't remember."

"Liar."

"It's true. The memories are gone."

"No memory is ever gone. You can't remember because you don't want to."

His voice, his eyes, his grip—it's all meant to hurt me.

It's working.

I shake my head. "I've tried to remember."

"Have you, though?"

Maybe he's right. I didn't try to remember. In fact, I tried actively to forget. Because I knew I wouldn't like the revelations those memories would unveil. I wanted a fresh start, and I didn't think I could attempt one without putting all that ugliness behind me.

"Phoenix," I sob. "Please…"

He flings me back onto the sofa. I cry out as I collapse into it and the wind is knocked out of my lungs.

"Tell me."

"Please stop…"

"Tell me!"

He hasn't hit me but it feels that way. His voice is a whip, flaying me open again and again and again.

"You remember what happened. Tell me… fucking *TELL ME!*"

I put my hands up to cover my face as the echo of his bellow bounces around the office. Is the foundation of the house shaking? Or is that just me?

"You will tell me; do you understand? You're mine. You're mine!"

You're mine... The words reverberate faintly in my ears. I can feel something threatening to unleash inside of me.

And just like that, my memory cracks wide open. I fall into it like sliding beneath the surface of a dark, frozen lake...

∼

The Sanctuary—One Year Ago

"Mama?" I ask nervously, biting my lip.

"Hush now," Mama says. "Don't ask questions." She fiddles with the lace trim on the wedding dress I'm wearing.

"Mama, I'm scared."

My mother fixes me with a hard stare. "Scared? Why should you be scared? This is Father Josiah. Our shepherd. He's going to be your husband. I thought you were excited. It is an honor, Elyssa."

"I know," I say. "I am. It is. I just… don't feel right."

I can tell she's uncomfortable. She's fidgeting a lot, and she's not paying attention to my hair when she fastens the veil on my crown.

"Ouch!"

"I told you to hush," she snaps. "I can't concentrate when you keep talking."

I stop asking questions.

Mama finishes prepping me. There's a knock on the door. It swings open, reveals Papa standing there.

"Is she ready?" he asks, as if I'm not even there.

"Yes," Mama says.

"Then let's go." Papa grabs me by the upper arm and steers me out of the room, out of the house. We step out into the night.

Our footsteps whisper through the desert sand. It's quiet. No one, not even insects, making noise.

It's a short walk. Everything is close here. The house I've seen a thousand times but never entered looms above. It looks bigger than I remember.

"Come on, girl," Papa tells me gruffly as we near it.

I'm glad I have this veil on. It feels like a mask. Something to keep me safe from the future I'm tumbling into.

The door opens before we can knock. Standing on the threshold is Father Josiah, looking at me with an approving glint in his eye.

"Ah, Elyssa," he says with a small nod. "You are right on time. We have much to do."

"Of course, Father Josiah," I murmur. "I am your servant."

Those are the words I'm supposed to say. But I keep my eyes down as I mumble them. This all feels so wrong, so out of place.

"Thank you for bringing her, Solomon," Josiah says. "You may go."

Papa nods and shuffles away. He doesn't look back at me even once.

When he's gone, I feel Father Josiah's gaze settle on me once more. "Come, Elyssa. We don't want you standing in the doorway the whole night. As I said, there is much to do."

When I still don't move, he takes my hand and pulls me inside the house. His eyes are sparkling under the bright lights of his home. Everything is so grand and beautiful here.

It's a far cry from the house I've lived in all my life.

I happen to know that Father Josiah has a full staff. Of course he would, given the sheer size of this place. But tonight, the place looks empty.

"Where are your maids?" I ask, my voice shaky and hesitant.

"Off for the night. It's just you and I, my dove."

I've always thought his smile was comforting. He has that easy, reassuring nature about him that makes trusting him easy. But tonight, his smile feels different.

Or maybe nothing is different and I'm just reading too much into everything.

"Come," he says again, offering me his hand.

I stare at it, feeling extremely uncomfortable in the dress. "Where are we going?"

"You'll see."

Left with no choice, I slip my hand into his and he leads me up the stairs. It takes forty steps to reach the top. I count every single one of them.

When we arrive at the landing, he takes a left and leads me down a candlelit corridor. "Where are you taking me?" I squeak.

He ignores me this time. Then he pushes open a large white door and gestures for me to go inside.

I move in slowly, realizing that we're in a large bedroom that overlooks part of the commune and part of the desert outside the Sanctuary's boundaries.

"Father Josiah?" I say, turning around to face him.

CLICK. He snaps the door shut and turns the lock.

"Oh, my frightened little dove," he says, taking a slow, deliberate step towards me. "I am to be your husband. I want you to call me Josiah."

I can't bring myself to speak. That feeling of wrongness has only grown.

He smiles as he closes the final distance between us. "You are a good woman, Elyssa," he murmurs, taking my hand and bringing it to his lips. "It's exactly why I chose you. Why you were chosen for me, rather. Well, that and your beauty of course. You really are the most beautiful woman I've ever seen. Beauty is a blessing from the powers that be."

I give him a shaky smile when he meets my eyes. "Thank you."

His words are honeyed, dripping with flattery. But they fall flat and grating against my ears. My skin tingles.

We shouldn't be here. I shouldn't be here.

"Let me remove that veil so I can gaze at your beauty."

He undoes the pins and pulls back the veil, leaving it half in and half out. Without the partition between us, I feel exposed.

"Those eyes," Josiah sighs as he drinks me. "What beautiful, innocent eyes. They can drive a man insane. I'm sure they have…"

He reaches to the bedside table and picks up a heavy goblet. "Drink this," he orders.

"What is—"

"Drink it."

I tense. Something bad is hurtling towards me like a shooting star. I can sense it, even if I don't know yet what it is.

"Yes, Father Josiah," I murmur. I raise to my lips and take the tiniest sip possible.

His smile sours. "More."

"I don't want—"

"It wasn't a question."

I hesitate. I'm locked in. Not just into this room but into this life. Into this marriage. I never had a choice. I thought I wanted it in the beginning, but I was wrong about that.

It's too late for that, though.

I raise the goblet to my lips once more and drain it of whatever is inside.

"That's a good girl," he croons as he takes it back from my trembling fingers. "Now, tell me, Elyssa—are you a good daughter of the Sanctuary?"

"I—I don't know what you mean." My head is swimming already. What did he make me drink?

"Have you ever laid with a man?" His voice crackles strangely at the end.

"No!" I blurt. "Of course not."

It's the truth. Since I was a little girl, I've been taught what is right and what is wrong in this world. A woman's place is with her husband. And if she is not yet married, she is to wait for him.

Once plucked, a flower withers. Isn't that what Father Josiah and the other elders have lectured time and time again? It's a lesson to the women of the Sanctuary: once you've been touched, once you've lost your purity… you're worthless.

"Why are you asking me this, Father Josiah?" I say, trembling.

He doesn't bother explaining himself. He pulls me against him suddenly, his eyes lingering on my lips.

"Listen to me very closely, Elyssa," he says. The honey is gone from his voice. It's hardened and venomous now. "There is only one man who kisses you from this day forward. Only one man who touches you. You understand?"

"You," I whisper.

"Precisely," he says, with an approving nod. "Me. You are mine now, Elyssa. Mine always."

I shiver. Perhaps he interprets that as desire, because the next thing I know, he's kissing me.

His lips feel like sandpaper. His breath is minty but I can taste the ash of cigarette smoke just beneath it. His beard is sparse and uncomfortable against my cheeks.

It hurts. It's wrong. I hate it.

I try and break away from him but his grip is firm. When he finally pulls away, his breath comes out ragged. His lips fall against my neck, and he starts sucking wildly.

The wrongness overwhelms me. This needs to stop. I need space to breathe, to think, to figure out what's happening.

I try and push Josiah off me but his eyes glaze over with lust and it looks like he's a million miles away from here. Lost in a place where he can't or won't hear me. Can't or won't listen. Can't or won't stop.

That's when he tosses me on my back against the four-poster bed and starts unbuckling his pants.

I pale, my hands digging into the sheets. "No! Please, not like this…"

"Shut up. Weren't you listening? You're mine. They gave you to me. The powers that be said I could have you…"

He unbuttons his pants and wriggles them down around his hairy, skinny legs.

"So I'm taking…"

His penis springs free. I gasp at how strange and grotesque it looks.

"… what's mine."

He starts scrabbling up the hem of my dress as I struggle and scream. "No! No!"

But I might as well not be speaking for all the good it does. I close my eyes when he rips my panties down my thighs.

I feel his hardness on the inside of my knee as he clambers on top of me.

"Please stop…!" I cry. "Please…"

He thrusts himself inside me and I wail in pain. My body shudders, trying to reject the alien thing that has just entered me.

Then, when I see how useless it is to push back, I stop fighting. I give in. I slump down onto the duvet and drift out of my skin so I can be anywhere but here.

The one saving grace is that I don't have to wait long. Eight thrusts later, and Josiah moans low. He quivers in a strange spasm and then he collapses next to me.

The slipperiness of the comforter sends me sliding down to my knees without his weight to skewer me in place. I hit the hardwood floor with a tiny *oof*. It's only when I touch my cheek do I realize I've been crying.

My eyes lock on a mote of dust caught in a moonbeam. It floats, shimmies, pirouettes. For a moment, I'm sure that it's the most beautiful thing that's ever existed.

I follow it as it drifts over and settles on top of something on the bedside table. The object is metallic and dark. It seems to swallow up the moonlight, blacker than all the shadows around it.

Between my legs, I'm vaguely aware of the sticky mess that Father Josiah left behind.

And in my chest, I'm vaguely aware of a hot, roaring rage bubbling up in me.

I've never felt anything like this before. My whole life, I've been taught that women must not let their feelings control them. That men are logical creatures, that we women are slaves to our emotions. That sadness and happiness and anger are not permissible.

Now, though, there's no way I can resist it. I knew this was wrong and this anger, this wrath, is my body reacting. I'm powerless to stop it.

The moon shifts just enough that the metallic object on the bedside table is lit up. It's a swan, I see now. A paperweight or something like that, curved and graceful. Its sleek, cast iron head is aimed in my direction. Looking. Observing. Judging.

My hands are starting to shake with this foreign feeling that's burning me up from the inside out.

It wants to take over.

It wants control.

And so I let it.

When Father Josiah entered me, I felt myself dissociate from my body. This is the exact opposite of that. I've never felt more alive, never felt more like myself, as I rise to my feet.

The trembling has stopped. In its place is molten certainty. Hot fire in my veins.

My hands close around the swan. I fondle it, feeling the cool metal against my fingertips. Hefting the weight in my palm.

I turn in place. Father Josiah is struggling to an upright position on the bed. His penis hangs limp and shrinking on the front of his linen pants. His eyes are dreamy, distant.

But when they see me, he freezes.

"What are you doing?" he demands. "Elyssa, what are you—"

I don't answer as I take one huge stride forward and slam the swan against the side of his head.

There's barely a sound, but the impact is immediate. His skull gives way. Something sickening crunches, spurts. It's almost enough to make me throw up.

He slumps back against the bed. And then, just like I did, he slides to the ground, moaning softly.

I'm still holding the swan when he hits the floor hard.

Then, like water down a drain, the anger rushes out of me. And I'm left there, pale and bloodied and trembling, wondering what on earth I've done.

48

ELYSSA
PHOENIX'S OFFICE

I blink. Phoenix starts to come back into focus. The memories catapulting around in my head feel like scenes from a movie. Imperfect scenes, strangely choreographed and heartbreakingly acted. They don't feel like they belong to me.

"Elyssa…"

There's a grudging concern in Phoenix's tone as he kneels in front of me and shakes me by the shoulders. I blink a few more times, trying to pull myself back from the nightmare that's not a nightmare at all.

"I remember," I whisper.

Phoenix stills a little. "You remember?"

"Not everything," I amend. "Just… what happened that night."

He removes his hands from my shoulders. But he doesn't get off his knee. I can't help thinking that it almost looks like he's about to propose. Except, instead of a ring, he's got bloody hands.

I suppose in a way, that's fitting.

"Tell me."

So I do. I tell him in a halting, jerking voice everything I just remembered. I don't even recognize my voice as I tell the story. It sounds like it belongs to someone else.

"… I just wanted him to stop touching me," I whisper in the end. "The paperweight was right there. It was heavy. I just wanted him to stop touching me."

I raise my gaze to his. His jaw is clenched so tight I wonder if his teeth will shatter. The storm in his eyes rages harder than ever.

"Then you set the fire and ran?"

"Yes."

"You stumbled into Wild Night Blossom and met me."

"Yes."

"And when we found ourselves alone together, we had sex."

I wince. "Yes."

"Elyssa?"

"Yes?"

"Theo… Who is his father?" he asks bluntly.

Nausea swells inside my gut. But I already know I have nothing left inside me to come out.

"Phoenix…"

"Answer the question, Elyssa. Answer the fucking question."

"I don't know," I sob, looking down. "I'm sorry. But I honestly don't know." I can't bear to look at his face.

"Get up."

I listen. I obey.

"Look at me."

I do. His face is terrifying. He looks gaunt and sinister. A wild animal who's just been set free. My wildest fantasy disguised as my worst nightmare.

"Get out," he tells me in a slow, creeping drawl. "You are never to return to this house again."

"Phoenix…"

"You heard me," he says coldly. "Get out now. Stay any longer and I'll do what I should have done a long time ago. I'll kill you."

"Theo could still be yours," I stammer desperately.

"I have only one son," he snaps, making me jerk back. "And he died five years ago, at the hands of this mad bitch. So I'm done trusting anyone. It's not a luxury I can afford any longer. And with you, there are too many lies. Too many unanswered questions."

I want to go to him. I want to beg for his mercy, his forgiveness, his understanding.

But I can see it in his eyes: Nothing will move him. He's lost too much and fallen too far to see past his pain.

"I'm sorry," I tell him, hoping the words will reach him even while knowing that they won't.

He turns from me. I feel fresh tears surface. I blink them back and turn to the door. I won't break down. Not here.

I move quickly through the house, searching for my son. I find him two doors down with a pair of maids. I rush forward and grab him from the pretty blonde who's rocking him in her arms without saying so much as a word. Theo cries in protest but I ignore both him and the maids.

I strap him back into the baby carrier and make my way out of the house as fast as I can. The car is parked in the same position I left it in the driveway. The moment I have Theo secured in the back seat, I get in and start to drive.

For a second, I think I spot a tall silhouette in one of the windows. But before I can focus my gaze, it's gone.

Wishful thinking—that's all it is.

I drive for twenty minutes before Theo starts bawling in his carrier and I'm forced to pull over. I get in the back and pull him out of the carrier.

As I try to soothe him, I realize that I don't have anything to comfort him with. And that's when it hits me: I left the duffel bag at the mansion.

All my earthly possessions were in that thing. Including the money I was going to use to get out of Las Vegas.

"No," I whisper. "No…"

And as Theo cries, I join in.

My breasts ran dry a long time ago, so I have nothing to offer him. I look down at my sweet baby boy, realizing that we have no one in the world to turn to. The one person we could count on is dead.

"Charity," I whisper. "I wish you were with us now. I have no one else."

I kiss Theo's head, leaving my tears on his soft skin. "I'm sorry," I whimper. "I'm sorry. You deserve better, my little angel…"

Then, as if it is giving up along with us, the car shudders and grinds to a halt. The engine whines like a dying creature. I don't even have to look to know that it's never going to start up again.

I'm in a daze as I step out of the car. My feet carry me down the sidewalk. We leave the vehicle behind, keys still in the ignition. I hold Theo close to my chest and walk, looking at everything and seeing nothing.

Bright lights. People—partiers and hookers, gamblers and addicts, tourists and nobodies. Not a single one of them gives me so much as a second glance.

I'm not in control of my body. It's piloting me somewhere, pulled along by fate or luck or something worse. So I shouldn't be surprised when I look up and find myself staring at a sickeningly familiar neon sign.

Wild Night Blossom. The place where it all began.

The red and black neon glows and hums against the Las Vegas night sky. It looks too bright to be real. Too garish. Too otherworldly.

The door to the club swings open. It's a black rectangle. A man steps out of it.

I recognize him, too.

"Hello, Elyssa," says Father Josiah.

I blink against the onslaught of confusion. "How... how...?"

"When you trust in the ways of the Sanctuary, all things arrive when they are supposed to," he explains. "I am here because you needed me. Isn't that right?"

Theo is asleep in my arms. I look down at him and wonder how this is all happening.

The recovered memory is fresh and sharp in my head. I remember how it felt when Father Josiah's skull broke beneath the paperweight. I remember the smell of his blood and the burning curtains. I remember the feel of the sand beneath my feet when I ran and ran and ran.

But none of that matters anymore. I left home and look what happened to me?

I fell in love with a killer.

I became a killer myself.

Father Josiah was right all along—the outside world is full of horrors. The Sanctuary is the only place where I can be safe. The only place where my baby can be safe.

So the Sanctuary is where I belong.

Just like they always taught me.

As if reading my thoughts, Josiah steps aside and ushers me into the darkened hallway. "Come inside, Elyssa. It's time for you to return to the flock."

I swallow. Take one step forward. Then another. And another. Father Josiah offers me his hand and helps me up the final steps. I cross the threshold into the shadowy nightclub, delirious and shaking and powerless to do anything but obey.

And as I pass him, that's when I smell it. Just the faintest whiff of it, but it's there, mingling with the desert sand.

The scent of patchouli oil…

Welcoming me home.

TO BE CONTINUED

The Ripped duet concludes in Book 2, RIPPED LACE, coming Monday, October 18th!

MAILING LIST

Sign up to my mailing list!
New subscribers receive a FREE steamy bad boy romance novel.

Click the link below to join.
https://sendfox.com/nicolefox

ALSO BY NICOLE FOX

Romanoff Bratva

Immaculate Deception

Immaculate Corruption

Kovalyov Bratva

Gilded Cage

Gilded Tears

Jaded Soul

Jaded Devil

Ripped Veil

Ripped Lace

Mazzeo Mafia Duet

Liar's Lullaby (Book 1)

Sinner's Lullaby (Book 2)

Bratva Crime Syndicate

*Can be read in any order!

Lies He Told Me

Scars He Gave Me

Sins He Taught Me

Belluci Mafia Trilogy

Corrupted Angel (Book 1)

Corrupted Queen (Book 2)

Corrupted Empire (Book 3)

De Maggio Mafia Duet

Devil in a Suit (Book 1)

Devil at the Altar (Book 2)

Kornilov Bratva Duet

Married to the Don (Book 1)

Til Death Do Us Part (Book 2)

Heirs to the Bratva Empire

Can be read in any order!

Kostya

Maksim

Andrei

Princes of Ravenlake Academy (Bully Romance)

Can be read as standalones!

Cruel Prep

Cruel Academy

Cruel Elite

Tsezar Bratva

Nightfall (Book 1)

Daybreak (Book 2)

Russian Crime Brotherhood

Can be read in any order!

Owned by the Mob Boss

Unprotected with the Mob Boss

Knocked Up by the Mob Boss

Sold to the Mob Boss

Stolen by the Mob Boss

Trapped with the Mob Boss

Volkov Bratva

Broken Vows (Book 1)

Broken Hope (Book 2)

Broken Sins *(standalone)*

Other Standalones

Vin: A Mafia Romance

Box Sets

Bratva Mob Bosses (Russian Crime Brotherhood Books 1-6)

Tsezar Bratva (Tsezar Bratva Duet Books 1-2)

Heirs to the Bratva Empire

The Mafia Dons Collection

The Don's Corruption

Printed in Great Britain
by Amazon